CAUGHT
in TIME

CAUGHT in TIME

A Kendra Donovan Mystery

JULIE McELWAIN

PEGASUS CRIME

NEW YORK LONDON

CAUGHT IN TIME

Pegasus Crime is an imprint of
Pegasus Books, Ltd.
148 West 37th Street, 13th Floor
New York, NY 10018

Copyright © 2018 Julie McElwain

First Pegasus Books mass market paperback edition May 2022
First Pegasus Books cloth edition July 2018

Interior design by Maria Fernandez

Library of Congress Cataloging-in-Publication Data is available.

ISBN: 978-1-63936-221-9

10 9 8 7 6 5 4 3 2 1

Printed in the United States of America
Distributed by Simon & Schuster
www.pegasusbooks.com

To Jeff and Holly

1

The fog came without warning, swift skeins of milk-white vapor curling across the Yorkshire countryside, ethereal in its beauty. And utterly dangerous, especially if you happened to be barreling down an unfamiliar road in a carriage drawn by a team of four horses.

The carriage began to slow. Kendra Donovan understood the precaution. It would be hazardous to go faster. And by faster, she meant a top speed of ten miles an hour. *Christ*, she thought, *I've driven faster golf carts.*

Impatience had her twitching in her seat. She tore her gaze away from the amorphous cloud that had settled on the landscape, obscuring the rolling hills and moors, and glanced at the carriage's two other occupants. But if she thought they'd exchange commiserating looks, the kind that commuters shared whenever their journeys were unexpectedly delayed, she was disappointed. Molly, a small figure bundled in cloak, bonnet, and blanket, had managed to wedge herself into the corner next to Kendra and had fallen asleep an hour ago, lulled by the tedious motion of the carriage. Kendra looked next at the man on the seat across from her. Albert Rutherford, the seventh Duke of Aldridge, was calmly reading a book, seemingly unaware of their now glacial pace. But then this was normal for him, she knew. Hell, it was normal for anyone in 1815. She was the odd one out.

Kendra shifted in her seat again, unable to get comfortable. She'd lost count of the hours they'd spent on the road today, but she knew the days. Three days ago, they'd begun their journey from Aldridge Castle. They still had one more day left before they reached their destination—Monksgrey, one of the smaller estates the Duke owned in Lancashire. *Four days*, she thought. Four days to travel a route that would have taken her roughly five *hours* to complete more than two months ago.

Two months ago—and two hundred years into the future. She should have been used to the concept of time travel by now, but those two words still had the power to make her feel punch-drunk. The natural laws of the universe meant time flowed in a linear fashion—*forward*. If you ladled hot soup into a bowl, the soup would eventually cool. It couldn't warm up again—or it *shouldn't*.

But in the field of quantum mechanics, scientists were just beginning to explore the possibility that time could flow both ways. The natural laws of the universe broke down on a quantum level, with subatomic particles behaving oddly, including leaping back and forth in time. But Kendra didn't exist on a quantum level. She was a person, not a subatomic particle. She should have been fixed on the plane governed by the natural laws of the universe, not thrown into the past, where it took four damn days to travel across England.

She'd been born at the tail end of the twentieth century. Chuck Yeager's test flight, which had broken the sound barrier by exceeding speeds of 662 miles per hour, had already been in the history books for decades. By the time she'd graduated Princeton to become a special agent at the FBI, that milestone had looked positively antiquated compared to the military jets that routinely pushed speeds above Mach 3—2,280 miles an hour. Time was the most valuable commodity in her era. Billion-dollar industries had been created by shaving off a second here, a minute there—microwaves, cars, texting, the Internet. In the twenty-first century, speed was as natural as breathing.

Kendra drew in a deep breath, held it, and let it out slowly. Her gaze traveled back to the fog-shrouded window. Her stomach twisted.

This isn't my world.

She leaned back against the seat and closed her eyes. In her world, she'd been the youngest person ever to be accepted into the FBI. The Bureau's Cyber Division had been interested in her tech skills. Her ambition had eventually propelled her into the Behavioral Science Unit, where she'd been successful in carving out a career as a criminal profiler. She'd been happy . . . well, maybe *happy* wasn't the right word, she conceded. But she'd been damn good at her job. Then her life had gone sideways.

The scars on her body began to throb, hot and itchy. A psychosomatic response, she was certain, to being shot and nearly dying. Bile rose up, hot and bitter, as Kendra thought about the man responsible for her injuries and getting half her task force killed. Sir Jeremy Greene. The British billionaire had all the trappings of respectability. But you had only to scrape off the surface shine to uncover the filth and muck beneath. Illegal narcotics, weapons smuggling, human trafficking—Sir Jeremy had his pointy fingers in plenty of nasty pots.

Was *that* when her life had skittered sideways? At the time, she only knew that she couldn't accept the deal that the government had made with Sir Jeremy, allowing him to keep his freedom and luxurious lifestyle as long as he fed them valuable intel against his viler associates. Such deals were done. Kendra wasn't naïve.

And if her own team members hadn't been casualties in the mission to capture the asshole, would she have looked the other way? Gone on with her life?

God help her, she didn't know.

But hindsight wouldn't change a damn thing. She hadn't looked the other way. She'd made plans to take Sir Jeremy out. An eye for an eye was too Old Testament for her. She preferred to think of it as justice.

She'd planned it so well, so meticulously. But how could she have known that Sir Jeremy's criminal associates had become suspicious of him, had hired an assassin to put a hole in the bastard's chest? She wouldn't have objected to that, if she'd been in her apartment in Virginia, and not standing in the room that Sir Jeremy had been entering. Even now, more than two months later, she could feel the jittery zing of adrenaline coursing through her bloodstream. Her memory wasn't quite eidetic, but it didn't need to be for this particular event. The scene was frozen, with stark clarity, in her mind.

She could still hear the impatient snap in Sir Jeremy's voice outside in the hallway, still see him as the door swung open. The sheen of silvery hair. The patrician profile. He'd been wearing a nineteenth century costume like everyone who was attending the costume ball at Aldridge Castle. Ice danced down her spine as she recalled the sound—a muted *pfft*—that had changed everything. The next moment, Sir Jeremy was falling into the room, his once snowy-white shirt blooming crimson. She could smell the raw, coppery scent of his blood filling the air.

Shock had robbed her of any mobility. She remembered that, too, the endless moment, stretching like a rubber band. The assassin had moved into the room, and his eyes, dark and cold, had locked on hers. Without hesitation, he'd lifted his gun, the barrel elongated by a silencer.

This was where her memory failed her. She couldn't actually remember moving when he'd fired the weapon. She only remembered hearing the deadly *pfft* again, and the Chinese vase shattered into a million pieces next to her as she frantically dove through the hidden door in the study. Her only thought had been to climb the stairwell that had been used for over a thousand years by the castle inhabitants to flee from their religious and political persecutors.

A cold, prickly sweat broke out on her body now as she recalled the unnatural darkness, the sudden sensation of going around and around on an excruciating spike of pain. The sensation that she was being shredded into a million strands had seemed endless. Her life had changed in that moment. Maybe forever. Unless she figured out how to return to her own time.

Kendra shivered. The cloth-wrapped warming brick next to her feet that had radiated heat two hours ago was now a block of ice. Yet that wasn't responsible for the goose bumps. That was due entirely to her bizarre predicament, which kept her trapped in the nineteenth century, like an insect in amber.

"Does your arm pain you, my dear?"

The Duke's voice jolted her out of her reverie, and she opened her eyes. She realized she was absently massaging the arm with the old wound.

She dropped her hand, and straightened. "No, I . . . it's nothing. Just thinking."

The fog outside cast an uncertain light inside the carriage, playing across the Duke's longish face and rather bold nose, and making his thinning hair more gray than blond. His blue eyes, pale enough to sometimes appear gray, glinted with intelligence. He was a man who held immense power in this world, with his title and wealth. He was also one of the kindest people that Kendra had ever met, regardless of century.

He asked, "Are you contemplating . . . your America?"

The careful way he said it made her smile. *Her America* had become their code for the twenty-first century. She might not be an expert on all the theories of time travel, but she understood human behavior. In her time, if anyone professed to being a time traveler, they would have ended up in a lunatic asylum. Or given their own reality TV show. It was sort of a toss-up. In the early nineteenth century, it would definitely be the madhouse. Fear had kept her quiet about her circumstance. Only two people knew her secret—the Duke and his nephew, Alec, born Alexander Morgan, the Marquis of Sutcliffe.

"It's a little difficult *not* to think about my America," she confessed, and glanced out the window. If anything, the fog had become thicker. "This is going to delay us, isn't it?"

Aldridge shifted his gaze to the window, studying the gray landscape. "I'm afraid so. We'll need to put up for the night, I think. However, if we begin our journey early tomorrow morning, we ought to arrive at Monksgrey by nightfall. 'Tis only a half-day delay. Unless . . ."

"Unless?" Kendra wasn't sure she wanted to know.

He shrugged. "Unless we encounter more fog on the highway tomorrow afternoon, and are forced to seek shelter in another hostelry until Monday morning."

Kendra frowned. "Why would we have to wait until Monday?"

"No well-bred person travels on the Sabbath."

How could she argue with that? Sundays in "her America" had become a day of recreation as much as spiritual reflection.

"We must stay optimistic," the Duke added.

Yet whatever optimism Kendra may have had vanished the next minute when the carriage rolled to a stop, swaying slightly as the coachman jumped off his perch. Kendra could hear him muttering to himself, his boots stomping loudly on the ground as he came around to the carriage door. He gave a brief knock before yanking it open. His broad face, ruddy with cold and gleaming with moisture from the swirling mist, peered in at them.

"'Tis wicked weather, we're 'aving, yer Grace."

Aldridge smiled slightly. "Yes, I can see it is, Benjamin. Yet somehow I don't think you stopped the carriage to impart your keen observation. Are you about to suggest a course of action? Shall we wait here until it lifts?"

"Nay. We'd most likely be 'ere till mornin'. And the 'orses are getting skittish, even with their blinders on. Oi thought me and Dylan'll walk the poor beasts. We got lanterns." Benjamin hesitated. "Oi'm afraid we ain't gonna make it far before evening sets in, sir. It's about five now.

But if Oi recollect properly, there's a village down the road with a good-sized 'ostelry."

The Duke nodded. "Let us hope it is not too far down the road."

"Aye, sir."

Benjamin stepped back, but Kendra scooted forward before he could close the door. "Wait. I'll walk with you." She needed to move. Her ass had gone numb from sitting for so long.

The coachman eyed her the same way that most of the servants who worked at Aldridge Castle did. Like she was a freak. Ironically, that was the one thing familiar to her in this era of horse-drawn carriages and homespun clothing. She'd been viewed in a similar fashion by many people in her own time. Her parents had believed that humanity could be improved if intellectually gifted people would marry and procreate, and she had been the result of their personal test of their hypothesis.

Here, though, she had to deal with another layer of suspicion. When she'd first arrived in the nineteenth century, she'd been mistaken as a servant. Now she was the Duke's ward. That kind of meteoric rise in status was often met with disapproval and distrust by every level of this society, including the servant class.

Benjamin scowled at her. "'Tis not a day for walkin', miss."

Kendra could have pointed out that he would be walking. Instead, she said, "I can carry a lantern."

The coachman's jaw jutted out. "'Tis cold outside, miss."

"It's cold inside too."

"Actually, walking is an excellent notion," the Duke said, effectively ending the argument. He set aside the book on his lap and picked up his gloves. "I could use the exercise myself."

Benjamin glared at Kendra, obviously holding her responsible for the Duke's decision. "But it ain't safe, yer Grace," he protested, his hand going to the blunderbuss tucked into his belt, nearly hidden by his greatcoat.

"In that case . . ." Kendra lifted the silk embroidered reticule off the seat beside her, and fished out the muff pistol that Alec had given her two weeks ago. It was a far cry from the Glock that she'd used as an FBI agent, but she knew the dainty weapon, with its polished walnut stock and engraved gold plate, could do some damage—as long as she was within fifteen feet of her target.

She caught the Duke's eye, and grinned. "Don't worry. I know how to use it."

"I have no fear on that score, Miss Donovan." He tugged on his gloves. "This is what you and my nephew have been sneaking off to do in the woods, is it not?"

Kendra wasn't given to blushing, but she felt her face grow hot under the Duke's scrutiny. She and Alec had done more in the woods than perfect her shooting skills with the archaic weapon. Against her better judgment, they had become involved. Just thinking about the marquis made her heart rate increase. *Talk about insanity.* She didn't belong in this world with Alec, any more than Alec belonged with her. He belonged with one of the pretty debutantes that the London social season churned out annually. He needed a young lady who knew how to dance a cotillion, ride a horse sidesaddle, and embroider or play the pianoforte, someone who had pretty manners and would never think to utter an expletive.

Someone who could give him a boatload of kids.

That, more than anything, was the prerequisite to marriage among the Beau Monde. A young lady must be able to provide a male heir, preferably an heir and then several spares. Infant and childhood mortality were frighteningly high in this pre-inoculation age. Kendra knew she couldn't promise anything in that regard. One of the injuries that she'd sustained on her last mission had drastically cut down on her odds of conceiving and carrying children.

In truth, she'd never thought about having kids. She'd been too busy with her career. Now, the possibility of not having children was like a shadow on her heart.

She shook herself free of such musings. She hadn't given up hope of returning to her own time, even if she didn't have a clue how to accomplish that. She was an FBI profiler, not a quantum physicist. But she clung to the hope that something would present itself.

"I've become a very good shot," she said carefully.

The way the Duke looked at her, she had a feeling that he was aware of just how involved she'd become with his nephew, but he was at a loss as to how to handle it.

Benjamin shook his head and mumbled something under his breath about improper females as he withdrew, trudging back to the horses.

In the corner, Molly stirred. Her eyes fluttered open, and she yawned widely as she sat up. "W'ot's 'appening?" Her hand flew to her mouth. "Oh, beggin' yer pardon, yer Grace. Oi didn't mean ter nod off on ye!"

Aldridge smiled at the maid. "Do not concern yourself. 'Tis an exhausting journey."

Molly rubbed her nose, red from cold, and looked around. "Are we done fer the night?" Her gaze fell on the gun in Kendra's hand and she gave a frightened squeak. "'Ave we been 'eld up by 'ighwaymen?"

"No," Kendra assured the girl, "we just ran into fog. Benjamin is going to walk the horses, and the Duke and I are joining him."

The maid blinked. "Yer goin' ter walk?"

"Yes."

"Oi'll come with ye, then." She began folding her blanket into a tidy bundle.

Kendra said, "That's not necessary, Molly. You can stay inside."

The maid looked horrified at the suggestion. "Oh, but it ain't proper. Oi'm yer lady's maid, miss. Oi can't sit while ye walk."

Kendra stifled a sigh. Molly had been a tweeny at the castle, basically a maid-of-all-trades. But circumstances—and Kendra's own preference—had elevated the fifteen-year-old to lady's maid. While Kendra would have preferred not to have one, it was damn near impossible for any woman in the upper levels of society to dress without assistance. Molly had been the best choice, though she tended to guard her new rank by being over-zealous in her duties.

"Okay," Kendra finally said with a shrug. "Suit yourself."

They climbed out of the carriage. Benjamin had already lit two lanterns, which he passed to the stable boy, Dylan, and another man, a groom named Stanley. Kendra suspected Stanley didn't just help Benjamin with the horses, but acted as a bodyguard as well. He had his own blunderbuss pushed through his wide leather belt. Traveling in this era wasn't just slow, it was fraught with peril, with gentry and mail coaches targeted by highwaymen.

The Duke's valet, Wilson, stood nearby, viewing the proceedings with the standoffish attitude prevalent among the upstairs servants. But when he saw the Duke, his eyebrows flew up and he hurried over. "Your Grace, may I be of assistance?"

Aldridge waved away his solicitation. "Thank you, no. Miss Donovan and I shall be walking—and carrying lanterns, if Benjamin needs assistance."

"But, sir . . ." The manservant's face twisted with horror. "Benjamin said the nearest village is three miles. Your hessians, your Grace. Think of your *hessians*!"

Aldridge cast a rueful glance at his gleaming black boots. "Yes, well, it can't be helped. If I had known we would be walking, I would have worn my older boots. As it is, they're at Monksgrey, along with the staff."

A day before they'd left Aldridge Castle, the senior staff, including the butler, Mr. Harding, the housekeeper, Mrs. Danbury, and the Duke's temperamental French chef, Monsieur Anton, had departed for Monksgrey to assist the skeleton staff that lived at the manor year-round to prepare for the Duke's arrival. At this moment, Kendra imagined Mrs. Danbury was whipping everyone into shape, sort of like a drill sergeant during basic training.

Even though they traveled with a lady's maid and valet, several trunks of clothing, and their own bed linens and necessities for staying in the public hostelries en route, Kendra was aware that this was actually considered traveling light by aristocratic standards. She'd never get used to it.

"'Ere. Ye can carry a lantern, Mr. Wilson." Before the valet could protest, Benjamin thrust a lamp into his gloved hands. Kendra caught the thin smile on the coachman's face as he turned away from Wilson to march back to the horses. The rivalries and petty jealousies between the upper and lower servants cut both ways.

They formed a ragged procession as they moved forward. Despite the lanterns, the fog was at times so thick that Kendra could barely make out the landscape ten feet in front of her. It created a strange sort of isolation, as if they were the last survivors in an apocalyptic world. Even the sounds—the rumble of wooden carriage wheels, the clomping of the horses' hooves, the jingling of bridles as the beasts periodically shook their heads and snorted, and the shuffling of human feet—were strangely muted.

Kendra had to strain to hear noises beyond their immediate group. It took a moment, but eventually she made out the whispering grass from the surrounding moorlands. The shriek of a bird circling high above them broke through the odd atmospheric bubble they were in.

"'Ow long will it be till we meet other folks?" Molly asked nervously. She was walking so close to Kendra that their skirts brushed. "'May'ap this place is cursed."

"There are no such things as curses, my dear," the Duke said. "Do not fall prey to superstitious nonsense. Fog is a natural phenomenon produced by moisture in the air. You've seen it often enough at Aldridge Castle. Quite frankly, I find this fog preferable to the miserable brown muck in London."

"Oi've never seen anythin' like this, yer Grace," Molly whispered.

Kendra swiped at the cold moisture forming on her face. "Why don't you go back in the carriage, Molly? I can hear your teeth chattering. You can keep warm if you cover yourself with all the blankets."

"Are ye goin' inside, miss?"

"Not yet."

"Then Oi'll walk for a bit too."

Kendra wanted to insist, but she knew that it wouldn't do any good. She decided to give herself another fifteen minutes, then she'd go inside the carriage, for the girl's sake. Everyone fell silent again, seemingly disinclined to talk in this peculiar gray world.

After about twenty minutes, Benjamin broke the oppressive silence. "We're losin' daylight, sir."

"We only need to keep to the road," Aldridge said, forcing a note of joviality into his voice. The Duke considered himself a man of science—a natural philosopher—but Kendra suspected the atmosphere was getting to him too. "We ought to be in the village soon enough. And the inn. I must say, I am famished. I am imagining a nice bowl of leek soup, and a warm brandy or hot buttered rum to take the chill out of my bones. What say you, Miss Donovan?"

"I wouldn't mind a hot drink," Kendra agreed.

"Ooh, do ye think they 'ave pigeon pie?" Molly wondered wistfully.

"I am certain they do. Any innkeeper worth their salt—" The Duke broke off abruptly, and came to a halt.

Kendra stopped, as well, which caused Molly to plow into her. "W'ot?" Molly demanded, straightening the bonnet that had slipped over her eyes.

The procession had stopped, their gazes transfixed by the shadows flickering in the gray fog ahead. Like shape-shifters from ancient tales, the images seemed to twist and lengthen until they took human form.

Molly shrieked, and grabbed Kendra's coat.

Kendra ignored the maid, keeping her gaze focused on the apparitions ahead. Her ears picked up the sound of running feet just before the men burst through the mist. There were at least a dozen in rough clothes, their faces blackened by what looked to be soot. Clutched in their hands were axes and sledgehammers.

"'Old on ter the 'orses!" Benjamin shouted at Stanley and Dylan, as the beasts began to sidle nervously. "Keep their 'eads down!"

Grim-faced, the coachman yanked out his blunderbuss, and held it at the ready as the men ran toward them. Kendra's own pulse leaped in her throat, but her hand was steady as she lifted the muff pistol. She shook off the cowering Molly, and grabbed the Duke's arm, shoving him behind her.

"Get into the carriage," Kendra hissed.

"'Ere now, w'ot's you lot about?" Benjamin cried out at the men.

Kendra braced herself, her finger curling around the trigger of the elegant gun. If it wasn't for the smeared faces and the air of violence that clung to the mob, the men would have reminded Kendra of marathon runners, their expressions intent on some finish line that only they could see. The lead runner, a burly man carrying a pickaxe, his blue eyes startlingly pale against his blackened face, saw them. He didn't stop, or even slow. But as she watched, he veered off the road. The rest of the men followed his lead—and one by one, they were swallowed up by the dense fog, vanishing into the countryside. For a few seconds, the sound of their feet could be heard thundering across the moor. Then that, too, faded away, and the only thing that pierced the silence was a bird's plaintive caw high above them.

"Holy crap," Kendra breathed. Her heart thumped against her chest. Carefully, she eased her finger off the trigger, and lowered the muff pistol. She glanced around. Only then did she realize that the Duke hadn't retreated into the safety of the carriage, but had taken up a defensive position beside her. She decided not to waste her breath on a lecture.

"What the hell was that?" she asked. "Some sort of militia?"

The Duke shook his head. Even in the diminished light, Kendra could see the uneasy expression in his eyes. "Not exactly," he said. "But let us make haste to the village. These roads are more treacherous than I realized."

2

By the time they reached the outskirts of the village thirty-five minutes later, darkness had fallen completely, the lanterns barely penetrating the vapor pressing against them. Kendra didn't realize how tense she'd become until she saw the blurred glow from the lampposts, which marked the boundary of the village, and released a sigh.

"At last," Kendra heard the Duke breathe softly. He glanced at her, relief softening his mouth into a smile. "You ought to be able to put away your weapon now, my dear."

Kendra hesitated, but then shrugged and slid the muff pistol back into the pouch that dangled from her wrist. She knew the Duke was concerned about her reputation. A wasted worry, as far as she was concerned. Her reputation had been damaged beyond repair a month ago, when she'd scandalized London while saving Alec from a murder charge.

"Blessed be—'tis a lovely 'ostelry, it is," Molly cried, staring at the large building looming ahead.

The inn was, smartly, located near the public road. The structure had a cobbled-together appearance, with the main building a half-timbered Tudor style that most likely dated back to the fifteen or sixteenth century. Two wings of red brick had apparently been added on during a later period, and bespoke a certain prosperity. The roof was steeply pitched and thatched. The windows were set back, small and perfectly square. A good many were dark, but a few flickered with a warm, buttery light.

Oil lamps hung on poles outside, casting a soft amber glow across the courtyard. Off to the right was a stable yard. The eerie atmosphere created by the cocoon of fog was suddenly broken by normal activities. A handful of stable hands were busy brushing and feeding the horses, vigorously shoveling up the dung their four-legged guests left behind.

The youths abandoned their work as soon as they noticed the newcomers, rushing forward to assist Benjamin and the others as they guided the team of horses into the courtyard. Kendra had a feeling that their enthusiastic greeting had a lot to do with the Duke's crest on the carriage door rather than being particularly happy to have more work to do on a bleak night.

Leaving Benjamin to deal with the stable hands, Aldridge ushered Kendra to the inn's entrance. Molly and Wilson followed.

"Let us pray no other travelers have been stranded by the fog, making rooms scarce," murmured Aldridge as he opened the door.

Inside, the foyer appeared smaller than it really was because of the low ceiling, which was bisected by ancient, gnarled beams. The walls had been painted white, a stark contrast from the dark wood floor and staircase. Voices drew Kendra to the open doorway on the right. It was a public dining room, families and single men occupying half the tables. No lone women, Kendra observed. But she knew that even married ladies and widows, who had more independence in this era, would balk at dining alone in public.

More voices—low and obviously male—came from the door on the left, which opened to the tavern. A quick glance revealed men crowded around sturdy wood tables and lined up along the tap, smoking pipes and drinking. Kendra noticed a few of the men were well-dressed, probably guests of the inn. The rest, she assumed, were locals. Given their work attire, she thought this was a familiar routine, the men ending their day with a few pints, catching up on whatever passed as news in the village. The orange-yellow light from the fire in the stone hearth and lanterns on the walls limned the men's faces, young and old. The only woman in the room was a dark-haired barmaid, her hands nimble as she pulled the taps, replenishing the mugs and laughing with easy camaraderie as she moved around the bar.

"Good evening. Good evening!"

Kendra turned around to see an older man trotting down the hall toward them, smiling. She judged him to be in his late sixties or early seventies, but still robust, with a florid, round face framed by bushy gray side whiskers that were only slightly darker than the thinning strands on top of his head.

His blue eyes were bright, and quick to size up the cut and quality of the Duke and Kendra's clothes. "Welcome ter the Green Maiden." He bowed, and his smile widened. "I am the proprietor here, Mr. Bolton. How may I serve ye, good sir?"

"Good evening," Aldridge returned. "I am the Duke of Aldridge, and this is my ward, Miss Donovan. We are journeying to my estate in Lancashire, but unfortunately the fog has forced us to seek shelter for the evening. Do you have rooms available . . . and a meal, preferably served in a private parlor?"

Mr. Bolton's eyes gleamed at the mention of the Duke's title. Kendra had a feeling that even if all the rooms were taken, Mr. Bolton would have evicted someone in favor of having a duke as a guest.

The innkeeper bowed again. "Of course, yer Grace. 'Tis an honor ter serve ye! Rest easy, we shall prepare two of our best rooms for ye and yer ward. The servants will even change the linens for ye, if ye want. The Green Maiden boasts the highest standards of cleanliness."

"Thank you, Mr. Bolton, but we have brought our own linens. Our servants will see to preparing our rooms."

"Certainly, sir," Bolton said, nodding. It was common practice for the gentry to supply their own linens, so he didn't view it as an insult. He glanced over his shoulder at a woman hurrying down the hall toward them. "Madam wife, we have guests—the Duke of Aldridge and his ward, Miss Donovan."

Mrs. Bolton was probably near her husband's age. Years had carved lines into her face and softened her jawline, but Kendra imagined she'd been beautiful in her youth, given her excellent bone structure. A mop cap covered her head, allowing only the smallest glimpse of hair, which in the dim light could have been an ash blonde, but Kendra imagined was a silvery-gray in the strong light of day. Her eyes were a dark gray. Her figure was petite, barely hitting the five-foot mark, and spritely. She had no difficulty dipping into a deep curtsy for the Duke.

"Oh, this is indeed an honor, your Grace," she said, her speech surprisingly cultured. "Pray tell, what brings you to East Dingleford, sir?"

Aldridge said, "Wicked weather, I fear."

"The Duke was travelin' ter his estate in Lancashire, but the fog has waylaid him," the innkeeper told his wife.

She clucked her tongue in sympathy. "Yorkshire has the most unpredictable weather in all the kingdom, I fancy."

"We must see ter our guests' comfort," Bolton said, and looked at the Duke. "Mrs. Bolton will take ye ter our private parlor. Ye can warm yerself by the fire and have a glass of sherry or brandy—my wife makes an excellent apricot brandy . . ." His gaze traveled to Molly and Wilson. "Yer servants can ready yer bedchambers, and are welcome in the kitchen for a meal there or in the public rooms. I caught a couple of hares this very day, so we have fresh meat on hand. Our cook, Mrs. Platt, makes a most excellent rabbit stew."

Kendra didn't know what was worse, eating rabbit or pigeon, but the tantalizing aromas wafting out of the public dining room were beginning to make her stomach growl.

"Thank you. You are a most gracious host." The Duke hesitated, then asked, "If I may inquire, do you happen to have a textile mill in the near vicinity?"

The innkeeper's eyebrows rose in surprise. "Aye, that we do. Bancroft Mills. 'Tis a cotton mill owned by the Lord Bancroft—Lord Nathan Bancroft—the Earl of Langfrey. His lordship's estate, Falcon Court, is nearby. Why do ye ask?"

Aldridge pursed his lips. The uneasiness returned to his eyes. "I think I shall need to have words with the village magistrate and constable."

"Our magistrate and constable?" Mrs. Bolton's gray eyes widened. "Good heavens. Whatever for?"

"I'm afraid there has been mischief tonight." The Duke looked like he was going to say something more, but then reconsidered. "Miss Donovan and I shall await the magistrate and constable's arrival in the parlor."

It was almost twenty minutes before the innkeeper escorted two men, their hats in their hands, into the private parlor. Kendra and the Duke were sitting in front of the fireplace, sipping from glasses filled with Mrs. Bolton's apricot brandy as they waited for their dinner to be served.

Mr. Bolton introduced Constable Jameson, a tall, barrel-chested, brawny man in his mid-thirties. His hair was dark, with a hint of red, and curly, and he wore it a little longer than was fashionable. He had thick brows that formed a ledge over deep-set brown eyes. Kendra was a little disconcerted to learn during the introductions that

Jameson had a full-time job as one of the village's three
blacksmiths, although that explained the leather apron
she noticed beneath his tattered wool outer coat. Apparently, there was more of a need in East Dingleford for
blacksmiths than constables.

The other man was Mr. Oliver Matthews, the son of
the local squire, who was also the village's magistrate.
According to the innkeeper, Squire Matthews was laid
up with a terrible case of gout, and had sent his son to act
as magistrate in his stead.

Matthews looked to be the same age as the constable,
but that was the only thing the two men had in common.
The squire's son was the opposite of the burly Jameson in
every way. He was short—barely five-foot-five, Kendra
estimated—and as thin as a stalk of wheat. His face was
pale, and his flaxen hair was cut into the fashionable
Brutus style popular among gentlemen, though his hair
was too thin and his hairline too receded to really carry
it off. Unlike the constable, he was dressed fashionably in
a dark umber multi-caped greatcoat layered over a well-
cut, bottle-green coat, ivory embroidered waistcoat, and
snug tan trousers tucked into gleaming boots. The points
of his shirt were sharp and high, his cravat exquisitely
tied. Since arriving, he'd pulled out a lace-trimmed
hanky, which he clutched like some sort of talisman.

Matthews's watery blue eyes were fixed on the Duke,
listening as he told them about their encounter with the
band of men on the road, but the constable was the first
to react.

"Luddites!" There was no mistaking the anger in
Jameson's voice. "By God, they're the scourge of England!"

"Are you absolutely certain, your Grace?" Matthews
asked, in such a way that Kendra felt like he was hoping
the Duke would change his story. "The fog has a tendency
to play tricks on one's eyes, you know."

Aldridge shook his head. "This was no illusion, sir.
I'd say there were about a dozen men. Miss Donovan,
what do you say?"

"Yes. They were carrying axes and hammers," she added. "Their faces had been blackened in an attempt to disguise themselves."

The Duke said, "I have read newspaper accounts about your troubles here in the north with men calling themselves Luddites."

"Aye," Constable Jameson acknowledged with a scowl. "But we ain't had any of those troubles in East Dingleford."

"There's always a first time," Kendra murmured. Both men shot her a brief look before turning back to the Duke.

Jameson scraped a beefy palm across his chin. "I suppose it'd be wise ter gather a couple of men and go take a look around the mill, see if any damage has been done."

"The earl ought to be informed." Matthews lifted his handkerchief to his nose, a worried frown creasing his brow. "And Mr. Stone, of course. They'll not be pleased."

"Nay. And why would they, eh?" Jameson's mouth curled at the other man. "Havin' their fine new machines smashed. No sense botherin' his lordship or Mr. Stone until after we look around the mill first, ter see if there's anything damaged." He looked at the Duke again. "Thank you, your Grace, for bringin' the matter ter our attention." He didn't look particularly thankful.

"Yes, thank you, sir," Matthews put in, and gave an abbreviated bow.

The Duke inclined his head. "Certainly. I believe this movement is beginning to weaken, but England cannot be held hostage by those bent on destruction, regardless of the cause."

Jameson and Matthews left the parlor, brushing past Mrs. Bolton as she arrived with bowls and silverware. She was followed by a serving girl juggling a large cast iron pot and a silver platter bearing thick brown bread and a dish of yellow butter.

"Would you like more brandy, sir? Miss?" Mrs. Bolton glanced at them as she set the table. "We also have wine, if you prefer that with your meal. Or ale."

Aldridge smiled. "Do not trouble yourself, Mrs. Bolton. We shall serve ourselves." He eyed the dishes that the girl had set on the table. "The stew smells delicious. Convey my deepest appreciation to your cook."

"I shall, your Grace. Mrs. Platt will be most pleased. We have never had a Duke visit the Green Maiden before. This is my granddaughter, Tessa—she made the bread."

The old woman smiled at her granddaughter, who looked to be about fifteen. Tessa exuded a wholesome prettiness, with her sandy blond hair and bright blue eyes.

"Tessa and her sister, Lizzie, live here now with us and help with the inn's work. If you need anything, they will be happy to assist."

The young girl gave a quick smile and curtsy.

Kendra returned the maid's smile. Bread, made from scratch, had become her greatest weakness.

Mrs. Bolton retrieved the bottle of apricot brandy from the sideboard. "Your servants have finished preparing your rooms, and are taking their meal in the kitchen. Your coachman is having his dinner in the tavern." She waited until they sat down at the table before refilling their glasses, then cut a sideways glance at the Duke. "Did Constable Jameson and Mr. Matthews help you, your Grace?"

"Yes." The Duke lifted his glass, pausing. "I suggested that they inspect the mill. I believe we crossed paths with men involved in the Luddite movement."

The hand holding the bottle of brandy gave a small jerk. Mrs. Bolton hurriedly set it on the table. "Forgive me, your Grace." She rubbed her palms down her apron in a nervous gesture.

"You have nothing to fear, Mrs. Bolton," the Duke assured the innkeeper's wife in his most gentle tone. "I'm certain the ruffians are gone, regardless of what happened at the mill."

Mrs. Bolton lowered her gaze. "Yes, of course. I'm being a silly old woman."

The Duke said, "I cannot hold with their destruction of property, but I have not heard of any incident where the Luddites have targeted citizens specifically for violence."

"You are right, of course," she said, and curtsied. "Enjoy your supper, your Grace . . . Miss Donovan."

Once alone, Aldridge looked across the table at Kendra and smiled, lifting his glass in a silent toast. "I imagine our excitement for the evening is over."

Kendra would remember those words—and how wrong they were—thirty minutes later, when they heard a shout from the foyer, and raised voices. Surprised, the Duke lifted his brows. Kendra looked in the direction of the commotion.

"I wonder what's amiss?" The Duke set down his fork and knife, and picked up his napkin to pat his lips quickly before rising from the table.

Kendra shoved herself to her feet and joined him as they left the private parlor, venturing down the hall to the foyer. Mr. and Mrs. Bolton and three other men had gathered around the new arrival, a skinny kid of about twelve. He was trying to talk and suck in great gulps of air at the same time.

As they came closer, Kendra heard him say, ". . . smashed, they were. But Mr. Stone . . . Mr. Stone . . ." The kid lost his breath.

"Out with it!" snapped a lanky man wearing a knit cap. "What about the bleedin' bastard? Did one of the Luddite's draw his cork?"

"Nay."

"Well? What about him then?"

The boy's chest expanded as he drew in air before announcing, "'E's dead!"

The news was met with a stunned silence. Mrs. Bolton's hand flew to her throat, and she shot a glance at her husband.

"*Dead*?" she echoed. "Dead. But . . . how?"

"Probably had a seizure when the Luddites arrived," a shorter man muttered, not looking too concerned about it. "Good riddance to bad rubbish, that's what I say!"

"Nay!" The kid shook his head, even as his voice rose to a squeak. "Ain't no seizure that stopped 'is claret. 'Twas murder! Somebody done beat 'is soddin' 'ead in!"

3

Aldridge took a step forward. "*Murder*? Are you absolutely certain?"

Everyone in the foyer swung around to stare at him, surprised by the interruption. Or more likely, Kendra thought, surprised that anyone who belonged in the higher circles of society would be interested in a conversation between common folk.

The innkeeper was the first to collect himself. "Oh, nay, sir. I'm certain it's a mistake—"

"Ain't no mistake," the boy piped in. His nose had begun to run, and he wiped it with the sleeve of his threadbare wool coat. "Oi *told* ye. Mr. Stone got 'is 'ead walloped good. A right bleedin' mess it is too! The constable and Mr. Matthews are at the mill. Matthews cast up 'is accounts. Constable Jameson wants me ter tell the menfolk 'ere so they can go after the Luddites!"

"How do you know that the Luddites killed this man, this Mr. Stone?" Kendra asked, drawing the boy's attention.

"Gor! Oo else do ye think it would be? They smashed up the mill's machinery jest like they done Mr. Stone's 'ead! The constable says ter round up men ter find the fiends and we'll 'ave a 'anging!"

"*No!*" Mrs. Bolton yelped. She frowned, her gaze darting to her husband, the boy, and the men. "No. I—I cannot countenance that the Luddites would have done such a thing."

One of the men gave a contemptuous snort. He was tall, with a broad, rosy face and salt-and-pepper hair. "They're a bunch of ruffians, Mrs. Bolton. Likely murder us all in our sleep, they will, if we don't stop them."

"Aye. They murdered that mill owner only a couple of years ago," said the man wearing the knit cap.

"I read about that incident," Aldridge put in, his expression concerned. "Three men, if I recall correctly. The authorities managed to capture and hang them."

"The mill owner had cheated them out of their wage," Mrs. Bolton protested. She looked as though she wanted to say more, but her husband pressed a hand on her arm.

"Laura," he said, giving her a look, and his wife subsided.

Salt-and-Pepper's eyes narrowed. "Your brother used ter work at the mill, didn't he, Mrs. Bolton? Until he had a fallin' out with Mr. Stone."

Mrs. Bolton's fingers nervously plucked at her apron. "That was ages ago."

"Oye!" the boy cried impatiently, drawing everyone's attention again. "Are ye gonna go after the Luddites, or not? Oi need ter get Dr. Poole and bring 'im ter the mill!"

"Aye, we will," said Salt-and-Pepper. He glanced at the other men beside him. "Let's round up some men ter go after the fiends!"

"Wait!" The word was out before Kendra could stop herself. But she was bothered by the lynch mob mentality thickening the air around her; she recognized too well the whiff of blind violence in the mix. "What about an investigation? There might not be any correlation between the murder and the Luddites other than bad timing."

Salt-and-Pepper stared at her, eyebrows raised. "Don't be daft. 'Course they killed 'im."

"Ah, Freddie . . ." Mr. Bolton cleared his throat, and cast an uneasy glance at the Duke, probably trying to gauge his reaction to hearing his ward being called stupid. "This is Miss Donovan. She's the Duke of Aldridge's *ward*."

Freddie's lip curled as he studied Kendra. "Ye're not from around these parts, Miss Donovan. And ye sound like a Yank. Ye don't know who the Luddites are and w'ot they're about."

"I know exactly who the Luddites are, and what they're about," Kendra shot back, keeping her tone cool and measured even though she could feel her temper rise.

In the twenty-first century, it was common to call anyone who was against or unfamiliar with technology a Luddite. But those involved in this era's Luddite movement weren't against technology per se. Most were actually highly skilled men—craftsmen and machine operators—fighting against the technology that had begun taking away their jobs and depressing their wages.

Kendra had to shake off the sense of déjà vu that crept over her. It was impossible not to think about her own era's protests and fights over stalled wages and lost jobs to technology and artificial intelligence. Economist Joseph Schumpeter called the cycle Creative Destruction. Industries were destroyed, but new ones were created. Autoworkers decried automation, but forgot that their industry had wiped out the livelihoods of blacksmiths, saddle makers, and stable hands. Progress was never easy, especially if you were the one losing your job.

She kept her gaze on Freddie. "There's a big difference between destroying property and killing a human being."

Mrs. Bolton spoke up. "They only desire a decent wage to feed their families."

The old woman shot her a grateful look, but Kendra felt uncomfortable. Jumping to conclusions without any sort of examination was anathema to her, but she wasn't a big fan of coincidences either. The Luddites being at a factory around the same time a man was murdered didn't look good.

Freddie studied the old woman with suspicious eyes. "Ye sound like yer a sympathizer, Mrs. Bolton."

"We don't hold with the Luddites," her husband put in quickly.

"I believe we ought to go to the mill, and assess the situation ourselves," said the Duke. He hadn't raised his voice, but Kendra saw the impact his announcement had on those in the foyer. Shock rippled across their faces. Even Mrs. Bolton appeared disconcerted.

"Why would ye be wantin' ter do that, your Grace?" Mr. Bolton said. "Luddite or not, it is *murder*, sir. 'Tis unseemly fer a gentleman such as yerself ter become involved in such a dreadful thing."

Aldridge smiled slightly. "I am aware that it's unorthodox, Mr. Bolton. But it is not the first time my ward and I have become involved in such matters."

"But yer a *duke*—" Mr. Bolton began, and then did a double-take as the Duke's words hit home. His gaze cut over to Kendra. "Ye *ward*?" He appeared uncertain, as if he doubted he'd heard correctly. "Miss Donovan? Or do ye have another ward?"

And by that, Kendra knew, the innkeeper meant a ward who was male.

"I speak of Miss Donovan," the Duke said firmly. "Her services are invaluable in these matters, I assure you." He met their dubious eyes, and shrugged. "She's an American. They have different sensibilities than we have here in England."

Kendra managed to keep a straight face, even as she came under inspection. When no one said anything, she decided to move things along. Georgian police procedures were basically nonexistent, and God only knew what the constable was doing right now to destroy the crime scene.

"We're wasting time," she said firmly. "We need to go."

The Duke nodded. "You are quite right, Miss Donovan." His gaze traveled back to the innkeeper. "How far is the mill, Mr. Bolton?"

The innkeeper seemed a bit bewildered by what was happening, so his words came slowly. "Ah . . . half a mile, no more."

Aldridge pointed at the child. "You, boy—what's your name?"

The kid swiped at his nose again. "Andrew, sir!"

The Duke said, "I will hire you to escort us to the mill."

"Ye will? Oi mean, aye, sir! But w'ot about Dr. Poole?"

Mr. Bolton recovered from his shock, and said, "I'll have one of the stable hands fetch Dr. Poole."

"Hold on! Yer goin' ter the mill?" Freddie stared at the Duke. "Ye and the gentry mort?"

"We are," the Duke said.

Mr. Bolton said, "I'd loan ye a gig, sir, but with the fog, 'tis best ter walk. I'll send a couple of me stable lads ter accompany ye with torches."

"Thank you, sir," the Duke replied. "The torches will be most welcome. I shall have my own whip take the journey with us. Mrs. Bolton, please inform my servants that Miss Donovan and I will return in due time."

"Yes, of course, your Grace." She made a brief curtsy, the worried look still on her face as she hurried down the shadowed hall.

Kendra followed the Duke into the private parlor, where they put on their coats, gloves, and hats. Kendra picked up her reticule, automatically checking the muff pistol. Satisfied, she replaced the weapon inside the pouch, making sure the strings were loose enough for easy access. She looked up to find the Duke's eyes on her.

"Hopefully you shan't be required to shoot anybody this evening, Miss Donovan," he said, his mouth lifting into a small smile.

Kendra considered his words, then shrugged. "Hope is good. Being prepared is better."

Bancroft Mills rose up in the foggy night like an ancient dragon's lair straight out of the pages of a Grimm fairy tale. In the flickering torchlight and swirling mist, Kendra got the impression of the mill's massive size: almost as long as a football field, with its height staggered between four and six stories, and topped by a slate-covered, gambrel-styled roof. Two enormous smokestacks thrust upward from the center of the building, lost in darkness and fog. Nearby, she heard the rush of water—a river. They were essential sources of energy, she knew, feeding the factories during the early Industrial Revolution.

As they entered the mill's graveled courtyard, their footsteps crunching on the tiny pebbles, Kendra paused to glance upward. Small bits of white fluff were spinning in the night air. *Perfect . . . snow*, was her first thought. It certainly felt cold enough for snowfall. Only when she lifted one gloved hand and watched the white bits land on her outstretched palm without melting did she realize that she was actually seeing bits of cotton fiber floating on the night air.

Kendra caught the Duke's frown as he stood regarding the mill. Benjamin's eyes darted around uneasily, but his hand remained steady on his blunderbuss. Kendra understood his apprehension. The lanterns and hissing torches did little to combat the thick shadows and fog around them. Her own neck tingled with the sensation of watching eyes. She wished that she was holding one of the FBI's kickass LED tactical flashlights instead of a sputtering oil lantern.

The kid—Andrew—was the only one who didn't seem affected by the atmosphere, racing up the steps with youthful exuberance. The door must have been well oiled, because it only made a whispering sound as Andrew yanked it open and disappeared inside.

"'Ere now, wait fer us!" Freddie called out after the child, a quiver of nerves in his voice. He'd insisted on accompanying them to the mill instead of joining the band of men who were now pursuing the Luddites. If she had to guess, Kendra thought curiosity had motivated him over anything else. She wondered if he was regretting his choice now.

She hesitated, then gave in to instinct, dipping her hand into her reticule and closing it over the muff pistol's small grip. It made her feel marginally better as they resumed walking, following in the boy's wake.

The spooky vibe wasn't any better inside the building. Their footsteps echoed in the cavernous space, and the scent of wood, dust, and linseed oil was thick in the air. The glow from their lanterns and torches bobbed through the darkness, touching briefly on the wreckage caused by the Luddites.

Kendra sighed quietly. *I can't believe I'm dealing with freaking Luddites.*

They continued forward, down a short, wide hall and up a flight of stairs. A glass window ran along one side of the hallway, allowing anyone standing there to observe the workers in the factory below. On the other side of the wall were two open doorways.

Kendra ignored the first darkened room, hurrying to the one from which light spilled into the corridor. She caught the murmur of voices inside. Her stomach tightened as the distinctive meaty scent that marked fresh death hit her nostrils.

Kendra hung back near the threshold as the men moved inside. First impressions were crucial in investigations, and so she scanned the room carefully. Every wall sconce had been lit, including two lanterns on the desk, revealing an office larger and more luxurious than she'd have expected to find in a textile mill. In fact, it reminded her more of a gentleman's study, with gleaming mahogany furniture, including a credenza with decanters and crystal tumblers arranged on top of it. A single hat dangled from one of the hooks of a rather ornate coat stand in the corner, next to the door. Bookshelves lined three walls. Here was her second surprise. Instead of books, the shelves were filled with porcelain figurines—all cats.

Kendra forced her gaze to move beyond the unusual display, surveying the two gold-and-brown damask-upholstered sofas that sat facing each other; the heavy leather club chairs; and the massive oak desk. Her mouth tightened as she studied the area. Blood was splattered on the desk, the ceiling, and the wall behind the desk. Her eyes lowered to the floor, where a chair was turned over; a man's boot extended beyond the desk leg and overturned chair. Mr. Stone, she presumed.

Near the desk stood Constable Jameson and another man, the latter wearing a dirty coat and smock, and a hat that had lost its shape a long time ago. Matthews, Kendra noticed, was standing on the other side of the office, as far away from the corpse as he could get and still be in the room. His complexion had a greenish tinge, and he was pressing his lace-trimmed hankie to his nose. She caught the hint of vomit in the air, and traced it to another corner of the room, and what she assumed was left of Matthews's dinner.

At their entrance, Jameson barreled forward, his hand raised like a police officer on traffic duty. "Wot—your Grace! Hold! Don't come any closer, sir. There's been a murder."

"Yes," Matthews spoke up from the back of the room. His voice quivered. "It is . . . it is quite dreadful."

Kendra eyed him with concern. "Maybe you should stand out in the hall?"

"I am—I shall be fine . . . now."

Still, he averted his eyes to stare at the collection of cats.

"Take deep breaths and bend over if you think you're going to pass out," Kendra advised, before crossing the room to get a closer look at the body.

Jameson stepped in front of her. "Miss Donovan, you don't want ter come any nearer. 'Tis not for female eyes." When Kendra simply walked around him, he puffed out his chest in indignation. "Now see here, yer Grace, I ain't gonna be responsible for any female hysterics!"

"I shall take full responsibility for my ward if she should become hysterical, rest assured," the Duke told him, and followed Kendra to look at the corpse.

Kendra focused on the body, sprawled on the floor face up. Mr. Stone had been a big man. Fat, not muscle, strained the seams of the pantaloons, coat, waistcoat, and shirt he was wearing. His stomach plumed over his breeches. He was also a lot older than Kendra had expected him to be. Late sixties, she deduced. His face was heavy and jowly. His eyes were open and filmed over. He still had a decent head of hair, once dark, but now silver. There were no marks on his forehead, but the left side of the head was matted with blood. His cravat, shirt, and coat were soaked in blood as well. A few blowflies were already buzzing around the body, crawling across the man's face.

"You moved the body," she said.

It wasn't a question, but Jameson answered. "'Course we did! Me and Bernard here." Jameson jerked a thumb at the man standing next to him. "Mr. Stone was flat on his face. Hard ter imagine that he'd be alive with his head caved in like that, but we had ter check. It wasn't easy rollin' him over either. He's as fat as Prinny."

"Nah, the Prince Regent's fatter!" the man next to him chortled.

Kendra bit back a sigh. She would have liked to have seen the body in its original position. When it came to homicide investigations, the crime scene was vital, every detail important. Still, it wasn't difficult to piece together what had happened here.

"What about the chair?" she asked. "Did you move that as well?"

"No reason ter do that," said Jameson.

"So the chair was overturned. And you found him lying beside it, facedown?"

"Aye." Jameson scowled. "Wot's this about, anyways?"

Kendra didn't say anything. Her gaze traveled across the pool of blood near the mill manager's head to the telling splatter on the back of the chair, the desk, the wall behind the desk.

The desk was the most interesting, both because of the blood spatter and one particular item upon it—a bronze lion. It was roughly the size of a small toaster, and cast in the style of the famous lions, Patience and Fortitude, flanking the entrance of the New York Public Library.

Even from where she was standing, Kendra could see the
flecks of blood and brain matter on the lion's base.

"And what about that?" She pointed at the bronze.
"Was that on the desk?"

The constable shot her an exasperated look. "It was on
the floor. 'Tis the weapon, you know. One of the Luddites
used it ter bash Stone's head in."

"I don't think so."

Jameson stared at her. "Wot do you mean, *you don't
think so*? There's blood on that statue, and a sodding hole
in Mr. Stone's head. Even a blind man can see that it's
the murder weapon!"

"It's the murder weapon used to bludgeon Mr. Stone,"
Kendra agreed calmly. "But the Luddites were not responsible for Mr. Stone's murder."

Jameson thrust out his chin, immediately aggressive.
"'Course they were!" He looked to the Duke. "Sir!"

But the Duke was regarding Kendra intently. "What
are you seeing, Miss Donovan?"

Kendra squatted down next to the victim. She wished
that she had latex gloves, but pushed away her revulsion
as she reached for the victim's elbow. She lifted it, testing
the tractability. She dropped the arm, then pressed her
fingers against the neck and jaw.

"W'ot's the gentry mort doin'?" whispered the man
named Bernard.

"The victim is in the beginning stages of rigor mortis,"
she told them, withdrawing her fingers. She turned her eyes
to the blood around the man, and wanted to curse as she
noticed the streaks caused by moving the body. She could
even see footprints walking through the blood. Footprints
that could be the killer's—or could be the constable's.

She pressed her fingers to the bridge of her nose in
frustration. Unfortunately, saying something on the point
wouldn't change any minds. *Christ.* She dropped her hand
and surveyed the body again. There was nothing stopping
her from rolling the victim back to its original position,
except that the man weighed a ton.

"I need help turning him over again." She lifted her gaze to her audience.

"W'ot for?" demanded Jameson, not moving.

The Duke started forward, and was joined by Freddie and Benjamin. Grunting, they rolled the dead man until he was facedown again. The new position clearly revealed the mortal injury. Mr. Stone's skull had been bludgeoned so savagely that it had shattered, caving in the back of his head. Blood and bits of brain matter clung to the back of his coat. The flies that had buzzed up when they rolled him over now swarmed onto the exposed wound.

Someone gasped. Matthews had braved a closer look, but the sight of the insects using the back of Stone's head for their breeding ground made him gag again. Pressing his hankie against his lips, he fled the room.

"Dear God . . ." the Duke breathed, staring at the damaged head. "The poor wretch."

"Wot's this about?" Jameson repeated. His hostility hadn't dissipated, but he now appeared more puzzled than angry. "Beggin' your pardon, your Grace, but this ain't your concern. Yours . . . or your ward's."

Kendra pushed herself to her feet. "It's our concern if you're going to hold the wrong person responsible for this man's death. The Luddites didn't kill him."

"Oh?" the constable cocked his head, regarding her with an expression both smug and challenging. "And who do you think killed Mr. Stone, Miss Donovan, if the blasted Luddites didn't do it?"

Kendra said nothing for a long moment. She allowed her gaze to sweep the room once more before returning to the pulverized skull of the victim. "I don't know the killer's identity—yet," she said finally. "That will require a much more thorough investigation. But offhand? I'd say we're dealing with a killer who didn't intend to kill. But once he started, I don't think he could stop."

4

Constable Jameson stared at her. Then he summarily dismissed her by turning to look at the Duke. "This is why ladies shouldn't involve themselves in such weighty matters, your Grace," he said. "They get fanciful notions."

Kendra drew in a sharp breath. She'd dealt with plenty of assholes in her career, but this man was a moron. "Okay, then," she snapped, "answer this: Was Mr. Stone deaf?"

Jameson grunted. "Wot kind of question is that? 'Course he wasn't!"

"Really? Because he'd have to be if he stayed at his desk while the Luddites were downstairs smashing the looms."

The constable blinked.

Bernard shifted his cap to scratch behind his ear. "The gentry mort's got a point. Oi reckon there'd 'ave ter been a godawful racket goin' on with them Luddites breakin' the frames."

Kendra kept her gaze locked on Jameson. "So why didn't Mr. Stone leave his office to investigate the noise? Unless you think he hid here while the Luddites vandalized the factory."

Bernard shook his head. "Nay. Mr. Stone ain't no bugaboo."

"Coward," Aldridge clarified, for Kendra's sake.

"Aye." Bernard nodded now. "He ain't—*wasn't* no coward."

The Duke said, "I see what you are getting at, Miss Donovan. The noise would have been enough to draw him downstairs to investigate. And if such a thing had happened, the Luddites would have set upon the poor man in the factory. Thus, his body would have been discovered downstairs."

Anger flared in the constable's brown eyes. "Doesn't mean one of those Luddites didn't sneak up here before they started ter break the frames. They could've clouted the poor sod then."

Kendra held onto her patience with an effort. "Mr. Stone was sitting here, behind his desk, when the unsub—when the killer picked up the bronze and struck the first blow. Has anyone been to Mr. Stone's office before?"

The men shook their heads.

"I'm going to hypothesize that the bronze was on the desk. It's the most reasonable assumption. Based on the angle of the head injury, the killer was standing on Mr. Stone's left, slightly behind him when he reached over to grab the bronze, hitting the victim and striking the parietal bone." She looked at Jameson. "Based on your theory, Constable, Mr. Stone continued to sit at his desk while a violent Luddite barged into his office. He didn't stand up or do anything to fend off the intruder."

Jameson's brows lowered as he stared at her.

She went on, sarcasm thickening her voice. "*No*, Mr. Stone, being the helpful soul that he must have been, just continued to *sit* there while the intruder picked up the bronze and walked around the desk to hit him on the back of the head."

Now Jameson's mouth knotted. "Mr. Stone was known ter drink. He could've been drunk and unaware when the Luddite snuck in and struck him."

Kendra eyed the man. He was *stubborn*. "The physical evidence doesn't support that theory," she said flatly. "If Mr. Stone had been drunk and passed out in his chair, with his head against the backrest, he would have been facing the killer. Mr. Stone would have been struck on the temple, crushing the frontal bone, not the parietal bone."

Her gaze traveled back to the dead man. "That's not what we have here. Mr. Stone was struck on the back of his head. And if the victim had been drunk, slumped over the desk when the first blow was struck, we'd be dealing with a different blood spatter pattern."

"How so, Miss Donovan?" asked the Duke, intrigued.

"Blood is dense; its surface tension basically creates a perfect sphere. For instance, if you cut your finger and let the blood drip on the floor, each drop will form a circle," she explained. "But do you see how the blood droplets on the desk are more oval—elongated, with what looks like a thin tail? The tail will point in the direction of the source of the blood spatter."

She watched as the men's eyes followed the invisible line across the desk to where Stone would have been sitting in the chair. "What we have here is a medium velocity impact," she continued. "The force of the bludgeoning would have propelled the blood to travel outward from the injury until gravity brought the droplets down across the desk."

The Duke nodded, and appeared to study the splatter of blood with fresh eyes. "'Tis basic physics. If Mr. Stone's head was already resting on the desk, the blood droplets would have little distance to travel—"

"And we'd be dealing with a ninety-degree impact, which is basically a free fall," Kendra cut in, nodding. "The splatter would be formed by round droplets, not oval."

Aldridge glanced at the back wall and ceiling. "What about there? It follows the same principle, I assume?"

"Yes and no. That was created when the murderer swung the bronze, contaminated with Stone's blood. It's called a cast-off pattern, which is exactly what its name implies. The blood was cast off from the bronze onto the walls and ceiling."

Jameson shifted impatiently, his brown eyes still regarding Kendra with skepticism.

"Look, it's not just the blood pattern," she said. "If Stone had been passed out with his head on his desk, you would also have found him in that position—not on the floor. Nor would the chair have been toppled over."

The constable crossed his arms and glared at her. "That's jest guesswork, Miss Donovan. You can't know any of that."

"It's more than guesswork. I'm looking at the *evidence*. There's other evidence that disproves Mr. Stone was drinking."

"Like w'ot?" he demanded.

"Where's the glass he was drinking from?" She flicked a glance at the sparkling crystal decanters and tumblers on the credenza that she'd noticed earlier. "I doubt the killer washed his glass and put it back."

The Duke's blue eyes brightened with admiration. "*Yes*. Yes, a brilliant observation, Miss Donovan. What you are saying is the most plausible explanation, with the fiend standing next to Mr. Stone, and using the bronze to strike him."

"They were both looking at something on the desk—"

"How can you know where a dead man was lookin'?" the constable interrupted, his eyes narrowed.

She said, "Because blood tells a story. Do you see this area here?" She pointed at the center of the desk.

The Duke frowned, inspecting the area she'd pointed at. "Yes, but I do not see any blood, Miss Donovan."

Kendra nodded. "Exactly. But there's blood spatter elsewhere on the desk. It's called a void pattern. It means something was on the desk, which protected that area from becoming contaminated."

Bernard and Freddie had come forward to study the desk as well. "Aye," Bernard said. "There's no blood there."

"Approximately twenty-six inches in length, sixteen inches in width," calculated the Duke. "We can only assume the height—"

"Yes and no," Kendra interrupted. "I'd say we're dealing with something no more than four inches high.

Anything higher would have interfered with the trajectory of the blood spatter. But there's something more important represented by the void pattern."

The Duke lifted his eyes from the desk to meet hers. "The killer took whatever had been on the desk after he murdered Mr. Stone," he said softly.

"And in that, the unsub made his first mistake." She scanned the area again. "The murder was disorganized, impulsive. The unsub took whatever was on the desk, so it means something."

Jameson scowled at her. "W'ot's this unsub you keep speaking of, eh?"

The Duke answered with a touch of pride. "Unknown subject—the perpetrator."

Freddie spoke up for the first time, looking at her. "How'd ye know it was impulsive?"

"Because the killer didn't bring a murder weapon with him. He acted rashly, using whatever was handy." She swung her gaze to Jameson. "It's another point against the killer being one of the Luddites, you know. The men that we ran into on the road were armed with axes and hammers. They brought potential murder weapons with them to the mill. Why not use them against Mr. Stone?"

Bernard gave a grunt of acknowledgement. "They'd 'ave used them, right enough."

Kendra circled the desk, her gaze roving over the black dots and drips against the wall, the smears on the floor. "I think Mr. Stone invited his killer inside his office. The person was someone he knew, or someone he didn't feel threatened by."

The constable was still standing with his arms crossed, his attitude hostile as he regarded Kendra. "Wot witchery is this, for you ter know such a thing?"

"No witchery or any magical nonsense, Constable Jameson," the Duke said, his voice hardening. "'Tis keen observation. Go on, Miss Donovan."

The Duke's defense of her hadn't won her any favor, Kendra realized. The constable's jaw tightened.

"I don't see any defensive wounds on Mr. Stone's hands," she said. "He didn't try to defend or protect himself. He had a level of trust with the unsub, allowing the killer to stand next to him, even slightly behind him." She shrugged. "If he didn't trust the killer, he was overly confident in his ability to fend off an attack." She eyed the body. "The victim was advanced in his age, but he's a big man. Men who are physically imposing like Mr. Stone often have a false sense of security."

Out of the corner of her eye, she saw Jameson straighten his spine, push his shoulders back, his chest out. The constable was a big man, too, though more muscle and less fat than the victim. Still, in this matter, he related to the victim, and he wasn't even aware that he was adopting a don't-mess-with-me stance.

As if adopting a swagger would allow him to avoid Stone's fate, Kendra thought. But she didn't let her lip curl with annoyance.

"The way I see it," she said, "Mr. Stone was sitting in his chair, angled forward slightly, which exposed the back of his head to the unsub. His attention was on whatever was on the desk. The killer was standing over him, picked up the bronze, and hit Stone. But the first blow didn't kill him immediately." She was visualizing it now. "Mr. Stone attempted to stand. He would have been stunned by the blow. Maybe he put his hands on the armrests of his chair to push himself up, and the killer struck again. That second blow sent Mr. Stone falling sideways to the floor. His grip on the chair would have caused it to tip over. The killer then continued to bludgeon his victim." She thought of the adrenaline pumping through the unsub, typical of high-stress situations. "It might have taken the killer a moment to even realize Mr. Stone was dead."

"Bloody hell," whispered Freddie, and made the sign of the cross.

"The killer then dropped the bronze." Kendra didn't want to think about the fingerprints from the unsub that were probably still on the murder weapon. She had no way to access the evidence. And even if she did, it wasn't like she could run them through any database or begin fingerprinting potential suspects. "He took whatever had been on the desk before he left."

She turned to the men and asked, "What was Mr. Stone like?"

Freddie spoke up. "He was a right bastard, that's what he was." His gaze settled on the body, his face twisting in distaste. "But I can't hold with this, nay. This ain't right."

"The Earl's gotta be informed," Jameson said ominously. "About the attack on the mill and Mr. Stone being killed."

"I shall send word to Falcon Court," said Matthews, who'd apparently crept back into the room. He still looked ashen, his face sweaty, but Kendra gave him points for returning. "No sense in disturbing his lordship's peace this evening though. Not like anything can be done about Mr. Stone now."

Kendra had almost forgotten about the boy until Andrew piped up. "Aye," he said, "'is Lordship'll be terrible upset that 'is fancy new frames 'ave been smashed."

She raised her eyebrows as she considered the boy. "More upset than to learn that his employee was murdered?"

"The frames are valuable," the boy pointed out, his thin shoulder jerking in a shrug.

Life was cheap in 1815, she knew. Then again, she couldn't exactly feel superior to her nineteenth-century counterparts. She'd investigated too many senseless killings, read too many accounts where a company's quest for profit had knowingly cost lives. Looking at history, backward and forward, the sad truth of it was that life had never been too valuable.

The sound of footsteps coming down the hall drew everybody's attention. A second later, an older man carrying a leather bag, cracked and faded with age, swept into the room. Beneath his tricorn hat, his face was long and sagged heavily, giving him a perpetually grumpy expression. His eyebrows shadowed his eyes like fuzzy awnings, but Kendra caught the gleam of blue from his irises. He wore a multi-caped greatcoat over a brown wool jacket. His breeches were baggy, his boots scuffed, and his cravat carelessly tied. Another young man in wool coat, hat, and scarf followed him, carrying a lantern.

"Dr. Poole—thank you for coming," Matthews greeted him.

"Ain't a social gathering, Oliver," snapped the doctor. He made a *tsk*ing sound in the back of his throat, and continued to walk forward until his boots hit the desk. "I saw what the damned vandals did downstairs." He stopped and peered down at the dead man. "Looks like they did a fair amount of damage up here too."

Dr. Poole pivoted suddenly to stare at Kendra. "Who are you, madam?"

"This is Miss Donovan," introduced Matthews. He dabbed the beads of sweat on his upper lip with his balled hankie. "And this gentleman is the Duke of Aldridge—Miss Donovan's guardian."

Poole's fuzzy brows lifted fractionally. "Maybe this is a social gathering after all," he muttered, and gave a short bow in the Duke's direction. "Apparently my wits have fled, but what's a duke and a lady doing in a place such as this?"

"Aye, that's wot I've been wantin' ter know," muttered the constable.

"We were in the inn, and heard about Mr. Stone. I wanted to assess the situation for myself," the Duke said carefully, earning a surprised look from the doctor.

"Curiosity?"

"Justice," Aldridge said.

The doctor was silent for a moment as he absorbed that. "Tom here said that Mr. Stone was killed by the Luddites," he said finally.

"The evidence suggests otherwise," Kendra said, shaking her head. "I think Mr. Stone was already dead by the time the Luddites arrived at the mill. Can you determine whether the statue is the murder weapon, Dr. Poole?"

Poole regarded her quizzically. Then he set his bag on the ground and walked over to the desk. He picked up the bronze, studying the blood crusting its base before glancing at the dead man. He set the statue down.

"Aye. It's the murder weapon, I'd say."

"Well, as long as you conducted a detailed analysis," Kendra said drily.

But then, what had she expected? She suddenly wished that she could call in Dr. Munroe, the London anatomist that she'd had dealings with twice before. The first time she met him, she hadn't expected much from a nineteenth-century doctor. But she'd quickly learned that he was very clever, and meticulous in his job. Despite the bronze obviously being the murder weapon, Munroe would never have assumed it without comparing the base of the statue to the wound. Apparently, she wasn't going to get Dr. Munroe's professionalism in East Dingleford.

Poole turned to inspect the body again. "A detailed analysis, you say? Looks like Stone was hit with something hard and heavy." He swiveled back to pick up the bronze. "This statue is hard and heavy. And do you see that there? That's blood. What else do you require as proof, Miss Donovan?"

Kendra huffed out a breath, made to feel foolish for her desire to implement twenty-first century procedures. She needed to let it go. It wasn't like she was building a case for the courts, and needed to keep the chain of evidence sacrosanct. For that matter, all she knew of law and order here was that there were two court systems, one for the commoners and one for the aristocracy.

"What about Mr. Stone?" she asked Poole. "Can you give an estimate of time of death?"

"You fancy yourself a doctor, do you, Miss Donovan?"

"She fancies herself a Bow Street Runner," the constable said.

Kendra shifted impatiently. "Narrowing down the time of death might be helpful in actually catching Mr. Stone's killer."

Poole squatted, examining the body in much the same way Kendra had. "Given the way he's stiffenin', I'd say he's been dead less than four hours. Probably was killed around four or half-past this afternoon."

He shook his head, and shoved himself to his feet. "I'll examine the body tomorrow. Constable, I'll need a man to help haul him away." He paused, his gaze on the rotund figure on the floor. "Make that several men."

Bernard gave a snorting laugh. "Aye, Mr. Stone was all guts and garbage, for sure."

"W'ot about the inquest?" the constable asked. "Shouldn't we leave him here for the jurors to see?"

"His lordship won't want him fouling up the air here. I'll write my statement for the inquest, and they can come to look at him in my room, if they feel the need. Seems pretty straightforward. Mr. Stone certainly did not have a visitation by God."

Kendra eyed the doctor. "A *what*?"

"'Tis a natural death, Miss Donovan," the Duke explained. "When someone dies naturally, the inquest finds that the deceased had a visitation by God."

"Oh." She looked at Poole. "When do you plan to do the autopsy, doctor?"

"Not sure if that's necessary. We already know how he died. Someone hit him over the head with that bronze on the desk. What more do you want?"

What more indeed? Kendra said nothing as the doctor picked up his bag. She wondered why he'd even brought the thing; it was obviously an unnecessary accessory for this particular house call.

"Good evening, your Grace . . . Miss Donovan." He gave Kendra a longer perusal, shook his head, then moved toward the door.

"One second, Doctor," she said, and waited until Dr. Poole glanced around at her again. "Did you know Mr. Stone?"

The fuzzy brows twitched, though with surprise or irritation, Kendra couldn't be sure.

"There ain't nobody in East Dingleford that I don't know, miss," he said.

"Any idea who would want to kill him?"

Dr. Poole eyed her. Kendra wasn't sure if he was trying to figure out the answer to her question, or if he was just trying to figure her out. "You might want to ask Lavinia that question."

"Lavinia?"

"Mrs. Stone—the victim's wife. She might have an idea. Or maybe not. Most everybody around these parts who knew Mr. Stone despised the bugger. But you're asking the wrong question, Miss Donovan."

"What's the right question?"

"Mr. Stone's been living in East Dingleford for nigh on twenty years, without anyone feelin' the need to brain the man." Poole's eyes gleamed from beneath the shadow of his eyebrows. He held her gaze for another beat without speaking. "Maybe the question you should be askin' isn't who wanted him dead, but why it took so long to do the deed."

5

Matthews accompanied Kendra and the Duke back to the posting inn, following them into the private parlor that Mr. Bolton had kept open for the Duke's use. New logs crackled in the hearth, placed there and tended by Mr. Bolton himself, before the innkeeper had left them to their privacy.

"This isn't London, or even Manchester," Matthews said, his gaze troubled as they entered the parlor. "To the best of my recollection, we've never had a murder in East Dingleford. People cock up their toes, to be sure. But we never had anyone being helped into their grave."

"Murder is innately disturbing," agreed Aldridge. He removed his greatcoat, hat, and gloves, and approached the sideboard. He removed a decanter's stopper and selected a goblet. "Would you care for a glass of Mrs. Bolton's very excellent apricot brandy, Mr. Matthews? I confess I could use a libation after seeing Mr. Stone."

Matthews swallowed hard. "Yes, it was quite horrifying. Thank you, a brandy would be lovely."

Aldridge splashed a generous amount into a glass and handed it to Matthews. He glanced at Kendra. "Brandy, Miss Donovan?"

"Sure." She dumped her outerwear on a chair and moved to the fire, holding her hands out to warm them.

Behind her, Matthews cleared his throat. "And you, sir . . . you say you have investigated similar vile acts?"

"We have done so on occasion, yes," he said carefully.

Turning, Kendra accepted the goblet the Duke brought her, her gaze searching his. Something was going on here. He was being cagey with Matthews, his expression inscrutable.

The Duke gestured to the chairs positioned in front of the fire. "Shall we be seated?"

"Thank you, sir." Matthews dispensed with his great-coat, gloves, and hat. He picked up his brandy glass again and eased himself into a seat. He frowned as he gazed at the fire, his glass dangling from his fingertips.

The Duke said, "You seem to have something on your mind, Mr. Matthews. Why don't you tell us what it is?"

Matthews lifted his glass and took a dainty sip of brandy. Then he sighed. "It would have been so much easier if the Luddites had committed the murder," he admitted. "Now an investigation is required, and my father is laid up with gout, and I—I confess I am uncertain how to go about this entire process."

He pulled his gaze away from the flames to look at Aldridge. "I am aware that you are only here in East Dingleford by the most unfortunate of circumstances, your Grace. If this were the normal course of events, you would be on your way tomorrow morning . . ."

"But we are not dealing with the normal course of events," Aldridge supplied slowly.

"No, we are not." Matthews took another swallow of the homemade brandy. His cheeks went pink, from the fire or the brandy, or perhaps the conversation. "I am asking . . . no, I am *begging* you to postpone your journey tomorrow, sir, and investigate Mr. Stone's murder."

It didn't escape Kendra's attention that Matthews was not really including her in the conversation. His gaze was locked on the Duke.

The Duke inclined his head graciously. "We accept your invitation, Mr. Matthews. My ward and I shall stay on in East Dingleford to conduct the inquiry into Mr. Stone's death. I'll make the necessary arrangements with Mr. Bolton for our extended stay."

Relief washed over Matthews's face. "Thank you, sir."

The Duke held up a finger. "A word of warning—I shall be sending for assistance. My nephew, the Marquis of Sutcliffe. And Sam Kelly, a Bow Street Runner."

"A thief-taker?" Matthews frowned uneasily. "Do you think that is really necessary, your Grace?"

"I do. Mr. Kelly's help has always been invaluable in these matters."

Matthews said nothing for a moment. Then he nodded. "I shall not offer an argument. What is the next course of action, sir?"

Kendra leaned forward. She was done with being ignored. "It would be helpful if you told us everything you know about Mr. Stone."

He glanced at her nervously. "I—I actually know very little about the man," he said slowly. "East Dingleford may appear a small village by London standards, but we do have a social structure here, and Mr. Stone and I did not belong in the same circles. The few times we socialized were at local assemblies, the occasional ball at Falcon Court, and gatherings like the village's Guy Fawkes Night. That is held in my family's paddock on the outskirts of East Dingleford. I barely knew the man."

Kendra regarded Matthews. "I'm not asking if you were friends with him. Dr. Poole said he lived here for twenty years, and he was disliked by the community. Tell me what you know *of* him."

Matthews hesitated, as though weighing his words. "Mr. Stone was low born," he finally said. "He was gauche and often brutish. I do not have dealings with the mill myself, but through my father, I have heard of dissension among the workers."

"How many workers are in the mill?" asked Kendra.

He frowned. "I'm not certain. Possibly three hundred. Maybe less, now that Mr. Stone has been bringing in the new looms."

"People have been losing their jobs?"

Matthews nodded. "That is why the Luddites attacked the mill."

"A lot of disgruntled workers then." *And a lot of potential suspects.*

"I would think so, yes." Matthews paused, and gave the Duke a significant look. "There were rumors as well."

Aldridge lifted his eyebrows. "Of what sort?"

Matthews looked uncomfortable. "Of Mr. Stone's debauchery throughout the years, even after his marriage. I dare not repeat some of the gossip, for fear of offending Miss Donovan."

Kendra managed not to roll her eyes. This coming from the man who'd thrown up at the crime scene. "I'm not given to swooning, Mr. Matthews. If you want Mr. Stone's murder solved, you need to tell us everything, sensibilities be damned."

He frowned and looked at the Duke.

"Do not concern yourself with my ward," Aldridge said. "She is not an uppish female. Please, continue."

After a moment, Matthews nodded. "Very well. There was an incident last spring at the assembly. I was on the dance floor, so I did not witness it myself, but my father was forced to step in. A farmer accused Mr. Stone of being a cardsharp."

Aldridge looked surprised. "That is a very serious accusation. Was it true?"

"It could not be proven," Matthews said carefully.

The Duke glanced at Kendra. "Society has little tolerance for cardsharps. It is one of the primary reasons men end up in the dueling fields at dawn in London."

Dueling was a strange concept to her. There were codes of conduct involved, which basically made it a civilized way to murder each other. Then again, maybe it was a little like chamber pots; it would just take a little while to get used to.

"I'll bet alcohol has a lot to do with that, as well," Kendra muttered, and shook her head.

The Duke smiled at her. "I think you may be right, my dear."

She moved her attention back to Matthews. "What happened when the farmer accused Mr. Stone?"

"Since no one could prove that Mr. Stone had been cheating, I assume the farmer had to pay his debt to Mr. Stone." Matthews shrugged. "The incident set tongues wagging for a short time, because it took place at the assembly, but it was resolved peacefully and forgotten. I only mention it now because of your inquiry into Mr. Stone's background."

"The farmer will need to be interviewed," she said. "What's his name?"

"I don't recall. But my father or Constable Jameson ought to be able to tell you. The incident happened last spring, Miss Donovan. 'Tis a long time to wait to seek revenge."

Her lips twisted. "I don't think there's a statute of limitations over how long someone holds a grudge. And from my experience, the more money involved, the bigger the grudge. Have there been any more recent accusations of cheating leveled at Mr. Stone?"

"Not that I'm aware. But I can ask my father."

Kendra said, "Mr. Stone's wife may know. We'll need to speak with her tomorrow. And we'll need to interview Lord Bancroft."

Matthews raised his eyebrows. "You can't think Lord Bancroft murdered Mr. Stone?"

"I don't think anything at this point. That's why we need to conduct interviews."

He gave a reluctant nod. "I must inform his lordship first about Mr. Stone's death, then I can bring you to Mrs. Stone." He flicked a look at the porcelain clock on the table. He drained the thimble-full of brandy left in his glass, and pushed himself to his feet. "'Tis late. I must bid you goodnight, sir, Miss Donovan."

"Until tomorrow morning," the Duke said, rising. "Shall we say nine o'clock?"

"Yes, sir." Matthews shrugged into his greatcoat and picked up his gloves and hat. "Thank you for your assistance, your Grace."

"After we speak to Mrs. Stone, we'll need to go to the mill again," Kendra said. "We'll need to interview the workers. At this point, it looks like Stone was killed during work hours. That means we've got three hundred suspects . . . or three hundred witnesses."

Matthews gave a heavy sigh. "I assume Constable Jameson will be questioning the workers, but the whole thing seems rather overwhelming. I do not know how we will find the fiend who did this."

"That is why you asked for our help, Mr. Matthews," the Duke reminded him, tapping him lightly on his narrow shoulder as he walked him to the door.

Kendra lifted her eyebrows when the Duke turned to her after closing the door on the departing Matthews.

"You never had any intention of leaving East Dingleford," she said, "yet you let Matthews practically beg you to help with the investigation. What game are you playing, sir?"

"No game." But he began to smile. "You have impressed upon me that investigations involving murder tend to make people anxious. I thought it would be best if we were invited to pursue this matter, rather than pushing our way in. Now we can act with the authority from the local magistrate."

Kendra nodded. "A clever strategy, your Grace. Especially since I don't think we'll be getting any help from the constable."

"You were quite brilliant in eliminating the Luddites as the murderer," he said, retracing his footsteps to the side table to pick up his brandy. He eyed her over the rim of the glass. "Do you think this might actually turn out to be a simple robbery? Mr. Stone was killed for what was on the desk?"

"I don't know. But I plan to find out."

❖

Forty-five minutes later, Aldridge was in his room. He pressed his ring into the soft wax of the last letter he'd written, sealing it. He added the letter to the two others already written, glancing at the young boy hovering nearby.

"Two of these letters must be sent out at first light with your fastest riders." He handed over the thick stack and a coin for the boy's troubles. "Do you understand?"

"Aye, my lord—er, Oi mean, yer Grace." The lad shot him a gap-toothed grin, and bolted for the door.

Wilson glanced up from the corner chair where he'd been polishing the Duke's boots. "How long will we be staying in East Dingleford, sir?"

"I'm not certain." The Duke's gaze traveled around the darkly paneled bedchamber. It was the best the Green Maiden had to offer, although much smaller than he was used to. Still, it had a dressing room, which he appreciated, and a fire in the hearth. The bedchamber's furnishings included two upholstered chairs, a small table, and a writing desk, which was pushed against the window. The canopied bed looked comfortable enough.

Wilson set down the boot he'd been buffing, satisfied that he'd repaired its gleam, and stood up. "Is there anything you require before I bid you goodnight, your Grace?"

"No, thank you." Aldridge went to the fireplace, picked up the poker, and pushed the logs around, sending up a shower of sparks in the grate. "Please make sure I am awakened at seven. Miss Donovan and I shall have breakfast before we meet Mr. Matthews."

"Yes, sir." Wilson strode to the door, but hesitated there. His face was a careful mask. "Miss Donovan appears to attract a considerable amount of trouble, sir. I don't recall you ever being involved in murders before she arrived at Aldridge Castle."

Aldridge arched a brow at his manservant. "I do not think that is fair to leave at Miss Donovan's door, Wilson. Mr. Stone would have been murdered here in East Dingleford whether Miss Donovan was in the vicinity or not."

"That may be true, but would *you* have been in the vicinity?" The valet gave him a significant look, then bowed out of the room. "Pleasant dreams, sir."

Thoughtfully, Aldridge crossed the bedchamber to bolt the door. Wilson had helped him undress earlier, and he now shrugged out of his robe. The cold drove him toward bed, snuffing out the candles and turning down the oil lamps quickly before climbing in beneath the canopy.

He should have slipped easily into slumber. The day had been long and, with the murder, quite eventful. Even so, his mind continued to race. He thought of the three letters he had sent with the boy. One would depart on the Royal Mail, and take a full day to reach the staff awaiting their arrival in Lancashire. The other two letters would travel farther, but if the riders were truly the fastest, they should be delivered at varying times the next day.

The Bow Street Runner, who'd be coming from London, would probably be in East Dingleford on Tuesday morning. Alec, meanwhile, was currently settling business at his estate in Northamptonshire. God willing, he would receive the letter by nightfall tomorrow. Aldridge figured that Alec would ignore the rule about traveling on the Sabbath. He expected to greet his nephew by Monday afternoon, at the latest.

Alec would be quicker not only because his estate was closer, but his motivation greater. The fact that Kendra Donovan had become embroiled in yet another murder investigation would not sit well with his nephew, Aldridge knew. Alec's instinct would be to rush in to protect the American. Of course, he understood Alec's fear. His own inclination was to shield the gentler sex.

Not that Kendra Donovan wanted to be shielded. And she certainly never acted like the gentler sex. Good God, she'd actually pulled the muff pistol from her reticule while on the road, and had tried to push him behind her at the approach of the Luddites. If he didn't understand her good intentions, he would have been insulted by the gesture, which seemed to indicate that she thought he was so white-livered as to cower behind a female's skirts.

Concern pulled his brows together. There were some areas where he and the American would never see eye to eye, he knew. What he viewed as protection, Kendra saw as a prison. But whether she liked it or not, he felt the need to place himself as a buffer between her and the nasty slings and arrows of the Beau Monde. But how could he protect her from his own nephew?

He wasn't a fool. He bloody well *knew* that Alec wasn't only teaching Kendra to shoot when they disappeared into the woods. He'd been young once. He remembered what it was like to be in love. He recalled those heady days before he'd made Arabella his wife and gave a wistful sigh. It was embarrassing, really. Watching Kendra and Alec together, he'd begun to feel like one of those detestable matchmaking mamas who plagued the Season, desperate to marry their whey-faced daughters off to the first eligible bachelor that gave them attention.

Fiend seize it. He might not be Kendra's father, but he *was* her guardian. And by God, he refused to stand by and let his own nephew compromise her. She wasn't a light-skirt to be trifled with. It was within his rights to demand that Alec marry her.

Except—and this was truly the crux of the matter—he suspected that it wasn't Alec who was averse to marriage.

What to do? His frown deepened. Kendra was guided by a different set of principles, fashioned from another time. And as much as Kendra sometimes drove him to the brink of sanity, the future from which she hailed enthralled him. While the American remained annoyingly reticent about giving away too many details—because of a misplaced fear that she might somehow change the future—he knew that daily life in the twenty-first century moved at a much faster pace. She'd once told him that, in the future, they were no longer at the horse and buggy stage, that they'd even traveled to the moon. *The moon!* How marvelous was such a thing? He couldn't fathom a world without horses and carriages for everyday use, but he followed the current development of steam engines with keen interest. He'd invested in several steam ships himself. As far as he was concerned, it was only a matter of time before the vessels dominated the waterways, replacing sails. Steam engines had been much less successful on land, but someday, he supposed, that would change too.

But if he were truly honest with himself, the societal shifts that came with the passage of time and technological advancements left him uncomfortable. As much as he applauded the advancement of women—his own wife had been intellectually gifted and had deserved the same respect as her male counterparts—he still believed a gentleman had a duty to protect the fairer sex. Was that so wrong? Was it wrong to wish to protect Kendra's reputation from being shredded by the claws of society's more vicious cats? Was it so wrong of him not to want to see her crushed? And she *would* be crushed, if she didn't conform to the sensibilities of this time.

He drew in a deep breath, then exhaled. He knew that his sister, Caro, had noticed Alec and Kendra's closeness. Of course, she'd assigned the blame to Kendra. She was brazen, Caro said. She was odd. Caro had cornered him every chance she could get to discuss Kendra's fast behavior.

Aldridge Castle was enormous, and yet it hadn't been big enough to accommodate both Kendra and his sister. All of this had motivated him to arrange for the visit to the Lancashire estate. He'd inherited the land and manor from a cousin twice removed who'd failed to produce any male heirs. At the time, putting half of England between the two women had seemed the only way to stop them from murdering each other. How could he have foreseen that they'd stumble into a murder investigation in these remote regions of Yorkshire?

He was a man of science, but he was no atheist. He believed firmly in the existence of a deity. Of course, his faith veered more toward the Deism espoused by

Kendra's countryman, Thomas Jefferson, which envisioned a benevolent but ultimately uninvolved deity. Yet in the last two months, since Kendra's miraculous arrival, he'd begun to reconsider that, and wonder if a higher power might be involved.

Wilson was right. They wouldn't have been on this particular road at this particular time if it were not for Kendra. He'd only been seeking peace of mind by separating his sister and his new ward.

An image of Mr. Stone's savagely bludgeoned head came to mind. He wouldn't be finding peace of mind here in East Dingleford. But he'd settle for justice.

6

I received word from his lordship," Matthews said when he arrived in the public dining room the next morning, where Kendra and the Duke were finishing up their hearty breakfast of eggs, fried tomatoes, mushrooms, and oat cakes. "He will be at the mill. I have my gig ready."

Kendra nodded and took a last sip of coffee. The dining room was busy with travelers breaking their fast before setting off again on their disparate journeys. Given the sunshine streaming through the windows, it would be a good day to travel. Of course, blue skies and sunshine didn't mean balmy temperatures. In late October, temperatures in England fell a little south of fifty degrees Fahrenheit. Not bad, but cool enough for Kendra to be grateful for the navy wool spencer that Molly had given her to wear over the long-sleeved pale blue muslin walking dress.

Matthews went outside to await them, and Kendra and the Duke followed shortly after. The young man was standing next to a two-wheeled, open-air contraption that was harnessed to a single horse. Kendra liked to think that she didn't scare easily, but her heart picked up speed at the sight of the vehicle. The wheels were large, the seat set high off the ground. In fact, the entire thing looked dangerously wobbly. They'd be road kill if the horse got skittish and bolted.

"Why aren't we walking?" she asked. "We walked last night."

"We walked last night because of the fog, Miss Donovan," Matthews said, hoisting himself up onto the padded leather seat. "This will be faster. It's a two-seater, but I think we can manage."

Kendra swallowed hard, but took the Duke's offered hand and climbed up on the gig. The ground seemed very far away. Her fingers itched with the twenty-first century need to secure herself with a seat belt, or some other sort of safety harness.

"Do not fret, Miss Donovan," the Duke said, smiling as he met her eyes. "It's quite safe."

"Yeah? I'd like to see the statistics on that."

"Very few people have been killed in gig accidents," he said.

"What about maimed? *Shit*!"

The curse escaped when Matthews cracked his whip, as the horse trotted out of the stable yard and Kendra was jerked backward. Matthews gave her a sideways glance, startled.

Aldridge pressed his lips together, apparently holding back great mirth at her predicament. "Miss Donovan is unused to riding on gigs," he offered.

"Miss Donovan doesn't want to break all her bones," Kendra snapped. "It's bad enough that—" She broke off with an embarrassing yelp when the carriage wheels hit a rut and her ass went airborne.

"*Oh shit*." She made an instinctive move to grab onto anything that would hold her steady. Only when Matthews gave his own yelp did she realize that she'd latched onto his upper thigh.

"Sorry. Sorry." Still, it took half a minute for her to peel her hand away.

The Duke took pity on her, grasping her hand and looping it through the crook of his elbow. He winced only a little when her fingers dug through several layers of fabric into his forearm. Logically, Kendra knew that they would both be catapulted into the ditch if they hit a bigger pothole. Psychologically, though, holding onto something made her feel a little better.

She worked to steady her breathing, focusing on the landscape rather than the road beneath her. Yorkshire in the fall was truly breathtaking. Mother Nature had painted the sloping hills green, yellow, and brilliant gold, while the woodlands, separated by patches of field and moors, were a fiery red, amber, and burnt sienna. Hedgerows and low gray stone walls crisscrossed hills that were dotted with sheep. They passed a few cottages, stone barns, and outbuildings and she glimpsed the river, bright blue shot with silver beneath the blazing sun, through the trees.

Kendra was vaguely ashamed of her panic attack when they arrived at the mill without incident. If she stayed in the nineteenth century, she'd probably have to get used to traveling in such antiquated contraptions.

If . . . That implied she had a choice in the matter.

Narrowing her eyes against the glare of the sun, she focused on the brick building ahead. The mill was as enormous in the daytime as it had been at night, but not nearly as spooky, as it looked exactly what it was—a factory. A trio of men in rough worker's garb stood outside the door, smoking and talking, but the men stopped talking and their eyes narrowed with suspicion as the newcomers approached. No one said anything. Kendra didn't have to look back at the men to know that their eyes followed them into the building.

The windows flooded the interior with light, revealing more workers—young boys as well as men—in the process of cleaning up the mess left by the Luddites. Some of them stopped what they were doing to stare at Kendra, Matthews, and the Duke; others continued their work, hammering at the water frames, picking up the tangled skeins of cotton off the floor, hanging from the machinery, seemingly uninterested in their visitors. It reminded Kendra of the morning after Halloween, when people were left to clean up after tricksters decorated their houses and trees with streams of toilet paper. No one in the mill appeared particularly friendly.

Kendra found herself retracing her footsteps from the previous evening. The mill relied mostly on sunlight to lighten its gloomy interior, but here in the hallway, a few wall sconces had been lit. She heard voices coming from the first open door in the hall, and followed Matthews into the room. A quick glance revealed an office, the kind that Kendra expected in a mill. It definitely wasn't a gentleman's study, like Stone's office. Here bookshelves were filled with thick ledgers, and rolled folios that appeared to be blueprints and maps. In the corner of the room, a simple wooden coat stand was festooned with a greatcoat and hat. On the desk was a pewter inkstand that held quill pens, a vial of ink, a penknife, a taper stick for candles, and two boxes, one for sprinkling sand, the other for the wafers used to seal letters. The rest of the desk was a chaotic mix of sheets of foolscap and letters. A pair of gray kid gloves, a black beaver hat, and a walking stick with an ornate polished silver handle had been thrown on top of the chaos.

An old man sat behind the desk, still wearing his greatcoat. He held one of the rulers, bouncing it in an angry tattoo against the edge of the desk. There was only one chair facing the desk, unoccupied, but there were two other men in the room, standing in front of the desk. One was Constable Jameson. The other man looked to be in his early forties, with dishwater blond hair, light blue eyes, and a clean-shaven face with average features. His complexion was pale, suggesting a life spent indoors. Average height. Neither fat nor thin. Kendra got a managerial vibe off him—not upper management, but mid—except for his clothes, which were exquisitely tailored and tasteful.

Jameson was speaking. "I've got men huntin' for the ruffians, have no fear, sir. Their necks will be stretched or it'll be off ter Botany Bay for them!"

"Good," the old man said, his voice as hard and cold as polished granite. "Their vandalism has cost me a bloody cod of money." Though he was sitting, and at least double the age of the men facing him, he held himself with the unyielding strength of a much younger man. His spine was ramrod straight in the chair, his shoulders squared in the expertly tailored coat.

Lord Nathan Bancroft, the Earl of Langfrey, Kendra assumed. He'd lost almost all of his hair except the half-moon gray fringe at the base of his skull. His weathered face was lined and speckled with age. His eyes, beneath iron-gray brows, were cold, dark, and intense. Kendra felt the jolt all the way down to her toes when he flicked a look in their direction as they entered the office.

The old man's gaze fixed on Kendra and the ruler that he'd been rapping on the desk suddenly froze, midair. No one said anything. Then the old man stood abruptly, his gaze still locked on Kendra. "Who the bloody hell are *you*?" he demanded.

Matthews had retrieved his hanky, and now clutched it in his hand like rosary beads. He cleared his throat nervously. "Lord Bancroft, may I introduce the Duke of Aldridge and his ward, Miss Donovan. I—I sent word to you that they would be inquiring into Mr. Stone's death."

Bancroft's expression was enigmatic. Then he gave himself a little shake, dropped the ruler, and came around the desk, his step agile.

"Forgive me for staring, Miss Donovan," he said, even as he continued to stare. "But a mill is not the normal environment for ladies. Did I hear Oliver correctly when he said you would be investigating Mr. Stone's death?"

Maybe someday she'd get used to the men in this era gawking at her like she was a succubus from hell, Kendra thought. "You heard correctly. The Luddites didn't kill your manager, my lord," she said, keeping her voice firm. *Don't let them see you sweat.* She shot the constable a pointed glance. "I want to make that clear to you in case it hasn't been: the evidence suggests that Mr. Stone was killed by somebody else."

"The evidence?" the other man in the room said. "*What* evidence?"

Kendra was disconcerted to realize she'd forgotten about the third man. Bancroft had commanded her complete attention. Matthews introduced the other man as Mr. Biddle—Mr. Stone's assistant, and Kendra knew she'd been right; mid-management.

Biddle executed a brief bow. "Your Grace, Miss Donovan. Forgive me, but I don't understand. The Luddites destroyed the factory at the same time Mr. Stone was killed. How can the two not be connected?"

Kendra gave Jameson a pointed look. "Didn't you explain how the murder happened?"

The constable's chest rose. "Now, see here, why should I go on and tell them all yer hysterical notions, Miss Donovan? It ain't like you can prove it."

"I believe Miss Donovan proved it last night," the Duke said, his tone cool and razor-sharp. Under the nobleman's regard, Jameson's face reddened. The earl's dark eyes regarded them without expression.

Matthews spoke up. "As you are aware, my lord, my father is incapacitated at the moment."

Bancroft's thin mouth twitched. "Still has the gout, I take it?"

"Yes, sir. I am acting as magistrate until my father recovers. As such, I have given leave for the Duke to make inquiries."

"I see."

Kendra eyed Bancroft. "I'm sorry for your loss," she said, even though he didn't seem particularly upset over Stone's death. When he said nothing, she asked, "How long did you know Mr. Stone?"

"He has worked for me for twenty years."

"Were you close?"

"No."

She had already suspected as much. She glanced at their audience, then looked back to Bancroft. "I will need to speak to you. Perhaps somewhere more private?" She needed to keep the interviews separate, the statements uncontaminated.

"I'm afraid I cannot accommodate you at the moment, Miss Donovan. Mr. Stone's death and the blasted Luddites have left me with a bit of a mess." He picked up the gloves, tugging them on. "Work must be done."

Kendra stared at him in disbelief. "So does an investigation, sir," she said. "You do want to find out what happened to an employee who worked for you for twenty years, don't you?"

His thin lips curved into a smile, although Kendra wasn't sure what he found funny. "I do. Certainly, I do. I shall make myself available for you to quiz me later. I would be delighted if you . . . and your Grace"—he paused, and inclined his head to include Aldridge—"would come to dine with me and my daughter tonight at Falcon Court."

Kendra didn't like how Bancroft had taken control of the situation, but the Duke was already nodding. "Thank you, sir. What time shall we arrive?"

"We dine at seven." Bancroft picked up his hat and walking stick. "I can send my carriage for you."

"Thank you, but I have my own carriage," said Aldridge.

A gleam of amusement came into Bancroft's dark eyes as they shifted from the Duke back to Kendra. "I shall look forward to our evening together, sir. Miss Donovan."

His gaze lingered for a moment on Kendra, then he turned abruptly, the movement sending the three capes on his greatcoat fluttering as he disappeared out the door.

7

Kendra wasn't sure what to make of the Earl of Langfrey. He gave her what one of her colleagues in the
Bureau would call the heebie-jeebies. She hadn't
expected him to break down in tears over his employee's
death, but his utter lack of distress struck her as odd.
Of course, some people reacted to trauma in different
ways, and, in all fairness, he'd had a couple of hours
to absorb the shock before coming to the mill. Maybe
that accounted for his cold behavior. Or maybe he was
just an asshole.

Bancroft reminded her of other suspects she'd encountered who were wealthy and well-connected. They were
the ones who always thought they could charm, manipu-
late, or maneuver their way out of any situation. And if
that failed, they'd pull out their checkbooks. Or, worse,
they'd call in their lawyers. In the twenty-first century,
people like Bancroft always employed a battalion of
sharp-eyed, nattily dressed, high-priced lawyers, whose
sole purpose in life was to block inquiries from anyone
and everyone in law enforcement.

At least here—and she nearly smiled at the
thought—she wouldn't have to worry about lawyers. Lord
Bancroft wouldn't be inviting his legal team to dinner
tonight. The earl wasn't the only one who was looking
forward to the evening.

But for now, Kendra would settle for talking to Biddle.
She swung around to face the assistant manager. He was

nervous, she could see, fiddling with one of the gold buttons on his waistcoat.

She glanced at the Duke. "Your Grace, perhaps you, Mr. Matthews, and Constable Jameson could begin interviewing the workers downstairs? Find out when they last saw Mr. Stone alive, and if they knew of anyone who threatened him."

Jameson glared at her, and Kendra realized that she was taking control of the situation, much as Bancroft had. She couldn't blame the constable for being angry. It didn't mean she was going to back off though.

"And w'ot are you gonna be doing?" Jameson asked.

"I'll be interviewing Mr. Biddle."

"But—"

"'Tis a sound plan," the Duke interrupted briskly, aware of the rising tensions. "It will go much quicker if we divide the workers amongst ourselves, gentlemen."

The Duke maneuvered the two men out of the room, although not before Jameson shot Kendra a last, enraged look over his shoulder.

Biddle remained standing, still fiddling with the button on his waistcoat.

"Why don't we sit down, Mr. Biddle?" Kendra suggested. She didn't wait, parking herself in the one chair facing the desk. He hesitated, then shrugged and lowered himself into the chair behind the desk.

"How long have you worked with Mr. Stone?" she asked, eyeing him as he ran an agitated hand through his hair.

"Nineteen years," he said. "Forgive me, Miss Donovan. But this is such a shock."

"I'm sorry. I'm sure it must be. Are you from East Dingleford?"

"No. Wardle." He dropped his hands to the desk, and laced his fingers together. "'Tis a village a mile outside Manchester. In fact, I was working at a mill in Manchester when I saw Lord Bancroft's newspaper advertisement for the assistant manager position here."

"Lord Bancroft interviewed you and hired you? Not Mr. Stone?"

"No. I mean, yes. The earl hired me," he clarified. "Why is that significant?"

"It might not be." She summoned a smile, even as she studied him. Some people were just anxious during interviews. Others were anxious because they had something to hide. She wondered which category Biddle fell into. "Tell me about Mr. Stone."

"What do you wish to know?"

"Did you two get along?"

"Yes."

"No disagreements? No arguments? That has got to be some kind of world record—nineteen years working for someone, and not one disagreement." She let that hang for a moment, then pressed, "Especially someone like Mr. Stone. We've heard that he wasn't a pleasant person. He was even accused of cheating at cards, which, I've been told, is a serious offense."

Biddle licked his lips. "I suppose we had a few disagreements, but . . . he was the mill's manager. I reported to him."

"You're saying that you were business associates, not friends?"

"Yes. That is exactly what I'm saying."

"Okay, then what was he like to work for? Was he even-tempered, or did he come to work in a bad mood?"

"He could be even-tempered, and he could be in a foul mood."

Kendra sighed. "Mr. Biddle, do you want his murderer caught?"

"Of course!"

"Then build me a picture. Don't lie or soften it. What was Mr. Stone like?"

He was silent for a long moment, staring at his tense hands. "Mr. Stone was complicated," he finally said. "He could be in a jovial mood . . ."

"But," Kendra prodded.

Biddle took the bait. "But his jovial mood often came at the expense of the mill workers."

"How so?"

Biddle unlaced his fingers and spread his hands on the desk. "He was the manager of Bancroft Mill. We employ nearly three hundred workers, Miss Donovan. It's the largest mill in the area."

"I see. In other words, he held a lot of power."

"Yes, he did."

"And how did he use his power?"

Biddle pursed his lips as he considered the question. "He . . . he enjoyed threatening workers with dismissal—without references. His humor could be cruel."

"Cruel to you?"

"No." He met her eyes, and shrugged. "I served a purpose, Miss Donovan. I handle the day-to-day operation of the mill, something which Mr. Stone had no interest in doing. He would never have dismissed me."

Kendra wondered if that was true. No one was indispensable. And if Stone turned on his assistant of nineteen years, what would Biddle have done?

She asked, "Did he threaten to fire workers, or did he actually fire them?"

"Both. We've had to dismiss workers with the addition of new frames."

"That must have angered a lot of your employees."

"Yes, but Lord Bancroft was the one who made the decision to order them, not Mr. Stone. It is essential for progress, you must understand."

"How many workers were fired recently?"

Biddle hesitated. "Seven."

"We'll need you to give us the names of all the workers who were dismissed. Did any of them threaten Mr. Stone, or seem particularly angry after they were let go?"

"I can't say that I recall a specific threat, but all the workers are angry, Miss Donovan. As the ward of someone like the Duke of Aldridge, I suppose you don't see it." His lips twisted, and something flashed in his blue eyes. It took her a moment to recognize it as bitterness.

"Most of the people in this country are angry," he continued. "At the government. At the Prince Regent. At our world." His hands curled into tight fists. "Our betters have become blind to the difficulties of the common folk. The Corn Laws and Enclosure Act have made life difficult, if not impossible, for many, while the Prince Regent depletes the royal coffers on such extravagances as Brighton Palace!"

He thumped his fist on the desk, and Kendra revised her opinion of Biddle. He no longer appeared to be one of the nameless people languishing in mid-management, a cog in a wheel to clock in and out. In his unremarkable face, she saw the kind of passionate fury that, if multiplied, could seed insurgencies.

"*Vive la révolution*," she murmured softly.

The rage died instantly, leaving Biddle pale and shaky. "No. No, I do not speak of revolution—"

"Hey, my country was born out of a revolution," she reminded him, summoning what she hoped was a soothing smile. But inwardly, she metaphorically kicked herself for not keeping in mind the sensitivities of this era. Even though France had ended its bloody revolution sixteen years ago, she knew that the British government still feared the possibility of England following a similar path and overthrowing the monarchy. To keep tabs on any populist sentiment, the English government had been known to plant spies throughout the country, listening to conversations in taverns, inns, coffee shops, and public squares, the nineteenth century version of the NSA. No wonder Biddle looked a little nervous.

"I would never advocate revolution," he said quickly. "Or the fall of the monarchy."

"I don't really care." She didn't. *Maybe I don't care because I know that the British monarchy is still going strong more than two centuries from now*, she thought.

Biddle blinked at her in surprise.

She shrugged. "What I *do* care about is who killed Mr. Stone. Can you think of anyone who might have killed him?"

"No." He shook his head vehemently. "Mr. Stone was not well liked, but, as I already told you, there were no recent threats against him."

"What about not-so-recent threats? We heard about a farmer who accused Mr. Stone of cheating at cards. Did Mr. Stone tell you about the incident?"

"I think you are under a misimpression, Miss Donovan. Mr. Stone was the mill manager, but he rarely came to the mill. I am involved in the day-to-day operation, not Mr. Stone. He and I had very little to do with each other."

Kendra allowed her gaze to travel around the office, again noting the sheaves of foolscap and stacked ledgers. Silently, she compared it to Stone's office, which was all for show, definitely not for work. Apparently the only work Stone had done was as the hatchet man, firing employees. He enjoyed the rush of power it gave him. *What a guy.*

She looked at Biddle. "Why did Lord Bancroft keep Mr. Stone on if he didn't do his job?"

"I cannot say."

"What was their relationship like? Were they friends?"

He shook his head. "No. I . . . No."

Kendra waited. Silence was as powerful a tool as asking the right question or applying the right pressure. Most people rushed to fill the void with words.

Biddle swallowed, and his gaze bounced nervously around the room. He looked back at Kendra. "I don't precisely know how to describe their relationship," he finally said. "His lordship is not a man to be trifled with, and yet I felt Mr. Stone took liberties."

"Liberties? How?"

"It's difficult to explain, but Mr. Stone wasn't as deferential to the earl as he should have been, given his station. There were times when he even appeared to mock him. Not overtly, but . . . I cannot explain it. Perhaps I imagined the slight."

"I see." She regarded him closely. "Let's say you didn't imagine it. How did Lord Bancroft react to Mr. Stone when he wasn't being . . . respectful?"

Biddle rubbed his jaw. "He didn't really react. His lordship ignored him."

"Maybe Lord Bancroft didn't want trouble."

He frowned at her. "Perhaps."

Yet the way he said it sound like he couldn't imagine such a thing. Kendra understood. In this world, Bancroft wasn't only Stone's employer, he was an earl. That meant something. For him to ignore Stone's insubordination would be unusual.

She said, "Tell me what happened yesterday at the mill, Mr. Biddle. What time did Mr. Stone arrive?"

Biddle blinked at the sudden change of subject. "Ah . . . I think it was half past twelve."

"You said that he doesn't often come to the mill. Why did he come yesterday?"

"I don't know."

Kendra stared at him. "Mr. Stone didn't give you a reason why he decided to come in yesterday?"

"No."

"What was his mood like?"

Biddle hesitated. "I don't know. He seemed . . . preoccupied."

"Over what?"

"I don't know."

"Okay. He arrived at half past twelve. Then what did he do?"

"He went into his office."

"Did he stay there?"

"Yes. I didn't see him again until two. Perhaps half-past two? It's all so muddled."

"You saw him—how? From a distance? Did he speak to you?"

Biddle interlocked his fingers again, and stared at them intently. "He came into my office because he needed to speak to me. He informed me that he would be away for a few days."

Kendra raised her brows at the news. "He was leaving town?"

He shrugged. "He told me that he would be traveling to Manchester. This was not unusual, Miss Donovan. I believe he found East Dingleford quite dull."

"Leaving you in charge," she remarked.

"Also not unusual."

Kendra tilted her head to the side as she surveyed him. "Will you become the mill manager now, Mr. Biddle?"

"I do not know Lord Bancroft's plans."

"You ran the mill, really, but Mr. Stone held the higher position. That must have been annoying. But his death sort of clears the way for you, doesn't it?"

He drew in a sharp breath. "What are you suggesting? That . . . that I wanted Mr. Stone dead? I may remind you, I have been the assistant manager for many years. I am quite content."

Kendra shifted gears again. "Is that all he wanted to tell you? That he was going to Manchester?"

Biddle frowned and looked away. "We spoke about business: buying more frames, cotton prices in America."

"How long was he in your office?"

He glanced up at her, beginning to look annoyed. "I don't know. I wasn't looking at the clock."

"Guess."

He gave a put-upon sigh. "Possibly fifteen minutes."

"That's a lot of conversation for fifteen minutes."

"Perhaps it was twenty. Why does it matter?"

"What did you do after he left?"

"I returned to business."

"And Mr. Stone?"

"I assume he returned to his office."

"And you were in your office? Was your door open or closed?"

"I understand what you're getting at, Miss Donovan. The killer would have to walk by my office to get to Mr. Stone's next door. But my door was closed. I didn't see anything."

"What were you working on?"

Another flicker of annoyance. "New shipment routes, invoices. There's quite a lot of paperwork in running a mill."

"Did you hear anything? As you said, your office is right next to Stone's."

"Have you ever been in a cotton mill when the machinery is in operation? The noise is ear-piercing. In fact, many workers on the floor become deaf over a period of time if they don't stuff their ears with bits of cotton fluff. I heard nothing."

Kendra nodded. "When did you leave the mill for the day?"

"The mill closes at half past five, but we closed the mill earlier yesterday, at five."

"Why?"

"We rely on sunlight to work profitably, and the fog made it impossible. It was cheaper to close the factory early than to spend the money on oil lamps and tallow candles."

"Did Mr. Stone make the decision to close the mill early?"

His hesitation was so brief, she probably wouldn't have caught it if she hadn't been staring at him so closely. "I did."

"Did you tell Mr. Stone what you were doing?"

"No." Another hesitation, this one longer. "His door was closed. I thought he must have already left."

"But you didn't know? You didn't check?"

"If he was still in his office, I did not want to interrupt him. He does not like to be disturbed. We had already settled our business."

It was possible, Kendra supposed. There'd been a couple of supervisors in her early days at the FBI who were such hard-asses that she'd tiptoed by their offices if their doors were closed. Why invite trouble? Maybe that kind of caution was how Biddle had lasted nineteen years working for a man like Stone.

"What do you know about Mr. Stone cheating at cards?" she asked suddenly, circling back to the earlier subject. He seemed lost in the topic change, which is what she intended. Set a rhythm, and then change it up.

"I told you, I don't know anything."

"But you wouldn't put it past him?"

"No," he admitted at length. "That is just the thing that would have amused Mr. Stone."

The door opened behind her, and she glanced up as the Duke and Matthews walked into the room. She stood to greet them. "Where's Jameson?"

"He left to see my father," Matthews said.

Kendra said nothing, but suspected the constable went to the magistrate to complain about her interference. She suppressed the flash of irritation, keeping her face neutral as she turned back to Biddle. "Thank you for your time, Mr. Biddle."

He was already standing. "We're finished?"

He looked a little bewildered. She made sure their eyes met as she smiled. "We're done. For now."

Kendra waited until they were outside and walking toward the gig before she asked, "Did you learn anything?"

Matthews said, "Everyone said that it was a normal day, except for the fog. Mr. Biddle let them go home earlier than usual."

Kendra nodded. "Biddle said he made the decision to close early. It's reasonable, I suppose."

"I heard a lot of speculation as to why Mr. Stone came in yesterday," said the Duke. "Apparently, he did not make a habit of it. According to the mill workers, they believe that Mr. Stone spent more time at another kind of mill—boxing mills—and in various acts of dissipation."

"Mr. Biddle said that Stone came in yesterday to tell him that he'd be leaving for a couple of days." She determinedly clamped down on her nerves when the Duke helped her into the gig and then settled beside her. "We'll see what Mrs. Stone has to say—" She broke off when Matthews cracked his whip, and the gig jerked forward.

"Did you learn anything of value, Miss Donovan?" Aldridge asked.

Kendra had a feeling that the Duke had asked more to distract her from falling off the gig and breaking both her legs rather than from any immediate interest. She drew in a deep breath and let it out slowly. "I found out the same—Mr. Stone was not a conscientious boss, he left Mr. Biddle to shoulder most of the responsibilities of the mill. However, he did like to come in personally to fire workers. Apparently he found that quite entertaining."

The Duke frowned. "He sounds like a thoroughly reprehensible gentleman, to play ducks and drakes with people's livelihoods."

"Thoroughly reprehensible, yes. Gentleman, no. Makes you wonder why Lord Bancroft kept him on. According to Mr. Biddle, Bancroft and Stone weren't friends."

"Lord Bancroft had another manager before Mr. Stone," Matthews spoke up suddenly. "An Aminadab."

Kendra leaned forward to curl her fingers around the seat to give her some semblance of control. She looked over at Matthews. "A what?"

The Duke answered, "A Quaker."

"Mr. Murray. An excellent manager, from what I recollect. Pious. A hard worker."

"What happened to him?" Kendra asked.

"I don't rightly know. My father never understood it. By all accounts, the mill was successful because of Mr. Murray. He was the manager when it opened in 1789." Matthew shook his head, puzzled. "Never made much sense, to dismiss Mr. Murray in favor of a man of Mr. Stone's character. One can only assume that Lord Bancroft and Mr. Murray had some sort of altercation."

"Interesting," Kendra murmured.

They'd entered the village and were traveling slower, so Kendra unclenched her hands from the seat and straightened up. "Did anyone give a time on when they saw Mr. Stone last?" she asked her companions.

The Duke shook his head. "Everyone was focused on their jobs. 'Tis dangerous work, and distraction could cost a finger or toe—or worse."

"I was told Mr. Stone came in around one o'clock, and went upstairs to his office. No one remembered seeing him after that," Matthews said.

"That tracks pretty much with what Mr. Biddle said," Kendra said, nodding. "It appears that he was the last one to see Stone alive. Except the killer, of course. They might be one in the same."

Matthews seemed startled by that comment. "Do you truly think Mr. Biddle could have done such a horrendous act against Mr. Stone?"

"Biddle really did Stone's job, for nineteen years. And Stone was a bastard who enjoyed exerting his power over people. I don't know if Biddle was compensated fairly for his work, but it's something to find out. He wasn't pro-moted." Her heart leaped into her throat as the gig swayed around a corner, and she clutched at the seat again. She found her voice again after a moment and added, "Where I come from, that would tick off anyone. Yet Biddle says he was content with the status quo."

"You don't believe him?"

Kendra met the Duke's eyes. "Nobody's that content."

8

Someday East Dingleford would be swallowed up by Manchester's urban sprawl. But in 1815, the village was larger than Kendra had first realized, dominating the countryside in its own right. From a distance, as they approached, she could see a haphazard collection of gray stone buildings tilted over narrow, twisting streets and pretty whitewashed, thatched cottages mixed with buildings that probably had been new two centuries ago. Ivy, still green and lush, crawled across stone walls and climbed up buildings. Rising above vivid red and gold treetops was a church spire on one end of the village and the crenellation of an ancient Norman church on the other.

The vibe of East Dingleford reminded her of Aldridge Village. The sunshine and daily routine brought the villagers outside. Women wearing plain dresses beneath wool coats and mop caps on their heads stood in doorways chatting with each other. Many had large straw baskets hooked over their arms. Five boys and one girl, ranging in age from about seven to twelve, laughed as they chased each other and several squawking chickens down a narrow lane. The last time Kendra had seen a bunch of kids together in her era, they'd all been on their phones, their thumbs a blur as they texted. She wondered what these kids would think of their future counterparts.

Kendra clutched the seat as the gig bounced along the cobblestone streets. She heard the clang of metal on metal from somewhere nearby, and figured that she'd be able to trace the sound to the blacksmith shop. If it had been a normal day in East Dingleford, untainted by murder, that's where she'd have found Jameson. Instead, he was likely filling the magistrate's ear with poison against her.

She drew in a deep breath. The air was crisp, with a vague scent of manure—as common in this time as the whiff of diesel and gasoline in her own—and the more pleasant odors of grass and sunshine-warmed earth. East Dingleford wasn't prosperous, but it didn't look poor either. At least there wasn't the grinding poverty that she'd witnessed in London the month before.

Matthews finally stopped the gig at the end of a narrow lane, in front of an Elizabethan-styled house with a deeply slanted slate roof, traditional, half-timbered stucco on the upper level and red brick on the ground level. The house was set off the street, larger and more private than the other houses in the neighborhood. The gardens surrounding it were overgrown, a variety of bushes and flowers opening up to a grassy field, dotted with cows, and in the distance the forest and river.

After climbing down from the gig they followed the flagstone path to the door. Matthews made use of the heavy brass knocker. It took several persistent knocks before the door finally creaked inward. A dour-looking, middle-aged woman in servant's garb glared at them.

"'Ere now, what'd ye want, then? This 'ere 'ousehold is in mournin'. Mr. Stone done cocked up 'is toes."

Matthews eyed the servant with disapproval. "We are aware of Mr. Stone's demise, Mrs. Trout. We have come to speak to Mrs. Stone. Please announce us—Mr. Matthews, the Duke of Aldridge, and Miss Donovan."

Kendra had met her fair share of butlers and house-keepers in this time period, but she could honestly say that Mrs. Trout was unlike any of those upper-class servants. In truth, she was unlike any servant Kendra had met in this era, period. The general rule for the hired help was to be acquiescent when dealing with their so-called betters. Apparently no one had told Mrs. Trout the rules.

The housekeeper huffed out her cheeks in a sign of extreme aggravation. "I suppose ye be wantin' tea too. I'm busy in the kitchens, ye know, dyin' Mrs. Stone's dresses in ter proper mournin' colors."

"Your duties are of no concern to me," Matthews snapped. "Now please let your mistress know that she has callers waiting."

"If you would give your mistress my card"—Aldridge produced one of his embossed calling cards, and handed it to the housekeeper—"I would be appreciative."

She eyed the card suspiciously. "Yer truly a duke? Don't reckon I can recall a duke ever vistin' East Dingleford in all me time 'ere."

Amused, Aldridge inclined his head. "I am the seventh Duke of Aldridge, madam."

Mrs. Trout finally seemed impressed. "Oh, my, yer Grace," she said, and even attempted a curtsy. Halfway down, she clutched her back. "Ooh, this cold weather 'as me joints seizing up somethin' fierce!" She straightened with a scowl. "C'mon, then. I'll get ye settled in the drawing room before I fetch the missus."

The servant led them down the narrow hall to an arched doorway. The drawing room was small, but strangely ornate, with a preponderance of marble and gilt. The sofas and chairs were tufted red silk. The patterned red, white, and gold wallpaper reminded Kendra a bit of a tacky Las Vegas hotel. Yet what really drew Kendra's attention were the shelves. Like the office, these were filled with a variety of porcelain cats.

She walked over to survey the astounding collection. Some were beautifully carved and high in quality, while others looked like cheap prizes handed out at traveling carnivals.

"Mr. Stone was a cat lover," she remarked, eyeing one figurine that was about the size of a man's shoe, a cat curled into a sleeping position. In college, she'd

participated in a study group at the home of her criminology professor whose wife had been a huge collector of
Hummel figurines. They'd been everywhere in the house,
even on the vanity in the bathroom. It had kind of creeped
her out. Stone's collection reminded her of that.

"Bah! Not that I ever knew. 'Twas one of the master's
peculiarities." Mrs. Trout scowled at the figurines. "Terrible things ter tidy up around." She paused, looking at
them. "I suppose I should be takin' yer coats."

"If you would be so kind." Matthews's tone was like
acid.

"Well, then, 'and 'em over." She waited impatiently as
they divested themselves of their outerwear, then stomped
out of the room.

"Can you countenance such a creature?" Matthews
complained, glaring after the woman. "She is truly one
of the most uncouth females I have ever encountered. She
didn't even invite us to sit down."

The Duke said, "Mrs. Trout is rather odd, I must say.
Wherever did Mr. Stone find her?"

"*Mrs.* Stone brought the creature with her when she
married Mr. Stone," Matthews remarked, and added
darkly, "Mrs. Trout reflects her mistress in many ways."

A moment later, Lavinia Stone swept into the room.
Trophy wife was Kendra's first thought. The widow had
to be at least forty years younger than her late husband,
which put her somewhere in her early thirties. She was
tall for this era, maybe five-ten, with a lushly curved
body that she'd displayed to her advantage in a hunter
green silk gown. The rounded neckline showed off both
her décolletage and an emerald teardrop pendant nestled
between her breasts. The bodice glittered with delicate
beadwork. Her long sleeves were edged with French lace.
More French lace was sewn at the bottom of her skirt in
a two-tiered ruffle.

She was very pretty, with a triangular face dominated
by light sea-green eyes, and even features. Her hair was
flaxen, and pulled into a loose topknot. As an added

decorative touch, she wore a green velvet bandeau around her head.

Aside from her relative youth, the most startling thing about Mrs. Stone was her obvious use of makeup. Her cupid's bow mouth was painted crimson, her face was powdered white and rouged, and her brows and lashes were noticeably darkened. None of that would have earned a second glance in the twenty-first century—or even in the eighteenth, for that matter—but the trend now was toward a more natural look. Some older women, like the Duke's sister, might judiciously apply a bit of rouge and powder, but society frowned upon younger women using cosmetics. Women who broke that taboo were considered brazen. Kendra got the feeling that description might not be too off the mark with Mrs. Stone.

There were no telltale sign of tears on the other woman's face, Kendra noticed. No red, puffy eyes or blotchy complexion beneath the powder. If the housekeeper hadn't mentioned dyeing gowns for the imposed mourning period, she might wonder if Mrs. Stone had been notified of her husband's untimely death.

A marriage of convenience? Kendra knew that was normal for the time period, but usually among the upper classes. And marriages of convenience could become inconvenient for one spouse.

She thought of the murder weapon. The bronze was heavy, but she didn't think Mrs. Stone would have any trouble picking it up.

"Good day." Mrs. Stone's gaze skimmed over Kendra and Matthews to zero in on the Duke. The crimson lips curved into an unconsciously seductive smile. She lifted her skirt to reveal her embroidered slippers and dropped into a perfect curtsy. "Your Grace. Mrs. Trout is not mistaken, is she? You *are* the Duke of Aldridge?"

"I am." Aldridge put one hand behind his back, and gave a courtly bow.

"Oh, my." Mrs. Stone's hand fluttered to her throat. Three fingers glittered with semiprecious stones, one diamond wedding ring, and two emeralds. "I could scarcely believe it when she told me. Pray tell, what is a duke doing here in East Dingleford? Did you know Harry?"

Aldridge kept his expression neutral. "Harry?"

"Mr. Stone. My husband."

"No, we were not acquainted." He hesitated. "My condolences on your husband's death."

"Thank you. Although Harry *was* old."

Kendra wasn't sure she heard her correctly. "Your husband didn't die of old age, Mrs. Stone."

The widow finally glanced at her. "No, but he would have. One must prepare for such an eventuality when you marry an older man. Shall we sit?"

Kendra had to admire the graceful way Mrs. Stone carried herself as she crossed the room, and settled into a delicate gilt-painted chair with claw-and-ball feet. She exchanged a bemused glance with the Duke before taking their seats on the sofa opposite Mrs. Stone. Matthews chose another chair, his face pinched with censure as he regarded the new widow.

"Mrs. Trout said she'll bring in tea," Mrs. Stone told them. "She's in a bit of a temper. Poor Harry's death has added to her workload, I'm afraid. I have no mourning gowns, you see. Until I am able to travel to my modiste in Manchester, Mrs. Trout will be dyeing most of my wardrobe. It is not a simple matter. Still, a duke ought to have tea."

Aldridge smiled, his blue eyes twinkling. "Thank you, madam. You are very considerate."

Kendra leaned forward slightly, her movement drawing the widow's eyes. "Who informed you of your husband's death?" she asked.

"Constable Jameson came to the door early this morning to inform me." She hesitated, and for the first time a shadow darkened her eyes. "'Tis difficult to believe. Who would want to murder Harry?"

"That's what we aim to find out," Kendra said.

The powdered forehead puckered in a faint frown. "I actually hadn't realized until the constable came that Harry was not in his bed. I thought he was asleep in his bedchamber."

The Stones weren't gentry, Kendra knew, but apparently they followed the custom where wives and husbands slept in different bedrooms. She regarded the widow steadily. Kendra didn't know if the woman stood to inherit anything, but there was a reason wives, like husbands, were always subject to greater scrutiny when their spouse met with foul play. "Where were you yesterday afternoon, Mrs. Stone, from three to six?"

Mrs. Stone didn't seem to find the question odd. "I was at home. Where else would I be? Nothing exciting ever happens in East Dingleford."

Kendra decided not to point out that she'd been in the town less than twenty-four hours, and the mill had been attacked by Luddites and Mr. Stone killed by an unknown assailant. She didn't think East Dingleford could afford any more excitement.

"Can anyone confirm your whereabouts yesterday afternoon?" she asked instead.

"My whereabouts? Why—" Mrs. Stone broke off when Mrs. Trout lumbered into the drawing room, carrying the tea tray.

The servant surveyed the room with a disgruntled expression, seeming to notice for the first time that every surface was cluttered with objects, mostly cats. Either there was another, more guest-friendly parlor, or the Stones didn't get many visitors.

"Where should I put this 'ere, then?"

Mrs. Stone's gaze traveled the room as though seeing it for the first time too. "Set it down there, Mrs. Trout." She gestured to the damask-covered footstool near her chair.

China teacups rattled as Mrs. Trout deposited her burden.

"Thank you, Mrs. Trout. I shall serve. Before you go, can you tell Miss Donovan where I was yesterday afternoon. She has expressed an odd curiosity about my activities."

"Ye spent most of the morning in bed." Mrs. Trout glanced at Kendra. "She's never been one ter get up before noon."

Out of the corner of her eye, Kendra saw the Duke's lips twitch. "What about between three and six?" she asked.

"I served 'er nuncheon around two." She looked to her mistress. "Ye sat down, and complained that the roast wasn't seasoned ter yer likin', remember? Afterward, I tidied up. Course it takes a considerable time, seein' I 'ave all those pots and pans ter wash, without me 'aving any 'elp w'otsoever. Not even a scullery maid."

Mrs. Stone rolled her eyes. "You manage quite well, Mrs. Trout. Better than when you were cleaning up after the patrons at the Queen's Theater—at half the wage, I might add. Now, off with you!"

Mrs. Stone turned to smile at the Duke as her servant sniffed loudly and shuffled out of the drawing room. "Do you take cream and sugar, your Grace?"

Mrs. Stone took her time filling cups with cream, pouring the tea and stirring in lumps of sugar. Aware that all eyes were on her, she smiled as she passed around the teacups.

Kendra waited until the duty was finished to ask, "How long were you and Mr. Stone married?"

"Three years."

"Where did you meet your husband? I don't think you are originally from East Dingleford."

"Oh, heavens no." She laughed at that. "I'm from Manchester. As soon as Mr. Stone's affairs are settled, I shall return there. Or mayhap I shall travel to London. I have always fancied living in that grand city." She lifted her teacup and eyed the Duke. "I suppose you have a house there, your Grace?"

"I do, yes. Personally, I prefer the country."

"Well, East Dingleford qualifies as country."

"Mrs. Stone was an actress in Manchester before she married Mr. Stone," Matthews spoke up.

Mrs. Stone lifted her chin, hearing the condemnation in his voice. "'Tis nothing I'm ashamed of, sir."

Matthews pressed his lips together, and said nothing.

"The Queen's Theater?" Kendra guessed.

"Yes. I was on the stage when I met Harry. He might not have been in his prime, but he was loose with his purse strings, if you know what I mean. We had a grand time." She took a swallow of tea, and then set down her cup. "You could have knocked me over with a feather when he asked me to marry him."

The Duke raised his eyebrows. "You didn't think he had honorable intentions?"

Mrs. Stone laughed loudly. "Oh, dear. There was nothing honorable about Harry's intentions, even after we married, your Grace. I wasn't looking to become leg-shackled, mind you, but I'd have been a simpleton to turn him down. I barely made twenty pounds a year on stage!"

Aldridge concentrated on his tea for a moment. "And what is—was Mr. Stone's annual income?" he asked, lowering his teacup.

"I'm not certain. I quizzed him about it, of course. Wouldn't have been right if I didn't, would it? Seeing how I was giving up my career. But Harry always told me that we'd be provided for. And he did seem well set. Just look at all these things!" Her gaze roved over the surfaces crowded with porcelain felines. "Harry was forever buying notions and putting them about."

Kendra eyed a ceramic cat licking its paw. "So this was your husband's collection?"

Mrs. Stone gave an inelegant snort. "Oh, yes, the *collection* was Harry's. Personally, I wouldn't give a farthing for the entire lot! It's not like a pretty gown or a sparkler you can wear around your neck, now is it?" Her ringed fingers toyed with the emerald pendant. "Don't know why Harry had such a fondness for such things either. Thought he was going daft. Old age does that to a person, you know."

"Just because he collected objets d'art . . ." Kendra's gaze was drawn to another cat, this one on its back, batting a ball of yarn. Okay, perhaps calling these ceramic figurines *art* was stretching it. "That doesn't mean he was going senile."

Mrs. Stone shrugged. "It wasn't so much him collecting the things. But when he'd bring home another one, he'd find it all so bloody amusing. Harry has—*had*—a sly sense of humor. But I never understood *this*." She waved a hand, jewelry glittering. "Thought he must have had one as a pet when he was a boy. I told him that we should get a real cat—better that than to spend all his blunt on these things. At least a cat could be a good mouser. But Harry told me that he couldn't abide the things. He said they made his eyes itch something awful."

"Did your husband have any enemies, Mrs. Stone?" Kendra asked, bringing the topic back to the reason they were there. Stone's fetish for cat knickknacks was strange, but she doubted he'd been killed because of it. "Did someone threaten him recently?"

The widow bit her lip as she considered the matter. "Harry was a rogue, for sure. Wasn't no secret. There wasn't a dogfight or card game he wouldn't gamble on, or a wench he wouldn't bed at the twitch of her skirt. Yet for all his gaming, drinking, and whoring, he was a good husband."

Kendra stared at her. What would the widow consider a *bad* husband? "Those are a lot of vices," she finally said. "You're saying he was unfaithful?"

"Oh, I would be surprised if he *wasn't*. The man was a rascal."

"And that didn't bother you? I know plenty of wives who would've been angry to learn that their spouse was cheating on them." *Angry enough to bludgeon their husband to death, in fact*, Kendra thought.

But Lavinia Stone didn't seem to be one of them. Her ruby lips curved, the pale green eyes lit with bawdy humor. "Me and Harry had fun the first year, but I never expected him to become a proper husband. Not *Harry*."

Was she lying? Kendra couldn't tell. *She's an actress,* she reminded herself. *She's used to fooling people for a living.*

Kendra switched subjects. "Do you know why he went into the mill yesterday?"

Mrs. Stone frowned. "No, but he was in a bit of a temper yesterday morning, muttering under his breath."

"What about?"

"I didn't hear. I always found it best to ignore Harry when he was in a foul mood."

"Were you leaving East Dingleford for a few days?"

"No." She looked surprised. "Whatever gave you that idea?"

"Your husband told Mr. Biddle that he was leaving town for a few days. Maybe a business trip? He didn't mention it to you?"

"Business—ha! Most likely ladybird business!" The widow scowled. "Blast him. He knew I would want to leave for a few days too!"

"Do you have any idea who the—the ladybird could have been?" Kendra asked. Mistresses, after all, had jealous streaks too.

Mrs. Stone shook her head, still looking put out over her dead husband's inconsideration. "No, but I doubt the old devil planned to spend the time alone."

Kendra waited a beat, then asked, "Did you hear about a farmer accusing him of cheating?"

"Hear about it—I was there! Oh, not in the card room. I was dancing, of course. But it caused quite a scene at the time. The constable and magistrate had to step in." She flicked a look at Matthews. "Your father's the magistrate, isn't he?"

"Yes, he is," Matthews acknowledged stiffly.

Kendra eyed the other woman. "You don't seem particularly upset that your husband was accused of cheating, or that he caused a scene."

"Nothing was proven, was it?" Mrs. Stone huffed out a laugh. "And East Dingleford could use more scenes, if you ask me. Old Harry always knew how to cause excitement. Seems to me he still is."

"Do you know the farmer's name?"

"Hmm. Tanner? No, Turner! Yes, Turner, I think."

Kendra switched to another line of questioning. "Can you tell me about Lord Bancroft? What kind of relationship did your husband have with him?"

Mrs. Stone made a face. "Oh, that one. Very high on the instep, isn't he?"

"What do you mean?" asked Kendra.

"Mr. Stone and I have been married for three years, but I was only invited out to Falcon Court once for their ball. *Once*—when Lord Bancroft's wife was still alive. She died of the fever shortly afterward." For the first time, a note of bitterness crept into the other woman's voice. "The earl is a cold, prideful man."

"You and your husband never socialized with Lord Bancroft?"

"His lordship came here a few times to speak with Harry in his study. He barely acknowledged my presence, like I was dirt on his boot." Mrs. Stone's face tightened. The widow was clearly someone used to being flattered by male attention. "And his daughter, Lady Winifred . . ." She gave a sniff. "She is as cold and ill-mannered as he. We were introduced at the local assembly, but has she ever called upon me? Or left her card here for me to call upon her? *No*. The entire family is a bit stiff-rumped, if you ask me. I never met his other daughters, but I expect they're like Lady Winifred. The only decent one in the lot is the viscount. I met him in the Assembly Rooms a year ago when he was down from Eton."

Kendra eyed Mrs. Stone over the rim of her teacup. "The viscount?"

Matthews spoke up. "The earl's son, Phillip—Viscount Drake. Lord Drake is studying at Eton, and will be going to Cambridge next year."

"Harry found that amusing as well," said Mrs. Stone.

"Why?" Kendra asked.

Mrs. Stone shrugged. "Harry wasn't one for books. Maybe he thought anyone who was bookish like Lord Drake was a bit of a chucklehead. We didn't discuss it, but I always thought the viscount was a sweet boy. He brought me a lemonade and we took a turn around the ballroom."

"Lady Winifred lives here in East Dingleford?" asked Kendra, aware that they'd be dining with her and her father later tonight.

"For the moment. Lady Winifred's husband died almost two years ago." Mrs. Stone picked up her teacup and took a sip. "Lady Winifred married the Honorable Terence Hayward, who was in line to eventually inherit an earldom. But she only managed to produce a daughter, so, of course, there was no chance to inherit. She returned to Falcon Court." She paused, and the ruby lips pouted. "I suppose she's out of her widow's weeds by now."

The topic of Lady Winifred was obviously a hot button for Lavinia Stone.

"She acts as though I'm beneath her touch, because I was once on the stage, and had many admirers," Mrs. Stone went on, tossing her head back in a defiant gesture.

Matthews muttered something under his breath, and Mrs. Stone turned on him, her green eyes flashing in temper. "I am *not* ashamed of my past, Mr. Matthews. Lady Winifred ought not forget that her own family isn't without scandal. I *know* about Lord Bancroft. Harry told me all about *his* past!"

That caught Kendra's attention. "What do you know about Lord Bancroft?"

She laughed, but even that had taken on a razor-like edge. "'Tis difficult to credit, but there was a time when his lordship was not so high in the instep as he is now. When he mixed with the common folk. *Intimately.*"

Matthews scowled. "'Tis ancient gossip."

"It isn't gossip," Mrs. Stone said, her gaze locked on Matthews. "Everyone in East Dingleford knows about his indiscretion with Mrs. Bolton."

"*Mrs. Bolton*?" Kendra exchanged a startled glance with the Duke. Whatever she'd expected the widow to say, that wasn't it.

"Well, she wasn't Mrs. Bolton back in those days. She was a farmer's daughter. I heard that they were all set to elope to Gretna Green. Can you imagine? A farmer's daughter running off with Quality?"

Kendra had a more egalitarian view of such things, but she had to admit that she was having a difficult time imagining the innkeeper's wife in an illicit romance with the earl. "I guess that didn't happen," was all she said.

"Oh, no, Mrs. Bolton never ran away with the earl." The widow's lips curled, and Kendra recognized malice in the pale green eyes. "The high and mighty Lord Bancroft ran away instead."

9

Only the most common minds would still be talking about such a thing," Matthews sniffed, as they rode back to the Green Maiden. "The scandal happened well before I was even born. I am shocked that tongues continue to wag over the ancient incident."

Kendra wasn't shocked at all. A love affair between two people with such different pedigrees would capture the imagination. The affair's unhappy end would serve well as a cautionary tale for those who wanted to keep the status quo in the country's rigid class system. Kendra could imagine it being passed down from generation to generation, like family heirlooms—*This is what happens to those who reach above themselves.*

"What did Mrs. Stone mean when she said that Lord Bancroft ran away?" she asked.

"*I* actually do not know any specifics." Matthews sounded affronted, as though she had accused him of being one of the gossipmongers.

"What do you know—in general?"

Matthews maneuvered the gig around two men unloading casks from a wagon outside a tavern. "I know that Lord Bancroft left East Dingleford for many years," he said. "I believe he sailed to India. Or was it South America?" He shrugged. "Well, no matter. He returned when his father was dying. By then, he was the heir to the earldom, and Falcon Court is entailed. I was scarcely out of leading strings when this took place. If you are truly interested in the tale, you ought to quiz Mrs. Hearnshaw."

"Who's she?" asked Kendra.

"She used to be the housekeeper at Falcon Court until the old earl's death. I think Lord Bancroft pensioned her off. She went to live at Goose Hill with her son's family."

"Goose Hill?" Kendra echoed. "Is that another village?"

"No, 'tis the name of her son's farm, west of here, near the river. If you wish to speak to her, you should consider attending the local assembly on Monday night. She always attends with her family. Pray tell, what does any of this have to do with Mr. Stone's murder?"

"Probably nothing," Kendra admitted. But she filed away the information. In her experience, homicide investigations never followed a straight line, instead meandering through the past and present lives of suspects, witnesses, and victims. At the moment, Lord Bancroft interested her as a suspect. Maybe his former housekeeper could shed light on the man, introduce a viewpoint that his current staff, too afraid of dismissal, would be reluctant to share.

Matthews brought the gig to a halt next to the Green Maiden, and looked at the Duke. "What is our next course of action, sir?"

Kendra's back stiffened with resentment. Sensing her annoyance, Aldridge put his hand on Kendra's arm, and squeezed lightly. She didn't know whether he was offering her sympathy, or stopping her from punching Matthews in the nose.

"We shall need a place of privacy," the Duke replied. "I shall speak to Mr. Bolton about securing the private parlor or another chamber for the duration of our stay here. And we will need supplies. I can find most of them at the inn, I'm certain. But there is one thing . . ."

Matthews said, "I shall procure whatever you desire."

"Excellent. Then would you be so good as to find us a slate board?"

10

Sitting at the vanity back in her room at the inn later that day, Kendra saw that the sun, framed by the bedchamber's windows, was doing a swan dive toward the horizon. It had taken three hours to find a slate board and then set it up in the private parlor that would serve as their war room during the course of the investigation. Kendra had postponed filling the board with any notes, because she had to begin the long process of preparing for their evening at Falcon Court.

In the twenty-first century, it would have probably taken her forty-five minutes to prepare for a work function or date. An hour, tops. A hot shower. Toweling herself dry. Rubbing in body lotion, her standard routine for skincare. Blow-drying her long hair had been the most time-consuming part of the preparation. Styling it had been simple. For most of her life, her idea of the perfect hairstyle had meant pulling her hair into a ponytail. She'd never been heavy-handed with makeup, just a light application. The rest of her time would have been shuffling through her closet to select the appropriate clothes and shoes. Maybe she'd add a few pieces of jewelry.

Here, she wore no makeup, and her clothes were selected for her. But nothing else was so easy. Setting up a bath was not a simple matter. It involved servants trudging up and down the stairs, hauling hot water for the copper bathtub. After washing her hair, the only way to speed up the drying process was to light a fire in the hearth and

scoot her head as close as she dared without setting her
hair ablaze or infusing it with a smoky stench. Once dry,
Kendra submitted to Molly's ministrations, which meant
sitting in front of the vanity while the tweeny brushed her
hair until the raven strands gleamed like starlight.

"They say 'is 'ead was gone," Molly said, her voice
caught on the sliding scale somewhere between enthralled
and horrified.

Kendra met the maid's wide eyes in the vanity mirror.
"Jesus, is that what they're saying?"

"Aye." Molly set aside the brush and went to the
fireplace, where she'd been heating up the curling tongs.
"They also say that 'e was a regular rake." She divided
Kendra's hair in sections, and began curling the ends.

"Well, that appears to be true," Kendra conceded.
"Did any of the gossip include an altercation with a farmer
several months ago?"

Molly's brow wrinkled. "An alter—w'ot?"

"An altercation—a fight."

"Oh. Not that Oi remember. But the on dit is the bloke
fought with a lot of people. Except maybe the ladies, if ye
know wot Oi mean."

Molly was fifteen. In many ways, Kendra found her to
be fresh and innocent. And yet she wasn't sheltered like
many of the young girls in the upper classes. After all,
the servants cleaned up after their so-called betters; there
weren't a lot of secrets that could be kept hidden from
them, including infidelities and affairs. There were times
when she wondered if Molly knew about her and Alec.

"And Oi 'eard that 'e didn't care if they were *married*
ladies either," the maid added slyly.

"So there might be a jealous husband in the picture?"

"From w'ot Oi 'eard, more than one."

Kendra sighed. "We might need more than one slate
board."

Molly's eyes widened. "Truly?"

"Let's hope it doesn't get to that point." Kendra
watched Molly put aside the curling tongs and begin

coiling her hair into a low chignon. "Are they saying anything else?"

"Just that 'e got wot 'e deserved."

"I guess no one's planning his memorial service, then."

They fell silent as Molly continued to fuss with Kendra's hair, twisting it into a chignon, anchoring it with long pins. She tucked and pinned in silky amber rosettes and ribbons, which matched the evening gown she'd pressed earlier for Kendra to wear.

The chignon felt heavier, Kendra thought. Her hair had always grown fast, and now it was three inches longer than when she'd first come through the vortex. Then, her hair had been cut into a bob, with blunt cut bangs. When the bangs had grown long enough to get into her eyes, she'd wanted to cut them again, but Molly had been fiercely opposed to continuing such an odd style. She'd suggested curling them into tight ringlets on the side of Kendra's temples instead, which was more fashionable. Kendra's response had been a simple *hell, no.* They'd ended up compromising, with Molly managing to weave the loose strands into the rest of the hairstyle.

As she regarded her reflection in the mirror, Kendra realized that it wouldn't be long before Molly would be able to arrange her hair into the popular topknot worn by so many women. Her chest tightened unexpectedly. *I'm slowly disappearing,* she thought. *Bit by bit, I'm becoming absorbed into this timeline. How long before I look in the mirror and don't recognize myself at all?*

"Ye look lovely, miss," Molly said, stepping back to survey her handiwork with a satisfied expression. "Let me 'elp ye into yer gown."

Kendra forced herself to push aside the anxiety. *Breathe in; breathe out.* She rose, allowing Molly to help her into the amber silk gown with tiny cap sleeves and a rounded neckline. The sleeves, bodice, and bottom of the skirt were lavishly decorated with loop cord braiding in the same burnished shade as the gown. A scattering of seed pearls, sewn throughout the bodice, shimmered in the candlelight.

"'Ow long do ye reckon we'll be stayin' 'ere in East Dingleford, miss?" Molly asked, as she finished buttoning up Kendra's dress.

"I'm not sure," she admitted, pushing her feet into thin golden slippers. "You can't rush a murder investigation."

Molly nodded, looking resigned. "Oi'll unpack the trunks then, and see about pressin' more of yer dresses."

Kendra wanted to assure the maid that their stay wouldn't be long. But the words stuck in her throat when she thought of their victim. Harry Stone had led a complicated life. He was a libertine, and, based on how he'd treated the workers at the mill, he had sociopathic tendencies.

She remembered Stone's shattered skull. It had been an impulsive crime, filled with panic and rage. But when the killer had left, he hadn't left empty-handed. What had been on the desk? It had obviously meant something important, for the killer to take it. But had it been the trigger that had set him off? Or had something else triggered the murder, and the killer had taken whatever had been on the desk as an afterthought? Two men could get into a violent argument, with one killing the other impetuously, in the throes of a red-hot rage. Afterward, the murderer could notice an expensive Rolex on his victim's wrist, and take it. That was one possibility. The other was a robbery, where the killer noticed the expensive Rolex first, and then murdered the victim to steal the watch. *What am I dealing with here?*

Kendra closed her eyes and summoned the crime scene in her mind's eye. The gentleman's office. The strange collection of cats. The blood on the walls, on the desk, except for the clean surface area, a rectangle shape, the—

"Miss?"

She held her breath. Something was teasing at her senses now, something she should be seeing . . .

"Miss?"

She opened her eyes to find Molly frowning at her as she held up her cloak.

The teasing sensation grew stronger . . .

"The Duke'll be waitin'," said the maid.

Kendra's let out her breath, annoyed. Whatever had been there was gone. *What was it?*

"Miss—"

"All right." She let Molly settle the dark blue velvet cloak on her shoulders while she tugged on her gloves. Kendra picked up her reticule and left the bedchamber, her stride brisk and sure, even though she couldn't shake the nagging sensation that she had just missed something vital.

11

Falcon Court was less than a mile outside of East Dingleford, a striking mansion of Flemish bond brick, with pale sandstone framing mullion-paned windows and arching over the entrance. An icy waning moon revealed a slanting slate roof with five chimneys. High on ledges and tucked into dark niches, gargoyles grinned manically or glowered with menace down at the arrivals. It was certainly atmospheric, Kendra thought, as her gaze drifted over two of the frightening stone creatures.

A footman in full red livery hurried forward to open the carriage door.

"My God, gas lighting," the Duke murmured as soon as he stepped down. His expression was filled with awe as he studied the more than a dozen lampposts surrounding the courtyard, the steady flames casting the area in a golden haze. "Just look at it, Miss Donovan. It's been more than two decades since Mr. William Murdoch installed gas lighting at his manor in the wilds of Cornwall, but 'tis not something you would expect in the wilds of Yorkshire. Apparently Lord Bancroft is as progressive as Mr. Murdoch."

He tapped his chin, still staring. "I think I must investigate installing gas at Aldridge Castle. What do you think?"

"Since I've yet to master using a flint to light anything, I'd be thrilled." She looped her hand through the crook of his elbow, pulling him up the steps. Otherwise, she knew the Duke could spend the rest of the evening gawking at the gas lamps.

A butler was waiting at the open door, and ushered them into the enormous entrance hall, also lit with gas lamps. The room had been designed to impress. Given the Elizabethan architectural elements in the oak beam ceiling and wide, hand-carved oak stairs at the end of the long foyer, Kendra suspected she was seeing the ambition of Bancroft's ancestors. The floor was a polished white-and-black marble. Paintings and medieval weapons hung from the walls. The current earl's handiwork could be seen in the gas wall sconces, although a large bronze chandelier in the center of the ceiling flickered with traditional candlelight.

Four footmen in full crimson livery stood at attention, spaced evenly along the foyer's wall. Bancroft's predecessors weren't the only one who wanted to impress.

"Good evening, your Grace, Miss Donovan. I am Crawford." The butler bowed. "Let me relieve you of your coat and cloak." He looked at a footman, who immediately shot forward to take their outerwear and gloves, Kendra's bonnet and reticule, and the Duke's hat and walking cane. If the footman thought Kendra's reticule was heavier than normal, with the muff pistol inside, he gave no indication.

Crawford inclined his head. "If you will follow me . . . his lordship is in the Chinese salon with Lady Winifred."

They followed the butler up the stairs and down a long hallway. Their footsteps were muffled by a rug woven in muted shades of red and brown. The Chinese salon was aptly named, Kendra decided a moment later when Crawford opened the double doors. Red and gold lacquered walls, vases—from the Ming dynasty, she was sure—and a lotus chandelier hanging from the plastered ceiling evoked a Far Eastern mood. The legs and arms of the furniture around the room were carved into serpent tails. The marble chimneypiece bore a dragon motif. The fire burning in the grate, if she wasn't mistaken, carried a whiff of frankincense and myrrh.

Lord Bancroft was sitting in a chair, head tilted back, eyes closed, engrossed in the classical melody that a woman with honey-colored hair piled high on her head was playing on the pianoforte. His fingers tapped on his knee, the ruby in the heavy gold ring that he wore on his little finger flashing in the drawing room's muted light.

Bancroft opened his eyes the instant they entered the room, and was already pushing himself to his feet when Crawford announced their names.

"Good evening, your Grace . . . and Miss Donovan." His cold, dark eyes flicked toward the Duke before settling on Kendra, his regard as intense as she remembered from earlier. "You are in fine looks this evening, Miss Donovan."

"Thank you." Kendra ignored the prickle of ice that slid down her spine. Definitely the heebie-jeebies.

The playing stopped and the woman rose, gliding around the pianoforte to join them.

"My daughter, Lady Winifred," her father introduced.

"Good evening, Lady Winifred," the Duke offered. "You play beautifully."

She executed a perfect curtsy. "You are kind to say so, your Grace."

Kendra eyed the woman. Even though Lady Winifred appeared to be about her own age, Kendra had to remind herself that the other woman had married, given birth, and was already a widow. Kendra's gaze slid over the waif-like figure in a gown of dark purple, its cut demure, with no excess embellishment. The color and style reminded Kendra of what Lavinia Stone had said. Lady Winifred was out of full mourning, and could dispense with the black widow's weeds that she'd been required to wear for a year and a day. She was now in half-mourning, giving her a choice of colors between purple and gray.

Of course, Lady Winifred didn't need any embellishment. She was quite beautiful, with a pale, oval face framed by tawny tendrils. She'd inherited her father's eyes, Kendra noticed, dark brown and deep-set. Her nose was straight, if a little long, above a wide, pink mouth that was curved in a wintry smile.

Bancroft looked at Kendra. "Do you play, Miss Donovan?"

"Unfortunately, I'm not musically inclined."

"How does a gently bred female avoid music lessons?" he wondered, gesturing for them to come into the room. "'Tis a prerequisite for being a good wife. I required all my daughters to play the pianoforte."

"And what of your son? Does he play a musical instrument?"

The dark eyes lit with amusement. "Like yourself, my son had no aptitude for music."

"I guess he's not good husband material then."

Bancroft smiled. "Ah, you are teasing me, I think. The role required of a gentleman is quite different than that of a gentlewoman." He paused. "Forgive me, my manners have abandoned me. I have not even offered you an aperitif. I have an excellent Ratafia. Or perhaps I can tempt you with a sherry, Miss Donovan?"

"Thanks, Ratafia is fine."

"Your Grace? Ratafia, or something stronger?"

"Thank you, sir. A brandy would be most refreshing."

Kendra had forgotten the butler's presence until he materialized by her side with the glass of wine.

"I shall prevail upon my daughter to continue to play . . ." The look Bancroft gave his daughter was enough to send Lady Winifred gliding back to her seat at the pianoforte. "Let us be seated. Dinner shall be served shortly."

Lady Winifred began playing a lively sonata while Kendra and the Duke settled into the sofa opposite Bancroft.

Bancroft cocked his head and regarded Kendra with eyes as bright as a raven's. "How do you know that I have a son, Miss Donovan?"

Kendra sipped her wine, refusing to look away from the old man's piercing gaze. "Mrs. Stone mentioned him."

Something flickered in Bancroft's eyes. Kendra nearly shivered, but she couldn't say why.

The Duke broke the strange spell. "I cannot help but notice your use of gas lighting, your lordship," he said, lifting his brandy glass, and surveying Bancroft over the rim. "It is most impressive. You are to be commended. It's quite advanced to have it in one's home."

Bancroft shifted his gaze to the Duke. "'Tis the way of the future, your Grace."

"We are like-minded then. I, too, am interested in the future." Aldridge's blue eyes twinkled when he shot Kendra a brief look. His gaze returned to Bancroft. "I view myself as a man of science, and believe many wonders await us if we don't become diverted by superstition."

A smile as cold as the arctic touched Bancroft's mouth. "We are indeed like-minded men, sir. I, too, am eager for progress. Although a great deal can be said about the present as well."

"I would very much like to consult with you, your lordship. Aldridge Castle could benefit from gas lighting."

"Be prepared for your servants' opposition," warned Bancroft. "My staff was convinced that they would be poisoned or blown to bits. It took months to persuade them otherwise."

"I understand." The Duke smiled. "Not everyone embraces the latest techniques. I applaud you on your progressive nature, sir."

"I confess to having a bias. I was an early investor in the Gas Lighting and Coke Company."

Aldridge appeared impressed. "I was approached three years ago to invest, when the company was being formed. Alas, I foolishly declined." He glanced at Kendra. "The company is currently installing gas lighting on the streets of London."

Kendra made a sound in her throat that she hoped sounded like she was fascinated as well. But it was hard to get excited about gas lighting. If they were talking about the light switch and a multiple jet shower, she'd be there.

The Duke's eyes gleamed. "You, sir, must have turned a tidy profit."

Bancroft swirled his brandy, a smug look of satisfaction softening his mouth. "It has been quite lucrative," he drawled.

"Papa has the devil's luck in financial ventures." Lady Winifred surprised everyone by speaking up. Her fingers continued to caress the keyboards, switching adroitly from Mozart to Beethoven. "He was also the first to build a cotton mill."

Bancroft gave his daughter an indulgent look. "In this area, yes. I am but one of many to invest in textile manufacturing. There is a demand for good English cotton, which I believe will only increase in the coming years."

He shifted his gaze suddenly to Kendra. "Supplied by America's cotton plantations. Where exactly did your family originate, Miss Donovan?"

The question took her by surprise. "Virginia," she said finally. It wasn't the truth, but it wasn't like he could fact-check her story.

"Tell me of your circumstances, Miss Donovan," the earl encouraged. "How did a woman such as yourself, from Virginia, become the ward of one of the most powerful men in England? It would seem as though you, too, have the devil's own luck."

"I beg to differ, sir," the Duke remarked, and smiled. "I am the one with the good fortune. Miss Donovan has been a great comfort to me."

Bancroft looked at him. "And, pray tell, how long has Miss Donovan been a comfort to you, your Grace? When did she arrive at Aldridge Castle?"

"Two months ago," Aldridge answered.

That bit of information *could* be fact checked, if somebody wanted to do so, Kendra knew. Why they'd go to the trouble, she had no idea, but the Duke was being smart by not embellishing more than he had to. If anyone investigated, they'd learn that she'd been a servant for a week, then a companion. Her elevation to Duke's ward had come just the month before.

Aldridge took a moment to sip his brandy, probably to give him time to get the rest of his story straight. "Miss Donovan's father and I were childhood friends," he continued. "We made the arrangement before he and his wife immigrated to America. If anything should happen to them, I would become the legal guardian to their child."

Kendra dropped her eyes to her wineglass, keeping her expression neutral. The Duke had invented the cover story as a way to explain suddenly becoming saddled with a ward. A *twenty-six*-year-old ward, which in this era, Kendra knew, put her firmly in spinster territory.

When she lifted her gaze, she found Bancroft regarding her with quizzical fascination.

"You are the most fortunate of men, your Grace," he murmured. "And you, as well, Miss Donovan, to have found yourself in the warm embrace of the Duke." He paused. "My condolences on the death of your parents. When exactly did they die?"

Kendra frowned, disconcerted by the blunt question. "When?"

"His Grace mentioned that you have been under his care for only two months . . . and yet you are clearly not in mourning." He gestured to the dress she wore. "Or even half-mourning."

Ah. Now she understood Bancroft's curiosity and confusion. She took a swallow of the Ratafia. It wouldn't take her a year and a half to sail from America. And if she fabricated some story about having her journey delayed, that falsehood could be eventually discovered. Or lead to more questions: Why was your journey delayed? *To settle my parents affairs.* What law firm helped you settle their affairs? *None of your goddamn business.*

"My father disapproved of funeral rituals. He made me promise not to dress in mourning colors." That seemed a safe enough lie. There was no way to query a dead man.

"Hmm." Bancroft pursed his lips as he regarded her. "Your father appears to be an unusual man."

"Yes, he was." At least in that she could tell the truth.

Kendra decided that it was time to seize control of the conversation. "How long did you know Mr. Stone?" she asked Bancroft.

The earl's black eyes gleamed, clearly aware of what she was doing. "I believe I already told you that he was my mill manager for twenty years."

Kendra smiled. "Yes, you did. But I'm not asking how long he worked for you. I'm asking how long you *knew* him. That's a different question entirely."

And you know it, she thought.

Instead of answering, Bancroft looked at the Duke. "You must confess, your Grace, this is rather uncommon. A man of noble birth such as yourself, sir, and a . . . a gently-bred female, to meddle in such a grisly matter . . ."

"'Tis not the norm," agreed Aldridge. "Still, we do not intrude for our own amusement."

"Why do you do it, then?" Bancroft sounded genuinely curious.

"Because murder is an aberration in polite society," said Aldridge. "We are civilized men, sir. If we look the other way, we are complicit in barbarism and society crumbles. Justice *must* be sought, for the good of all."

Lady Winifred abruptly quit playing, and in the sudden silence, the Duke's words seemed to hang in the air, a dark promise. For just an instant, Kendra wondered if that had been the other woman's intent, to create drama by her sudden cessation at the pianoforte. Then she noticed that Lady Winifred's attention was not on them, but on the door, where the butler had materialized.

"Dinner is served," Crawford announced quietly.

Bancroft was the first to get to his feet. His black eyes glinted as he offered Kendra his arm. She had no choice but to stand and slip her hand through the crook of his elbow.

"Shall we continue this fascinating discussion in the dining room, Miss Donovan, your Grace?" the old man said. "I believe my appetite has been wheted."

12

They were seated at a dining room table that looked as though it could easily seat thirty people. Like the courtyard with its gargoyles, Kendra thought the room had a certain gothic atmosphere in its preponderance of dark mahogany, from its paneled walls to the heavy furnishings, to the fireplace mantel intricately carved with winged dragons. Gas lamps hissed on the walls, but the white-clothed table held several silver candelabras, the flickering light from the long tapers passing over the bone china bowls and wide silver spoons.

The butler brought the wine forward for Lord Bancroft to approve, and then moved silently around the table, filling their goblets. A tall footman arrived, carrying a silver tureen. Another footman accompanied him to serve the brisket of beef soup, its tantalizing aroma curling around the table.

"I knew your father, your Grace," Lord Bancroft told the Duke.

Aldridge was seated across from Kendra. He looked at their host. "Oh? How were you acquainted with my father? I don't recall him mentioning you."

"No, I should rephrase. Our meeting was brief." Bancroft picked up his spoon. "Thirty-seven years ago, at Aldridge Castle," he ruminated, and a small, funny smile played around his mouth. "You were not in the castle at the time, but two of your sisters were there, as was your brother."

Aldridge's blue eyes softened. "I would have been eighteen. I imagine I was in London at the time, where I had the great fortune of meeting my future wife during a lecture at the Royal Society."

"That is a happy memory. I apologize—I don't recall her name."

"Arabella," Aldridge said quietly.

"No doubt you swept her off her feet."

The Duke smiled. "No, I was forced to wait. Arabella was only fifteen at the time. Her father was a squire at a small estate in Somerset, and had only been visiting London. We spent the next three years corresponding until she was launched into her first season. I was determined to make it her last."

"Her family would hardly turn down the heir to a dukedom," said Bancroft.

Lady Winifred looked at the Duke. "Where is your wife, your Grace?"

"My wife died many years ago."

"I'm sorry," she murmured with a certain coolness, which indicated that her sympathy had more to do with social etiquette than any genuine feeling.

Kendra looked at Bancroft. "You never said how long you knew Mr. Stone, my lord. Did you know him before he came to East Dingleford and served as the manager to your mill?"

Bancroft dipped his spoon into the soup, then brought it to his mouth. Kendra wondered if he was doing what she and the Duke had done in the drawing room, deliberately sipping their wine to buy time to get their stories straight.

"No," he finally said. He plunged his spoon into the soup again. His black eyes glittered. "Why do you ask?"

"I heard that you had employed another mill manager before Mr. Stone." She paused to taste the soup as well. "A lot of people were surprised when you fired him and hired Mr. Stone."

"You have uncovered a lot of information in a short time, Miss Donovan."

Kendra smiled, and said nothing. Again, her skin prickled as she met his dark eyes, and caught the mocking gleam in them.

"Of course, not all your information is correct," he continued. "I did not dismiss Mr. Murray. He offered his resignation, and I accepted it—with much regret, I might add. He had been the manager of Bancroft Mills from the day it opened in 1789. However, Mr. Murray recommended Mr. Stone as his replacement."

Kendra frowned. "I was under the impression that Mr. Murray was a rather pious man. And Mr. Stone was . . . not."

Bancroft's lips curved into something near a smile. "One does not offer employment recommendations because they admire another man's soul, Miss Donovan, but rather on that man's skill in business."

"From what I've heard, Mr. Stone wasn't very good at either."

The earl set down his spoon and picked up his wine-glass. "Mr. Stone was not well-liked, in many ways because he *was* good in business."

"You mean because he was good at laying people off."

"Such things must be done." Bancroft shrugged. "Especially with the advancements in machinery. The mill is not a charity house."

"Still, I heard he enjoyed that part of his job."

Bancroft returned his attention to his soup. "As I keep telling you, Mr. Stone was my mill manager, but we were not friends."

Lady Winifred gave a small, tight smile. "The very notion is absurd. We do not share the same social circles as Mr. Stone and his wife."

The way she said *wife*, with a note of sharp conde-scension, reminded Kendra of the resentment Lavinia Stone had displayed when she spoke of Bancroft and his daughter. Looking at Lady Winifred's scornful expres-sion, Kendra could see why Lavinia Stone had disliked the other woman.

"But you must have known that Mr. Stone wasn't a conscientious worker," she persisted. "You hired Mr. Biddle."

Bancroft pushed away his empty bowl. "I had been planning to hire an assistant manager for Mr. Murray. Bancroft Mills is a large enterprise; it makes sense to have more than one manager running it."

"Will you promote Mr. Biddle now to the top manager position?" asked Kendra.

"Possibly. I haven't given it much thought."

"He's handled the majority of the responsibilities of running the mill. We heard Mr. Stone spent most of his time in other pursuits."

Bancroft regarded her with what looked like amusement. "Again, I am in awe of the amount of information you collected in such a short time, Miss Donovan."

Kendra was saved from making any sort of retort by the return of the butler and footmen to clear the table for the second course. She sat back and watched, still fascinated at the grand production the aristocracy made of their evening meal. Savory scents blanketed the room as the servants returned with platters boasting squab pigeons and stewed hares, and side dishes of julienned carrots, boiled potatoes, and brussels sprouts. Gravy boats filled with dark brown sauce, melted butter, and an assortment of jellies accompanied each dish.

"Did you know that Mr. Stone had a reputation at cheating at cards?" she asked after the butler had replenished their wine and withdrawn.

"Rumors and innuendo," Bancroft dismissed. He picked up his knife and fork, making short work of the pigeon on his plate.

"Rumors of being a cardsharp should not be dismissed lightly," the Duke said. "Did you at least investigate the accusations, my lord?"

Bancroft chewed and swallowed the slice of meat before replying. He seemed to weigh his words carefully. "I think you are referring to the incident in the Assembly Rooms. Last spring, I believe it was."

"Yes," Kendra said.

The earl stabbed a sprout with his knife. He took a bite of the vegetable, and chewed thoughtfully. "A farmer accused Mr. Stone of cheating him during a game, from what I recollect. Winifred, do you recall the man's name?"

"Really, Papa." She gave a pained smile, picking up her wineglass. "You do not expect me to know the name of a farmer, do you?"

"Turner! Yes, Mr. Turner." Bancroft looked at Kendra. "I do not have more than a passing acquaintance with him, but he has a reputation for being a thoroughly disagreeable character. You would do well to look into him."

"We'll do that." Kendra sampled the julienned carrots. The food was decent, but she decided that she'd become spoiled by Monsieur Anton. "Where were you yesterday, my lord, between three and six?"

There was no way to soften the question, and she was curious to see Bancroft's reaction. Realizing that one had come under scrutiny in an investigation elicited various reactions from shock to insult.

Bancroft merely looked curious. "Is that when Mr. Stone is thought to have died?"

"It is."

"How do you know Mr. Stone was killed within those hours?" he wondered.

"The physical evidence suggests that's the window we're working with," she said, choosing her words with care. "Mr. Biddle said he was with Stone until approximately two-thirty—half past two." She opted for the British usage, then continued. "The constable is in the process of interviewing workers to see if anybody saw Mr. Stone after that time. Maybe we can narrow down our window even more."

Bancroft eyed her. "You are a most unusual female, Miss Donovan."

What did you say to that? It was, as far as Kendra was concerned, equal to being called a freak.

The earl picked up his wineglass, hesitated. "Hmm. Between three and six, you say?"

Bancroft swirled his glass, his eyes lowered to the eddy he created inside the cut crystal. Candlelight was supposed to be kind to women after a certain age—it wasn't kind to Lord Bancroft. The light played across his face, deepening the lines around his eyes, and across his forehead. The loose flesh of his jaw hung over his cravat. In this setting, he had the look of a feeble old man. But Kendra knew that was deceiving. The earl might be old, but there was nothing feeble about him. Beneath his aged flesh was a strength and purpose that made her watch him as if he was a coiled snake, ready to strike.

"I worked in my study the entire afternoon," Bancroft said finally, lifting his gaze to lock on hers. "At six, I retired to my dressing room to prepare for dinner. Naturally, Winifred joined me for the meal. We dined at seven, as we do every evening. Is that not correct, Winifred?"

"Yes, Papa."

"Can anyone verify that you were in your study all afternoon?" Kendra asked.

"My land steward was with me in the early hours, but, unfortunately, he departed at around half past two. My valet can confirm that I was in my bedchamber at six. You have my permission to quiz my manservant if you don't believe me, Miss Donovan."

"What is this?" Lady Winifred's dark eyes moved from her father to Kendra. She suddenly seemed to understand the direction the conversation had taken. Her nostrils flared in indignation as she looked at Kendra. "Are you suggesting that my father may have anything to do with Mr. Stone's death, Miss Donovan? That is outrageous!"

Kendra met the widow's dark eyes. If the evening progressed in the typical fashion for this era, the men would stay behind at the table to take port and possibly smoke, while the women moved into the drawing room. She hoped that particular ritual would be abandoned this evening.

"Do not fuss, Winifred," said Bancroft. "I have nothing to hide."

His daughter let out a sharp breath. "Of course you do not."

The Duke asked, "Where is your study located, my lord?"

"On the ground floor, near the morning room. It would be easy enough, I imagine, for me to sneak outside. It has French doors that lead to the verandah and the gardens in the back of the manor." He smiled at them as he sipped his wine. "But to sneak off the grounds and make my way over the moors to the mill without being seen? I do not think so."

As the butler and footmen returned to clear the table for the third course of fruits and cheeses, Kendra regarded the old man. He didn't seem to care whether he was a murder suspect. She wondered if that was because he was innocent, or because he was very clever.

The wineglasses were filled again. She sipped, and summoned a mental picture of the surrounding geography. The mill was less than two miles away. By Bancroft's own account, he had at least three hours to make it to the mill, kill Stone, and return home for dinner.

"Oh, I don't know," she murmured, and met his dark eyes with a smile as cool as his own. "It would depend on the motivation, I think."

"Ah, but you make my point, Miss Donovan." He picked up his refilled glass, and wagged a playful finger at her. "I have no motivation to kill the manager of my mill. In fact, the entire incident inconveniences me dreadfully."

"Inconvenience has never been a good alibi for murder."

Bancroft's mouth curved into a thin, sharp smile. "Nevertheless, I had no reason to murder Mr. Stone."

Kendra held his eyes for a beat. "Do you know why Mr. Stone went into the mill yesterday? Was he working on anything specific?"

"No. Mr. Biddle would be the person to ask."

She asked, "Who do you think may have had reason to kill him?"

"I can't imagine. Although now that I think of it, Mr. Turner certainly had a grievance against him. I had thought the whole incident was in the past, but perhaps not. Mr. Turner has a reputation as having a violent temper. What was done to Mr. Stone was certainly violent." He paused, then smiled. "Of course, if anyone else comes to mind, I shall certainly send word. Now . . . shall we retire to the drawing room and have another drink?"

"What are you thinking, my dear?" the Duke asked from the opposite seat as the carriage rolled back to East Dingleford. He'd turned on the small brass lamp in the corner, enough light to see the frown on Kendra's face.

"I'm thinking I shouldn't have had that last glass of wine." Kendra leaned forward. Her head was swimming; the godawful swaying of the carriage wasn't helping matters. She gripped her head with both hands. "God."

Aldridge eyed her warily. "If you are going to be ill, I shall tell Benjamin to pull off to the side of the road immediately."

"No . . . well, I'll let you know." She slid her hands to her cheeks. "It's actually embarrassing to know that someone like Lady Winifred can drink me under the table."

The Duke smiled slightly. "I don't think you are giving Lady Winifred a compliment."

Kendra pulled herself upright. "I'd like to know a lot more about the Earl of Langfrey. You never met him in London?"

"Even before Arabella—before the accident, we preferred the country. Though the Langfrey name does ring a distant bell. I find it interesting that he is not the local magistrate, given his obvious wealth. Then again, financials are easy to disguise." He cocked his head. "What troubles you about him, my dear?"

She had to think about that. "He's arrogant, condescending."

"Unfortunately, that is typical of men in his position."

She regarded him. "You're in a higher position, but you aren't like that."

"I had an older brother until I was thirteen," he said. "I was never meant to inherit Aldridge Castle, and was allowed to develop my interests in natural philosophy. I only came in line to inherit the dukedom after Richard was struck down with brain fever while at Cambridge."

There was so much they didn't know about each other.

"It was a long time ago," Aldridge continued. "My point is, I wasn't being groomed to be a duke from birth. And I fell in love with Arabella. Her father was a squire—landed gentry, not nobility. Our view of the world is shaped by the people around us and our experiences, is it not?"

Kendra was quiet for a moment. "I wonder what shaped Bancroft while he was gone from East Dingleford?" she said. She shook her head. "I don't like him. I feel like he's toying with me in some way."

Aldridge considered that. "I didn't find Lord Bancroft particularly evasive."

"You think it's my imagination?"

"Not necessarily."

She frowned. Was she letting her dislike for Bancroft cloud her judgment? "He certainly pushed Mr. Turner as a possible suspect, didn't he? He barely remembered the man initially, but then suddenly recalled his violent temper."

"You think Lord Bancroft is being devious?"

"I think everyone is being devious. I also think that the simplest way to deflect suspicion away from yourself is to point a finger at somebody else."

13

The next morning, Kendra found herself in the private parlor, a cup of coffee in hand, in front of a newly acquired slate board. She wondered where Matthews had dug it up. There was a hushed quality to the Green Maiden that reminded her of the preternaturally still hours just before dawn, though sun poured through the window. Many of the travelers had left on Saturday, not wanting to offend God—or society—by being caught on the highway on Sunday. The remaining guests had either left for church services, like the Duke, or were still in bed.

Kendra lifted the coffee cup and took a long swallow. She closed her eyes and sighed with pleasure, appreciating the jolt of caffeine as much as the silence. When she opened her eyes, her gaze fell on the first column on the slate board: victimology, filled with scribbles.

She sighed again, but this time there was nothing pleasurable about it. She could easily just write *asshole*. Mr. Harold "Harry" Stone was the kind of victim that law enforcement dreaded, a guy whose personality and lifestyle generated a long list of suspects. He'd been a womanizer and libertine, before and after his marriage, and jealousy was always a motivator. Wives were normally at the top of the suspect list, but Lavinia Stone's alibi was solid. And she wasn't ringing any bells for Kendra. Mrs. Stone had displayed more jealousy and anger toward Lady Winifred and Lord Bancroft than her husband's infidelity.

Kendra's gaze slid down the list. Stone had been a gambler and, if the rumors held, not averse to cheating. Gambling was high-risk behavior. Even if Stone hadn't swindled anyone, Kendra often found that people didn't like losing their money. And if he had cheated . . . She thought of what the Duke had said, that many gentlemen resolved their differences on the dueling field. Maybe the offended party in this case had chosen to bludgeon Stone with a bronze statue, rather than challenge him with dueling pistols.

She finished her coffee, her eyes moving down the list. Based on everything she'd learned, Stone would've likely been diagnosed as having an antisocial personality disorder in the twenty-first century, the disorder of moguls and megalomaniacs in her era. His wife had talked about his charm, as much as she'd talked about him being a rogue. Exploitation, cheating, lack of remorse, a certain irresponsibility—all those characteristics fit the diagnosis. So did Stone's desire for power, to have control, to boast. Even his office, fashioned into a gentleman's study, was a form of boasting.

But what's up with the cats? They were more than a fetish. Whether they had anything to do with his murder, though, she didn't know.

Stone had used his position as the mill manager ruthlessly, cruelly. He'd enjoyed threatening the livelihoods of those beneath him, enjoyed firing people. Kendra thought of the French Revolution—all revolutions and revolts, really. People could be suppressed for only so long before they rose up, angrily, sometimes violently. She'd seen riots in her own era, revolutions in other parts of the world. This was nothing new. Had one individual risen up against Stone in an equally angry, violent way?

Mr. Biddle came to mind. He had several checks against him, which put him at the top of the suspect list. He'd been the last person to see Stone alive, and she'd worked plenty of cases where the last person to be seen with the victim usually turned out to be the murderer.

He also had no real alibi, and his office was right next to Stone's. After his meeting with Stone, Biddle said he'd stayed in his office, claiming that the noise from the mill would have drowned out any sound that came out of Stone's office.

He was probably right. The crime had been brutal and bloody—but, Kendra thought, fairly silent. She doubted whether Stone would've cried out even when the first blow landed—too stunned—and he'd been dead after the second blow. Biddle could have been in his office and heard nothing but a muffled thud when Stone and the chair fell over, and even that might have been covered up by the noise of the factory.

She lifted her coffee cup to take another swallow, and scowled when she realized it was empty. She set the cup down, and paced instead.

Biddle had been doing Stone's job, without the title, most likely without the same pay. That would piss anybody off. Except he'd been doing it for nineteen years. If it had been him, why now? Did it have to do with whatever had been on the desk?

Her thoughts shifted to the seven workers Stone had recently fired. The timing worked out for them. One of those men might have stewed about it long enough to come in to confront Stone. Except . . . that kind of confrontation meant raised voices. Surely Biddle would have heard that kind of commotion? Plus, the killer had been standing slightly behind Stone. A confrontation between Stone and a recently fired worker would have taken place face-to-face. Stone would never have turned his back on him.

That didn't mean the fired workers were off the hook completely. Biddle had supplied the list to the constable, who had yet to give it to her, but she wanted to follow procedure and tie off that thread, even if, in her mind, she'd already crossed them off the list.

Kendra's jaw clenched when she thought about Jameson. He was dragging his heels and blocking her

work, every step of the way. *Sexist son of a bitch.* She wished
Sam would get here. The Bow Street Runner had regarded
her with suspicious eyes initially, but that was because she'd
lied to him, not because she was a woman. She needed
Sam's help tracking down the previous manager. Mr.
Murray had known Stone before he'd shown up in East
Dingleford, and she needed to find out who Harry Stone
was, really, not just his personality traits or vices. Who was
he? What was his background? Where was he from?

Lord Bancroft said that he'd hired Stone on Murray's
recommendation, which made sense. What didn't was
that Bancroft had kept Stone around for twenty years.
The earl didn't strike her as someone who would hesitate to fire an incompetent manager. Yet he hadn't fired
Stone—he'd enabled him by hiring Biddle to do the job
that Stone couldn't.

Blackmail. It was the simplest explanation. Proving it
would require digging into Stone's past, a time-consuming
process in the early nineteenth century, especially when
you didn't even know where the potential blackmailer was
originally from.

But she knew Bancroft's origins. She had an entire
community who could talk to her about *his* background.

Her gaze fell on her empty coffee cup, and she smiled
suddenly. Yes, she had an entire community. And one
person who had nearly run off to Gretna Green to marry
Bancroft.

Kendra got lucky. She found Mrs. Bolton alone in the
kitchen, the room filled with the tantalizing aroma of
baking bread. The innkeeper's wife was peeling and slicing
turnips and carrots into a big copper pot. She glanced up
at Kendra's entrance, and gave a dramatic start.

"Miss Donovan! You mustn't come in here. 'Tisn't
proper!" Mrs. Bolton dropped the knife, and wiped her
hands on her apron. She hurried forward to intercept her.
"What do you require? I shall bring it to you in the parlor."

"Please, don't concern yourself, Mrs. Bolton. I was just
hoping for some more coffee." Kendra held up the empty

cup, then scanned the kitchen. "I also need to speak with you. Where is everybody?"

"At church services. I said my prayers earlier, of course. Someone needs to stay here for the guests. Why don't I bring you a tray?"

"I'd rather talk now."

The old woman hesitated, but seemed to realize that it would be useless to argue. She moved to the cupboard and retrieved a burlap sack. She plopped it down next to an old fashioned, industrial-looking grinder that was about the size of an outdoor motor, with gears and wheels on the side and a crank handle.

"What do you wish to talk to me about?" she asked finally.

"Lord Bancroft."

Mrs. Bolton's hands froze on the burlap sack. As Kendra watched, the old woman's fingers slowly relaxed, untying the sack to scoop out the aromatic coffee beans and pour them into the funnel at the top of the grinder. "Why are you asking me about the earl?"

"I was told that there was a time when you and Lord Bancroft were quite close." Kendra observed a series of emotions flicker across the old woman's face, too fast to identify.

"That was a long time ago," Mrs. Bolton said.

"Then you've known Lord Bancroft for a long time."

"I've known him all my life. When my father was alive, he rented one of the earl's farms that bordered Falcon Court." She began to turn the crank of the coffee mill. "We were children together. And then . . . we were no longer children."

Kendra saw the soft look enter the other woman's gray eyes. "You became involved."

Mrs. Bolton paused in turning the crank, and looked at Kendra. "You see an old woman before you, Miss Donovan, but I was young once. Young, and very, very foolish."

Kendra said diplomatically, "I can't imagine you being foolish, Mrs. Bolton."

Mrs. Bolton smiled. "You are being kind. Unfortunately, youth tends to make us all foolish. It was long ago—I was sixteen and Nat was seventeen—but I still remember the day he rode his big bay out of the woods separating our properties. It was like the boy I had known had become a man overnight." She let out a long sigh, and began turning the crank again. "Although now I look back and see only a boy."

"Nat?" Kendra prompted.

"Nathan—the Earl of Langfrey. Oh, I know, 'tis brazen of me to address him in such a manner, but everyone in East Dingleford called him Nat back then, even his father. He hadn't yet come into the viscountcy. His grandfather was still alive. When I recollect those days, I still think of him as Nat."

"You were in love with him."

"Yes," she admitted softly. Now that she'd opened up, the words came more easily. "He was so handsome, my Nat. Dark curly hair and those dark eyes, always laughing. I swear, Nat could have charmed a miser into giving up his gold."

Kendra said nothing. The romance between Mrs. Bolton and her Nat had taken place more than a half century before, she knew, but she still had a difficult time imagining the cold, arrogant old man she'd dined with last night as the handsome, charming boy that Mrs. Bolton remembered.

"I loved him," Mrs. Bolton continued in a whisper, "and he loved me."

"What happened?" Kendra asked quietly, affected by the pain she observed in the old woman's eyes.

"What happened? Why, what was bound to happen, of course." Her lips twisted in a combination of sadness and bitterness. "I was the daughter of a simple farmer. My mother's father was a vicar, and she was a governess until she married my father. She educated us. But still, my people are not gentry. 'Tis the curse of the very young, I suppose, to dream of things that can never be."

Kendra thought of Alec, and her own heart squeezed. *Not just the curse of the very young.*

"For the span of one summer, we were very young," Mrs. Bolton continued, "and, as I said, very foolish." Her face softened, her gray eyes holding a strange glow as she recalled that fateful summer. In that instant, Kendra could see beyond the lines, loose skin, and age spots, and imagine Mrs. Bolton as a young, beautiful girl.

"Nat asked me to marry him," she murmured, lips curving upward. "We were aware that such a thing was scandalous, even in East Dingleford, but Nat wanted to run away to Gretna Green, and God help me, I agreed to go."

The older woman fell silent. Kendra waited.

"My father learned of our elopement, and sent word to the earl," Mrs. Bolton whispered. "Well, he was actually only a viscount, then—Lord Drake—since his father was alive." The light slowly faded from her eyes. "My father depended on renting the lands, you see. Poor Nat. He and his father had a dreadful row. His father threatened to cut him off if he didn't leave East Dingleford and go away to school. Cambridge or Oxford. I cannot recall."

"Away from you."

"Away from me, yes," Mrs. Bolton murmured. "But Nat could be as stubborn as the devil. He told his father that he could go to Jericho; he intended to seek his own fortune. There were riches to be had in India, or one of the many foreign lands. He'd hire on as a privateer. He promised me that he'd return and we would marry, with or without his father's consent." She drew an unsteady breath, and let it out slowly. "He was such a lovely, courageous, silly boy."

She began to turn the crank again, as though needing to release pent-up energy. "I waited, you know. One year, then two. He sent letters. From India, Egypt, Barbados . . . so many foreign places. I thought I could wait forever."

"Forever is a long time."

"Yes . . . particularly when you are young and yearning for marriage and babies." Mrs. Bolton's smile was filled with sorrow. "The letters stopped. I waited. Five years, Miss Donovan. I watched my sisters and brothers marry and set up their nurseries. I was true to Nat, but God forgive me, I didn't want to be a spinster."

She quit turning the crank, and drew out the small drawer at the bottom of the coffee mill, now brimming with fresh grounds. Mrs. Bolton dumped the grounds into the tin coffee kettle and glanced at Kendra as she lifted a nearby pitcher. She poured water into the kettle, replaced the lid, and set it on the stove.

"Plenty of men asked for my hand, but I sent them on their way. Five years . . . and then Mr. Bolton offered marriage." Mrs. Bolton sighed. She took a tinderbox, and went about lighting the stove. "Charles wasn't as handsome as my Nat, nor so charming. But he was—*is*—a good man. A good husband and provider. I accepted his proposal. What else could I do?"

"I heard Lord Bancroft left East Dingleford for a time," Kendra said. "When did he finally return?"

"In 1780. It was the year after his father took ill. Poor Nat. He returned, but less than a week later, his father died. Fell down the stairs and broke his neck. I only pray they mended their relationship before the earl's accident."

Kendra lifted her eyebrows. "He . . . Lord Bancroft never told you if he did?"

A shadow passed across Mrs. Bolton's face. "You must understand, everything had changed, Miss Donovan. It had been sixteen years since I had said my goodbyes to Nat. So much had happened." She pressed a hand against her breastbone, as though it ached. "I haven't spoken more than a handful of words to him in all the years since he returned. I knew . . . I knew he was no longer my Nat. From the day he came to the inn after burying his father, and forever more, he was Lord Bancroft to me."

"He changed," Kendra murmured. She felt oddly affected by the story.

"We both changed. I was no longer the young girl he'd promised his heart to. I was married with four children.

And he was no longer the charming boy that I remembered. I scarcely recognized him. He still had those dark eyes and dark hair. But he was so . . . *hard*. The sixteen years he'd spent overseas had turned him into a different person. Angrier—no, not angry." She shook her head, and said, "Colder. More like his father. Or his grandfather, who never cared for East Dingleford, and spent his days in London Town. I think . . ." Mrs. Bolton's voice dropped so low that Kendra had to strain to hear. "I think I hurt him very badly. He returned home and found that I had married and set up my nursery. I think that is one of the reasons he turned so cold."

Kendra frowned. "He was gone for sixteen years. He could hardly have expected you to wait for him, especially when he stopped writing letters."

Mrs. Bolton said nothing.

Kendra asked, "Did Lord Bancroft ever find his fortune?"

"I don't know. He inherited the title and the family money after his father's death. The old earl and his father before him weren't wise with money, and the late earl was forced to sell some of the land. Lord Bancroft worked to rebuild the estate, although the squire refused to sell the land he'd bought from the old earl. A year or two after he returned, Lord Bancroft went off to London to hunt for a bride. He found an heiress—the daughter of an earl . . . Do not look at me like that, Miss Donovan," she said sharply. "'Tis how it should be. How it was *meant* to be. We're better off with our own kind."

The anger rose up inside Kendra, taking her by surprise. "And who determines what that should be? Who decides where a person belongs in society, and who with? Exactly *who* are the gatekeepers, and why should anyone accept their edicts?"

The older woman's eyes widened, and she reached out to grasp Kendra's arm, squeezing it surprisingly hard. "Hush, Miss Donovan," she hissed. "I know you are an American, but you must hold your tongue in these parts, lest you be thought a radical. There are spies everywhere."

Kendra thought of Biddle's response when she'd mentioned revolution yesterday. "I wasn't talking revolution."

"I apologize, miss, but 'tis a sensitive time in England." Mrs. Bolton let go of Kendra's arm. The kettle began to spurt and rumble, and Mrs. Bolton snatched a rag off the counter, using it as an oven mitt as she lifted the kettle. "Many fear radical propaganda."

Kendra leaned back against the counter, considering the matter. "I don't consider equality for everyone such a radical philosophy."

"That is because you are an American. You were born into a radical philosophy. I see much of my brother in you. You share the same sentiments . . ."

Mrs. Bolton pressed her lips together, as though she'd said too much. She shook her head and poured the coffee into an ornate silver coffeepot, which she set on a tray. "That is neither here nor there. Why are you concerning yourself with things that happened so long ago?"

Kendra hesitated before explaining, "There's a possibility that what happened to Stone has roots in the past. I'd like to know more about Stone's background. Do you know where he was from before he came to East Dingleford?"

Mrs. Bolton frowned. "No. But I did not have much association with Mr. Stone. We are of the same age, but I was always too old for him, so he never paid me any mind." Her gray eyes glinted. "I was careful to keep Tessa and Lizzie well out of his reach."

Kendra was shocked. "Tessa is only . . . what? Fifteen? Lizzie can't be much older."

"Seventeen."

Kendra pushed aside her anger. She didn't know what irritated her more: Stone's lecherous, possibly predatory behavior, or the fact that no one in East Dingleford stopped him.

"What can you tell me about the relationship between Lord Bancroft and Mr. Stone?" she asked.

Mrs. Bolton looked puzzled. "Lord Bancroft owns the mill, and Mr. Stone is—was—his manager."

"From what I've learned, Stone wasn't a very good manager. Why did Lord Bancroft keep him on rather than finding someone better? Do you think they could have known each other before Stone arrived in East Dingleford?"

Mrs. Bolton was quiet for a long moment. She concentrated on retrieving a creamer and sugar bowl, adding them to the tray. "It's possible, I suppose," she admitted finally. She made a move to lift the tray, but Kendra put her hand on the other woman's arm. It was thin, but Kendra could feel the corded muscles beneath the brown linen fabric of her dress. How different would her life have been if she'd married Lord Bancroft and eventually become a countess? Kendra imagined the arm beneath her hand would have been rounder and softer, with very little of the muscle tone she could feel beneath her fingertips.

"Let me help," she offered.

"You shall do no such thing!" Mrs. Bolton looked aghast. "A gently bred female such as yourself does not go about hoisting trays like a commoner." She lifted the tray, then paused and gave Kendra a direct look. "What is it that you are really asking me, Miss Donovan?"

Kendra nodded. No more niceties. "You know Lord Bancroft. Do you think he could have killed Mr. Stone?"

Mrs. Bolton bit her lip, and her gray eyes darkened. She was silent for so long that Kendra began to wonder if she'd answer the question at all.

Then the old woman gave a soft sigh. "The boy I knew and loved could never have killed anyone," she said. "'Tis vile to even imagine such a thing. But the man that the boy has become? I do not know that man. I do not know what he's capable of. I—" Her breath caught, and she simply shook her head unhappily. "I simply do not know."

14

The Duke lifted his teacup, his gaze speculative as he scanned the notes Kendra had written on the slate board. "You think Mr. Stone may have been holding something over Lord Bancroft's head to keep his position as manager of the mill."

It was not a question, but Kendra shrugged. "It fits. Lord Bancroft left East Dingleford for sixteen years. Mrs. Bolton said he left when he was seventeen after a falling out with his father—"

"You spoke to Mrs. Bolton about Lord Bancroft? About their . . ." The Duke appeared to struggle for the right word.

"Love affair? Yes."

"I was going to say 'youthful indiscretion.'"

"I think it was more than a youthful indiscretion. I think they loved each other. It's heartbreaking, really." Kendra remembered the sadness in the old woman's eyes. "She called him her Nat."

"Nat?"

"Short for Nathan. He left East Dingleford to strike it rich. He promised to return and marry Mrs. Bolton. He was so . . ."

"Chivalrous?"

"Actually, I was thinking something more along the lines of stupid," she said drily. "Apparently he didn't realize that it's not easy to get rich. He was thirty-three when he returned home."

"A man. And you think in that time away, Mr. Stone and Lord Bancroft became acquainted?"

"I can't prove it, but yes. I also think there's a hell of a lot of testosterone pumping between seventeen and thirty-three."

"Indeed." He took a sip of tea, and put the cup back on the saucer. His eyes were bright when he looked at her. "And what, may I ask, is testosterone?"

Oh, hell. She was suddenly exhausted that she always had to consider her words. "It's a hormone—a male sex hormone," she finally said. Hormones wouldn't be identified until the early twentieth century, but she didn't know how giving the Duke this kind of information would affect the space-time continuum. "It's what turns boys into men, giving them their bulkier muscle and deepening their voices. And testosterone accounts for more aggressive behavior."

"Fascinating." The Duke's blue eyes glinted as he leaned forward. "This is not entirely unknown to me, my dear. John Hunter—a Scottish surgeon and a brilliant man of science—conducted experiments by castrating roosters."

"Now that's the kind of guy you want to invite to a party."

The Duke laughed. "I read that he transplanted roosters' testes into capons to study the effects. It changed what was a docile creature into an aggressive one. The experiment proved a link between male testes and aggression, just as you say. In the future, they will call this a *hormone*, with the proper name *testosterone*?"

Kendra sighed. "Yes, but we're getting off track here."

The Duke looked briefly disappointed not to pursue the scientific discussion, but he waved his hand. "You are quite right, my dear. What you are referring to as testosterone, we identify here as young bucks sowing their wild oats. You see, we might not know the scientific reason underlying the behavior, but we *do* recognize it. Your world and my world are not really that dissimilar."

"And yet I'm the one wearing skirts and can't vote," she countered.

"Point taken."

She smiled as she walked over to the coffeepot and refreshed her cup. "Now we really are getting off track. The point I was trying to make is, Lord Bancroft was gone during some pretty formative years. There's a lot of temptation in the world."

"Young bucks are often tempted to engage in all sorts of mischief."

A shadow dimmed the Duke's eyes. He didn't say it, but she knew he was remembering his late nephew, Gabriel—Alec's half-brother. He'd been typical of many wealthy young men of this era—hell, in any era, really—who'd been lured into alleviating his boredom in a hedonistic club. Drugs, sex, and rock 'n' roll. It had eventually killed him.

Kendra nodded. "Let's say Lord Bancroft and Stone got into some mischief together. If it was egregious enough, Stone might have held it over Lord Bancroft's head."

"Hmm. But Lord Bancroft returned years before Mr. Stone arrived in East Dingleford."

"They could have run into each other after that. Or Stone waited to blackmail him. Right now, I have more questions than answers."

"One of those questions Dr. Poole brought up: why now? If Lord Bancroft is our villain, why did he wait twenty years to dispose of the person threatening to expose him?"

"I don't know. Maybe it has to do with what was taken from the desk." She pinched the bridge of her nose. The missing item continued to bother her.

Aldridge rubbed his jaw. "I have another point of contention. We interviewed the workers at the mill, but no one remembered seeing Lord Bancroft that day."

"That actually doesn't bother me as much. People see what they want to see; you know that. Lord Bancroft could have disguised himself as a worker, so anyone who saw him would have assumed it was another worker going up to Stone's office. I did it myself when I put on Molly's clothes in London." That had been liberating, she remembered. Women in the lower classes had much more freedom than those in the upper echelons of society.

"No one knew you in London," the Duke pointed out. "East Dingleford is much smaller, and Lord Bancroft is well-known."

"You'd be shocked by how blind human beings can be, especially when they're concentrating on their work." She lifted her coffee cup, her gaze on the Duke. "It's called inattentional blindness. We can be so focused on the task at hand that we don't see anything else. If you were involved in one of your experiments, you might not see a naked woman walk through your laboratory."

The Duke looked startled. "I confess to becoming involved in my experiments, but I can assure you, Miss Donovan, that I would notice an intruder without clothes!"

Kendra smiled. "Everybody thinks that. There have been experiments done, you know. The visual cortex filters out all sorts of information so we're not distracted. Look at your nose. What do you see?"

"My nose? All right." He laughed, but lowered his eyes, shifting them side to side. "I can see its outline, depending where I look. But then, I have a rather large nose."

"Everyone can see their nose if they want to look at it. Even when you're looking straight ahead, you can see a little bit of it. But we don't. Our visual cortex makes certain we are not constantly distracted by our own noses."

"Fascinating! And you think that the mill workers may have filtered out Lord Bancroft's presence at the mill?"

"I think it's a possibility that we shouldn't ignore. Maybe he slipped in without anyone noticing him, maybe he dressed like another worker, or maybe they saw him but didn't really process seeing him."

"You said there have been experiments done? Where someone is working and they have a . . . a lady who is unclothed walk by?"

Kendra had to stifle a laugh at the Duke's inability to say *naked*. "Not a naked lady. But there were experiments done where a man dressed in a gorilla costume walked across a room, and nobody noticed because they were focused on something else."

"What is a gorilla?" asked the Duke.

"Oh." Kendra paused, a little thrown that something so common in her era wasn't known here. "It's a large ape."

"Ah. I see." After a moment, the Duke shook his head. "Regardless, I don't see how that's possible."

"Our brain works in mysterious ways."

"And *no* one saw the man dressed as an ape?"

"*Most* participants didn't see him."

"Ah. But it was not one hundred percent."

"No, but it was pretty high. Maybe seventy-five percent." She recognized the glint in the Duke's eyes. "I see what you're getting at. Even if the majority of workers didn't process seeing Lord Bancroft, one or two would have seen him and said something."

"I would think so, yes. Still, it is another matter if he undertook some type of subterfuge. Unfortunately, I take issue with that as well."

Kendra raised her eyebrows. "What issue?"

"Your original hypothesis is that the crime was impulse—spur of the moment, as it were. However, if Lord Bancroft disguised himself in some way, doesn't that suggest some sort of premeditation?"

Kendra's lips parted in surprise. "Christ, you're right." She shook her head, and laughed. "Who's the FBI profiler here? I'm an idiot."

"No, you were focused on another part of the equation. Maybe that is another form of inattention blindness."

She narrowed her eyes at the Duke. "You're being generous, but I sense smugness."

His eyes twinkled, but he remained silent.

She laughed again and set down her coffee cup, crossing the room to stare at the slate board. "Bancroft stays on the list, but he just dropped down to the bottom. Let's go and find someone to replace him."

"You speak of Mr. Turner."

"That's exactly who I speak of."

The Duke pushed himself to his feet. "I have his address. Shall I have Benjamin bring around the carriage? Or shall I send word to Mr. Matthews to come around again with his gig?"

"Smug I can take. Now you're just being nasty."

15

From a distance, the Turner farm looked like a scene taken straight off a tourist postcard. Beneath the brilliant blue sky, trees were dressed in dusky autumn colors around a cluster of gray buildings: a stone barn, stables, and a scattering of smaller outer structures. Set further back was a two-story cottage, its stucco whitewashed and its windows framed by shutters that were painted the same dark hunter green as the door. A low wall made out of stacked flat gray rocks circled the property and snaked up the sloping hill, where several dozen sheep appeared to be sleeping in the late-morning sun. Near the barn, about half a dozen white and brown chickens clucked and pecked at the ground.

It was only when they drew closer that some of the charm ebbed for Kendra. She'd grown used to the faint scent of dung that was prevalent in this era, but the stench that hit her now was something else entirely. It was a pungent, musky scent, earthy and a little wild.

She also realized the farm was more rundown than it had first appeared. The roof of the barn sagged slightly on one side, giving it a listing appearance, and the paint had begun to fleck off the cottage's door and shutters.

The carriage rolled to a stop. Benjamin leaped off his perch, hurrying around to unfold the steps for them to descend. As she and the Duke walked the path to the front door of the cottage, Kendra glanced up in time to see the curtains in the middle upper-story window twitch.

There was no brass knocker so Kendra rapped on the door with her gloved fist.

"Who are you?"

The harsh voice came from behind them, raised to bridge the distance between the house and barn. Kendra and the Duke turned and watched a tall man emerge from the gloomy depths of the open barn door, carrying a sack of grain across one of his broad shoulders. He looked to be in his mid-thirties, with wheat-colored hair matted with sweat and sticking to his temples. Sweat stained the homespun smock he wore. His trousers were torn at the knee and patched at the hip, and his boots were scuffed white around heel and toe.

It occurred to Kendra that the man resembled his farm. At a distance, he could be perceived as handsome, tall, and broad-shouldered. But upon closer inspection, the effects of time and what looked like an indulgence for drink gave him a florid face and heavy jowls. Of course, the scowl darkening his brow didn't help give a good first impression either. As he stepped closer, Kendra noticed that his eyes were blue and slightly bloodshot. Allergies, sleepless nights, or drink. Any of those factors could have contributed to his appearance, but her gut told her it was the last.

Now his eyes narrowed into a squint, roaming over them, then over to the carriage to study the Duke's crest on the door. Kendra expected his expression to change then, to become obsequious. She'd grown accustomed to that reaction in the two months that she'd been here. People grew deferential—or at least cautious—when anyone crossed paths with the Duke of Aldridge. Yet in this, Turner surprised her as well. Instead of looking impressed or wanting to ingratiate himself with the nobleman, his expression hardened.

If the Duke noticed the hostility in the other man's demeanor, he hid it well. "Good morning, sir," he greeted, his smile polite, his tone measured. "I am the Duke of Aldridge. May I introduce my ward, Miss Donovan?"

Turner gave a grunt as he jerked his shoulder forward in a movement that dislodged the bag of grain. It landed at his feet, sending up a small cloud of dust. In a flurry of feathers and excited cackles, the chickens began strutting toward the bag. Turner gave the nearest one an impatient kick, sending it squawking and flapping its wings in the other direction. "W'ot do you want?"

Kendra decided in that moment to cut out the pleasantries. "We're here about Mr. Stone."

Turner wiped the sweat from his brow with his forearm as he turned his head to look at her. "W'ot about him?"

"He's dead." She watched him carefully. "He was murdered on Friday."

Kendra didn't expect Turner to be surprised by the news. A full day had passed since Stone had been murdered on Friday night, and she knew that gossip traveled shockingly fast even without 24/7 cable news and the Internet. Still, she was interested in gauging his reaction.

He lifted a beefy shoulder. "Aye? And w'ot's that got to do with me?"

Before she could answer, the door behind them opened. A young woman, probably about her own age, stood in the doorway, wearing a serviceable cotton dress that had been washed so many times that it was now more white than its original yellow, its paisley print ghostly images splayed across the material. She wore a mop cap that covered most of her hair, but a few ash blond tendrils had escaped to float around a delicate, fine-boned face. She was lovely, except for the ugly purplish bruise marring her high cheekbone, swelling the skin beneath her right eye.

"Mrs. Turner?" Kendra asked.

The woman's eyes, a pretty aquamarine shaded by long lashes, flicked a look in Turner's direction before shifting her gaze to Kendra. She licked her lips nervously. "Aye. Can I . . . can I help ye?"

"They don't need your help," Turner growled, taking a step forward. Anger emanated from him like invisible light waves. "Get back ter your chores!"

"Wait." Kendra didn't know if she stopped the woman because she wanted to ask her questions, or to defy Turner, to show him that not every woman would cower before him. "Mrs. Turner, I'm Kendra Donovan, and this is the Duke of Aldridge. We're here about Mr. Stone."

The other woman's complexion was the color of freshly churned cream, but at the mention of the mill manager's name, she turned gray. A flash of fear leaped in her pretty eyes.

Kendra kept her voice gentle when she asked, "Did you know that he was murdered on Friday?"

Mrs. Turner brought her hand up to her throat. Her gown had a high neck and long sleeves. When she moved her arm, the sleeve shifted lower, revealing a delicate wrist. And five purplish smudges darkening her skin.

Kendra couldn't stop herself from shooting a piercing look at Turner. She slid her gaze pointedly from his face down to his hands. They were big hands, with thick fingers. And Kendra knew that she'd be able to match each digit to a corresponding contusion circling his wife's wrist.

"Aye. I heard," Mrs. Turner mumbled behind her. "'Tis a . . . a dreadful thing."

"W'ot do you want?" the sheep farmer demanded again, his face reddening. He took another step toward them, his chin jutting out in an aggressive manner. But then he hesitated, his gaze flicking to the Duke. He might not be inclined to show the same deference as others, Kendra realized, but he wasn't quite willing to take the Duke head-on either.

Classic bully, thought Kendra. *You can pick on someone smaller, who can't fight back, but you always think twice before taking on a stronger opponent.* The Duke might not be physically stronger than Turner, but in this world, any action against the nobleman could have drastic consequences for Turner.

She had to tamp down her raw dislike before she asked bluntly, "Where were you between three and six on Friday afternoon, Mr. Turner?"

"W'ot do you want ter know for?"

She kept her gaze locked on his. "Because Mr. Stone was killed around that time, and we heard that you two had a disagreement," she said.

"My ward and I are investigating the murder of Mr. Stone," the Duke spoke up beside her. His upper-class accent had sharpened dangerously—a sure sign of his ire. "We would appreciate an answer as to your whereabouts on Friday afternoon, sir."

The sheep farmer stared at the Duke, frowning. "Why would someone of the Patrician order such as yerself soil yer hands in the business of murder, eh?"

Aldridge met the other man's hostile gaze. Kendra had seen the Duke's grayish-blue eyes reflect many emotions, but she'd never seen them quite like this, with this icy, slightly contemptuous—no, *aristocratic*—look in them. It was scary impressive.

"'Tis no concern of yours as to why I involve myself in these matters, sir. I *am* involved, at the behest of your magistrate, Squire Matthews. Answer the question, if you please."

Turner's nostril's flared and his eyes blazed. For just a moment, Kendra thought the man was actually going to challenge the Duke. But then he crossed his arms in front of his chest, and regarded him stonily. "I was here, yer Grace. All day and all night. Jest ask me wife." He jerked his chin at her. "Wife, tell his Grace that I was here."

Mrs. Turner lowered her eyes and whispered, "Aye. My husband was at home, yer Grace."

"Speak up, woman!" Turner ordered.

Mrs. Turner gave a start, her eyes darting to her husband's red face. She stared at him as she repeated, louder, "Aye! My husband was here with me, yer Grace."

Kendra was surprised by the rage that all but boiled her blood. She had never been a beat cop, who witnessed a tragic amount of domestic abuse situations. But during the course of her career, there had been a handful of times when she'd suspected a woman was being abused by her husband or boyfriend. Her stomach had curdled and, if she'd had a chance to get the woman alone, she'd recommended that she seek help at a woman's shelter. As far as she knew, the women had never followed her advice. It had been depressing. But she couldn't remember any of those situations driving her to a point where she'd lost her temper.

She had to take a moment to make sure her voice was under control before she said, "We heard that you accused the victim of cheating during a card game."

The memory had Turner's lips thinning. "The bleeding bastard fleeced me!"

"You were angry." *Still are angry.*

"Aye. W'ot man wouldn't be? Common folk I might be, but I gotta right ter be angry!"

An anger that he took out on his wife when he got home, Kendra would bet. "It's a serious accusation, sir. I doubt Mr. Stone took it lightly to be called a cheater. How did he react?"

He snorted. "Denied it, of course!"

"You brought in the magistrate," she stated.

He gave an ill-tempered shrug. "W'ot good it did! Squire Matthews and Constable Jameson ain't gonna go against his lordship."

"What does Bancroft have to do with it?"

"W'ot do you think? Stone worked for Lord Bancroft. Bah! W'ot does it matter? It was months ago. I've gotta get back ter me chores, same as me wife." The steel in his eyes made Mrs. Turner jerk upright, her eyes going painfully wide. "We don't have time ter talk ter the like of you."

"Aye. Forgive me, but I—I must . . . do me chores," Mrs. Turner said. "Good day to ye, your Grace, Miss Donovan." Mrs. Turner dipped into a quick curtsy, her gaze fixed on her shoes. She didn't raise her eyes again as she stepped back and closed the door in their faces. It was a little like witnessing a beaten dog slink away from its master, fearing a fresh thrashing.

Kendra glanced at Turner. "I suppose you're going to tell me your wife walked into a door."

"W'ot?"

"Miss Donovan, this is not why we are here," the Duke murmured, putting a hand on her arm. "Mr. Turner, how deep was your play?"

The farmer shifted on his feet, he gaze sliding away. "'Tis nobody's business but mine."

"By the authority of the magistrate, it is our business, Mr. Turner," the Duke said coldly.

Turner's face took on a mulish look, but after a moment, he admitted, "We came ter an arrangement."

"To pay off your debt?" the Duke pressed.

"Aye."

Kendra asked, "What sort of arrangement?"

He glared at her. "Ain't none of your business!"

She tried a different approach. "Was that the first time you played cards against Mr. Stone?"

"Why? Are you a Quaker?" he sneered. "Here tryin' ter interfere in a bit o' harmless fun?"

"Harmless fun?" She arched her eyebrows. "A second ago you were complaining that he'd swindled you. The magistrate and constable became involved to prove that he hadn't cheated you. Doesn't sound harmless—or like much fun."

He pressed his lips together and remained silent.

She studied him. It wasn't just anger she saw, but a sullen resentment at all perceived injustices. "When was the last time you saw Mr. Stone?" she asked.

His eyes narrowed. "W'ot's that gotta do with anythin'?"

"Maybe nothing. If you could answer the question."

"I can't say I rightly remember."

They stared at each other for a moment, a silent battle of wills. "Your alibi is crap," she finally said.

His eyes twitched at her blunt assessment, his lips tightening, but he rolled his shoulders and said nothing. The chickens had gamboled back, scrambling around his feet. He glanced down, and as swift as a snake, he swooped down, grabbing one bird while kicking the other viciously.

"I think we're finished here." The Duke curled his hand around Kendra's arm, and gave a little tug. "Come along, Miss Donovan. Good day to you, sir."

Reluctantly, Kendra allowed the Duke to guide her back to the carriage. As she walked, she could feel Turner's eyes burning a hole between her shoulder blades. *Don't look back.* She actually accomplished the feat until she was seated in the carriage; then she couldn't stop herself from peering out the window. Turner was still staring. Their gazes met. Kendra watched a slow, unpleasant smile spread across his face. And with an ease that sent a chill arrowing through her, he shifted the bird he was holding, and calmly wrung its neck.

16

The bastard." Kendra fingers curled into a tight fist. "He's beating his wife." She gave the Duke a sharp glance. "What can we do about it?"

Aldridge spread his hands in a gesture of sympathy and helplessness. "Unfortunately, she *is* his wife."

"So that means he can *beat* her?"

"Wives have taken their husbands to court and won a divorce on the basis of physical cruelty, but it is rare," he said carefully, well aware of her temper. "The common law of coverture makes these matters sensitive. Under the doctrine, a man and a woman becomes one in the eyes of God and the law."

Kendra drew in an unsteady breath. "So women become property, with no rights against their husbands." But she already knew that.

"Coverture views husband and wife as one, and expects the husband to act accordingly. To physically harm one's wife is to do harm against himself."

Kendra rolled her eyes, and gave a harsh laugh. "Oh, yeah, I can see that's working well. Christ."

"A wife does have rights if the abuse is deemed excessive."

"And what exactly is *excessive* abuse?"

"That is a matter of debate," he conceded. "There is an acceptance of corporal punishment to correct a wife's behavior, as long as her life is not endangered."

Kendra opened her mouth but no sound came out. It took a few minutes. "So he can beat the hell out of her as long as she stays breathing," she said. And that didn't even touch on the husband's right to treat his wife like a child. *Correct her behavior?* Dear God.

"No, I think that would be deemed excessive force," the Duke said. "Regardless, wife-beating is an abhorrent practice. I cannot imagine ever having lifted my hand against my wife. And, quite frankly, I cannot imagine Arabella ever allowing it." He paused, his eyes meeting hers across the carriage. "I am aware that you sometimes view this world—*my* world—with frustration, Miss Donovan. But we are not barbarians."

"It's just . . ." *Unfair.* But life was unfair, and not just here. In her job, she'd encountered the worst of humanity. It wasn't always easy to remain objective, but it was important. You had to care to do a good job, be a good agent, but if you cared too much, you burnt out, with fantasies of eating your gun.

Or you went rogue and ended up in the nineteenth century.

Kendra sighed. "Turner's alibi is his abused wife. Which means he has no alibi," she pointed out. "He was also evasive about the debt he owed Stone."

"Yes, I am aware. His debt to Mr. Stone must have been fairly substantial. If he was playing deep, he could have even put up his farm as collateral against the bet."

"And if he didn't pay or couldn't pay, he would have lost everything."

"Unfortunately, it's been known to happen, especially among young bucks in the Ton."

"Sounds like a good motive for murder. We need to find out more about Turner's debt, and the arrangement he mentioned to pay it back. Maybe Turner decided to renege on it—"

She broke off as the carriage began to slow, and came to a swaying halt.

"What's amiss, I wonder?" Surprised, the Duke leaned forward to look out the window. "It's too early in the day to be concerned about highwaymen."

"It looks like Mr. Matthews," Kendra said, staring out the window at Matthews—wearing a dashing red riding habit, gray pantaloons tucked into polished boots, and a black beaver hat—galloped toward them on a bay roan.

Aldridge unfastened the latch to the window, and slid it down. "Good day, sir," he called out as the other man drew his horse to a halt beside the carriage.

"Good day to you, sir, Miss Donovan," Matthews greeted them, removing his hat. "Forgive me for waylaying you in such a high-handed manner. I sought your company at the Green Maiden, but Mr. Bolton informed me that you were out. It is most fortuitous that I happened to spy your carriage in the distance."

"We were calling upon Mr. Turner," said the Duke.

"Pray tell, did you learn anything?"

Kendra slid down her window to answer. "Not really. He says that he was at home when Mr. Stone was murdered. He remains a suspect."

Matthews raised his eyebrows. "You have cause to doubt his word?"

"I have cause to doubt everything about the man," she said drily.

"My ward and I discovered that Mr. Turner is a thoroughly reprehensible character," the Duke put in.

Matthews didn't appear surprised by the assessment. "I have had little cause to deal with the man myself, but I think I told you that he has come to the attention of my father and Constable Jameson, beyond his accusation that Mr. Stone was a cardsharp." He shifted in his saddle. The bay roan tossed its silky mane, its long ears twitching. "Actually, my father is the reason I sought you out, your Grace—and Miss Donovan. As you know, he is laid up with gout, so traveling is rare. However, he would be delighted if you would join us for supper tonight."

Kendra nodded. "Thank you. I need to talk with your father."

"He is quite interested in speaking with you as well, Miss Donovan." Matthews glanced at the Duke for confirmation.

The Duke said, "We would be delighted to dine with you and your father, Mr. Matthews. 'Tis good of the squire to invite us when he's feeling so poorly."

"My father does not invite you out of the goodness of his heart, sir—but tedium at being laid up for the past fortnight," Matthews said, and grinned unexpectedly. "To be frank, he has been quite devoured with curiosity. We have never had a duke visit East Dingleford before. Or a woman such as yourself, Miss Donovan."

Kendra arched her eyebrows, not entirely sure that was a compliment, but the Duke smiled and said, "Well, whatever the reason, we shall accept your invitation."

"It's settled then. I left the invitation with Mr. Bolton, along with directions to Acker Manor. We keep country hours, your Grace, and dine at half past six. Tomorrow evening will be a different story, of course."

The Duke looked at him. "Tomorrow evening?"

"Our assembly."

"Of course. You mentioned it."

"We tend to do town hours when we hold the assembly. East Dingleford is not without its frivolity, sir. Mr. Bolton used to open the public dining room for the evening, but we now have real Assembly Rooms for that purpose on High Street. The festivities begin at eight o'clock—the moon should be still bright. Pray the weather cooperates.

"Admission is a pound," Matthews added. "Your presence would be most welcome."

"We'll be there," Kendra promised. "Who else do you think will come?"

"Oh, the assemblies are quite well attended." His lips twisted into a wry smile. "It is our one source of proper entertainment in East Dingleford." He put his hat back on, and tapped its brim. "I look forward to seeing you both this evening. Good day."

17

After a light lunch of thinly carved, cold roast beef and ham, honey cakes, sliced apples, and Wensleydale and Lancashire cheeses, the Duke went riding while Kendra spent the rest of the afternoon hunkered down in the private parlor, working on the slate board and murder book. She added the timeline. According to Biddle, Stone had come into the mill around twelve-thirty. But why? Lavinia Stone had said he'd been in a bad mood; Biddle had said he was preoccupied.

At two or two-thirty, Stone went into Biddle's office to tell him that he'd be leaving for a few days. They spent fifteen to twenty minutes talking about business, before Stone went back to his office. No one but the killer saw Stone alive again after that. Sometime between three and six, someone had gone into Stone's office, and bludgeoned him to death.

If Kendra had to guess, she'd place the time of death between three and five. The mill had closed at five. The Luddites had to attack shortly thereafter, since she and the Duke had encountered the band of men on the highway at around six. That gave the Luddites an hour to vandalize the frames in the mill. Still, the timing of the attack was interesting. The Luddites either had someone watching the mill, or they had someone on the inside to feed them information. Could they have seen the killer?

Kendra's gaze fell on her most recent addition to the suspect list: Turner. God, she wanted it to be Turner.

He rang every bell. He had the strongest motive, and no real alibi for the time of the murder. It wasn't hard to imagine Turner's beefy hand wrapped around the bronze . . . just as she could imagine it wrapped around his wife's delicate wrist.

But wanting Turner to be the killer because she didn't like him was a dangerous path to follow, one that was filled with her own confirmation biases.

People see what they want to see. It was way too easy to fall into that trap, to focus so intently on the one suspect that she missed evidence pointing in another direction.

She paced, hoping the activity would jog something loose in her brain. She stopped again in front of the slate board. In the twenty-first century, the board would be white, and filled not only with notes but photos, of the victim, when he'd been alive and dead; of suspects; of the crime scene.

The crime scene . . . The whispery sensation was back. *What am I missing?*

"Do you have a headache, my dear?"

Kendra hadn't heard the door open, but the Duke was standing in the doorway, gazing at her inquiringly. Only then did she realize her fingers were at her temples, moving in a circular motion. She dropped her hands.

"No. I'm trying to visualize how the crime scene was, exactly."

The Duke walked to the sideboard and pulled out a stopper from one of the decanters. "And . . . what do you see?" he asked, pouring a splash of brandy in a crystal tumbler.

"A lot of blood. On the wall. The victim. The chair. On the desk, except for where it wasn't."

"Bludgeoning is not a tidy crime by its very nature," agreed the Duke, taking a sip.

"No, it's not." Kendra tapped her chin, concentrating. "We're dealing with medium velocity impact and passive blood spray, and transfer. The killer was standing behind, slightly to the side of our vic. He had to have gotten a lot of blood on himself."

"I would imagine so."

"So he couldn't have left without cleaning up. What if he ran into somebody? Even if he waited until the mill was closed—before the Luddites arrived—he was taking a chance of being seen."

The Duke's eyes narrowed as he considered it. "Mr. Stone had decanters in his office. The killer could have cleaned up using the spirits."

"Yes. But not his clothes . . ." She drew in a sharp breath. She knew what was bothering her now. "There was a coatrack. There was a hat on it—and nothing else."

"What? Ah!" Understanding flashed in the Duke's eyes. "The weather has turned chilly. Mr. Stone would have worn a greatcoat into the office."

"I'd think so," she nodded. "And that's another point that tips the scales to suggest this crime was not calculated. Something set the unsub off, and he picked up the first weapon at hand—the bronze statue—and struck Stone over the head. The frenzied nature of the attack indicates a surge in adrenalin. Temporary insanity, if you will. When sanity returned, the killer realized he was covered in Stone's blood."

"He wore Mr. Stone's coat to cover the blood on his own clothes," the Duke concluded. "Yes, that makes sense. You said something set the fiend off. It must have been what was on the desk, since the killer took it with him when he left."

"Maybe. Maybe not. I don't want to jump to that conclusion just yet. But we do know it was important enough to the killer to take after the fact. If we can figure out what it was, it could help us identify the killer."

He gazed at her, a frown behind his eyes. "How do we figure such a thing out?"

Kendra shrugged. "Keep asking questions. We might just get an answer that will be the break we're looking for."

❖

Kendra lifted her long skirts, a delicate silvery gauze that swirled over the green-and-silver striped underskirt, and stepped down from the carriage. The moon above was still plump enough to light Acker Manor, a beige stone mansion, as she and the Duke made their way up the stairs to the portico. The squire's elderly, stoop-shouldered butler was already waiting, overseeing a footman who took their coats and gloves. She hesitated before handing over her embroidered reticule with the muff pistol tucked inside. But like the footman at Falcon Court, this one didn't seem to notice its extra weight either.

Then again, maybe all ladies in this era secretly carried muff pistols.

"If you'll follow me, your Grace, madam," the manservant said. "Squire Matthews and Master Oliver are in the library."

As they climbed the staircase, the flickering light from the wall sconces danced across paneled walls and paintings, most of which looked to be J.M.W. Turner seascapes of glorious crashing waves and ships in turmoil. The elderly butler shuffled over to a pair of double doors and swung them open, his voice carefully modulated as he announced their presence, stepping aside.

The room was lit only by a handful of candle braces. Kendra's first impression was height, dark shelving filled with books and collectibles soaring to a shadowy third story, wrapped by a balcony. Three tall, mullioned windows took up the farthest wall, glinting with moonlight. Another wall was bisected by an enormous fireplace, its cherry hardwood mantel carved in scrolls and leaves surrounding a cave-like hearth. There were many logs stacked within, ablaze. Comfortable chairs in heavy damask were arranged near the fireplace to take advantage of its warmth in the cold room. The air was scented with melting tallow wax and burning wood.

"Your Grace . . . Miss Donovan." Matthews leaped up from his seat, bending in a deep bow. "Good evening. May I introduce my father, Squire Matthews."

"Forgive me for not rising," the squire said, using his cane to point to his stockinged foot propped up on a stool. "My blasted toe has been causing me grievous injury for a fortnight."

Squire Matthews was short like his son, but rather than thin, he was round. And unlike his son, who was dressed in a fashionable brown velvet jacket, starched collar points sticking out of an extravagantly worked cravat, and close-fitting trousers, the squire's clothes looked like they might have been fashionable a decade ago, including the stockings and knee breeches. He had lost most of his hair—a future, Kendra predicted, that his son would most likely share. His eyes, beneath wiry brows, were the same watery blue as his son's. All in all, Squire Matthews resembled a fat old gnome.

"Do not fret, Squire Matthews," the Duke said, eyeing his host's toe. The stocking may have concealed the red, swollen joint, but through the material they could still see the protruding shape, round like a golf ball, had attached itself to the squire's big toe. "I am aware how painful the disease of kings can be for a person."

The squire's eyebrows rose. "Have you been afflicted, your Grace?"

"Not I personally. However, my father and brother suffered from it at various times in their lives."

"Please be seated, sir, Miss Donovan." Matthews gestured to the chairs. "Claret?"

"Thank you," the Duke said.

Kendra thanked Matthews when he handed her a glass, and noticed that the squire held out his to be refreshed. Matthews promptly brought the decanter over, replenishing his father's glass. She wondered if the squire realized alcohol exacerbated his gout. She lifted her gaze and met the squire's shrewd eyes.

"You don't look like you approve, Miss Donovan," he remarked.

Kendra shrugged. "It's not for me to approve or dis-approve, but you might want to cut back your alcohol consumption—"

"Yes, yes, that and red meat. Poole has already lectured me in tedious detail." He waved that away and took a defiant swallow of his claret. Lowering his glass, he fixed her with a considering look. "Poole also says that you fancy yourself a doctor."

"Not really."

The squire continued as though he hadn't heard her. "And my boy here says that you fancy yourself a Bow Street Runner. A peculiar desire for a young lady, I must say."

"My ward and I are investigating the murder of Mr. Stone," the Duke put in. "I was under the impression that you had no objections with our involvement. Was I misinformed?"

"I have no objections, your Grace. But you have to confess that it *is* peculiar, for both Miss Donovan and an exalted nobleman such as yourself to involve yourself with the criminal element. Constable Jameson is quite put out."

Kendra said, "That's because Constable Jameson wanted to pin the murder on the Luddites. It's probably inconvenient for him to have to consider other theories."

The old man laughed. "No doubt, no doubt. The Luddite movement has caused no end of annoyances here in the North."

"They didn't murder Mr. Stone," Kendra said.

"No," the squire agreed. "Oliver explained your theories, and I cannot argue with them." He drank his claret, a little more slowly this time. "'Tis all very curious, I must say."

The Duke asked, "How well acquainted were you with Mr. Stone, Squire Matthews?"

He didn't answer right away. "Not well," he finally admitted. "East Dingleford is a small village compared to the grandeur of London, or even the sprawl of Manchester. But we conform to the standards of society in much of our daily life."

"You mean, Mr. Stone was not in your social sphere," Kendra said.

"Mr. Stone, like many of his class, attend our local assemblies, but he was not a man one would invite into their home, nor would one break bread with him."

"You must have developed some impression of him over the last twenty years."

He smiled. "I did indeed. Mr. Stone was more interested in pursuing his vices than his work at the mill."

"Vices like gambling," Kendra said. "Possibly cheating at cards."

"You are referring to Mr. Turner's claim that Stone cheated him out of hundreds of pounds."

The Duke looked startled. "Good heavens. *Hundreds*, you say?"

"Yes. I am of the mind it was sheer desperation that had Mr. Turner accusing Mr. Stone of being a cardsharp. He wanted the debt voided, of course."

"You don't think Mr. Stone cheated?" Kendra asked.

"I have heard that Mr. Stone has—*had* the most prodigious luck in cards and dice, but in that particular game, I believe Mr. Turner simply got caught up and failed to keep track of his chits. And, of course, when one is on a losing streak, there is the unnatural belief that one's luck will change with the next hand." The squire shook his head. "Such behavior happens even in the best of families, and I think we can agree that Mr. Turner cannot lay claim to a Quality pedigree."

He paused to take another swallow of wine, then said, "The constable and I inspected the cards. There was no evidence of anything irregular about them. Our findings did little to calm Mr. Turner, and we had to evict him from the Assembly Rooms."

"I must say, sir, that I am surprised you allow such deep play at your local assembly," said the Duke. "I imagine altercations are a regular occurrence."

"No, sir." The squire shook his head. "Most of the young bucks prefer the dance room. Men of my age, who are not so nimble on our feet anymore, prefer to spend our time in the card room. And we are not as hotheaded as the lads."

"You were in the room when the argument between Mr. Turner and Mr. Stone occurred?" Kendra sipped her claret. "Do you know what arrangement the two men came to?"

"I was, but I do not. I was more concerned with avoiding bloodshed," he said. "At the time, Mr. Turner was too furious to see reason, which is why we were forced to put him out."

"How did Mr. Stone react when Mr. Turner accused him?" Kendra asked.

The squire pursed his lips in thought. "If we had not intervened, I think he would have happily engaged in fisticuffs, even though Mr. Turner is a much younger man. It was the type of man Mr. Stone was. A bit of a ruffian, I always thought."

He paused, lifted his glass to his lips, and realized it was empty. He only had to shoot his son a look to have Matthews jump up to retrieve the crystal decanter.

"I confess, I expected more to come of their argument," continued the squire. "Mr. Turner lost hundreds of pounds. By rights, Mr. Stone could have taken his farm. I do not know what arrangement the two men formed, but Mr. Turner never came to me to issue a formal complaint. I imagine he realized he had no proof against Mr. Stone." He raised his glass so his son could refill it. "You might ask Mr. Biddle if he knows anything about the arrangement. He was involved in the card game as well."

That surprised Kendra. "Mr. Biddle? Are you sure?"

The squire gave a derisive snort. "I may not have had many dealings with Mr. Biddle, but I *do* know who he is."

He lied, Kendra thought. Actually, Biddle had remained silent, not mentioning that he'd been involved in the card game himself: a lie of omission. *Why?* Because he didn't want to get involved in the criminal investigation any more than he had to? Some witnesses did that. Others distanced themselves for less benign reasons.

"In fact, I seem to recall that Mr. Biddle lost to Mr. Stone as well," the squire said. "He didn't accuse Mr.

Stone of cheating. But then that would have been stupid of him, what with Mr. Stone being his overseer at the mill."

"How much blunt did Mr. Biddle lose?" asked the Duke.

"He didn't say, and since he wasn't the one making the accusations, the constable and I never asked. Still, I can't imagine Mr. Biddle was happy with losing."

The squire's son huffed out a laugh. "My father is notoriously tightfisted with his purse strings. 'Tis why we're still using tallow candles, and his wardrobe is more in line with Mad King George's tastes. He'd still be wearing a periwig if the government hadn't begun taxing hair powder. Quite frankly, I'm surprised that he is willing to lose a few coins when he partakes in the card games at the assemblies."

"You'd do well to be more frugal with your allowance, as well," the squire snapped. "Too much like your mother, I say. Always wanting something new rather than making do with what we have. I swear, if she hadn't expired from consumption when you went up to Eton, we'd be in the poorhouse. And do *not* call the King mad. 'Tis disrespectful."

Matthews said nothing, retreating behind his wineglass.

Kendra waited a beat. "Was Lord Bancroft at the assembly when the argument with Mr. Stone happened?" she asked the squire.

The old man shifted in his seat and snorted. "Not likely. Lady Winifred attends often, but his lordship rarely graces us with his presence."

"A bit high on the instep, is he?" the Duke murmured.

The squire said nothing for a moment, then said, "Yes, but he wasn't always such. Nat and I grew up together. Never put on airs. Course, that might've been the thing to get him in mischief."

"You're speaking of his involvement with Mrs. Bolton," Kendra guessed.

He shot her a look. "You know about that, do you? She was Laura Thackeray then. Fetching little thing. I might've been interested in her myself, except she had no dowry to speak of, and she was a bluestocking."

"A scholarly woman," the Duke translated.

"Can't abide them myself," the squire huffed. "My wife didn't need to fill her head with books and such to be able to plan the meals and darn my stockings, did she?"

Kendra said, "Lord Bancroft must not have had a problem with, ah, bluestockings."

"Apparently not, much good it did him. But Nat had his head in the clouds in those days. Thought his father would accept Laura if he brought her home as his bride. Ha! Laura—a countess. Can you imagine?" He shook his head and chuckled. "The old earl—Nat's grandfather—would have disowned him before he did that. As it was, Nat was the one who disowned his family. Took himself off to become a privateer. No one heard from him for sixteen years. The old earl passed away, and Nat's father became the earl. I imagine someone sent word to Nat that he'd become a viscount. Still, he didn't return home. Then the earl took poorly, and hired a Bow Street Runner to find his son. It took almost a year. But God was good to keep him alive until his son returned home."

Kendra said, "I heard the earl fell down the stairs right after Lord Bancroft returned."

"Yes, but I doubt if he'd have survived much longer." His brow furrowed. "Pardon. Didn't mean to go off on a tangent. None of this can have anything to do with Stone's murder."

"Lord Bancroft was gone from East Dingleford for more than a decade." Kendra turned her wineglass in her hands. "Do you think he might have encountered Mr. Stone during that time?"

The squire's eyes held a perceptive gleam. "I have to say that the thought crossed my mind over the years. They never seemed particularly friendly with each other, but Bancroft had a perfectly good mill manager in Mr. Murray. He was a Quaker, but also Scottish. No one is thriftier than a Scot. Why get rid of him, especially when the replacement is someone like Mr. Stone?"

"Lord Bancroft says that it was Mr. Murray's choice to leave," Kendra said. "And Mr. Murray recommended Mr. Stone as his replacement."

The squire frowned, perplexed. "Never heard that, but I suppose it could be true." He drained his glass and set it aside. "I heard tell that Mr. Murray got another position as a manager of a larger mill in Manchester, so it could be true, indeed."

He took a moment to hunt around for his cane. Grasping it, he used it to hoist himself to his feet, careful to keep his bad foot off the ground. "Their gain is our loss, I must say," he grunted. "Stone may have been a lucky devil with cards, but he was a bloody poor manager." The squire hesitated, and shook his head. His shadowed gaze met Kendra's. "I suppose Stone wasn't so lucky after all."

18

Kendra came awake with a start, mouth dry and heart pounding from a nightmare that faded from her consciousness the second she opened her eyes. For a long moment she lay in bed, staring at the moonbeams slanting across the ceiling while the wind outside rattled the windowpanes. She could hear the rustle of leaves outside as branches stirred in the trees, and the ancient inn creaked and settled. From inside the walls came the skittering of mice. At least she hoped it was only mice.

She turned over and squinted at the small porcelain clock on the writing table in the corner. But it didn't glow like the digital clocks she was used to, and the shadows were too thick for her to make out anything.

She swallowed. Her heart may have resumed its normal pace, but her mouth still felt uncomfortably dry—the result, no doubt, of the countless glasses of wine she'd drank at the squire's table earlier. Or maybe it was from the fear chasing her in her dreams. She didn't know, but the last thing she wanted to do was get out of the warm bed. But her mouth felt like the damn Sahara.

Sighing, she pushed aside the heavy blankets, and the icy draft that washed over her nearly sent her straight back. Across the room, the fireplace was too dark, only a few embers glowing demonically amid the heaps of ash. Gritting her teeth against the cold, she forced herself to swing her feet out of bed and moved to the rack of logs next to the fireplace. She pulled off two logs and tossed them into the hearth, which caused a shower of sparks . . . and then nothing. Shivering in earnest now, she prayed that she hadn't accidentally smothered the embers. She grabbed the poker, and nudged the logs into a better position. Nothing.

Why is everything so damn hard in this era? Impatient, she moved forward to prod the logs again, but she noticed an embryonic flicker first. She held her breath and prayed. The flicker suddenly leaped, morphing into a flame. Surprised, Kendra watched as tongues of fire suddenly wrapped themselves around the log. *Kendra Donovan—Girl Scout-in-training.* To think that her idea of starting a fire used to mean pressing a remote to ignite the gas logs in the fireplace in her Virginia apartment.

The warmth from the fire was practically nonexistent though. The floor was covered by a threadbare rug, but that wasn't much protection for her bare feet. Her toes were already tingling from the icy draft. Shivering, she hurried over to the pitcher and poured water into an earthenware mug. The water was cold enough to make her back molars ache, but she drank deeply.

Her gaze drifted to the window. The moon was still bright enough to flood the back area of the inn and the four outbuildings, including a stone barn and chicken coop. Vaguely she had a memory of hearing a rooster crow early the previous morning.

She began to put down the mug, eager to dive under the covers again, when movement below caught her eye. Curious, Kendra leaned forward to press her face against the windowpane, and watched a cloaked figure—a woman, judging by the skirts—emerge from the shadow of the inn, making her way toward the barn. The skirts and the hem of the cloak swept behind her, leaving a trail on the frost-covered grass. She wondered if she was watching Mrs. Bolton's granddaughter, Lizzie, on her way to a romantic rendezvous. What else would entice someone to haul their ass out of a warm bed in the middle of the night?

Kendra's breath caught in her throat as she was assailed by an intense longing for Alec. She'd thought of him often since they'd gone their separate ways. She'd known she'd miss him, but she hadn't anticipated this hollow sensation in her chest. It was like a piece of her was missing too.

She'd made a mistake by becoming involved with him. She wanted to feel his arms around her, to be able to press her face against his chest and breathe in the clean, masculine scent that was uniquely his. But that was physical desire, and physical desire could either be overcome—or would fade. What terrified her was that she missed *him*—talking to him, laughing with him, watching those green eyes framed by spiky lashes brighten with amusement, narrow with interest, darken with passion.

She lifted a hand to rub the center of her chest, as though that could ease the ache inside. She'd never been in such a situation before, and quite honestly didn't know how to handle it. When her parents had cut her loose at fourteen, she'd survived the only way she knew how—by moving forward, one step at a time, first by focusing on her college studies, and after that, her career ambitions. Her personal life had been pretty pathetic. Her few love affairs had never been strong enough to go beyond a promising beginning, before they crashed and burned thanks to last-minute cancellations caused by her busy schedule. How did you maintain a relationship when you were flying across the United States at the last minute to set up a war room, to investigate the latest atrocity?

One canceled date was acceptable. But three? Or five? If she had met Alec in the twenty-first century, would their relationship have become just another casualty of her career? Her stomach knotted. She didn't know. How could she?

He made her happy. And sad. And confused. Was that love? And even if she was in love with Alec—and that was a big *if*—that didn't mean she was willing to forget about returning to her own era. If the opportunity to return to the twenty-first century presented itself—again, another big *if*—she'd take it. Of course she'd take it.

Wouldn't she?

The cold returned her to the present, and she looked outside again. The mystery woman had disappeared into the barn. At least she was probably getting warm now.

But then, there she was, already emerging from the building. Kendra frowned. How long had the woman been inside? Five minutes, maybe; less than ten, definitely. So not a romantic rendezvous, after all. Or a very disappointing one.

Kendra watched the woman retrace her footsteps back to the inn. Her head was bent, her face obscured by the shadow of her hood. Then, as though sensing eyes on her, the woman lifted her head to look up. With some surprise, Kendra stared at Mrs. Bolton's upturned face, illuminated by the light of the moon.

As her gaze locked on the old woman's face, Kendra remembered an article she'd read once about how the human eye couldn't actually detect wrinkles. What the eye saw was the shadow created by a wrinkle. It was why aging actresses often had their lighting cranked up to a white-hot glare. Now looking down at Mrs. Bolton, with her face tilted up and washed bright by the moon, Kendra saw the young, beautiful girl that had captured Lord Bancroft's heart a half century ago.

Kendra didn't think the other woman could see her in her darkened window, but she found herself holding her breath. Then Mrs. Bolton ducked her head down and resumed walking, quick, furtive. In the next second, she disappeared from view.

Though her feet were now numb with cold, Kendra lingered at the window, waiting to see if anyone else came out of the stone building. She didn't know how long she stood there, but no one appeared. Discomfort finally drove her back to the bed, and she hauled the blankets over her chilled body.

Kendra was an urbanite. The only farms she'd spent any time at were the six body farms in the United States, each holding dozens, if not hundreds, of bodies in all states of decomposition. Gruesome, certainly, but hugely educational for anyone in law enforcement. But she'd never been on a traditional farm. Maybe Mrs. Bolton had chickens to feed, or animals to tend to. It was possible. But Kendra didn't think so.

She closed her eyes, wanting to drift into slumber. She thought of picturesque East Dingleford, with its twisting cobblestone streets and aged gray stone buildings. But beneath that pretty image was something else: secrets and lies, and a bubbling anger.

And something insidious.

Something dangerous.

Some*one* dangerous.

19

Sometime during the night, the clouds scuttled in, leaving the morning a dreary gray beyond the windows of the private parlor where Kendra and the Duke sat having breakfast.

"We're all hopin' that by later this afternoon the sun will shine again," said Tessa, Mrs. Bolton's grand-daughter. She poured coffee into Kendra's cup, and cast a worried look at the window. Her lips were threatening to pout. "If it doesn't clear up, we may have ter cancel tonight's assembly, and that would be most unfair. We've been waitin' ever so long for it. The next bit of fun will be Guy Fawkes Night. The squire allows us ter build a bonfire in his paddock near the river, and tinkers and hawkers from all over come ter set up. There's music and dancin' and fireworks." She stood for a moment, coffeepot clutched to her chest, her pretty eyes glazed. Then she seemed to recollect herself. "Oh, pardon me. More tea, your Grace?"

"Yes, thank you." He held up his teacup, while the maid switched pots. He glanced over at Kendra. "Guy Fawkes was a seventeenth century revolutionary who attempted to blow up the House of Lords."

"I know who he is."

"Oh. I wasn't certain if his memory survived in . . . your America."

"He's in the history books," Kendra decided it was safe to say that in Tessa's presence. "It's not a known celebration in America. I think they celebrate it in Canada. I've never participated."

"Oh, it's ever so exciting, miss," Tessa said after pouring tea for the Duke, and setting the pot down. "It'll be next Sunday. Will you still be here for the celebration?"

Next Sunday—November 5. That was the day the British had marked on the calendar to celebrate the failed gunpowder plot. Kendra's stomach tightened. *November. Time is moving too fast.*

The Duke answered, "It is entirely possible, my dear."

Kendra noticed how the girl's gaze traveled to the slate board, its contents hidden behind a linen sheet.

"Will you be at the assembly tonight?" Tessa asked, her bright eyes swinging back to them.

"Yes. I'm looking forward to it." Kendra hid her smile as she picked up her coffee cup. She wasn't telling a lie. The way she saw it, the local event would give her unprecedented access to interview the villagers.

"Who usually attends the assemblies?" she asked Tessa.

The girl shrugged. "Most everybody. We used ter hold them here at the inn until the Assembly Rooms were built. Will you be needin' anything else, your Grace, Miss Donovan?"

"No, but thank you." The Duke picked up a bun, and began buttering it.

Tessa curtsied, and moved to the door. She nearly ran into her grandfather, who came into the room. "Sir, Lord Bancroft sent a messenger to deliver this to you, sir." He held out a folded piece of paper.

The Duke put down his buttered bun, and wiped his fingers with his napkin before reaching for the note. Mr. Bolton waited while he scanned the scrawled words. He looked at Kendra. "The earl is inviting us to Falcon Court later this morning to show us the gas lighting installation designs."

"Oh, wow. The fun just never stops, does it?"

The Duke's lips twitched. "Do not mind my ward, Mr. Bolton," he told the innkeeper when he caught the other man staring. "Miss Donovan has a perverse sense of humor. Please send word to the earl that *I* shall be delighted to join him at Falcon Court after I have finished my breakfast. Miss Donovan, however, will decline. No doubt she has her pianoforte to practice."

Mr. Bolton looked startled. "But we do not have a pianoforte, yer Grace."

Kendra laughed. "Now who has the perverse sense of humor?"

"I was only joking," the Duke told the innkeeper.

"Ah. I see." He laughed even though it was clear that he didn't understand what the joke was. "I shall send word to Falcon Court, your Grace."

"I suppose gas lighting must appear antiquated to your eyes," Aldridge commented once they were alone again. He picked up his knife and fork to attack the thick slices of ham.

Kendra knew he was fishing, but she answered anyway. The Duke was powerful, but it wasn't like he could build an entire power grid in England, and change history. "Gas is still used in many things, including heating homes. But lighting is usually electricity."

"Electricity?" His blue eyes brightened. "When I was a boy, the Leyden Jar appeared almost magical. Of course, now I understand electrical currents. No one has been able to harness electricity with any reliability though. It makes sense that there will be innovation in this regard. Where does the source of the electricity come from? Water?"

"Some. It depends. Coal, natural gas, wind, solar, nuclear . . . it's become a matter of debate in my time on what method is the best to power our energy needs. Some power sources are very reliable but aren't necessarily good for the overall environment, others aren't very reliable but appear to be good for the overall environment."

"What is nuclear electricity?"

Leave it to the Duke to pick out that word. "It's . . . that might be a discussion for another time."

"I see. And you say people argue over these things?"

"Oh, yeah. Sometimes violently. Everybody has an opinion."

The Duke was silent for a moment. "It reminds me of the Luddite movement here," he said slowly. "Everyone has an opinion on that as well. Sometimes violently expressed. There appear to be many new inventions these days to make the factories run more efficiently."

"With fewer men."

"Yes. But mankind cannot stand still, Miss Donovan. Progress has a cost, I think." His gaze was troubled as he picked up his teacup. "Even the gas lighting craze will eventually eliminate the role of the lamplighters. What will happen to them?"

Kendra gave a shrug. There was no way to avoid the cycle of change, in this century or in hers. "Eventually there will be new jobs, new needs," she said. "It's never easy for people to make the transition to new industries. But eventually people adapt." *They had to.*

They were quiet for the rest of the meal. The gray world outside seemed to have an oppressive effect. Or maybe it was an awareness that the fundamentals never seemed to change. *Will mankind always be engaged in the same battles, over and over?*

The Duke pushed away his empty plate, striving for a lighter note. "What will you be doing while I investigate Falcon Court's gas lighting?"

"I'll work on my notes. I'd like to see Mrs. Stone again. Maybe she knows what arrangement her husband had with Mr. Turner to pay off his debt."

Aldridge gave her a dubious look. "Do you think she'll know? She didn't seem too . . ."

"Smart?"

"Involved with her husband's business," he finished smoothly.

"Maybe without the distraction of a duke in the room, she'll be more forthcoming," Kendra pointed out with a crooked smile.

Aldridge laughed, and rose to his feet. "Point taken. You are welcome to take the carriage. Benjamin will drive you. I'm certain Mr. Bolton will be able to loan me a horse."

"I'm certain too. But it's not necessary. I thought I'd walk. Get a feel for the village."

"You will take your lady's maid?"

"Worried about my reputation here in East Dingleford?"

He gave her a look. "Whoever murdered Mr. Stone is still out there. And the fiend most assuredly knows you are investigating, Miss Donovan."

"He knows *we* are investigating—and probably dismisses most of my contributions because I'm a woman. I think I'll be safe without Molly . . ." she waved her hand to stave off the argument she saw in his eyes. "But I could use the company. It's no fun walking alone."

The Duke smiled. "Thank you, Miss Donovan. I know you can protect yourself, but if the murderer is watching you, he may hesitate to attack two women."

"And what about you?"

"Me?"

"Yeah. Who's going to be accompanying you as you ride out to Falcon Court?" She stood up, some of her humor vanishing. It was frustrating that even someone as enlightened as the Duke didn't seem to understand how annoying it was to have such restrictions imposed on half of the population—*because the restrictions weren't placed on his half of the population.* "You'll be alone," she pointed out now. "The murderer knows you're part of the investigation."

He lifted his eyebrows. "I hadn't thought of it."

"I know."

"Miss Donovan—"

"Don't worry," she cut him off. "I'll bring Molly. Save the village of East Dingleford the shock of seeing a woman walking down the street all by herself. Oh, the horror."

"Actually, I was going to remind you to bring your umbrella. It might rain."

"Oh." Kendra glanced at the window, with its low potbelly clouds. "Good point."

20

It was standard practice for a lady's maid to walk several steps behind her lady. She was supposed to be seen by everyone but the lady she was accompanying, and not heard at all. While Kendra would have liked to ditch the chaperone thing altogether, she wasn't about to have anyone trail after her like some nineteenth-century Sherpa. Molly had adapted to Kendra's more modern sensibility fairly quickly, and strode enthusiastically beside her, her blue eyes darting left and right to take in the scenery of East Dingleford, her face shining with excitement. Kendra often forgot that the girl was only fifteen. Until a month ago, she had never been outside Aldridge Village.

"Do ye think there'll be an assembly tonight, miss?" she asked.

Kendra glanced at the sky. Gray—except she thought she could detect a faint ribbon of blue on the horizon. "If the wind doesn't change direction, it might clear some of these clouds out, so . . . maybe."

But Molly was no longer listening. The maid's attention had been drawn by three boys, who looked to be about her age, across the street. They were hauling down burlap sacks from a cart harnessed to a mangy-looking pony. A blush spread across Molly's face when they paused to return her regard with bold looks and leering grins. For just a moment, Kendra had a mental image of the same boys in her own era. They'd probably be wearing jeans and hoodies, sporting tattoos and maybe an earring or too. Different clothes, but their expressions would be the same. The Duke was right. They may not have given testosterone and hormones a name just yet, but they had always been a part of the human experience.

When Molly began to slow, glancing over her shoulder at the boys, Kendra grabbed the girl's arm and hurried her along. *Who's really the chaperone here?*

They walked along High Street with its collection of shops, passing a haberdashery and two coffee shops. Villagers were conducting business or walking along the street. But Kendra could feel the prick of curious eyes that charted her and Molly's progress up the slanting hill.

Kendra summoned up a mental picture of the route Matthews had taken. "This way," she said, and swerved right, down another winding street. The shops faded away and houses rose up in their place. At the top of another hill, Kendra recognized the narrow lane, which would take them to the Elizabethan-styled house at the end of the street. A breeze stirred the trees and a few brilliant red and gold leaves sailed on the current to the ground. Birds trilled from their nests. The faint cry of a baby drifted to them from one of the houses they passed.

The Stone residence had a forlorn look about it. Maybe it was the gloomy sky, but Kendra suspected the sensation of neglect came more from this era's imposed mourning rituals. All the windows were either shuttered or had the curtains drawn. A black ribbon had been tied to the brass knocker.

"Oi wonder if Mrs. Stone will be goin' back ter work on the stage," Molly whispered as they approached the door.

"How did you know she was an actress?"

"Tessa spoke of it. She said Mrs. Stone was at every assembly and festivity, and she's gonna 'ate 'aving ter be in mourning for an 'ole year an' a 'alf. She won't be able ter dance or nothin'. Oi don't even know if she's supposed ter 'ave any callers."

Kendra thought of the vivacious woman she'd met the other day, and silently agreed with young Tessa. Lavinia Stone was not cut out for the seclusion required of widows to honor their dead husbands. "She might be eager for our company, then," she said, lifting the knocker and banging it against the door panel.

They waited.

Kendra knocked again. "When we came the other day, Mrs. Trout—the housekeeper—was dyeing dresses in the kitchen. It took her a while to answer the door."

A minute passed. And another. Molly glanced at Kendra out of the corner of her eyes. "Maybe they don't want ter be disturbed, seeing 'ow they're in mourning."

"Or maybe they're down in the wine cellar because the mourning period here has got to be freaking boring." Kendra hesitated, then tried the door. It was locked. "Come on."

Molly stared at her. "Where are ye goin', miss?"

"Around back, to the servant's entrance. I might be able to get Mrs. Trout's attention better from there."

She had to push her way through the overgrown weeds and shrubs to the back of the house. The garden wasn't any better here. Apparently neither Mrs. Trout nor Mrs. Stone had a green thumb. Dying rosebushes and tall heather crowded the path that led to the portico and servant's entrance. The branches from the raggedy bushes snagged at Kendra's dark brown pelisse as she walked by. She used the umbrella to swat back the greedy vegetation as she approached the back door.

"Mrs. Trout?" she called out. Since there was no knocker here, she used her fist to thump on the door. "Mrs. Trout, are you in there? It's Kendra Donovan! I need to speak to you!"

Birds continued to chirp from the trees and eaves, and the wind whispered through the foliage. Had the temperature dropped? Kendra suddenly felt chilled.

"Maybe we should leave, miss," Molly said from behind her. "Nobody's 'ome."

Kendra ignored the maid. She knocked again, and rattled the doorknob out of habit. She was surprised when it actually opened. "Mrs. Trout? Are you here?" She poked her head in and froze.

"Miss, Oi don't think—" Molly began, and gave a shocked gasp when Kendra reeled back and dropped the umbrella. She slid the reticule off her wrist, opening its strings, and retrieved the muff pistol.

Molly's eyes widened. "W'ot are ye doin'?"

"Shush," she whispered. "Molly, do you know how to get back to the Green Maiden?"

"W'ot? Aye . . . w-why?"

Kendra snagged the maid's wrist and bent down to capture her frightened gaze. "Go to the Green Maiden, and ask Mr. Bolton to send for the Duke." She hesitated "And the constable."

"Miss?"

"Go!" Kendra dropped Molly's wrist. She waited until the maid finally stepped back, and then, in a flurry of skirts, fled. She inhaled sharply, held her breath, and let it out. Steadier, she automatically checked the small gun, and then stepped through the door into a hallway.

It was long and shadowed. On the right, there were three doors, all closed. Kendra saw that in one quick scan, her attention already focusing on the open doorway on the left—the kitchen. She could see cupboards lining one wall.

She drew in another breathe. Her heartbeat sped up, but her hand remained steady on the pistol as she moved to the door. The windows hadn't been shuttered here, so Kendra saw the figure crumpled on the kitchen floor about five steps from the doorway. The odor, of course, was more pungent, the coppery smell of blood mixed with a rancid whiff of decaying meat and defecation.

Kendra did a quick sweep of the kitchen, heart jackhammering in her chest, hand tightening on the gun before she circled to the body on the floor. She was careful not to step into the lake of blood, long since congealed into something like Jell-O, which surrounded Mrs. Trout.

The housekeeper was lying on her back, her cloudy eyes fixed on the ceiling, her dour features slack in death. Kendra's gaze slowly tracked from her face to the gaping wound below her chin.

Somebody had slit Mrs. Trout's throat, from ear to ear.

21

Kendra slowly backed away from the body and blood, retreating into the hallway. The trill of birds and stirring of trees drifted in from the outdoors, almost jarring in its normalcy. Kendra tuned them out as she moved forward down the shadowy corridor, her finger on the muff pistol's trigger. She nudged open a door on the right and took a quick peek inside. It was a small room that held shelves filled with jars of jellies and jams, and bottles of what appeared to be homemade alcohol, maybe brandies or ales. Kendra recognized it as a still room, although much smaller and simpler than the one at Aldridge Castle, which also stocked herbal medicines, potions, and the castle's soaps. No one was hiding inside.

Pulse racing, she returned to the hallway, and crept down to the next closed door. She held her breath, listening. *Nothing*. Even though she was certain it was empty, she led with the gun, sweeping the interior of the morning room.

She was deep enough in the interior of the house to no longer hear the birds or wind. Unfortunately, the very stillness amplified the rapid thumping of her own heart. Briefly, the thought flitted through her mind that maybe she should wait for backup. But what kind of reaction would she get from her nineteenth-century counterparts? Maybe it was arrogance on her part, but she knew how to deal with this type of situation better than anyone here.

Adrenaline made her skin tingle. She swung left, then right down the dark hall. She remembered this area of the house from their visit the other day, knew where this door would lead. She paused, her hand on the doorknob, her finger on the pistol's trigger, her ears straining to pick up any sound within.

Silence.

Though she didn't expect to find anyone inside the room—*alive*, she amended—she moved quickly, pushing open the door and going in low. Inside, her gaze swept the drawing room. Someone had opened the shutters a crack, allowing a gray beam of light to slice through the gloom. Kendra stopped, and stared at the destruction around her. The tufted red silk chairs and sofa had been viciously slashed, goose down feathers pulled angrily and strewn about. Porcelain chips covered the Oriental rug like confetti. Every cat figurine had been taken off the shelves and tables, and smashed.

Kendra forced herself to leave, closing the door again and continuing down the hallway into the foyer. It could have been midnight, the shadows were so thick in the small space. Kendra moved to the stairs and peered up into the darkness. She held her breath. Listened. Was that the creak of a floorboard? Or just the noise of an old house settling?

It was cold in the house, but a skinny line of sweat wiggled down her spine. She ignored it and focused on the darkness at the top of the staircase, and began to climb the steps. The only sounds were the dry whisper of her skirt trailing behind her, the scrape of her sole across the runner.

On the second-floor landing, her eyes strained to pierce the gloom. A credenza bracketed by two chairs hugged one wall in the wide hallway. On the other side of the wall were three closed doors. There was a window at the end of the hall, but it was shuttered. Kendra could see a seam of light bisecting the two panels.

She sucked in a deep breath, and opened the door nearest her. She kept the door between her and anyone lurking inside. It was another drawing room. Someone had gone through here with a sharp knife, as well, slashing the cushions and overturning furniture.

Pace quickening, Kendra moved to the other rooms—a library and formal dining room. Both had been tossed.

She returned to the staircase, and climbed to the third-story landing. Her pulse was settling down. She was almost certain the house was empty—

A woman appeared before her, her face ghostly white. Kendra gasped, jerking back as her heart nearly jumped out of her chest. It was only her training that kept her from pulling the pistol's trigger, and shattering the mirror in front of her. *Good job, Donovan. You almost shot your own damn reflection.*

Gritting her teeth, Kendra had to pause to get her racing heart under control again, before she could move forward to the first door. She swung it open. The smell hit her first, strong enough for her gag reflex kick in. She swallowed hard, and entered the bedchamber. The emerald silk curtains were open, and the gray light from the outdoors spilled inside, touching on the green-and-yellow striped canopy bed and the velvet settee, the cherrywood vanity and dresser. Kendra saw all of that in one sweeping glance, then her gaze settled on the woman in the chair. Lavinia Stone stared back at her, her eyes fixed and glassy in death. The woman had been killed like Mrs. Trout, her throat slashed, but there were more wounds on her flesh.

Kendra's first thought was that the Duke had been wrong. Two women together hadn't stopped the murderer from striking after all.

Kendra was ninety-nine percent certain the house was empty, but that one percent could kill you. She kept her finger on the pistol's trigger and crossed to the double doors, which led to a dressing room. The next set of doors led to another dressing room, masculine in its colors. She kept going, through to the bedchamber on the other side. The curtains here had been opened as well. Kendra scanned the room, no longer surprised to see the destruction. Feathers and glass shards carpeted the floor from the slashed mattress and chair cushions, the broken decanters and goblets. The whisky fumes were as strong here as the blood in the other bedchamber.

She exited through the doors that led to the hallway. She had to take a moment for her eyes to adjust to the gloom again, then she continued down the corridor. She hesitated where the hall branched off in an *L*-shape. Another door. She opened it to reveal a darkened room with no furniture. A guest bedchamber, Kendra assumed, which, from the looks of it, had never been used. The Stones apparently were not interested in entertaining overnight guests. She didn't venture into the room. Even in the gloom, she could see the thick layer of dust on the floor.

Closing the door, she walked to the servant's staircase tucked discreetly at the end of the corridor. Her Spidey-sense told Kendra that no one was upstairs. Still, she felt obligated to be thorough and finish her search. The steps creaked slightly as she climbed them. Mrs. Trout apparently hadn't felt any need to mourn Mr. Stone, as she hadn't bothered covering the windows on the third floor. Sensing the emptiness of the area, Kendra picked up her pace to check out the four small rooms. Two were filled with old furniture, rolled carpets—and enough dust to assure Kendra that no one had been inside for at least a decade. Another room was empty. The fourth room was clearly Mrs. Trout's sleeping quarters. Light from a single window revealed a single-sized bed, nightstand, wardrobe, washstand, and rocking chair.

Kendra caught a movement out of the corner of her eye and whirled around in time to see a brown mouse streak along the baseboards, disappearing behind the wardrobe. Suppressing a shudder, she retreated into the hall. She could still hear tapping, perhaps tiny rodent feet. She traced the sound to the windows. A light rain had begun to fall from the overcast sky, hitting the windowpanes in a sharp staccato.

Kendra drew in another deep breath, and let it out. Her chest felt tight, her skin clammy. The atmosphere was clearly getting to her. She retraced her steps to the second floor, debating whether she should begin processing the crime scene in Lavinia Stone's bedchamber, or wait for everyone in the kitchen. Even though Mrs. Trout's murder had been simpler, she didn't want that scene to be trampled over by her inexperienced nineteenth-century counterparts.

There really was no option, she decided. She'd wait in the kitchen. She moved down the hall, toward the stairs, and gave a reflexive jerk at the sound of crunching glass coming from Stone's bedchamber. *I'm not alone.*

Her heart slammed into her throat as she started to turn. Her peripheral vision caught a dark shape looming in the threshold. In the next instant, strong arms encircled her from behind. Letting out a cry, she reacted instinctively, whipping her elbow back as forcefully as she could into the man's diaphragm. The pain made her assailant exhale sharply and loosen his grip. She pressed her advantage, throwing her weight against him. She began to swing her arm up, her hand tightening on the gun. The man countered by grasping her arm, and spinning her around. Her body slammed against the wall, hard enough for her to lose her breath. Before she could move again, he was pinning her there with his hard body.

"Bloody hell," he muttered.

The only thing that stopped Kendra from stomping on her assailant's foot was the familiar voice. Her fear evaporated, replaced first by relief and then by anger. She considered still stomping on his foot, out of sheer annoyance.

"Goddamn it, Alec!"

She caught the gleam of his eyes. In the gloom of the hallway, they looked almost black, shaded even more by his spiky lashes. But they were green, she knew, like a cool lake in the middle of a forest, warmed only by the flecks of amber around the pupil.

"What the hell do you think you're doing?" she hissed. "I could have blown your goddamn head off."

He cocked a dark eyebrow at her. "Which is why I thought to embrace you, thereby disabling you. I thought if I called out, you might be startled into shooting. I foolishly forgot about your other skills."

"One more second, and you would have been limping for days."

"I was under the impression that you needed assistance. Mr. Kelly and I had only just arrived at the Green Maiden when Molly came running into the stable yard."

"Sam—Mr. Kelly's here, too?"

"He's downstairs with the maid. She had to show us the location of the house. We put her outside as soon as we walked into the kitchen. My God. What is it about you that always attracts murder?"

Insulted, she tried to shift back, but he still had her pressed to the wall. "Hey! I seem to remember last month *you* were the one attracting murder."

"Ah, the memory is coming back to me. So is this."

He dropped his hands from her arms, but only to bring them up to frame her face. He held her gaze for a long moment, long enough for heat to curl all the way down to her toes. Then he leaned in and kissed her.

Her mind went blank. He had always been a good kisser, but something welled up inside her—a strange sort of joy. She wrapped her arms around his neck and responded with enough passion that they were both breathing unevenly by the time he withdrew. His eyes were lit by an emotion that made her heart thump harder as he allowed his gaze to roam over her features. She'd never had anyone look at her like that.

"I missed you, sweet," he said softly.

"I missed you too."

She caught the flash of teeth, white against the darkness. He had at least a day's growth of beard, which surprised her, since he usually was clean-shaven. A dark lock fell over his brow, making him appear almost boyish.

Yet there was nothing boyish about Alexander Morgan, the Marquis of Sutcliffe, she thought. She couldn't resist the impulse to bring up her free hand, smoothing the curl back into place.

"You look like a pirate," she murmured, and dropped her hand to stroke the prickly stubble.

"I almost killed Chance in my quest to get here after receiving Duke's message," he admitted, referring to his prized Arabian. "Duke wrote that the manager of the mill had been murdered. However, this . . ." Alec eased back slightly, frowning. "Hell and damnation, Kendra, what have you gotten yourself into this time?"

"Seriously?" The bubble of euphoria evaporated. Glaring up at him, she pushed at his shoulders to force him to step back. It irritated her that it wasn't her shove that forced him backward but the pounding of feet on the stairs behind him. A moment later, Sam Kelly appeared on the landing. He gave them a quick, measuring look, then did the most sensible thing: He went to the windows and opened the curtains. It was still raining, hard enough to distort the windowpanes, but the dreary light spilling into the hallway was better than none.

"God's teeth, 'tis sheer wickedness that killed that maid in the kitchen," the Bow Street Runner said, shaking his head as he turned around. He was a short man, but muscular, which seemed an odd contrast to his elfin features. Like Alec, he hadn't shaved. His stubble was more gray than reddish-brown, matching his sideburns instead of the curls framing his face. His eyes were his most distinctive feature, Kendra thought, a brown so light they appeared golden. They could twinkle in good humor—or when eyeing a glass of whisky—or they could become as flat and hard as any cop Kendra had known in the twenty-first century.

"Mrs. Trout's murder was expedient," Kendra said now.

Sam regarded her. "Expedient? How so?"

Kendra allowed herself a moment of pleasure that the Bow Street Runner was looking at her like an equal. It hadn't always been like that, but two murder investigations had given them a mutual respect for each other. Was it any wonder she wanted to deal with him rather than the constable?

"She wasn't the intended victim, but she was a witness, so he had to kill her. His intended victim is in there." She tipped her head to the door that led to Lavinia Stone's bedchamber.

Sam hesitated, then, face grim, he walked through the doorway. Kendra and Alec followed. Sam was standing in front of the corpse. *Does he see what I see?* Kendra wondered as she joined him, her gaze once again settling on what had once been Lavinia Stone. Her throat had been slit like Mrs. Trout's, but that had only been the end of her ordeal.

"She's been tortured," Sam observed, his tone flat.

"Yes," Kendra said.

Alec walked to the window to open the curtains fully. In the new light, Kendra could see how drawn he looked. His normally olive complexion was pale, and lines of exhaustion were carved around his eyes and bracketing the sensual line of his mouth. He was wearing a dark green riding coat, spattered with mud and layered with dust. Sam didn't look much better, his black topcoat so dirty that it appeared to be gray. For the first time, Kendra wondered how they'd arrived at the Green Maiden together, since she knew Alec had been at his estate in Northamptonshire, while the Bow Street Runner's usual haunt was London.

But that was a question for later. The victim deserved their complete attention. Kendra had been too intent on searching the house in the off chance that the unsub was still on the premises, and so had only done a quick scan of the body and its wounds. Now she was prepared for a more detailed analysis.

Lavinia Stone had been tied to the chair, her wrists bound to the armrests, her ankles bound to the legs. She'd been held immobile while the unsub had sliced open the bodice of her gown—black, Kendra noticed; most likely recently dyed by Mrs. Trout. The unsub had continued cutting through to the chemise and stays, peeling them open to expose the soft flesh beneath.

"Jesus," Sam muttered, his gaze on the wounds.

"Burn marks," Kendra identified, glancing at the fireplace, and the poker that had been tossed carelessly aside. She knew that the tool would match the blisters and blackened flesh that marked Lavinia's torso.

"Why? Why do this?" Alec wondered. He shot her an angry glance. "How could torturing this poor woman be related to the man that was found murdered at the mill?"

"The man at the mill was her husband," Kendra said, and gazed at the angry red marks mutilating the woman's flesh. She murmured softly, "There are only a few reasons to torture a victim. Sexual gratification, for one—your garden variety sadist. Religious zealotry to coerce their victims to confess their sins, or convert to their faith. Martyrs were always tortured. Then there's the most popular reason—forcing the victim to give up information."

Alec met her gaze. "You believe this woman was tortured for information."

"Yes, that's what it looks like," she said, and pulled her eyes away from studying the victim to look at her audience. "We know that Mr. Stone wasn't murdered for religious reasons. And if a religious zealot had targeted Lavinia Stone, he would have also included Mrs. Trout in his torture. Sexual sadism . . ." She paused, and had to suppress a shudder. "We've dealt with a serial killer who tortured his victims for pleasure. As bad as what happened here, a sexual sadist would have done far worse. There would've been more mutilation, and, most likely, rape.

"This *has* to be connected to Stone's murder," Kendra added, frowning. "But it doesn't make sense. I interviewed Mrs. Stone. I could have sworn she didn't know anything about her husband's death. But she'd been an actress before her marriage—maybe she was better than I gave her credit for."

"Nay, I don't think so," Sam said, his eyes on the victim. "The fiend was trying ter find out something, I think. He spent a lot of time vandalizing the rooms. It wasn't all rage. He tortured Mrs. Stone ter get her ter tell him what he wanted. But the poor lass couldn't do it."

Alec regarded the Bow Street Runner. "How can you know that, pray tell?"

"Look at her. If she knew anythin', the bastard would have gotten it out of her after he burned her with that poker the first time." Sam's eyes darkened with pity. "She didn't talk because she couldn't. She didn't have the information the fiend was wantin' . . . and she died in agony because of it."

22

Bleeding hell." Constable Jameson's face twisted in horror as he stared down at Lavinia Stone ten minutes later. "W'ot's this about? What kinda fiend would do such a thing?" He shook his head as he stepped away from the body. "Mr. Stone was one thing—everybody hated the bastard. But who'd have call ter do this ter Mrs. Stone?"

The fact that he'd cursed in her presence told Kendra how shaken he was. Or he just might not view her in the same light as he viewed ladies of Quality. She certainly couldn't rule that out.

Kendra looked over her shoulder at him as she went through the dead woman's vanity. Unlike the other rooms in the house, the unsub hadn't caused any destruction here.

"That's what we need to find out," she replied.

"Maybe housebreakers . . ." Jameson began, casting his own look around the room.

Kendra held up the emerald pendant she'd dug out of the jewelry box on the vanity. "I don't think so. Stone's murder was impulsive and what was done in this house was premeditated, but the murders are obviously connected."

Jameson glared at her. "How can you know that?"

Kendra dropped the necklace back into the box and pointed at the corpse. "Do you think *that* was impulsive? He brought rope with him to bind her. He may have brought the knife, as well—the kitchen needs to be searched. The only instrument that he didn't bring was the fire poker, but there's hardly a shortage of those. Every room in this"—she'd been about to say *century*—"house has one."

She turned away from Jameson to look at Alec and Sam. "They've been dead at least twelve hours—possibly more."

"Dr. Poole will tell us what we need ter know," Jameson said, thrusting out his jaw in an aggressive manner. "Word's been sent ter him and the magistrate."

"I don't need Dr. Poole to tell me that Mrs. Stone is in full rigor mortis, which takes at least twelve hours to set in. But it's cold in here. I'd say it's probably sixty-two to sixty-five degrees Fahrenheit without any fires to heat up the house. It was colder during the night . . ." She thought of getting out of bed the night before. Her room had been freezing. "Rigor mortis can slow down if the temperature drops below fifty-nine degrees."

Sam glanced at the clock on the dresser. "'Tis half past twelve now. You think the lass was killed between ten and midnight?"

"It's an estimate," she said. "There's no way to pinpoint the exact time." Even in the twenty-first century, with all the technological and forensic advances, scientists still couldn't give the exact time of death without an eyewitness account. There were too many variables that could skew the results.

"Mrs. Trout was obviously killed first," she continued. "She's not wearing a nightgown and robe, so it was still early enough when she answered the servant's door. Mrs. Stone was most likely here in her bedchamber. Why bring her up here? He brought the knife and rope with him. He could have done . . . what he did to Mrs. Stone in almost any room."

Sam looked around the room, seeing it through Kendra's eyes. "You've got a strong point there, lass."

She moved back to the corpse, inspecting the face more closely. There were blowflies crawling across the dead woman's flesh. Given the timeline, Kendra suspected the insects had already begun their cycle of dropping fresh larvae into the body's soft tissue. "I don't see any bruising to indicate she was gagged." Her gaze fell to the violent branding that had been done to the woman's torso. "She would have been screaming."

The men behind her were silent. The entire house was silent. The rain had stopped, Kendra realized.

She straightened. "The house is set back from its neighbors, but maybe there's a witness who saw the killer arrive or leave."

"Aye." Sam nodded. "I'll be talking ter the neighbors. What about other servants?"

"I don't think there are any," Kendra said. "When the Duke and I came here the other day, Mrs. Trout complained about not having any help."

"Stone could be a miserly man, ter be sure," said Jameson.

"What about outdoor servants?" Sam asked. "Stable hands?"

"There's old Paddy," Jameson said, and his lip curled. "Irish. If you don't find him sleepin' off a drunk in the stables, you'll find him at one of the taverns in his cups. I doubt if the bog trotter saw anythin'."

Sam's golden eyes narrowed at the slur, but he chose to ignore it. "I'll find the man, and speak ter him, miss."

"Maybe he'll give us some insight into what Stone might have been hiding," Kendra said. "Mrs. Stone was tortured for a reason."

Jameson scowled. "Why didn't the fiend torture Mr. Stone, since he was the one who had whatever it was the monster wanted?"

"I told you, that murder was impulsive. I'm not sure what triggered it, but the unsub—the killer—acted precipitously. I suppose he thought that Stone shared his secrets with his wife."

"I wish to God that he had." Alec's expression was grim. "What this woman went through was barbaric. 'Tis the kind of punishment that the Anglo-Saxons used when they branded their victims."

Kendra had to suppress a shudder. The medieval period was notorious for the inventive ways human beings could be tortured. People often thought the torturers sick and sadistic to do such evil acts on another human being. But Kendra had often thought the true sadist wasn't the torturer, but the mind that had actually conceived the instruments to torture in the first place.

She looked at Alec. "If Stone had told her whatever it was the killer wanted to know, she would still have been killed."

"Yes, but it would have been a quick, merciful death, like that poor woman downstairs. Who knows how long this woman had to endure this brutality?"

Kendra's gaze fell to the bound wrists. Based on the blood and abrasions she saw there, it had been too long.

They heard footsteps out in the hall. Kendra expected the newcomer to be Dr. Poole, but instead the Duke and Lord Bancroft strode through the door. She frowned, and made an instinctive move to stop the earl from invading the crime scene. But it was already too late, so she hung back and watched Bancroft's face as he halted in front of the body. He was frowning, his eyes narrowed as he looked over the dead woman, but other than that, his face remained impassive.

The Duke was easier to read. His blue eyes reflected his shock as his gaze roved over the victim, and then came around to lock on Kendra. "Dear heaven . . . I was with his lordship when the Green Maiden sent a messenger for me. We came as soon as we heard. What is this madness?"

"We can only theorize at this point," Kendra said.

Bancroft regarded Kendra with an impenetrable expression. "And what theory have you come up with, Miss Donovan?"

"If I could have a word, my lord? Outside?"

Something flashed in the old man's eyes, too quick for her to identify. It could have been annoyance. Or amusement.

"Certainly." He waited until they were in the hall to ask, "What's this about, Miss Donovan?"

"Please don't take offense, but I need to know where you were between ten and midnight last night."

He stared at her. "Do you honestly think I am capable of what was done in there? Or to Mrs. Trout? In God's name, why would I?"

Kendra kept her gaze fixed on his. "I think anybody is capable of anything, with the right motivation. And, no, I don't know yet why anyone would do what was done to these women. Mrs. Stone was tortured. Not for pleasure, but because the unsub—"

"Unsub?" The dark eyes brightened with interest. "What is this word?"

"Sorry. It's American terminology. It's another name for the perpetrator."

"Ah. Interesting." He was studying her like a bug under a microscope. "Go on, Miss Donovan."

"Where were you last evening, sir, between ten and midnight?"

"I was in my study until the early morning hours. I am involved in many investments, many developing projects. This requires a great deal of correspondence, you understand."

"Can anyone verify your presence there? Your daughter, perhaps?"

"Regretfully, no. Winifred and I dined at our usual time—seven. I was in my study by nine. Crawford brought me in a tray of coffee and sweets at half past nine, because he was aware of the amount of work I planned on doing."

"When did he collect the tray?"

"Not until morning. My staff had orders not to disturb me."

"Is that usual? For you to work late into the night with orders not to be disturbed?"

"I've done it before, yes."

"Did your valet help you undress? Can he confirm what time you were in your bedchamber?"

"No. A man is less reliant on his valet than a lady is on her maid, I think."

She heard footsteps clamoring up the stairs, and turned to watch Dr. Poole appear on the landing, followed by Matthews.

"God in heaven . . ." Matthews said as soon as he saw them. His face was unnaturally pale and he had his hankie out, pressing it against his trembling lips. "Mrs. Trout . . . I never particularly liked the creature, but to see her like that . . ."

Poole shot the younger man a contemptuous look. "I told you to stay outside, Oliver. You nearly cast up your accounts all over the poor woman. It's not like she ain't messy enough, having bled everywhere. I don't need to pick through your last meal on top of it."

Matthews flushed a bright red. "I am acting as magistrate until my father is well," he reminded the doctor. "'Tis my duty."

"If your father doesn't subscribe to the diet I gave him, you will be acting magistrate forever," Poole grumbled, "and God help us all. Although we've never seen the likes of this." His blue eyes, nearly obscured by his fuzzy brows, landed on Kendra. "Three murders in East Dingleford . . . if I were a superstitious man, I'd say you are cursed, Miss Donovan. We never had such ill-luck before you came to the village."

Kendra glared at the older man. "I arrived with the Duke of Aldridge. Why do you blame me, and not him?"

The brows twitched. "Huh. I never thought of it like that."

"Huh. Maybe that's why more women were burned as witches than men," she shot back sarcastically.

He cocked his head and regarded her with a sour humor. "Mayhap it's because you are standing where most women would not be, Miss Donovan."

"Needlework and painting watercolors bore me, doctor. Did you have a chance to do the autopsy on Mr. Stone? Anything new to add?"

"No." He took a step toward the door, then paused and glanced back at her. "Except the last thing Mr. Stone ate was chicken, potatoes, and mincemeat pie. Will that help you?" he said mockingly. Then he turned abruptly and went through the door. Matthews seemed nervous, but he straightened his shoulders and followed the doctor.

Kendra shifted her gaze to find Bancroft eyeing her again with an inscrutable expression. Since she had nothing more to say to him, she started back to the bedchamber. She was nearly bowled over by Matthews, running out of the room, his handkerchief pressed against his mouth as he gagged.

23

Dr. Poole refused to let her attend the autopsy.

Kendra wasn't surprised. Annoyed, yes, but not surprised. Her surprise came when Dr. Poole maintained his position even when Aldridge stepped in, trying to convince him that she wouldn't swoon observing the gruesome procedure, that her nerves were steady. It was a rare day when someone's sensibilities proved stronger than the Duke's title. Poole lowered his fuzzy brows and proclaimed that a lady's place was in the drawing room, not at the autopsy table.

I've grown accustomed to the Duke smoothing the way for me, and providing me entrée into his world, she realized.

Still, she wanted to kick something. Preferably the doctor's ass.

Instead, she drew in a deep breath, counted to ten, and spent the next twenty minutes going through the crime scene. She didn't need the doctor's permission to procure foolscap and pencil to make her notes, as well as crude drawings of both victims, which depicted the wounds and positions of their bodies. Later, she'd add both to the murder book. Having civilians on the scene like Matthews and Bancroft was an irritant that she forced herself to ignore. Matthews was less of an issue. He spent most of his time outdoors, breathing in fresh air or throwing up in the bushes. Bancroft, on the other hand, seemed to take an inordinate interest in what she was doing, his beady dark eyes following her as she moved around the room. It bugged her. Not just because he gave her the creeps, but because he was a damn suspect.

Then again, what could he really do? Tamper with trace evidence that she had no access to and that meant nothing in this era?

When she finally stepped outside, the sky had lightened up in the east. A small crowd had gathered. Kendra was surprised that they hadn't come inside to satisfy their ghoulish curiosity.

She approached them. "Who lives in the house next door?"

A woman with light brown hair tucked under a mop cap looked at her. "I do, miss. Me and me husband." She probably would have been attractive if she hadn't looked so tired. Kendra attributed much of the woman's exhaustion to the chubby baby she had propped on her hip. The baby was chewing on a wet rag.

"Mrs.—?"

"Mrs. Hooper."

"I'm Kendra Donovan. Can we walk a bit, Mrs. Hooper?"

Kendra and Mrs. Hooper moved down the sidewalk, closer to the woman's whitewashed cottage and out of earshot of the bystanders.

"Did you hear or see anything last evening coming from the Stones' house, Mrs. Hooper?" Kendra asked.

"Nay, I don't recollect hearing anythin'. I was up late last evenin' with me boy. He's been fussin' somethin' awful because of his teeth." The woman shifted her son in her arms, smoothing down his flyaway hair. The baby's saucer eyes were locked on Kendra with the unblinking intensity that kids under the age of four seemed to share.

"What about your husband? Did he see or hear anything?"

Mrs. Hooper gave a snort. "Hah! Chester sleeps like the dead, he does."

"Did you happen to see Mrs. Stone or Mrs. Trout anytime during the day?"

"Nay. I thought ter call on Mrs. Stone, ter express my condolences, but . . ." She gave a shrug.

"How well did you know Mrs. Stone?"

The woman shook her head. "Not well at all. Mr. Stone married Mrs. Stone three years ago, but she . . . Did you know she was an actress in Manchester?" Mrs. Hooper lowered her voice, as though imparting scandalous information.

Kendra knew that actors during this time were often celebrated on stage and even popular guests in certain circles, but they were not considered respectable members of society. Actresses were even less respected than their male counterparts. No surprise there, given the parameters imposed on women. Actresses stepped outside those rules governing unmarried women, often by forming out-of-wedlock relationships with their patrons. Yet Kendra suspected that society's doors were closed to them more because of fear—fear that the sons of the Beau Monde would have their heads turned by a beautiful face, and elope with a starlet.

"Yes, she mentioned it," Kendra said. "So you and Mrs. Stone were not friends?"

"Oh, nay. I don't think she had much interest in forming a connection either. We sometimes spoke at assemblies, but her dance card was always full. There're plenty of men ready ter make cakes of themselves." A sour note crept into Mrs. Hooper's voice, and Kendra wondered if Mr. Hooper might have danced with the former actress himself.

She asked, "How well did you know Mr. Stone?"

Something flickered in the other woman's eyes before she shifted her gaze away. "We were only slightly acquainted."

Kendra eyed her more closely. "How long were you and Mr. Stone neighbors?"

Mrs. Hooper focused on the house across the street. "He was here when we came."

"And when did you move in?"

"After I married Mr. Hooper. He's an apprentice for Mr. Talbot, the local stone mason."

"And when was that exactly?"

"Oh. Five years ago."

"In that time, you never had any encounters with Mr. Stone?"

Mrs. Hooper stiffened. "Why would there be?"

Kendra studied the woman for a long moment, noting the defensive posture and wooden expression. "Five years is a long time." She waited, but when Mrs. Hooper didn't respond, she said, "You must have formed some opinion of Mr. Stone. What did you think of him?"

The baby began to squirm. Mrs. Hooper said, "I must tend ter my son."

Something in Mrs. Hooper's eyes sent a chill down Kendra's spine. Acting on instinct, she laid a hand on the other woman's arm, and waited until Mrs. Hooper's gaze lifted to hers.

"Mr. Stone has a certain reputation. Did he make a pass at you?"

"A what?"

"Did he try to take advantage of you?"

Mrs. Hooper flushed, and her gaze slid away again.

"Whatever you tell me here will go no further, I promise you," Kendra pressed.

The baby pulled the rag from his mouth and let it drop to the sidewalk. With a weary sigh, his mother stooped to pick up the wet cloth, then automatically teased her son's lips with a corner of the material until he opened his mouth like a baby bird and began gumming it again.

"He . . . It happened when we first moved into the cottage," she finally said. Her voice sounded tight, and she had to clear her throat before she went on. "I was coming home from the market, and Mr. Stone . . . he offered ter carry my basket. I—I never thought ter decline, never thought . . ."

"Mrs. Hooper, whatever happened, it wasn't your fault."

"But I should never have let him inside. He viewed it as an invitation. He misunderstood—"

"It wasn't your fault," Kendra repeated firmly. "He didn't misunderstand. He took advantage of your good nature and innocence. That's what men like Mr. Stone do."

Tears welled up in Mrs. Hooper's eyes. Blinking rapidly, she looked away. "I should have fought harder . . . I was jest so shocked . . ."

Kendra's chill deepened. "Did Mr. Stone assault you, Mrs. Hooper?" she asked slowly, keeping her voice neutral with an effort.

Mrs. Hooper flinched, but said nothing. Her gaze was now on the crowd standing outside Stone's house.

Kendra's throat tightened, and she had to take a moment to get her anger under control. "Did you tell your husband?"

Mrs. Hooper's gaze jerked back to Kendra, her expression horrified. "Nay! Nay . . . Chester—my husband . . . he would have flown into a rage."

"At you?"

"Nay. At Mr. Stone. He would have killed him—" She went pale.

"Are you sure he never found out?"

"Aye. I told no one, Miss Donovan. It was only that one time, and I was careful never ter be alone with Mr. Stone again." She paused. "When he married, I was happy. I thought I had nothing ter fear. But during our chance encounters, I could see the look in his eye . . . He was a wicked man, Miss Donovan. 'Tis evil of me, but I cannot help but be pleased he is dead."

"I understand." Kendra regarded the other woman. "Are you all right? Do you have someone who you can confide in about your . . . about what happened?"

She seemed genuinely puzzled over the suggestion. "Why?"

"It might help if you talk to someone." Kendra thought of how she'd handle this conversation if she were in her own era. *I'd recommend counseling or going to a rape crisis center.* She was pretty sure there was no such thing here, any more than there'd be a shelter for abused women like Mrs. Turner.

Mrs. Hooper was shaking her head. "'Tis over. I do not want ter think about it, Miss Donovan. You won't tell anyone?"

Kendra hesitated.

Mrs. Hooper's eyes widened. "Please, Miss Donovan. You can't tell anyone!"

"No one who lives in East Dingleford will hear it from me," Kendra said carefully. "You have my word."

24

Kendra didn't break her word. But there was no room for modesty in murder investigations. Lives were dissected in war rooms just as bodies were dissected on autopsy tables. Victims, suspects, witnesses—everyone's secrets were exposed and examined in embarrassing detail. Mrs. Hooper's secret had to be told to the Duke, Alec, and Sam. Kendra comforted herself that since none of the men lived in East Dingleford, she was technically keeping her promise of confidentiality.

Yet because guilt pinched at her, she emphasized, "This information stays between us."

They'd returned to the private parlor. Kendra had taken up her position in front of the slate board, which remained covered with the sheet, as she shared the news. She looked at the men.

"Certainly," the Duke stated. "Mrs. Hooper has suffered enough. She doesn't need to have the other villagers whisper about her." He moved to the bell-pull and yanked the tasseled cord, which was attached to a clever system of chains and cords snaking through the walls and ceilings to ring a bell in the kitchens. Distaste tightened his jaw. "The man truly was a monster. To attack a young woman in such a manner. I am of the mind to think Mr. Stone may have gotten what he deserved."

"Aye." Sam's golden eyes turned flinty. "I'm surprised someone didn't bash the bas—er, the bloke's head years ago."

"That's been mentioned," Kendra murmured. She picked up a piece of slate, but held off on removing the sheet from the board when someone knocked on the door.

Aldridge opened the door to Mrs. Bolton. "Your Grace. How may I help you, sir?" she asked.

"I'd like a tray brought in for nuncheon, Mrs. Bolton. And pots of coffee and tea." He glanced back at Alec and Sam. "Have you been given rooms?"

Alec sauntered over to the table with the decanters. "We arrived when the maid came running into the stable yard, and left as soon as she sent a boy with a message to you and the constable. Are there rooms available?"

Mrs. Bolton nodded. "Aye. I shall send Tessa and Lizzie to make up your beds. Did you bring your own linen?" She regarded both men doubtfully.

Kendra didn't blame her. Alec had taken off his grimy riding coat, tossing it over the back of one of the chairs around the table, but his coat, shirt, and cravat looked almost as dirty, and the heels of his hessians were caked with mud. Sam had a similarly disheveled appearance. Of course, with the Bow Street Runner it was more normal.

"Sadly, I did not," Alec drawled, as he pulled out the decanter's stopper, and poured a generous three fingers of whisky into a tumbler.

"Aye. I forgot ter pack me linens too." Sam grinned at the innkeeper's wife.

Mrs. Bolton frowned at the Runner, not entirely sure what to make of him. She decided to ignore him, turning to Alec. "No matter, sir. We keep tidy rooms at the Green Maiden, sir. We wash our linens at least once a week."

"Two rooms then, for myself and Mr. Kelly," Alec said, handing Sam a glass of whisky. "I'll toss in an extra guinea if you wash the linens before you make the beds. And if you could direct me to the nearest lake or pond to wash off the grime of travel or, better yet, have a bath awaiting me in my room after nuncheon."

"I will have a bath sent up, milord. And for you, Mr. Kelly?"

Sam lifted his glass in a toast. "'Tis better than a lake. Thank you, madam."

She gave him another frown, but said briskly, "His Grace and Miss Donovan already occupy our largest bedchambers that include dressing rooms. However, the Green Maiden has several comfortable rooms available. I shall inform Mr. Bolton that you will be staying with us. And I'll send in a tray as soon as it's prepared, your Grace." She curtsied, and departed.

The Duke glanced at his nephew. "Are you certain you don't want to find the lake now, Alec?"

Alec laughed as he splashed whisky into his own glass. "Are you suggesting that I am not in my best looks, uncle?" He crossed the room, and collapsed into the chair before the fire. He didn't drink the whisky, but balanced the glass on his flat stomach as he stretched out his long legs, crossing them at the ankles. It could've been a languid pose, but for Kendra it spoke of sheer exhaustion.

"Actually, you both look like hell," she said bluntly.

Sam gave a startled laugh. He was already getting used to the American's frankness and lack of feminine wiles, but there were times when her bluntness still took him aback. "I feel more alert than I was at four this mornin', when his lordship shook me awake and put me on my horse without me breakfast," he said, settling into a chair opposite Alec.

The Duke regarded them both quizzically. "That brings up an interesting point . . . How did you end up traveling together? I confess that I didn't expect you, Mr. Kelly, until many hours, if not a full day, after my nephew's arrival."

Sam was lifting the tumbler to his lips, but now lowered it as he peered up at the Duke. "You were calling me in ter investigate Mr. Stone's murder, your Grace?" Surprised pleasure brightened Sam's gold eyes. "I didn't realize."

"I don't understand." Aldridge raised his eyebrows. "You never received my message?"

"Nay. It was actually most fortuitous, your Grace. I was with Lord Sutcliffe when he received your letter."

"What?" Startled, Aldridge glanced between his nephew and the Bow Street Runner. "Why?"

"Bow Street wanted the marquis to sign an official statement regarding the incident last month." Sam hesitated, but they knew what he was talking about—the month before, Alec had come under suspicion of murdering his former mistress. "I offered me services as courier. If your rider for Lord Sutcliffe had come but ten minutes later, I would have missed him, as I was preparin' ter ride back ter London Town."

"We gave the papers Mr. Kelly had brought to your rider, to take to London in Mr. Kelly's stead," Alec spoke up. "And Mr. Kelly accompanied me to East Dingleford."

Sam made a wry face. "His lordship is an excellent horseman, but the pace he sets is punishing."

Alec lifted his glass, and offered a crooked smile. "But you kept up, Kelly. You are to be commended."

Sam returned the salute, and took a healthy swallow of whisky.

"How extraordinary." The Duke shot Kendra a pointed look. "It would appear as though Fate has taken a hand in events again."

"Or it's a coincidence," said Kendra. But it was weird, she had to admit. She didn't like the idea of some mysterious force pushing her around like a piece on a chessboard, even as the Duke seemed to embrace the idea. Still, now was not the time for a philosophical debate. She smiled at Sam. "I have to say that I'm happy to see you, Mr. Kelly. We can use your services."

"You shall have them." His eyes narrowed. "Anything ter stop the fiend that did what was done in the Stone household. Obviously the killer wanted something from Mrs. Stone, ter torture her like he did. Any notion what that might be?"

"Not exactly. But I'd say it's connected to whatever the unsub stole off Mr. Stone's desk." She went to retrieve the murder book, pulling out the crude drawings she'd made of the desk. She showed them to Alec and Sam. "This might take a little imagination, but this represents the surface area of Stone's desk."

"It might take a lot of imagination," Alec murmured.

Sam asked, "What are those little dots?"

"Blood spatter."

Sam grunted. "Why ain't there any of dots in this area?"

"Because that's what is known as a void pattern. When Stone was killed, something was on his desk that caught the blood. The killer took it."

"What was it?" asked Sam. "Any idea?"

"No. And this is where it becomes a guessing game. We only know the dimensions: twenty-six inches in length, sixteen inches in width. We can only estimate the height. But I wouldn't go higher than four, maybe five inches, otherwise that would interfere with the spatter pattern."

"A book?" Sam suggested.

"It would have to be open to explain the width," said the Duke.

Kendra nodded. "Or a painting. Or a map."

"A treasure map," Alec murmured. His eyes were at half-mast, but Kendra caught the gleam of amusement between his lashes. "I fancied finding myself a treasure map when I was a boy."

She could feel her lips curving into a smile. "How old were you?"

"Seven, I believe."

Envisioning Alec as a seven-year-old dreaming of treasure maps brought an unexpected lump to Kendra's throat. In many ways, Alec's childhood had been as lonely as hers. His mother, Alexandria, an Italian countess who'd married into the English aristocracy, had died. His father had remarried, but Alec's stepmother had been a cold woman who'd dealt with her stepson by shipping him off to boarding school. In hindsight, that had been a blessing; Alec's half-brother hadn't fared well in his mother's care.

Aldridge broke into her reverie. "It could have been a map—although I doubt a treasure map." Aldridge shot an indulgent smile at Alec. "Sorry, my boy."

"My dreams are shattered, but I cannot be too despondent. It appears as though I have enough adventure in my life at the moment." His gaze slid to Kendra. "I doubt if I could handle the excitement of a treasure map on top of everything else."

Kendra rolled her eyes. "Treasure maps are mostly a myth. The only one I've ever heard of is . . ." *The copper scroll from the Dead Sea Scrolls, which won't be discovered for another 137 years.* "I can't remember," she muttered lamely, aware of Sam regarding her with his cop-eyes. *Shit.*

Aldridge said, "Whatever was on the desk, it is obviously only half the puzzle. The other half was in the Stone household. It is why Mrs. Stone was tortured."

"No." Kendra set the drawing aside. "The unsub *believed* the other half was in the Stone household. We don't know if he found what he was looking for. Personally, I don't think that he did."

"Why?" asked Aldridge.

Kendra jiggled the piece of slate in her hand as she thought about that. Part was gut instinct, she realized. The other part . . .

"I can't be completely sure, you understand," she said slowly. "But we can reasonably assume the killer dispatched Mrs. Trout as soon as he entered the kitchen. There were no signs of struggle and the door wasn't forced open. I think she opened the door for him, and he followed her inside. Her body was just inside the kitchen, face-up, which is consistent with the unsub grabbing her hair from behind, yanking her head back to expose her throat, and slashing it. *If* I had been allowed to attend the autopsy, I might have more to say on the injury."

"Would she open the door to just anyone?" asked Sam. He took a hurried swallow of whisky, as though he had a bad taste in his mouth and needed to wash it away with something.

"I do not think Mrs. Trout was very . . . discriminating," the Duke said. "She was an unusual creature. I don't see her turning the killer away if he made a convincing argument as to why he was there at a late hour."

"And I'm leaning toward the attack occurring closer to ten o'clock," Kendra said. "I'm not sure what Mrs. Trout's daily routine was, but I don't think she'd retired for the night. She wasn't in her nightgown. And her bedroom is on the third floor—sorry, second floor. If she'd retired for the night, I don't think she would have heard the knock at the door. Or she would have ignored it."

The Duke nodded. "She was an odd creature. I can imagine both of those scenarios."

"Mrs. Trout's murder was the most cold-blooded of the three," Kendra continued. She began to pace, still jiggling the piece of slate in her hand. "She meant nothing to him. Her death was like stepping on a cockroach. With even less emotion."

"Quite different than Mr. Stone's murder," the Duke said, "which had rather a lot of passion."

Kendra nodded, but before she could respond, there was a knock at the door. The Duke opened it, stepping back as both Tessa and Lizzie came through with trays. The maids moved to the table, setting down the trays and uncovering platters. Instead of cold cuts for the normally lighter nuncheon, Kendra was surprised to see dishes of hot roast beef, peas swimming in butter, and mashed potatoes, with a loaf of brown bread.

"Praise heaven—'tis a feast," Sam said, clearly appreciative.

Lizzie smiled at him as she laid out the plates and silverware. She'd inherited her blond prettiness from her grandmother, Kendra realized. "Gran thought that with your hard ridin', ye might need something more ter fill your belly," she said.

"Your grandmother is the wisest of women." Sam gave an elaborate bow that set Tessa to giggling. "I'm so hungry that my guts have been thinkin' me throat's been cut." He winced, apparently realizing how inappropriate the expression was given what had happened in the Stone residence. But Tessa and Lizzie hadn't heard the graphic details about the murder; their expressions remained innocent.

"Will you be needin' anythin' else?" Lizzie asked, setting tankards of ale on the table.

"No," Aldridge said. "We'll serve ourselves. Please give our thanks to your grandmother for this excellent meal. And your cook, Mrs. Platt."

"Aye, sir," Tessa dipped into a hurried curtsy, and bolted from the room.

"Tessa!" admonished Lizzie, but the other girl was already out the door. She gave them an apologetic look. "Forgive my sister's hoydenish ways, but she's excited for the Assembly tonight."

Kendra had forgotten about the much-anticipated event, and shot a look at the window. It seemed brighter outside than when they'd returned to the inn, proving that nothing was more mercurial than English weather. "So the Assembly is on?"

"Aye. If the sky continues to clear, we should have a moon tonight. Will you be attending?" Her gaze encompassed the entire room. "It's ever so much fun."

"I wouldn't miss it for the world," Kendra said.

Lizzie curtsied and left the room.

Alec pushed himself to his feet, looking at Kendra. "I had no idea you are interested in attending country assemblies, Miss Donovan."

"I imagine there will be a lot of people talking about the murders."

The Duke pulled out a chair for Kendra, a chivalrous gesture that still surprised her. They all sat, then spent the next several minutes loading up their plates. Kendra cut the brown bread, and passed the plate around.

The Duke broke the silence, returning to the earlier subject. "Why don't you believe the fiend found what he was looking for, Miss Donovan?"

Kendra chewed her bread before answering. "The destruction of the crime scene. We can reasonably assume that the killer didn't start his rampage after killing Mrs. Trout, right?"

"Yes." The Duke smiled as he gazed at her. "'Tis the same argument you made regarding the Luddites. If this monster had begun his search immediately, causing the destruction that we witnessed, Mrs. Stone would have heard the commotion and come downstairs to investigate."

Kendra nodded. "And he would have tied her up downstairs to torture her. He killed Mrs. Trout and found Mrs. Stone in her bedroom. He brought rope to tie her to the chair. I assume he threatened her first, probably with the knife, but it escalated quickly when she didn't—*couldn't*—tell him what he wanted to know. I think after he realized Mrs. Stone didn't know anything, he killed her. Then he went through Stone's bedchamber, tossing it."

"And the rooms downstairs," added the Duke.

"Yes. But it was more than someone searching for something," she said. "That was temper. He became enraged when he didn't find what he wanted. That's my hypothesis, anyway."

"You mention his knife . . . why didn't he use that to inflict his torture?" The Duke forked up mashed potatoes. "Why go about the process of burning the poor creature?"

"Maybe he was afraid that she'd bleed out. It would have taken a considerable number of lacerations for that, and maybe he didn't want to take the chance. Or . . ." Kendra shrugged. "Burning inflicts more pain."

"'Tis also a well-known method of torture," said Sam, lifting his tankard and taking a swallow of ale.

"I don't know how long he tortured her, but when he finally realized it was pointless, he killed her in the same way he killed Mrs. Trout." Kendra looked at them. "What does that tell us about the unsub?"

"He's a devil," Sam muttered.

"Yes and no," Kendra replied.

The Duke raised his eyebrows. "What do you mean, *no*? He clearly is a monster, Miss Donovan."

"He's a monster, yes, for taking lives. For torture. But he didn't do it because he enjoyed it. He had a reason. It was a means to an end. We're not dealing with a sadist."

Kendra paused, letting that sink in, then continued, "Stone's murder was impulsive. Anger and panic made it sloppy, disorganized." She suspected that in the twenty-first century, that crime scene would have yielded a ton of trace evidence that would've been used to quickly apprehend the killer. Disorganized crimes were typically easier to solve. "But the murders of Stone's wife and housekeeper were highly organized. And that forces me to revise my profile. We're not dealing with a person who killed once, in a hot moment of temper and fear."

She allowed her gaze to roam across their faces, seeing their fierce concentration on what she was saying. "We're dealing with someone who will use any means to get what he wants," she said. "Someone who is very determined, very cold. And very dangerous."

25

East Dingleford's Assembly Room was a large brick building located on High Street. It reminded Kendra of the town halls she'd seen in Middle America, which were also used for community dances and socializing. It was eight P.M., and the street and sidewalk were already crowded with arrivals. Kendra heard the buzz of excited conversation as soon as Alec helped her down from the carriage. The citizens of East Dingleford had gotten lucky with the weather. Most of the clouds had blown away by late afternoon. Kendra tilted her head to look up at the moon, a waning gibbous, but still strong enough to allow night travel. Against the inky darkness, a scattering of stars winked down at them.

The Duke's gaze washed over the throng of people. "The event appears to be a crush. I suggest we leave our outerwear in the carriage."

Kendra shivered the second she discarded her cloak. The threat of rain may have dissipated, but it was still damn cold. *Especially for women*, she thought resentfully. After peeling off their greatcoats, men still had on their coats, layered over a waistcoat, shirt, and cravat. Women wore wispy, empire-waisted evening gowns that displayed a bit of décolletage. The evening gown Molly had selected for Kendra was a golden organza floating over a white satin slip. The tiny bodice was embroidered with sequins that twinkled in the moonlight. A gold satin sash was tied into a ribbon beneath her breasts. Embroidered white slippers peeked out from the skirt. Probably the warmest thing she was wearing was the long white kid gloves that ended above her elbows.

It was a wonder more women didn't end up with pneumonia in this era. Maybe that's why in another couple of decades women would embrace the fashion that Kendra had always thought looked uncomfortable: starched highneck collars, long sleeves, extra padding in the form of bustles, and several petticoats.

"Let's get inside before Molly and I freeze to death," she muttered.

The narrow sidewalk forced them to walk two at a time. The Duke offered Kendra his elbow. Alec followed behind them, but Molly kept three steps behind him. A country assembly was different than London, Kendra had been informed, less formal, allowing the different classes to mingle. But that didn't mean a lady's maid could act as though she were equal to a nobleman.

They were caught in the stream of people who were making their way to the Assembly Room's doorway. Inside, Kendra observed, "It looks like the entire village showed up." She appreciated the body heat that warmed up the foyer. There was a good bit of jostling as people removed their coats, hats, and cloaks. Young boys raced around to collect them.

Kendra caught the looks flicked in their direction. They were strangers to East Dingleford, which prompted many stares. But she also had a feeling the small-town gossip machine had kicked in. The villagers knew about the double homicide at the Stone residence, and that they were involved in the investigation.

"Your Grace, Miss Donovan!" It took Matthews a minute to push his way through the press of people. He gave Alec a once-over before recognition lit his eyes. "Lord Sutcliffe. I must say you've cleaned up nicely since we met earlier."

Alec smiled crookedly. "A hot bath and a twenty-minute nap does wonders. And, of course, borrowing the

Duke's valet." He scraped his palm against his now clean-shaven face. "If he can get the mud out of my riding jacket, you ought to increase Wilson's wages, uncle."

Aldridge gave his nephew a look. "I may have to do that to keep him. This entire adventure has taken the wind out of his sails. You look quite stylish as well, Mr. Matthews."

Kendra's gaze traveled over Matthews's navy velvet cutaway coat, which revealed a blue-and-silver striped waistcoat, and white satin knee breeches and white stockings. The points of his collar were high enough to dig into his chin, and his cravat was tied in another elaborate style. A sapphire as large as a robin's egg was pinned in its snowy folds.

The Duke's words made Matthews's slight chest swell. "Thank you, sir." He attempted to execute a formal bow that drew annoyed cries when his rump bumped into the people behind him as he bent over.

"Oh, dear. I beg your pardon!" Coloring, Matthews straightened hurriedly, casting an apologetic look over his shoulder. He turned back to the Duke. "'Tis an honor to have you at our fete, sir. We have never had a duke in attendance before. I dare say when word gets out to nearby villages, they shall be positively green with envy."

"You are too gracious," murmured Aldridge.

Matthews said, "I am the Master of Ceremonies this evening."

The Duke raised an eyebrow. "You wear many hats, Mr. Matthews."

"We do not put on airs in East Dingleford or pretend to be so grand as London Town, but we *do* have our codes. And those codes must be enforced here at our assembly." Matthews gave Kendra an approving nod. "I am relieved to see that your gloves are white, Miss Donovan, as they should be. You would be utterly scandalized to hear how many young ladies have been *brazen* enough to wear colored gloves these days."

Kendra had been in this time period long enough to know that society revolved around countless rules, but she hadn't heard this one yet. "Young ladies aren't supposed to wear colored gloves?"

"Good heavens, no. Not if they desire to dance." He paused, eyeing her with confusion. "'Tis the same in London, is it not? Or has there been a relaxing of standards?"

Alec said, "You have the right of it, Mr. Matthews. The restriction remains."

Matthews looked relieved. "Thank you. I . . . oh." He cocked his head to listen as the plucking notes of a violin drifting through the doorway. "Forgive me, but I must have a word with the musicians before they begin."

They watched him dive back into the crowd, fighting his way into the ballroom. Alec turned to gaze at Kendra. "You are considering ordering a dozen colored gloves, aren't you, Miss Donovan?"

She laughed. "Maybe more."

"And if they play the waltz?" Alec asked.

Kendra's breath caught as she recognized the heat in Alec's green eyes, and remembered that they'd danced the waltz last month in the Duke's study. The memory of it—and what had come after—burned through her, so hot that she wondered if she'd become the first documented case of spontaneous self-combustion in history.

"It's doubtful they will play the waltz," Aldridge said, unwittingly breaking the spell between her and Alec. "The dance has only begun to be accepted in London. It will undoubtedly be months before it arrives here."

"Yes, well." Kendra cleared her throat, and tore her gaze from Alec's wicked grin. "I didn't come here to dance. I came here to interview people."

Aldridge smiled, "Then let us begin."

The citizens of East Dingleford had splurged on the décor of the ballroom, Kendra thought as she stood in the corner. Enormous gilded mirrors hung against the patterned ivory silk wallpaper, doubling the people mingling inside the ballroom. Three chandeliers dropped from the high ceiling, their light reflecting against the tall windows and French doors that led out to the verandah. She could smell the more expensive beeswax melting from dozens of lit tapers.

The Assembly Room had indeed brought the different classes together, but Matthews was careful to introduce dance partners who shared the same rung of society. Kendra could now tell from the cut of a man's coat or the fabric of a woman's gown where they belonged in the social hierarchy. The Duke had been persuaded into honoring them with his presence on the dance floor, and was standing opposite a handsome older woman, who was wearing a four-tiered diamond necklace that spoke of, if not nobility, then wealth.

Kendra's gaze scanned the chairs that ringed the dance floor. Lady Winifred sat in one of them. There were other women around her, but the countess had a distant expression on her beautiful face that somehow set her apart.

"Miss Donovan." Bancroft moved into her line of vision. His dark eyes flicked to Alec, who was standing beside her. "Lord Sutcliffe."

"My lord," Alec greeted coolly.

"I was hoping to persuade Miss Donovan to take a turn on the dance floor."

"You'll thank me when I turn you down." Kendra summoned a polite smile. "I have two left feet."

The earl regarded her steadily. "I see. Well, then perhaps I can persuade you to take a stroll?"

Kendra sensed Alec stiffening beside her, but stepped forward immediately, putting her hand on Bancroft's arm. "I'd like that, my lord."

They said nothing as they joined the other couples circling the outer perimeter of the room. The string quartet had begun playing, the music swelling into a wonderfully upbeat tempo that encouraged the dancers. Kendra thought it was Haydn.

"Does your interest lie with Lord Sutcliffe?" Bancroft asked abruptly.

"*What*?" Whatever topic she thought the earl would introduce, this was not it. She turned her head to look at him.

"Do you and Lord Sutcliffe have an understanding?" His dark eyes locked on hers. She couldn't read his expression, but the intensity in his gaze once again made her uneasy. "He appears possessive of you, Miss Donovan. I wondered if a betrothal between you is imminent."

"No."

"It would be logical, of course. I am aware that Lord Sutcliffe is the Duke's nephew and heir. And you are his Grace's ward. I assume the Duke has made provisions for you. However, if you marry his nephew, the wealth remains in his family."

"That's very cold-blooded don't you think?"

He smiled. "Somehow, I don't think you are a romantic young maid, Miss Donovan. The business of marriage is just that—business."

Kendra narrowed her eyes at the earl. "Then how is it any of your business?"

"My wife is dead, Miss Donovan. I have been a widower for nearly three years. But I am not averse to the state of matrimony."

She stumbled, and for a moment her mind went blank. Was he saying what she *thought* he was saying?

"I find you a fascinating woman, Miss Donovan." He ushered her toward a shadowy corner near the French doors. He stopped, and fixed her with an unfathomable gaze. "I believe we have much in common."

Kendra stared back at him, and hoped that she didn't look as appalled as she was feeling. Christ, was he hitting on her? Such May-December marriages were done all the time, throughout history—and Hollywood. Still, she sensed something else was behind Lord Bancroft's sudden interest in her. A diversionary tactic? To throw her off her game?

She tried to pull her hand from his grasp, and was reminded that he had strength that belied his age. She glared at him until he let go, then took a step back, angered at his attempt at intimidation.

"I'm not entirely sure what you are saying, my lord," she finally said, and was pleased that her voice was cold rather than heated with temper. "We barely know each other."

"I disagree. I know who you are, Miss Donovan."

"Papa."

Kendra would never admit to the surge of relief at Lady Winifred's timing. She turned to meet Lady Winifred's dark eyes—the same dark eyes as her father—as she approached. Walking next to her was an old woman wearing a starched black bombazine dress that rustled as she walked, and an ivory ruffled lace cap pinned to her thinning white hair.

"Miss Donovan," Lady Winifred said, "I am surprised to see you here tonight."

"Really? Why?"

Lady Winifred arched a brow, pretending amazement. "Because this very afternoon you discovered Mrs. Stone's body, did you not?"

Kendra said, "And Mrs. Trout."

"Pardon?"

"I discovered Mrs. Trout's body, as well," Kendra said firmly, annoyed that the poor housekeeper had become a side note.

Lady Winifred's expression cleared. "Oh. Yes, certainly." She gave her small, cool smile. "I only know that if I had the misfortune to discover what you did, I would be prostrate in bed—not attending a local assembly some scant hours later. You are a wonder, Miss Donovan, to not be affected by the more feminine sensibilities."

Kendra felt that was a slight, but couldn't quite put her finger on it. "Oh, I have a feeling you'd be able to hold your own, too, my lady," she said, and smiled.

"Good evening, Lord Bancroft," greeted the old woman who'd accompanied Lady Winifred. Her faded blue eyes were pinned on the earl.

"Forgive me . . . Mrs. Hearnshaw, this is Miss Donovan," Lady Winifred introduced. "She is an American."

She made it sound like a disease, Kendra thought. She looked at the old woman, who was returning her regard with bright curiosity.

"Miss Donovan."

"Mrs. Hearnshaw." *Mrs. Hearnshaw* . . . It took Kendra a moment, then she remembered: Falcon Court's former housekeeper.

"Mrs. Hearnshaw." Bancroft inclined his head, his expression unreadable.

"Your daughter kindly offered to take a turn around the ballroom, as my daughter-in-law has abandoned me." The old woman gave a sniff, apparently not happy. "I suspect Jenny snuck into the card room again. She'll be losing her pin money, mark my words."

Bancroft looked at Kendra. "Would you like a refreshment, Miss Donovan? I'll escort you to the supper room."

Kendra wondered if it was her imagination, or if the earl was trying to avoid his former housekeeper. "Actually, I was going to ask Mrs. Hearnshaw if she'd like to walk with me," she said smoothly. It killed two birds with one stone, she decided. She had wanted to talk to Falcon Court's housekeeper, but even more importantly, she really didn't want to continue the strange conversation she'd been having with Bancroft, at least not until she figured out what he was playing at. Not for a second did she think he'd formed some sort of attraction to her. What was his game?

"I would like a refreshment, Papa." Lady Winifred spoke up, and looped her arm through her father's, looking at him expectantly.

Bancroft hesitated, then he inclined his head. "As you wish." He leveled a look at Kendra. "Please consider what I said, Miss Donovan."

Kendra said nothing, but saw Lady Winifred shot her father a questioning glance. Then Bancroft put his hand on his daughter's and they joined the strollers. Kendra watched them disappear through a nearby door that she could only assume was the supper room.

"Seeing how you desire to walk, Miss Donovan, perhaps we can walk to the card room to make sure my foolish daughter-in-law has come to no harm," said Mrs. Hearnshaw, her gaze appraising Kendra. "She has a fondness for games."

Kendra thought of Lord Bancroft. "I don't think your daughter-in-law is alone in that," she murmured. "I get the impression that there are a lot of people in East Dingleford who have a fondness for games."

26

Tell me, how long have you lived in East Dingleford, Mrs. Hearnshaw?" Kendra asked the old woman as they joined the other strollers circling the ballroom. Already the room was beginning to feel overheated with the number of bodies swirling around the dance floor. Kendra wished someone would crack open a window or one of the French doors to lessen the stuffiness, and bring in fresh air to diffuse the mingled odors of wax, perfume, and sweat.

"All my life," said Mrs. Hearnshaw, watching Kendra out of the corner of her eye. The blue eyes might have faded with age, but they were still sharp with intelligence. "I will be four score and two next month, Miss Donovan."

Mrs. Hearnshaw sounded triumphant. Kendra couldn't blame her. Eighty-two might be normal for women in the western world in the twenty-first century, but was unusual enough here in Georgian England to deserve applause. Hell, she deserved a parade.

"When did you become the housekeeper at Falcon Court?" she asked.

The old woman looked surprised. "How did you know I was the housekeeper?"

"Someone mentioned it."

"I began as a scullery maid," she said. "My father owned the local haberdashery. It did well enough, but with fourteen children . . . well, we could hardly all work behind the counter, could we? And East Dingleford was much smaller back then. My sister and I were fortunate to find work on the estate."

Kendra knew that a scullery maid was one of the lowest positions in a household, responsible for scrubbing the kettles, cutlery, and dishes, and blackening the stove early each morning. "How old were you?" she asked.

"My sister was ten and three; I was nine."

Kendra was no longer surprised at how young children were when they began working. Child labor was part of this world, and Kendra suspected it had been even worse when Mrs. Hearnshaw had been a little girl. "You worked your way up to become housekeeper. That's admirable."

"Nay." She shook her head. "I was eventually promoted to upstairs maid. That's when my Tom—Mr. Hearnshaw—began courting me." She glanced sideways at Kendra. "Tom and his brother farmed Goose Hill together, which made him quite the catch. He was a sturdy lad, my Tom was. When I resigned from Falcon Court to wed, I never thought to return. But we cannot know the future, can we?"

"It depends."

"Pardon?"

"Sorry—you're right, of course. What happened, if you don't mind me asking?"

"Ack, it was a lifetime ago." She sighed. "Silly man was hurrying home one evening. It was winter, and he crossed an ice pond. I dare say he thought it would make his journey quicker. He was always in a hurry, my Tom. He went through the ice."

"I'm sorry."

Mrs. Hearnshaw waved away Kendra's sympathy, and frowned. "Why am I telling you this? Oh, aye, you asked me about my position as housekeeper at Falcon Court. I was fortunate, Miss Donovan. I needed to support my children, and the earl required a housekeeper. He was still a viscount then, what with his father being alive, away in London Town. He was kind to me, even though he was going through challenges himself. He'd lost his wife before I lost my Tom, and then Nat taking off like he did." The old woman pursed her lips, disapproval stamped on her face.

"Nat—Lord Bancroft had already left when you became the housekeeper?"

"Aye. I knew him, of course, like everyone in East Dingleford. He was a right handsome lad. I can see why Laura became moon-eyed over the boy. But the silly chit reached above herself." She sniffed. "Nat ought to have been sent to Eton or Harrow, not schooled at Falcon Court. Then everything would have been proper-like. He would have eventually found someone befitting his station—just as he did when he came home after gallivanting around the world."

The censure in Mrs. Hearnshaw's voice reminded Kendra of the housekeeper at Aldridge Castle. Mrs. Danbury believed firmly that everything—and everybody—had a place.

They had walked the length of the room, and turned to walk the width. Kendra's gaze drifted to the dancers lined up on the floor, men facing women, the more affluent villagers on one end of the ballroom, the common folk on the other.

"You sound as though you don't approve of the earl's travels," she finally remarked.

Mrs. Hearnshaw pressed her lips together. "'Tis not for me to approve or disapprove of my betters' behavior," she said stiffly. "Still, I was serving the earl—he became the earl shortly after I returned to Falcon Court, when his father passed. I could see how heartsick he was over his son's desertion. It wasn't right that Nat hardly wrote his father either. Then the earl had a seizure."

"I heard that he'd been ill."

"Ill—he was at death's door, he was," she huffed. "Dr. Poole said he'd had an apoplectic stroke. The poor man was bedridden for nigh on a year, his body having seized up something fierce. Could hardly talk, slurring his words something terrible. Course, we pretended not to notice, the earl being such a proud man, and all. I attended him myself rather than hire a nurse."

"He was fortunate to have you," Kendra murmured.

"Well, as to that, it was my duty. We feared that his lordship would never lay eyes on his son—not in this world, anyway. Hired a Bow Street Runner to find him. It was a miracle when Nat walked through the door."

"I'm sure he was happy to see his son."

"Oh, aye. And probably relieved. I fancy he was worried about the estate. The earl never had a head for business, nor did his father. But he tried. The earl's cousin was in line to inherit. A rakehell if there ever was one." She gave a disapproving sniff. "If he ever got his hands on Falcon Court, he'd have it tumbling into ruin in less than a fortnight, I'm sure."

"But Nat wasn't dead. How could the earl's cousin have inherited?"

"Oh, he would have done whatever he could, by fair means or foul, you mark my words," she said darkly. "I'm certain the very thought kept the earl in a terrible state. Without Nat, there was no one else. The earl and the countess had five children, but not one of them survived, save Nat."

"That's terrible."

Mrs. Hearnshaw shrugged. "I'm only grateful that the earl's mind was put to rest when Nat returned," she said. "Didn't matter that Nat had grown from a stripling into an oak, and a tough oak at that. His lordship was content to have his son home, never matter the years he spent away with barely a letter. Poor dear was restless whenever Nat wasn't around."

Mrs. Hearnshaw fell silent, lost in her memories. "Even now, I can hear the earl call out for his son," she continued. "*Nat-son*, he would say. Oh, it was something awful, with his lordship's tongue being twisted like it was. Couldn't manage his *t*'s and *h*'s, you see. Oh, dear." Tears glistened in her eyes, and she fished out a handkerchief from her pocket. "I'm being positively mawkish. Forgive me."

"They're difficult memories."

She nodded. "They are, even if it was a long time ago. I'd send a footman to fetch Nat, and the earl would settle down like a pet. He'd just watch Nat with those dark eyes of his. Always got the feeling that the earl was afraid that his son would disappear again if he looked away."

"It's understandable, I suppose, after such a long estrangement," Kendra said.

Mrs. Hearnshaw nodded. "Aye. 'Tis a shame they had so little time together."

"I heard he fell down the stairs not long after Lord Bancroft's return."

"Aye."

Kendra asked, "How did that happen, if he was bedridden?"

Mrs. Hearnshaw frowned. "Only his left side had seized up, and he was as weak as a baby bird, especially after Dr. Poole bled him to restore his humors."

"Good God," Kendra muttered, appalled that she was stuck in an era when bloodletting was still a part of the medical field.

Mrs. Hearnshaw didn't seem to hear her. "I have my suspicions on what happened."

Kendra focused on the former housekeeper. "What do you think happened?"

Mrs. Hearnshaw shot a quick glance around to make sure she wasn't overheard. "I'm of the mind that the earl woke in the middle of the night, and became fearful that Nat had fled again. I think he dragged himself out of his bed to go to his son's bedchamber. But his strength gave out on him, and he went tumbling down the stairs."

"Who found him?"

"Falcon Court's butler, at the time—Mr. Darrow. It was quite a shock, but mayhap also a blessing. Everyone knew that his lordship was withering away in his bedchamber."

In the twenty-first century, rehabilitation and medicine could help stroke victims recover and live out a normal life. But here . . . Jesus, here they still practiced bloodletting.

"How did Lord Bancroft react to his father's death?" Kendra asked.

Mrs. Hearnshaw didn't say anything for a long moment, but her face tightened. "There were no tears, if that's what you're asking," she finally said. "But to be fair, it would have been ill-bred of a gentleman of the Ton to show excessive emotion."

Kendra remembered what Matthews had said about Lord Bancroft pensioning off the housekeeper after his father's death. She asked, "When did you leave Falcon Court, ma'am?"

"Shortly after the earl was laid to rest," she said. "Nat—the new Lord Bancroft—summoned me and Mr. Darrow to the study to explain that our services were no longer required."

"That seems like a strange thing to do. Why do you think he did it?"

The old woman hesitated. "It's not for me to presume about the behavior of my betters, but I dare say it was guilt. I think he blamed himself for his father's death, and thought Mr. Darrow and myself blamed him as well."

Kendra lifted her eyebrows. "Why would he think that?"

Mrs. Hearnshaw shrugged. "I have found that when one is feeling guilty, they take on odd notions and begin to think everyone is thinking the same."

Projection. "He let you go in order to quiet his own conscience."

"Aye. I was fortunate to be able to move in with my son and his family at Goose Hill." She straightened, and pushed the handkerchief back in her pocket. "Goodness, I have been rambling on like a doddering old woman."

"Not at all. Can you tell me if Lord Bancroft—Nat— ever talked about where his journeys had taken him?"

"He never spoke of it, no. But we knew from the thief- taker's accounts that he'd been all over the world. I think he was in India when he finally received the message we sent about his father. Of course, it took months before he made it back to England."

"Did he ever mention Mr. Stone?"

Mrs. Hearnshaw frowned. "His mill manager? But that was years before he even built the mill."

"I thought I heard that they knew each other from India," Kendra lied.

Mrs. Hearnshaw shook her head, still frowning. "Not that I ever heard. But I left only a few weeks after the earl died. And Nat—his lordship—has said about ten words to me since he returned home thirty-five years ago." The old woman looked shrewdly at Kendra. "You're asking me all these questions about Lord Bancroft and Mr. Stone because you're trying to find the murderer who killed Mr. Stone and his wife?"

"And Mrs. Trout." When Mrs. Hearnshaw stared at her, perplexed, she said, "Their housekeeper. She was killed too."

"Oh. Anyhow, 'tis a peculiar hobby for a nobleman and a lady."

Kendra decided there was nothing she could say to that.

"Lord Bancroft didn't kill Mr. Stone. You'll catch cold if that's what you're getting at, Miss Donovan," the old woman warned. "Nat may have grown up hard after he left East Dingleford, but he's been good for the village since his return. He built the mill and revived the estate, even if he has foolishly replaced candles with that noxious gas lighting."

Kendra switched the subject. "What do you know about Mr. Stone's background? You must have heard something in the twenty years he's been in East Dingleford. Do you know where he was originally from?"

Mrs. Hearnshaw thought it over. "I seem to recollect that he might have been from somewhere south of London. I don't know if that's true though." She pressed her lips together, once again radiating disapproval. "Mr. Stone was not a man to make one's acquaintance. He was very much a Man of Town, to be sure."

"I thought you didn't know if he was from London."

"Nay. I am referring to the man being a rake. A debaucher." She huffed. "Nothing like Mr. Murray."

"You knew Mr. Murray?"

"Well, of course. Or I should say that I made his acquaintance; I can't rightly say I *knew* him. Seemed to prefer his own company to socializing. We used to hold these assemblies in the Green Maiden's public dining hall, but Mr. Murray would stay in the tavern, scribbling something fierce in the mill's account books. He was a very *different* sort than Mr. Stone, who left everything for Mr. Biddle to manage. Mr. Stone never cried off any assembly if he was in the village. He enjoyed the card room and terrorizing the young ladies with his attentions."

It was Kendra's turn to press her lips together, wishing she could speak about the terror Stone had inflicted on Mrs. Hooper. And probably other women too ashamed to come forward. *Bastard.*

Instead, she said, "I heard that Mr. Stone was accused of cheating at cards during an assembly."

"Aye. Shocking public display, if you ask me. Personally, I think Mr. Turner was in his cups, and played too deep."

"I met Mr. Turner . . ." She attempted her own sniff, which sounded more like a snort.

An astute gleam came into the faded blue eyes as she gazed at Kendra. "Did you now? And what did you think of him, if I may ask?"

"I feel sorry for his wife."

Mrs. Hearnshaw nodded. "The poor creature has much to contend with. The Turner farm is near Goose Hill, but our families do not socialize. We have found Mr. Turner to be an unsociable fellow. He often attends the assemblies, but rarely brings his wife. It's not dancing that interests him, that's for certain."

Kendra glanced toward the card room. "Is he here tonight?"

"I have not seen him."

"Do you know what arrangement Mr. Turner might have made with Mr. Stone to pay off his debt?"

The old woman shook her head. "The only one privy to such a thing would be Mr. Turner and Mr. Stone. And possibly Mrs. Turner. You would do well to quiz her."

"I'd like to do that. The problem is getting her alone, away from her husband."

The old woman cocked her head as she regarded Kendra. "It's not a problem—it's timing, Miss Donovan. My Tom—my son; he was named after his father—is a sheep farmer too. And tomorrow is market day. He will be culling the herd, bringing the sheep to slaughter, as is the custom."

"I see . . . And Mr. Turner will be bringing his sheep to market too?"

"I expect so."

"When does this take place?"

"The market opens at eight A.M. Depending on their livestock, it could take two hours or more. There tends to be a lot of haggling. And I've found more often than not that haggling dries the throat. Most men stop by the tavern to wet it before going home."

Kendra grinned. "You are very observant, Mrs. Hearnshaw."

"After four score and two months on earth, I hope I have picked up a thing or two, Miss Donovan. Now I must venture into the card room to keep an eye on my daughter-in-law—despite her advanced years, Emma can be a goosecap." They started forward again, but Mrs. Hearnshaw paused, her gaze turning serious as she looked at Kendra. "Do you believe Mr. Turner is responsible for the murders of Mr. Stone and his wife?"

"Do you?"

"I certainly can imagine him doing what I heard was done to Mr. Stone," she said slowly. "Mr. Turner's vicious temper is well-known in East Dingleford."

Kendra said nothing. Temper, uncontrollable and vicious, might have been responsible for Stone's bludgeoning. But it wasn't temper that had killed his wife and Mrs. Trout. If the killer had been enraged, he'd suppressed it beneath icy control. Did the farmer have that kind of control, or could she rule him out?

Then she suddenly remembered how Turner had gazed at her as he plucked up the chicken, and calmly wrung its neck. No, she couldn't rule out Turner. At the moment, he was at the top of her list.

Dr. Poole entered the card room just as Mrs. Hearnshaw finished her introductions between Kendra and her daughter-in-law. Kendra quickly excused herself from the two women, and wove her way through the tables and card players, waylaying the doctor before he could sit down.

"Good evening, Dr. Poole. Would you stroll with me a bit?"

Blue eyes beneath fuzzy brows swiveled around to stare at her. "Miss Donovan." He flicked a look at the card table, then back to her. "This is a Hobson's choice, as it would be rag-mannered for me to refuse."

"Ah. You are too gracious, sir."

"I'm not." But a slight smile tugged at his mouth. He offered her his arm. "However, I beg your pardon. My manners appear to have deserted me."

Kendra kept quiet until they were out of the card room, and joined the continuing parade of strollers. "What can you tell me about the autopsy, doctor?" she asked, keeping her voice low.

Dr. Poole glared at her. "Of course, you would ask me that! Have you no sense of propriety, Miss Donovan?

"No, nor privacy, either, if you don't keep your voice down," she warned him, and steered him toward the corner where she and Mrs. Hearnshaw had recently conversed.

"What does it matter to you, eh?" Still, he lowered his voice. "You appear to have no delicate sensibilities whatsoever for a member of the fairer sex."

"You're right, doctor. I have none. But that doesn't mean I want everyone in this room to know the details of the crime." Now that they were standing in the corner, she dropped her hand from his arm and matched his glare. "And if you had let me attend the autopsy as I wanted, we wouldn't be having this conversation and you could be playing cards right this minute."

He simply stared at her. Kendra was no stranger to being stared at by a hostile witness. She fixed him with her gaze, refusing to back off.

He grunted, the fuzzy brows twitching. "You are an unnatural maid," he finally said, shaking his head. "What do you want to know, pray tell?"

"Mrs. Trout. Based on the position of her body, I would say that she let the killer inside the house, and he was following her when he cut her throat. Can you confirm that?"

"Aye. The monster wielded the knife from left to right, slicing open her carotid arteries, the jugular vein." He looked at her expectantly, as though waiting for her to express horror. Or swoon.

"Left to right. Our killer is right handed—if he was standing behind her."

"He *was* standing behind her. The position and curve of the wound prove this."

Kendra had suspected as much based on her initial examination, but she wanted it confirmed by an M.E. Of course, she'd have been more confident in Dr. Munroe's analysis, but she couldn't disregard what Dr. Poole was saying. "That's consistent with my findings," she said slowly. "The blood spray would have been outward; he would have been protected from any contamination from her body, and gotten very little, if any at all, on himself."

"Possibly," Poole agreed reluctantly.

"Were there any other findings with the housekeeper?" she asked.

Kendra doubted there would be much more. The woman's murder had been brutal and efficient. As she'd told the Duke, Sam, and Alec, Mrs. Trout had collapsed the minute the unsub released his hold. Massive amounts of blood would have been spurting out with each pump of her heart. She would have died shortly after hitting the floor."

Poole eyed her like she was crazy Aunt Hilda escaped from the attic. "Such as?"

Kendra shrugged. "I was just asking."

"'Tis a morbid curiosity of yours, Miss Donovan. Little wonder you are a spinster."

"It's my cross to bear," she agreed with a smile.

His eyes narrowed. "How does any of this help determine the fiend who committed the atrocity?"

"We've learned two things by Mrs. Trout's murder alone, Dr. Poole," Kendra said quietly. "We now know the killer is right-handed. I'd already determined that Mrs. Trout wasn't afraid of him. She let him in and didn't run from him. She walked ahead of him while he followed her into the kitchen. The fact that he came to the back door—not the front—and she brought him into the kitchen rather than the drawing room might be significant." *And possibly points at Turner over Bancroft*, she thought.

Dr. Poole said nothing for a moment, then his lips twisted. "You think you're a clever female, don't you, Miss Donovan?"

"Well, it's better than the alternative."

He grunted. "Figuring the fiend is right-handed ain't exactly clever, Miss Donovan. Mothers bind their babe's left hand as soon as the child shows tendencies toward left-handedness. A few folks around these parts still think it's a mark of the devil to be left-handed, you know."

Kendra frowned at this, and Dr. Poole gave a nasty smile. "So you'd be hard-pressed to find a left-handed killer in these parts, miss. As to what you already *determined* . . . ain't nothing to that either. Mrs. Trout was an uncommon housekeeper. I've been to the Stone residence on occasion myself, and know—*knew*—her queer ways. I have no doubt Mrs. Trout would have thought nothing of someone coming to the back door—peer or pauper—and would have shown him into the kitchen."

He wasn't telling her anything she didn't already know, except that left-handedness was the mark of the devil. "What about Mrs. Stone?" she asked. "What were your findings there?"

Dr. Poole's face sank into his habitually grumpy expression, although he appeared even more grim. "What that woman endured was beyond human. As you know, she was tortured by the monster pressing the hot fire poker against her flesh. After he was finished, the fiend went behind her chair to slit her throat, in much the same way he did the housekeeper's. I'd say he didn't want to be walking around with her blood on him. I guess that we've learned something about the killer, eh?"

Kendra knew a set up when she saw one, but she asked anyway. "And what is that, doctor?"

"The fiend ain't no pudding-headed fellow."

"No, he's not."

Dr. Poole regarded her from beneath his fuzzy brows. "We've finally reached a point of agreement, Miss Donovan."

27

While most of the villagers attended the assembly, Sam ambled up to the tap at the Ploughman, a tavern on the west side of East Dingleford that he had been directed to by the stable hands at the Green Maiden. He positioned himself at the end of the scarred wooden counter, which allowed him to keep his back against the smoke-streaked stone wall, and scanned the rest of the room. The space formed by the walls and the low, beamed ceiling could either be cozy or claustrophobic, Sam thought. At the moment, with a fire crackling in the blackened hearth and only seven men in the room, it was cozy.

Sam allowed his gaze to drift over his fellow patrons as he ordered a hot whisky from the rosy-cheeked, generously endowed lass behind the bar. Workmen, he deduced, with their rough, homespun clothes. Two were standing at the tap like himself, in the middle of a heated conversation about King George's failing health and whether the Prince Regent would destroy the monarchy with his lavish spending and hedonistic ways. Four more men were gathered around a table, smoking and playing cards. One man, still bundled in coat, hat, and scarf, was sitting alone at a table in one of the tavern's shadowy corners, his hands wrapped around a pewter tankard.

Sam could hear the rumble of men's voices from the other side of the back door, a few shouts, curses, and whistles punctuating the general noise. The Ploughman, he'd learned, ran a cockfighting match on a regular basis, which was popular with its clientele.

"Ah, bless you, lass." He smiled at the barmaid as she brought him the hot whisky. He tossed down a coin and picked up the glass, immediately appreciating the warmth seeping into his fingertips.

"Ye're the thief-taker brought in from London," she said, snatching up the coin.

Sam took a swallow of whisky, enjoying the smooth burn down his throat, then lowered the glass with a sigh. He was aware that the two men standing along the bar had fallen silent at the barmaid's identification and were now regarding him with hooded, suspicious eyes. There were times in the past when the Crown had employed Runners such as himself to slip into taverns exactly like the Ploughman to listen to disgruntled men argue about what was happening in the kingdom. He'd felt like a wraith, because his mission hadn't been to engage or even quiz anyone, but to report back to Whitehall if he heard anything that went beyond dissatisfaction. No one had known that he was a Bow Street man. He hadn't even brought his famous gold-tipped baton, for fear if he did stumble onto any plots, his bag could be searched and he'd be found out.

He wished now for the anonymity of those assignments. One could pick up all sorts of useful tidbits by staying hidden. But tongues had clearly been wagging here in East Dingleford, where even a barmaid in a small, out-of-the-way tavern knew that the Duke had requested his services.

Sam regarded her ruefully. "I'm from Bow Street," he admitted. He'd always disliked being called a thief-taker, which reminded him of Bow Street's past corruption, where men who carried the baton had been found to be working with the criminal element. Sam liked to think that such unscrupulous behavior had been rooted out, but he feared that a few of his colleagues might be lining their own pockets by continuing the practice. "How'd you know?"

"T'aint difficult, sir. Everyone in the village knew the Duke had sent for ye. And ye were at the Stone household askin' questions. Ye match the description goin' about." She picked up a nearby rag and began scrubbing the counter, an action that sent her ample breasts bouncing.

Sam eyed the movement appreciatively, then locked on the two men standing against the bar. One was large, with a moon-face beneath a dirty knit cap, while the other was shorter and wiry, with facial whiskers that made him look like a drowned rat. They both stared at him with barely suppressed hostility.

"Do you two work at the mill?" he asked.

The rat-faced man's lip curled. "And why should we be tellin' ye our business?"

"The way I see it, you've got a monster runnin' about killing innocent folk. I'd think you'd sleep safer in your beds if the monster was caught."

The big man grunted. "Oi sleep well enough—probably better with Stone dead. He wasn't innocent."

"Aye," his friend said. "'E was a sneaky bastard."

Sam gestured to the barmaid to fill up the men's tankards, then said, "I heard that he'd dismissed workers ter bring in those new machines." He lifted his whisky with studied ease. He'd learned a long time ago that one of the best way to get certain folks talking in taverns was to pretend to have little interest in what they were saying. He kept his eyes on his whisky glass, as though contemplating the quality of the amber liquid. "Still, can't blame *him*, specific-like. He was only the manager. It's his lordship's decision ter bring in the damn frames, ain't it?"

The moon-faced man said, "Ain't just that—although the earl's one for the future, that's for certain. Did ye know that 'e put in gas lightin' at Falcon Court? Mark me words, 'e's gonna have 'is own Guy Fawkes Night when 'e blows 'is old 'ouse up!"

Sam understood the man's fear, even though in London Town, Pall Mall had boasted gas lighting for eight years without incident. "What do you mean, it ain't just about the machines? What else is there?"

"It ain't only about the *new* machines," clarified Moon-face. "We used ter 'ave guards on the old machinery, so as ter keep us from losin' a finger or a limb. Mr. Murray insisted on it, as well as water buckets in the carding room in case of fire."

"Aye," the other man piped up, his eyes narrowing in his anger. "When the guards fell off, we told Mr. Biddle. But did Mr. Stone buy any replacements? Nay! Mr. Biddle said that Mr. Stone complained about the cost. W'ot about the cost of *this*?"

He lifted his right hand, and Sam saw that the man's index finger had been shorn off, leaving only a nub below his knuckle. "Little Nellie lost three of 'er fingers," he went on bitterly. "If she loses another on the same 'and, she won't be able ter card anymore. She'll be done at the mill and off ter the poorhouse!"

"Did you take your concerns ter Lord Bancroft himself?" asked Sam.

Moon-face snorted. "W'ot's gentry gonna care about our lot, eh? The mill is fallin' apart, it is, and the earl's solution is ter bring in new machines. Even the quality of the cotton they're bringin' in has declined in the last couple of years. Oi swear the yarns break more, and create more of that damn dust. Stone was cuttin' corners all around the mill. Mr. Thackeray confronted him about it at the Green Maiden last week, an' Stone acted all outraged. Like 'e was the wronged one! Bah!"

"Sounds like plenty of folks would want Mr. Stone dead," Sam said carefully. "Who is Mr. Thackeray?"

The two men eyed him warily. "Thackeray worked at the mill 'til Stone fired 'im a couple of years ago for speakin' up," Moon-face finally said. "'Is sister's 'usband owns the Green Maiden."

Sam raised his eyebrows. "Mrs. Bolton?"

"Aye." The man's face tightened with defiance. "Anyhow, everyone wanted Stone dead. But none of us did the deed."

Sam tapped the rim of his whisky glass, signaling the barmaid to fill it up again. "I believe you."

Instead of looking relieved, the two men's scowls deepened with distrust.

"Why?" Rat-face demanded, his eyes narrowing on Sam as though he sensed a trap. "Why'd ye believe us so quick-like?"

The barmaid brought Sam another hot whisky, and he took a moment to sip it before he responded. "In truth, I can see you wantin' ter brain Mr. Stone. But I don't see why you'd want ter kill Mrs. Stone, or her housekeeper." He let that sink in for a moment. Then he turned to fix his gaze on the men. "Who do you think killed the women?"

Moon-faced shook his head. "Gotta be a madman."

"Do you know where I can find Paddy, the Stones' groom?" Sam asked.

The barmaid spoke up. "Paddy won't be able ter tell ye anythin'. He's been on a drunk fer the past week. Probably dunno even that 'is mistress done cocked up 'er toes."

"But he knows about his master."

She laughed. "Everyone's 'eard about Stone! Paddy was probably celebratin' with the rest of the clodhoppers in the Red Sail. If ye want ter find him, he's probably in Mistress Dolly's bed. She owns that place."

Sam hesitated. "Anybody hear any rumors about Stone havin' hold of something valuable?"

"Like w'ot?" asked Rat-face.

"I don't know."

They shook their heads.

The back door suddenly burst open, and men of all ages poured into the tavern, their faces flushed from the chilly night and steady drinking. Sam watched them, easily separating the winners from the losers. The winners were rowdier, still puffed up from their success in betting over the cockpits, while the losers slunk into available chairs, hoping to drown their sorrows in another pint, or vanished out the door, scowling. The barmaid scurried over to the winners, obviously hoping they would share their generosity.

Sam shifted his gaze back to the two men. He was about to repeat his question when Moon-face anticipated him, and shook his head. "We don't know anything, and can't imagine why anyone would do such a dastardly thing ter his wife. Stone deserves ter be dinin' with the devil, but Mrs. Stone . . . she was a fine beauty, and didn't put on airs. No reason ter kill her. Or her maid. Doesn't make any sense."

Sam nodded. It didn't seem to make sense. Except it had made sense to someone.

28

Exhaustion settled like a weight on Alec's shoulders as he undressed himself in his bedchamber later that evening. He made use of the low washstand in the corner, wincing slightly as he bent forward, reminded that he'd spent more than fifteen hours in the saddle. The hot bath he'd soaked in earlier had eased much of his discomfort, but now, as the plain wooden clock on the fireplace mantel ticked past midnight, the aches and pains associated with hard riding were making themselves known again. Mrs. Bolton—God bless the woman—had the foresight to leave a decanter on the small table before the snapping fire.

He straightened, and toweled off beads of moisture that clung to his skin from the sponge bath. Tossing the towel aside, he moved to the bed and rummaged through his open satchel, pulling out the banyan that his valet had packed for his hasty journey to Yorkshire. He shrugged into the black silk robe, tying the belt as he crossed the room to the decanter. The fumes of apricot brandy assailed him as soon as he unplugged the stopper, and he smiled appreciatively. He splashed brandy into a glass. Instead of taking a sip, though, he swirled the glass, and watched the brandy spin, the reflection of glinting flames in the amber liquid.

By all rights, he should be crawling into bed. Hell, he should be deep in slumber. But despite the fatigue that wrapped around him like phantom vines, he was strangely on edge.

He would have liked to have attributed his tension to the moment the rider had handed him his uncle's letter. His heart really hadn't settled since he'd broken the seal and read the contents. The hours after that were a blur, with him and Sam riding hell for leather across the countryside. *And bollocks to all that.* But there was only one reason for his restlessness, and that was the woman in the bedchamber down the hall. Did he dare go to her?

Alec lifted the glass to his lips, and sipped the brandy as he contemplated taking such a foolish risk. This was not Aldridge Castle, where the servants may disapprove, but their loyalty to the Duke had them turning a blind eye on their suspicions. This was a public inn. There would be serious consequences if he were discovered coming out of Kendra's bedchamber early in the morning.

He knew well enough that Kendra would dismiss his concerns. He was quite familiar with her condescension regarding the rules that governed Polite society—governed *his* Polite society. *As though* her *world is so bloody superior,* he thought with sudden irritation. Because of her disdain, she was careless with her reputation. He raised his glass, his annoyance growing. More than careless; she was bloody defiant.

He took a healthy swallow of brandy, then, lowering the glass, let out a frustrated sigh. Damnation, Kendra had no idea what would be unleashed if their liaison was ever exposed. She was an unmarried miss, not a married lady or widow who could embark on discreet dalliances. The Duke of Aldridge's position and wealth had shielded her from vicious tongues regarding her peculiar behavior, but even his uncle couldn't save her if the old biddies that controlled the upper circles of the Ton should learn of their affair.

He could only imagine the Duke's wrath if that should happen. Society would place Kendra's ruin directly on her own shoulders, but his uncle would blame him. The Duke would no doubt remind him that Kendra had been raised to a different set of standards, but Alec had not. He *knew* what was expected of him by society.

Alec rolled his shoulders to loosen the tension knotting his muscles. Fiend seize it, why hadn't she accepted his offer of marriage like any normal woman? If she had, they wouldn't be in this predicament, forced to sneak around like thieves in the night to steal a moment here and there. He would have a husband's right to his wife's bed. There would be no fear of encountering servants on their nocturnal rounds or fellow travelers seeking their bed for the night, no fear of having the woman he loved treated like an outcast, noble houses barred to her, shunned by society.

Of course, he couldn't go to her, he knew. *Not here.* She had too much to lose. If she didn't protect herself, he would bloody well protect her *from* herself. Decision made, he raised his glass again, and drained the brandy. He set the glass down, and strode toward the bed.

Kendra glanced over as the door opened. Shadow and firelight played across the bedchamber's walls. Excitement knotted her stomach as she sat up, her gaze meeting Alec's.

"You didn't bar the door." His voice was low and raspy as he came to her.

"No . . ." She didn't think she had to tell him that she'd been expecting him; she was already feeling too vulnerable.

Impatient, she rolled onto her knees on the feather mattress, which brought her eye-level with him. His pupils were dilated, and she could see the pale cameo of her own reflection as she leaned forward, sliding her hands inside his robe to stroke his chest. He brought his hands up to frame her face, much as he'd done earlier.

"I only have one question," she whispered, and her hands slid upward to curl around his neck. She kept her eyes fixed on his as she shifted closer until she thought Alec's body heat would set fire to the thin cotton nightgown she was wearing. She smiled when he arched a dark brow.

"What took you so long?"

"This is dangerous," Alec murmured. "I should not have come."

Kendra didn't want to talk, especially if it was about fear or regret. She wanted to burrow against his side, her head on his chest, and listen to the strong, steady thump of his heart. She wanted to continue to breathe in his scent. She wanted to enjoy the way his fingers threaded through her hair, gliding in a butterfly caress around her ear, along her jawline and down the curve of her neck. If she had been a cat, she'd be purring.

"I told myself to stay away," he continued.

She kept her tone light. "I'm not complaining, you know."

"Kendra . . ."

"If you start talking about my reputation, you'll be killing the mood, fast."

Alec was silent for a long moment. "Shall we speak about you accepting my proposal instead?" he finally asked.

Kendra sighed. "Okay, now you *have* killed the mood."

He shifted so he could look into her eyes. "I love you."

Kendra's heart leaped into her throat. She should have been getting used to the words by now, but they still came as a shock. Who had ever loved her? Certainly, not her parents, only concerned with how well she'd score on the next test. Love didn't belong in the laboratory. How could she trust such a nebulous emotion?

"What do you want from me, Alec?"

"I want what most men want—to have the woman I love return my affection. To marry her, so as to not to hide or sneak around. Did I tell you that you looked beautiful tonight?"

Kendra frowned at the non sequitur. "I'm not looking for compliments, Alec."

He ignored that, skimming one long finger down her throat. "Still . . . I would have wished to give you my mother's jewels to complement your beauty."

"I'm not looking for jewelry either."

"I realize that. My point is that I am not free to give you my mother's jewels, or any other jewelry, because it would announce our relationship to the nasty gossips of the world. You would be viewed as my mistress—"

"I'm not your mistress," she cut him off, jaw tightening. "You are *not* keeping me. We're equal partners in this relationship."

"We would be equal partners in marriage."

Kendra gave him a wry look. "One thing that I've learned about this era is there is no such thing, at least not in England. Married women are property. Husbands control their wives' lives, their fortunes, their bodies, everything."

"You don't have a fortune to control."

"Thank you so much for reminding me," she snapped. But he was right. Alec might not be keeping her, but the Duke was. Everything she had was because of the Duke's generosity. She released a frustrated sigh. "I've always made my own money and controlled my own destiny, since I was fourteen. I don't want an allowance from the Duke, to know that everything that I have in this world is because he allows it."

Alec frowned. "Duke does not begrudge taking care of you, Kendra. He is not a cheeseparing man. In fact, I'm certain he has already considered settling a portion on you to ensure that you are not left penniless."

"That's not the point!" Kendra struggled to keep her voice low even as her stomach twisted in frustration. How could she explain to Alec, or anyone here, how important it was to have financial control over her own future?

She rolled onto her back and stared at the swaying shadows on the ceiling. Outside, the wind had picked up, making the trees creak and rattling the windowpanes. They should be cuddling or making love. Instead, Kendra was contemplating how money meant freedom, the one constant that held true, regardless of time and place. She broke out in a cold sweat when she remembered her parents' abandonment. She'd had a trust fund to ensure her education, but it had taken her a while to find her footing. A professor had hired her to help code a computer program. The money hadn't been much, only a couple hundred dollars. But it had come with the realization that she had the skills to take care of herself. It meant that she didn't need anyone. And now, as long as she lived here—in the *upper*-class world—that basic desire would always be denied her.

She sighed. "I want to earn my own money," she said. "I want to pay for my own dresses and food . . ."

She realized belatedly that she was talking as if she was staying here, as if she'd given up hope of going home.

"There's no need—"

"And what if I had the opportunity to return home?" she asked suddenly, turning to stare into his eyes. "What then, Alec?"

He shook his head. "It's a false hope, sweet."

"You don't know that."

He swung his long legs out of the bed and pushed himself to his feet.

"I can't just give up," she said softly, scooting up into a sitting position. She clutched the blankets against her breasts, and tried not to get distracted by the way his sleek muscles rippled in the firelight as he walked, naked, across the room. "You know I don't belong here, Alec."

"But you *are* here. Mayhap you ought to reconcile yourself to the possibility of staying." He shrugged on his robe, tying the belt with obvious irritability.

Kendra sighed and scrambled out of bed, dragging the sheet with her to stand before him. "If the opportunity presented itself for me to go home—"

"Sweetheart . . ."

"—would you come with me?"

"*What*?" His head jerked up and he stared at her.

"Would you come back to the twenty-first century with me?"

He raked his fingers through his hair, agitated. "Why are we discussing a hypothetical?"

She had to smile, but it was without humor. "First lesson in behavioral science: avoid a question by asking another question."

"I'm not avoiding your question. I simply see no point in having a discussion about something that has little chance of happening." He came toward her, sliding his arms around her waist. He leaned in and nuzzled her ear. "I love you."

"Second lesson: avoid the question by distraction," she murmured, but leaned into him, turning her head to meet his lips. She could feel her temper slip away.

He drew back slightly to peer down at her. His spiky lashes veiled his eyes, but Kendra thought she caught the gleam of humor. "Is it working?"

She grinned up at him and put her palms on his chest. "Hell, no. I'm a trained agent in the FBI."

He yanked her against him, kissing her hard. Without breaking the embrace, he walked her backward until her legs hit the bed, and she fell on the feather mattress. Alec followed, trailing biting kisses down her throat.

"Okay . . ." She was beginning to sound breathless. "Maybe now it's working."

The fire had almost died out by the time Alec left the bed for the second time. Kendra watched him through lowered lashes, careful to keep her breathing modulated as though she were still sleeping. He put on his robe and then kneeled down, adding another log and spending the next few minutes building up the fire again. When he stood up, she hurriedly closed her eyes. She heard the light slither of the silk robe, and knew he'd turned to look at her. Her skin prickled with awareness, but she continued her ruse. The moments stretched on endlessly. She was on the verge of giving up her pretense when she sensed him turning away from her toward the door.

"Is the third lesson on avoidance to pretend that one is asleep?" he asked, a thread of laughter in his voice. "Lock the door, my love."

Kendra opened her eyes, but he was already gone. Releasing a sigh, she turned and pressed her face into the pillow. Alec's scent clung to the fabric.

She'd always prided herself on being logical. But there was nothing logical about her relationship with Alec. Even if she factored in love, the negatives far outweighed the positives in that emotion. If she allowed herself to be persuaded into a marriage with Alec, how long would it be before he woke up one morning and realized he'd made a mistake? How long before he looked across the ballroom and saw a lady—a *real* lady—more ideally suited to be his wife? To be a marchioness . . . a future duchess?

She would always be a freak—in her own time, in this time. How long before Alec realized that and abandoned her?

And then what would she do?

29

The next morning, Kendra pushed aside her personal anxiety to focus on the investigation. They gathered around a buffet of salted kippers, stewed tomatoes, scrambled eggs, black pudding, mushrooms, and toast points. The grisly topic of murder never put off her nineteenth-century counterparts from their meal, she noticed. As her gaze drifted to her own plate, filled with everything except the black pudding—pork blood boiled with fat and oats and made into a sausage would never be appealing to her—Kendra reflected with some amusement that her appetite wasn't affected either. She was famished.

"I found the Stones' groom, but he didn't know anything," Sam informed them, lifting a tankard of ale and taking a swallow. "I also learned the name of the mill where Mr. Murray is employed, and thought ter ride to Manchester today."

The Duke looked at the Bow Street Runner as he reached over to splash cream into his empty teacup. "What information do you think to gain from the mill manager? He has been gone from East Dingleford for more than twenty years."

"Lord Bancroft said that Mr. Murray was the one who recommended Mr. Stone for the position at his mill," Kendra supplied. "He's the only one who may know of Stone's background."

"You're still hoping to find a link between Lord Bancroft and Mr. Stone before he became the mill manager," the Duke speculated, lifting the silver teapot and pouring the strong China blend into his cup.

"It's not a matter of hope. It's a matter of following threads and tying them off. Same reason I want to speak to Biddle again." She sipped her coffee. "He failed to mention that he was at the card game where Turner accused Stone of cheating."

Sam looked at her. "Why do you think that is?"

"I'm not sure. It could mean nothing. Or he might be trying to distance himself from the investigation. Or he might be hiding something."

"You know, there's another possibility why Lord Bancroft didn't dismiss Mr. Stone," said Sam, circling back to the earlier point. "He could have discovered somethin' about his lordship *after* he began his position at the mill, rather than a previous acquaintance."

Kendra thought about that, and nodded. "You're right, Mr. Kelly. But we'd still be dealing with blackmail, something Stone held over the earl's head. Maybe Mr. Murray will be able to shed some light on it. He worked for Bancroft for six years."

"Aye," Sam said. "Mr. Murray may have as much to say about the character of his lordship as he does about Mr. Stone."

"What about the seven mill workers who were recently dismissed?" asked the Duke.

"The constable said he spoke ter them, and their whereabouts are accounted for," Sam said. "He gave me the list, if you want me ter follow up with them as well."

"I don't think that's necessary," Kendra said. "They were never a high priority. The crime scene puts our unsub in a position behind Stone. Would you allow a disgruntled worker to stand behind you?"

"Nay." Sam shook his head. "You'd want ter keep your peepers on them."

"Exactly," Kendra said. "I also don't see why any employee—former or not—would have murdered Mrs. Stone and Mrs. Trout."

"I talked ter a couple of workers last night," Sam said slowly. "They're not jest angry about the dismissal of workers and new frames. They had plenty of complaints on how the mill's fallin' apart with shoddy equipment, and how they've been bringing in cheaper cotton—which, they say, is causin' more lung infections."

Alec leaned back in his chair, regarding the Bow Street Runner. "Is that Mr. Stone's fault, or Lord Bancroft's?"

"Aye, that's what I asked. They said they brought their complaints ter Mr. Biddle, and Mr. Biddle took them ter Stone. They seemed ter think Mr. Stone might not have even told his lordship." Sam stabbed a plump mushroom with his knife and popped it in his mouth. "With Mr. Stone gone, maybe Mr. Biddle will be able ter help the folks. Assuming his lordship promotes him ter manager."

They were quiet for a moment as they ate their breakfast.

Five minutes later, the Duke set down his knife and fork. "I think we mustn't forget about what was on the desk that the killer took."

"I'm not forgetting it," said Kendra. "It may have been the trigger." She glanced at the clock, and set down her coffee cup. "But right now, I need to interview Mrs. Turner. Maybe without her husband around, she'll tell us where Turner really was on Friday night."

Alec borrowed a cart and horse from Mr. Bolton to drive her to the Turner farm. But when they were near, she ordered him to drop her off so she could walk the rest of the way herself. Abused women like Mrs. Turner tended to be skittish, especially around strange men. She was already anticipating an interview process that would need a delicate touch; she didn't want to throw up any more obstacles than necessary.

As she approached the house, she thought that the farm looked the same as the other day. The chickens were pecking outside the sagging barn—one fewer than the day before.

The day was cool, but the sun was out. By the time she walked the distance to the house and knocked on the door, Kendra felt sweaty beneath the velvet pelisse and blue-and-white paisley walking dress. She waited. She knocked again, and listened. She imagined that she could hear breathing on the other side of the door.

"Mrs. Turner," she called out, and knocked again. "It's Kendra Donovan. We met the other day. The Duke of Aldridge is . . . is my guardian." Christ, she was twenty-six years old—it felt stupid to call the Duke her guardian. "Mrs. T—"

The door swung in so suddenly, she stumbled back in surprise.

Mrs. Turner clutched at the door, her aquamarine eyes anxious as she stared at Kendra. "Ye shouldn't be here."

Kendra studied the other woman's delicate face. The bruise had faded from purple into bluish green. She was wearing a mop cap and the same faded dress as the other day, beneath an apron dusted with flour.

"My husband—" Mrs. Turner tried.

"Is at the market. I know. That's why I'm here. I need to talk to you."

Mrs. Turner shook her head frantically. "Nay! He'll be displeased. He doesn't like it when I have visitors. A-and I have me chores ter do." She began closing the door, but Kendra stepped forward, wedging her foot and part of her leg between the door and the frame.

"Please, Mrs. Turner." She fixed her gaze on the other woman's. "I need to talk to you. This is important."

"I don't have anythin' ter say."

Kendra knew that she could easily push her way inside the house, but that wasn't the way to do it. Force was what Mrs. Turner was used to. Deliberately, she let go of the door and stepped back. "I think you have more to say than you realize, Mrs. Turner," she said quietly. "*Please.*"

Mrs. Turner said nothing. Kendra took it as a good sign that she hadn't slammed the door shut on her. Yet.

"This will be a private conversation—just between you and me," she promised, keeping her voice low and even, like she was approaching a wild animal caught in a trap. "What's your name?" Mrs. Turner frowned, puzzled, and Kendra clarified, "Your first name?" Familiarity was important to coaxing someone to let down their guard. "Call me Kendra."

Something flickered behind the aquamarine eyes. "Flora," Mrs. Turner finally whispered.

Kendra forced a smile. "Flora. That's a pretty name."

Flora said nothing. There was only the guarded look of someone trapped.

"I need to speak to you. Can I come in? Three people are dead, Flora—"

"Three?"

Kendra stared at her. "You didn't know?"

Flora shook her head.

"Mrs. Stone and her housekeeper were killed," Kendra said.

Flora's hand went to her throat. "Dear heaven. How?"

"May I come in?"

Flora hesitated, then stepped back from the door. "I still have ter do me chores," she said. "Mr. Turner could be back any moment."

"Thank you."

Kendra followed Flora inside. The door opened into a roomy kitchen. Sunlight streamed through the two windows, over whitewashed walls and oak cupboards that held a variety of bowls filled with onions, potatoes, and turnips. Kendra noticed a wooden bucket with a washboard sticking out of the grayish water near the stone fireplace. A man's smock shirt was spread out in front of the hearth to dry. A cast iron stove, much smaller than the one at Aldridge Castle or even the Green Maiden, was against one wall. It tilted slightly to one side, which Kendra attributed to a missing leg. Someone had shoved a stone in its place. A pot was on one of the burners. Kendra could smell cinnamon cloves, apples, and something spicy.

Flora hurried over to the sturdy oak table in the center of the room, which dominated the space. The surface was already dusted with flour and held a rolling pin, a large earthenware bowl filled with flour and what appeared to be two slabs of lard—Kendra recognized the thick, whitish substance from her time working in Aldridge Castle kitchens—and two other smaller containers with lids. Now Mrs. Turner lifted one of the lids to reveal either salt or sugar. She took a pinch and tossed it in with the flour and lard.

Kendra asked, "Was your husband at home between three and six last Friday afternoon, Flora?"

The other woman hesitated, then busied herself by rolling up her sleeves. Kendra saw again the bruises circling the other woman's wrist, before she plunged her hands into the flour and lard mixture, kneading it. "Nay." Her eyes were locked on her hands in bowl. "He left early . . . He didn't return until the next morning."

"Where did he go? Do you know?"

Another hesitation. Then Flora shook her head. "I thought the fog kept him away."

"Okay. Tell me about Sunday, Flora. What did you and your husband do?"

Flora finally lifted her eyes to look at Kendra. She didn't stop her movement, continuing to work the flour into the lard. "'Twas the Sabbath. We went ter church in the morning."

"And after church? What did you do?"

"There's always chores ter do on a farm, Miss Donovan." Her mouth twisted.

"Oh, I'm sure *you* always have chores," Kendra said, and couldn't quite keep the bite out of her voice. "But what about your husband?"

"My husband works very hard!"

"Yet he still manages to attend assemblies, doesn't he? Did he bring you with him the night last spring when he played cards against Mr. Stone, and lost?"

Flora dropped her gaze to the paste forming beneath her deft fingers. "Nay, I wasn't there," she finally said.

"How much did your husband lose to Stone, Flora?"

She didn't answer.

"What arrangement did your husband make to pay Stone back?"

A shadow rippled over the woman's delicate features. She kept her eyes down, her fingers still busy kneading the dough though she was probably finished with the task. "'Tis my husband's business."

"Okay, Sunday," Kendra said, circling back. "Where were you, Flora? What did you spend your day doing?"

"I told you. I was here, doin' chores. My husband is a particular man."

Kendra's gaze traveled around the kitchen. The stove was ancient, the cupboards and wood floor worn. But Mrs. Turner's domain was clean and tidy. Kendra's mouth tightened as she thought about the sagging barn and derelict outbuildings. While his wife was breaking her back scrubbing inside the house, what the hell was Turner doing?

"Where was your husband, Flora?"

Flora bit a trembling lip and Kendra began to feel like she was kicking a small kitten.

She sighed. "Flora, I promise this will go no further. I just want the truth."

Flora nodded. "H-he was here until the afternoon. I fear I displeased him. I can be very foolish, ye see, not keepin' a civil tongue in my head."

Kendra clenched her jaw to tamp down the fury racing through her veins. "When did your husband return?"

Flora shook her head. "I don't know. I was asleep when he came ter bed."

Kendra watched Flora skillfully separate the paste into two balls, dusting them with flour before reaching for the rolling pin. "You didn't speak to him at all?" she asked.

"Nay." Flora flattened the dough into two thin spheres. She set aside the rolling pin, and retrieved a tin pie plate from the cupboard.

"What was your husband's mood like yesterday morning?" Kendra asked.

Flora focused on scooping up lard and smearing the plate. Kendra could almost feel her arteries clogging up as she eyed the thick grease.

"Same as always, I reckon," the other woman murmured.

"What does that mean?" Kendra asked, though she was pretty sure she knew. Sullen. Pissed off at the world, at his wife. What other mood was there for a man like Turner?

"Angry," Flora whispered. She kept her eyes on her hands, as they pressed the dough into the pie tin. "He's always angry." Her eyes flicked to the small clock on the cupboard near the stove. She swallowed, and her expression turned apprehensive. "Ye need ter go, Miss Donovan. I've told ye everythin', I swear. My husband will be most displeased ter see ye. He doesn't abide folks stopping by."

"I'll bet he doesn't."

"Pardon?"

"Nothing. Thank you for your time, Flora." Kendra moved to the door. She opened it, but hesitated, looking back at the other woman. "Flora—"

The other woman was already shaking her head. "*Please.* I've told ye everything, Miss Donovan. I—I need ter finish this mincemeat pie and clean the pots before my husband returns. He doesn't like ter see dirty pots. Please, ye must leave."

Kendra nodded, and was almost out the door when Flora's words penetrated. Shock made her dig her fingers into the doorframe. She could feel her pulse leap into her throat as she stood there, staring out at the yard, where the chickens were poking the ground, searching for a stray seed. Kendra turned, surveying the kitchen with new eyes. Her gaze roamed over the potatoes and turnips on the counter again.

"W'ot is it?" Flora asked, worried.

Her gaze locked on Flora as Dr. Poole's words ran through her head. *The last thing Mr. Stone ate was chicken, potatoes and mincemeat pie. Holy shit.*

"Tell me, Flora," she said slowly, "why was Mr. Stone out here last Friday? What was he doing on this farm just hours before he was murdered?"

The blood drained out of Flora's face, leaving it the color of ash. For just a second, Kendra was afraid the other woman was about to faint. Flora reached out a trembling hand, clutching the table to steady herself. She licked her lips nervously. "Pardon?"

Any doubt that Kendra might have had vanished as she observed Flora's reaction. "Mr. Stone was here, in this kitchen, before he was murdered," Kendra repeated, keeping her tone neutral with an effort.

"N-nay. Ye're mistaken, Miss Donovan—"

"Please don't lie, Flora. He was here, and you fed him chicken, potatoes, and mincemeat pie."

Flora's lips parted in surprise. "How do ye know such a thing?"

Kendra waved that away. "What was Mr. Stone doing here? Did he speak to your husband?"

"My husband didn't murder Mr. Stone. Or . . . or anyone else. He's a good man."

"Good men don't beat their wives," she said bluntly.

Flora's hand went to the bruise on her cheek, an automatic gesture, as though she could conceal the wound and stop this conversation. "Ye don't understand," she whispered.

Kendra's jaw tightened. She was having a difficult time concealing her anger, and heard it seeping into her voice. "I understand that you deserve better. Where's your family, Flora? Do they live nearby?"

"Nay. They live in a hamlet in Cheshire."

"Maybe you should go to them."

Flora frowned. "Why would I do such a thing?"

"Your husband isn't going to quit beating you, Flora. You need to leave him."

"And ye think I can go ter me family?" The other woman's eyes widened. "They don't have enough food for their bellies. I was the oldest. Papa was grateful William took me off their hands when he came through our village."

"But they can't know that your husband is abusing you."

Flora gave a quick, bitter laugh. "Papa was never one ter go light on beatings, either, Miss Donovan. Nay, if I returned, he'd beat me for sure for disobeyin' my husband. I'm a married woman. 'Tis me duty ter submit ter William. It says so in the Bible."

"I think it also says that a husband is to treat his wife like she is his own flesh. Unless your husband is a masochist, I doubt that's happening."

"A mass-o . . . w'ot?"

"Never mind. Is there some other place you can go?" Kendra wasn't sure why she persisted. Even in her world, with the crisis hotlines and shelters, it was estimated that anywhere from a quarter to a third of all abused women stayed with the partner who was mistreating them.

Flora shook her head. "I have no money, Miss Donovan. I—I have no skills. I'm only a woman."

"You know how to cook. You obviously have domestic skills." Kendra's gaze traveled around the kitchen, with the washing in the corner and the scrubbed counters and floors. It wasn't lost on Kendra that Flora actually had more valuable skills for this time period than she did herself. "Maybe you could seek employment as a housekeeper, or a cook."

"I can't leave my husband, Miss Donovan. It wouldn't be right." Flora grabbed a rag as an oven mitt, and picked up the pot, transferring it to the table. She took a spoon, and began ladling the mixture into the piecrust.

Kendra couldn't shake the sensation that she was looking at a dead woman. Abusers didn't stop, and the abuse usually escalated until the woman ended up dead. And there was nothing Kendra could do to save her.

She pinched the bridge of her nose in frustration, then sighed. "Let's go back to my earlier question. Why was Mr. Stone having a meal at your table hours before he was murdered at the mill? What did your husband speak to him about?"

"I told ye, Mr. Turner wasn't here," whispered Flora. She kept her gaze on her task. "He . . . he left early in the mornin', before Mr. Stone came."

Kendra frowned, studying the other woman's averted face. Suddenly she thought of Mrs. Hooper and went cold. "Did Mr. Stone know that your husband would be gone?" she asked carefully.

Flora put the spoon aside, eyes downcast, and said nothing.

"Did Mr. Stone assault you, Flora?" she asked softly.

Flora lifted her eyes. "Nay."

Kendra stared hard at her, but she couldn't decipher the other woman's expression. She didn't seem to be lying, and yet . . .

"There's nothing for you to be ashamed of, Flora. If Stone hurt you—"

"He didn't," Flora said, her tone abrupt. She flushed. "He didn't do . . . do what ye are sayin'."

Kendra was silent for a moment, studying the woman closely. Denial? "Why was Mr. Stone here, Flora?"

Flora swallowed, but said nothing. Her delicate features showed strain. She laced her fingers together, the knuckles white with tension.

After a moment, Kendra tried a different tack. "I heard that he was in a bad mood that morning. Was that true?"

Flora hesitated, then gave a tiny nod. "He was thinkin' hard on somethin'. He said he was gonna speak ter Mr. Biddle about it."

Kendra silently absorbed that information, the way Flora had said it. Why would Stone share that information with Flora? Unless . . .

A memory surfaced. She'd been nine years old when she'd first seen the famous Charles Allan Gilbert drawing, *All Is Vanity*, in a magazine. It was a brilliant use of ambiguous optical illusion. Up close, the image was a woman in front of a mirrored vanity. But when you stepped back, the image transformed into a skull. At the time, she'd been fascinated at how two different images could emerge from one picture, depending only on where you were standing.

She felt like that now. What she'd imagined two seconds ago was being transformed into an entirely different picture.

"Were you having an affair with Mr. Stone?" she asked bluntly. Flora bit her lip, and Kendra pressed, "What was your relationship with Mr. Stone?"

Silence.

Kendra drew in a sharp breath. Flora's lack of denial spoke volumes. Kendra's gaze drifted back to the bruise darkening Flora's cheek. Had her husband found out that she was having an affair with Stone? She didn't have to imagine Turner's reaction. She knew he'd have taken his temper out on his wife. And then . . . what? Go to the mill to confront Stone? Turner wouldn't have been quiet in his rage. Somebody would have seen the sheep farmer at the mill that day. She could imagine Turner bludgeoning the other man. But what had been taken from the desk, and why would Turner torture Lavinia Stone two days later?

Kendra realized that the silence had dragged on for several minutes. She decided to take a different approach. "You were having an affair with Mr. Stone." She paused to give the other woman time to deny it. When she didn't, Kendra gave a nod at her confirmed suspicions. "Did your husband find out?"

Flora said nothing again, and Kendra felt herself becoming impatient with the woman's misplaced loyalty. "You have to stop protecting him, Flora!" she ordered sharply. "Did he find out about your relationship, and go after Stone?"

Flora flushed. "Ye don't know anything," she said softly.

"Then tell me!" She stepped forward, fixing her gaze on the other woman. "Tell me what you're hiding. Because right now, it looks like your husband had another reason to murder Mr. Stone besides his gambling debt."

Tears sprang up in Flora's eyes, and she wiped them away. "It's not that way at all. Ye don't understand. Ye've got it all *wrong*."

30

Mr. Murray will see ye now, Mr. Kelly! If ye will please follow me, sir!"

Even though the lad was shouting, Sam could barely make out his words above the thundering noise of the mill's giant frames slamming together, while other machines spun the cotton yarn. Men and lads darted around, plucking loose cotton thread from beneath the clattering machines.

He'd been waiting in the mill for less than ten minutes, but he was drenched in sweat, the shirt beneath his coat sticking uncomfortably to his body. "Why is it so bleeding hot in here?" he asked as he followed the lad up the stairs.

"W'ot?"

Sam raised his voice, and repeated the question.

"Oh, we need the damp, sir, ter keep the cotton thread from breakin'!"

His last word ricocheted loudly down the hall upstairs, where the walls buffered the noise from the bays below into a muffled roar. God's teeth, as far as he was concerned, working in a mill was a miserable existence, not fit for man nor beast.

There was a time, though, when these massive factories hadn't blighted the countryside. When he'd been a lad, there'd been crafters who spun their cotton and wool into yarn inside their cottages. Then they'd bundled the yarn, sending it to the next cottage, and a crafter would weave the yarn into cloth. It had been hard work, Sam

was certain. But it had been done by families skilled in
the craft, not these giant mills churning out cloth as the
machines pounded and workers toiled to feed the soul-
less devil.

The lad stopped at a door and knocked. If someone
bade them enter, Sam didn't hear it, but the lad opened
the door and gestured Sam inside. A quick glance around
revealed a small, spare office, with shelves filled with
neatly stacked papers, ledgers, and rolled folios. Two
chairs were positioned before a simple wood desk. More
papers and a writing tray were arranged on its surface,
as well as a porcelain bowl that had a cloth soaking in
water. Sunlight streamed in from a window behind the
desk. Because of the natural light, the tapers around the
room were left unlit, probably saving the mill owner a nice
sum. Candles were not cheap these days, even tallow ones.
The level of noise had also dipped several more notches,
thank heaven.

Sam's gaze landed on the old man who'd risen from
behind the desk. Mr. Murray was short and stocky, and
appeared to have the Quaker inclination to shy away from
adornment and bright colors. His coat, waistcoat, and
pantaloons were dark gray. His cravat was simply tied
and as white as the old man's mane, which hung straight,
touching his collar. His face reflected his seventy years,
with lines around his eyes and from nose to mouth. The
brown eyes, behind wire spectacles, regarded Sam with
shrewd intelligence.

"Mr. Kelly," the old man said now. "Please sit. To what
do I owe the pleasure of your company, sir?"

Mr. Murray's speech was slightly garbled. It took Sam
a moment to realize that his lower jaw appeared swollen.
He thanked the man, and as they settled into their respec-
tive chairs, Mr. Murray reached over for the cloth in the
bowl. He grimaced as he wrung out the material, and then
placed it gingerly against his jowl.

"Forgive me, Mr. Kelly, for this oddity. But the
pain is quite unbearable, and I have found that a cold

compress helps more than the poultice that the apothecary prescribed."

"Were you injured, sir?" Sam asked. Given the pacifist nature of Quakers, he had a difficult time imagining the mill manager getting into a physical quarrel with anyone.

The manager sighed. "I only wish some ruffian had planted me a facer. Those injuries heal. My difficulties will continue, I fear. The barber recently took most of my teeth, and gave me these infernal dentures." He opened his mouth to reveal the gleam of teeth and gold wires.

"Ah." Sam obediently looked into the other man's mouth. "'Tis better than nothing, I suppose."

Still, he had to suppress a shudder. Thank God, he had all of his own teeth. He'd known a magistrate in London who had to get dentures, which struck him as ironic, as most dentures were made from the teeth of executed criminals. Sam had always wondered if the magistrate's mouth was filled with the teeth of men he'd sent to the gallows. Of course, after the war, dentures were also made from the teeth of soldiers fallen on the battlefield—Waterloo teeth. Now, as he gazed into the Quaker's mouth, he wondered if he was looking at the teeth of some poor lad who'd perished on the Continent. He was grateful when Mr. Murray finally closed his mouth, and he could look away.

"Aye, you speak the truth, Mr. Kelly," Mr. Murray mumbled, shifting the rag along his jaw. "I'm partial to eating real food, not mush and broth. But you did not come here to discuss the troubles with my dentures, I suspect. What brings a man from Bow Street to Manchester? More Luddite concerns?"

"Nay. I'm here in regards ter the murder of Mr. Harold Stone."

Mr. Murray's brows shot up. "Mr. Stone of Bancroft Mills? In East Dingleford?"

"Aye."

"I hadn't heard. Murder, you say? You are certain it is not the work of Luddites? The group has been active throughout these parts for years. Not that they don't

have some cause for their anger." The brown eyes behind
the spectacles darkened in disapproval. "Too many mill
owners allow small children to work in their factories. 'Tis
disgraceful. Only last week, a poor lass had her apron catch
on the shaft of one of the frames. She was cut to bits.

"No one in *my* mill is younger than ten years of age,"
Mr. Murray added with a flash of pride.

"The Luddites had nothing ter do with Mr. Stone's
murder," emphasized Sam. "An investigation is underway
ter discover the fiend."

"I fail to understand how I can assist you, Mr. Kelly. Lord
Bancroft hired me as his manager when he first built the
mill." He leaned back in his chair, looking up at the ceiling,
the cold wet rag still clamped to his swollen jaw. "That was
the year of our Lord seventeen hundred and eighty-nine.
There have been considerable changes to the cotton industry
since then." He lowered his gaze back to Sam. "I have heard
rumors that Bancroft Mills is having financial difficulties."

Sam thought of the grumbling he'd heard last night
about how safety measures had been sacrificed to save a
half-penny.

"'Tis odd, that," said Mr. Murray as he switched the
rag to the other side of his jaw.

"How so?"

"I should say it is surprising. Lord Bancroft was unlike
any other nobleman that I've known when it comes to
business. The Ton invest their money, and expect returns.
High returns," he added wryly. "However, they never want
to give the impression that they are actively involved."

Sam grunted. "Aye. Labor is low-born."

Mr. Murray nodded. "Yet I found his lordship to be
different. He would come to the mill every morning. He
was actively involved in its operation. I always thought
that his time outside of England must have changed his
regard in that area. Made him less . . . typical, I suppose."

"Did he speak of his travels?"

"Nay, he always said that he was interested only in the
future, and he wanted Bancroft Mills to be part of that

future. I was under the impression that the earl's father hadn't been as wise in his business ventures as his son, and had to sell off parcels of the estate that were not entailed. Lord Bancroft wanted to rebuild the family fortune. He was quite ambitious, really."

"Ambition is not unusual in the Ton."

"True, but the gentry tend to marry to further their ambition. I suppose his lordship actually did such a thing when he left for London to seek his bride. The village gossip at the time was the future countess had a sizeable dowry."

Sam asked, "How did you and the earl get on?"

Mr. Murray seemed surprised by the question. "As well as one gets on with one's betters. His lordship was a deep man, but he kept his thoughts to himself. Our association was that of business, not friendship." He tossed the cloth back in the bowl of water, and put his arms on the desk, lacing his fingers together as he leaned forward. "Many years have passed, but I am amazed that a man of Lord Bancroft's ambition would have allowed the mill to falter in such a way. Of course, there are more textile mills today. More competition. It can be a difficult business."

"From my understanding, Mr. Stone was not the best manager."

Mr. Murray smiled slightly, enough to show off a glimmer of his new teeth, then grimaced at the movement. "As I said, 'tis a small enough industry, even with the new mills. Mr. Stone has—*had* a reputation for being a reprobate."

Sam frowned. "Did he always have that reputation, even before Bancroft Mills?"

Mr. Murray shrugged. "I would assume so. Men, in my experience, don't change. But my information comes from the chatter in coffee shops where suppliers and shippers are wont to go, and laborers who have left East Dingleford to make their way to Manchester. They have never spoken kindly of Mr. Stone."

Sam frowned. "Why did you recommend him if you have always regarded him as a rogue?"

"I beg your pardon? Pray tell, what would I recommend the man for?"

Sam eyed the Quaker, saying nothing for a long moment. "You didn't supply Mr. Stone's name and address ter Lord Bancroft when you resigned from the mill?" he finally asked.

Mr. Murray shook his head, the brown eyes narrowing behind the round spectacles. "You have been given misinformation, Mr. Kelly. I did not resign my position, nor did I know Mr. Stone. In fact, I have never met the man. My only knowledge comes, as I told you, from industry gossip."

"And Lord Bancroft let you go? For what cause, if I may ask?"

"You may ask . . . but I am unable to tell you. Six years after the mill opened, the earl called me to Falcon Court and dismissed me. I will say that it was quite cordial, and he included a generous severance and reference letter."

"You had no expectation that he was going ter let you go?"

"None whatsoever. He told me that he wanted me out of the house that I'd been given with my position as manager, and gone from East Dingleford in two days. At the time, I presumed the unseemly haste was because his lordship wanted me gone before he installed his new manager in my stead." He leaned back in his chair, frowning. "Why would someone tell you a falsehood?"

Sam smiled slowly. "That's an excellent question, Mr. Murray."

31

Flora's tears began to fall in earnest now. Kendra moved forward and gently guided the woman to one of the chairs around the table. Covering her face with her hands, Flora sank down on the seat, her thin shoulders shaking with gut-wrenching sobs. Kendra shot a quick glance around the kitchen. In the twenty-first century, she'd be getting the distraught woman a glass of water or offering to make a pot of coffee, maybe tea. But this kitchen was so ancient that there wasn't even a water pump and sink, and Flora was too distraught for her to leave alone.

Kendra crossed the room and began searching through the cupboards.

"W-w'ot are ye d-doing?"

Kendra glanced over her shoulder at Flora. "Trying to find out where you keep the brandy. Or whatever alcohol you have on hand."

Flora picked up a nearby rag, mopping up her tears. "I—I'm fine."

"Who said it's for you?"

That earned her a startled look—and a faint smile, gone so quickly that Kendra might have imagined it. Flora pushed herself to her feet and walked over to a low cabinet, retrieving an earthenware jug. Kendra took it, and went to a cupboard where she'd spied teacups. Uncorking the jug, she poured generous splashes of what smelled like brandy into two teacups. No one ever wanted to drink alone. She steered Flora back to the chair and handing her the teacup.

"I—I apologize, Miss Donovan," Flora whispered, casting an embarrassed glance in Kendra's direction. Her delicate features were puffy, her complexion blotchy from her crying jag. "What must y-ye think of me, sniveling in such a way?"

"I think that you've got a lot on your mind." Kendra pulled out a chair, and sat facing the other woman. "Take a drink, Flora."

She waited until Flora did so, and coughed a little as the brandy stung her throat.

"Why don't you tell me what's going on, Flora?" Kendra prompted. "Sometimes it helps to talk about your troubles."

Flora gave a watery laugh, so filled with bitterness and despair that it scraped across Kendra's nerves like a rusty razor. "Nothin' can help me."

Kendra regarded her. "Did your husband find out that you were having an affair with Mr. Stone?"

Flora laughed again, wildly this time, like she was on the verge of hysteria. "He didn't find out," she said, choking off her laughter. She lifted the teacup again, took another, longer swallow. "William knew. My husband *knew.* It was . . . it was his idea."

Only years of experience stopped Kendra from spilling her brandy. Shocked, she stared at the other woman. "Your husband suggested that you sleep with Mr. Stone?"

Flora's gaze fell to the teacup she held, but not before Kendra saw the misery swimming in her eyes. When she spoke, her voice was so low that Kendra had to lean forward to hear the word. "'Twas last spring."

Kendra drew in a sharp breath, and the jumbled thoughts rolling around in her head fell into place. "When your husband lost to Stone in the card game," she said slowly.

More tears sprang up, and Flora quickly brushed them away with one hand. "Aye. Maybe Harry . . . maybe Mr. Stone did cheat. I don't know. But Constable Jameson and Squire Matthews said there weren't no proof. They said William was responsible for the debt that he owed Mr. Stone." Her small hands clenched, white-knuckled, around the teacup. She set it down on the table and picked up the rag again, wiping her tear-streaked face. "T-the sum was too great. We would've lost the farm ter Mr. Stone and been sent ter the workhouse, or my husband would've had ter go ter debtors' prison."

That didn't sound like such a bad idea to Kendra. She bit her lip on the comment.

"Mr. Stone came ter talk ter William about the debt . . ." Flora continued.

"I see." And Kendra did. "Your husband said that he'd made an arrangement to pay off his debt."

Flora nodded, but kept her face averted. "William knew about Har—Mr. Stone's character with women. And he saw . . . he said he saw the way that Mr. Stone looked at me when he came ter call. He said I needed ter do it. That it 'twas past time for me ter work for my keep."

Kendra jerked her gaze away from the other woman's tear-streaked face to scan the tidy kitchen, skimming over the pie crust and dough on the table to the washing next to the fireplace. "I think you do more than enough for your keep, Flora," she said, her voice tight with anger.

Flora gave her a sideways look. "We needed ter do somethin', or else Harry would've turned us off the farm. William didn't have the money. We had no way ter raise it. What else could we do?"

Kendra didn't know what was more horrifying, the psychological and physical abuse that Flora had suffered at the hands of her husband, or the fact that Kendra had seen this kind of situation play out before, young girls lured into sex trafficking rings, not by strangers, but by their own boyfriends. Like Turner, they manipulated their girlfriends with false promises and emotional blackmail. Then they'd control their new recruits with drugs and beatings.

No, Flora's story was nothing new. It disgusted her, but now that she understood, it didn't shock her. She only wished that it would have.

"Your husband had no right to put you in such a position, Flora," she said, careful to keep her voice neutral.

Flora bit her lip. "He's me husband, Miss Donovan. 'Tis God's will that I obey him."

"Somehow I don't think God would approve of you sleeping with Stone in order to pay off your husband's debts."

"I'm not a whore," the other woman whispered, her shoulder's hunching in shame.

Kendra had to swallow the bitterness rising in her throat. "I didn't say you were."

Flora clasped her hands together, and bowed her head as if seeking salvation. "Harry was not unkind," she murmured. "I . . . I think he grew ter have some affection for me. He invited me ter go ter Manchester with him. I've never been ter Manchester." She sounded almost wistful.

Kendra studied her. Was this Stockholm syndrome? Everything they'd learned about Stone indicated that he wasn't a man who did anything out of the goodness of his heart. His agreement to take part in this hideous arrangement showed exactly what kind of man he'd been.

Then again, Flora's husband had abused her physically and emotionally. In comparison, someone like Stone might look like a goddamn prince.

"Did you tell your husband that Stone wanted you to go away with him?"

"Nay." She lifted her hands and let them fall helplessly. "I told ye, Miss Donovan, me husband left early that day. He . . . he knew that Harry would be callin'. William never stayed when Mr. Stone would visit."

"Yeah, I can see where that might be awkward."

"The arrangement *is* difficult for William. A man has his pride."

Again, Kendra had to clench her jaw to stop herself from exploding. Her gaze fell on the discoloration on the other woman's cheek. She wondered if Turner's *pride* made him beat his wife as soon as Stone left. Never mind the fact that it had been Turner's idea to loan out his wife to pay off his debt in the first place. Kendra knew men like Turner. He would have twisted the situation around like a goddamn pretzel, making himself the victim. If Flora meekly accepted Stone's visit, her husband would have viewed her capitulation as willingness. He'd put her in a no-win situation. *That bastard.*

"Pride can push a man over the edge," Kendra said finally, her gaze on Flora's face, trying to gauge her reaction. "It can push a man to do things that he never thought he'd do."

Emotion rippled over Flora's delicate features. Kendra waited, but the other woman said nothing. She went on, "The way I see it, your husband gained a lot with Stone's murder, Flora. One, he doesn't have to pay back his debt anymore. Two, he doesn't have to share his wife with another man."

Flora shook her head so violently that her mop cap fluttered. "William didn't kill Harry. He wouldn't. *He couldn't.*"

Denial? Desperation? In Flora's mind, she needed her husband. Maybe she needed to believe that he wouldn't have crossed that line.

"Flora—" Kendra began, but the door opened behind her and she turned to look, just as Turner entered.

He stopped when he saw Kendra, his jaw loosening in surprise. But he recovered almost immediately, an ugly gleam entering his eyes as he lurched forward, carrying with him the pungent aroma of sheep. "W'ot are you doin' here?" he demanded. He shot his wife an angry look. "W'ot's she doin' here?"

Flora scrambled to her feet. "M-Miss Donovan came ter call."

Kendra saw the storm take shape on Turner's face. "I've got eyes—I can see that she's come ter call! Are you a bleeding simpleton? She's standing right in front of me! Do you think *I* am stupid?"

"Nay. I—I didn't mean anything by it, William. I vow, I didn't!"

Kendra shot to her feet, and quickly moved to stand between the husband and wife. She kept herself still as Turner swung back to look at her, raw fury on his face. "I have a couple more questions for you, Mr. Turner," she said coldly. "Where were you on Sunday?"

He glared at her. "Why should I tell ye anythin' about my business, eh? 'Tis none of yer concern! Just because ye're with some fancy duke don't mean nothin' ter me!" He took a threatening step forward. "Ye're a brazen chit, comin' where ye're not wanted! Pryin' inter decent folks' business."

"This is a murder investigation, Mr. Turner, not a knitting party," she snapped. She didn't take a step forward like she wanted to do, but she didn't retreat either. She kept her gaze fixed on his, and saw the flame of anger light up his blue eyes.

Fleetingly, Kendra wished she'd brought her muff pistol; it would've made things simpler. But she'd been trained in a variety of martial arts, favoring Krav Maga, the self-defense method used by the Israeli special forces. It wasn't as elegant as some of the Eastern martial arts, but it was brutal and efficient. Brutal and efficient might be just what Turner needed.

She shrugged out of the pelisse she wore, as the coat would only hamper her movements, and ran her gaze over Turner, assessing his strengths and weaknesses. He was a big man, but his muscle was turning to fat. But his biggest disadvantage was his brain. Martial arts were more about strategy than strength—strategy and lightning-quick reflexes. She had both. Turner, she was sure, had neither.

"W'ot are yer doin'?" He watched her as she tossed her coat across a chair. "Ye're not welcome here."

"You haven't answered my question. Where were you on Sunday?"

He reddened. "Ye think jest because yer our betters, ye can come inter *my* home and talk ter me with no regard! Somebody oughta teach ye some manners."

"Please." Kendra forced a laugh. "Like that somebody could *ever* be *you*."

She heard Flora gasp, could all but feel the other woman's horror wash over her, but she kept her focus on Turner and saw his eyes blaze. Adrenaline pumped through her, making her skin tingle. Her heart pounded heavily in her chest, but her mind was clear, her nerves ice-cold and steady. She shifted to the balls of her feet, waiting for him to make the first move. Out of the corner of her eye, she saw his hand ball into a fist—

"You need to step away." The voice sliced across the room, cold and lethal. Kendra didn't glance at Alec in the doorway, but kept her attention on the sheep farmer to avoid a sucker punch. She only relaxed slightly when Turner spun around to stare at the new intruder.

"Who the bleeding hell are ye?" he roared.

"I am Alexander Morgan, the Marquis of Sutcliffe," Alec informed him, his upper-class accent infused with icy contempt. There was no mistaking the dangerous expression in his green eyes. "My uncle is the Duke of Aldridge. And you are standing too close to my betrothed."

Kendra controlled her start of surprise at his announcement. "Mr. Turner was about to tell me where he was on Sunday," she said, arching her brows at the sheep farmer. "Weren't you?"

He thrust his jaw forward, his expression mulish. "Ye ain't got no right ter come into my home and quiz me and me wife."

"The magistrate can pay you a visit, then." She picked up her coat and shrugged into it.

She waited, but when it became clear that Turner wasn't going to give an inch, she walked toward Alec. She wanted to invite Flora to leave with them, but she knew the other woman wouldn't go, just as she knew that she'd become a target for her husband's rage as soon as they were alone. Her heart was heavy as she allowed Alec to usher her out of the cottage and toward the cart and pony he'd left near the barn.

Turner followed to the doorway, watching them with hostile eyes. Kendra could have sworn that she felt the space between her shoulder blades burn as Alec helped her into the cart. He swung into his seat and picked up the reins, sending the horse trotting down the lane. The burning sensation didn't ease until they were out of sight of the house.

Kendra turned to look at Alec, lifting a brow. "Betrothed?"

Alec shrugged. "It got Mr. Turner's attention, didn't it?"

"Yeah, it got my attention too. But I don't need the protection of your name or an imaginary engagement to deal with someone like Turner." She could feel her frustration rising. "I can take care of myself, Alec. You didn't need to swoop in and save the day."

"Are you truly going to ring a peal over my head for my rescue?"

She sighed. "That's just it, Alec. I didn't need you to rescue me."

His mouth curved into a crooked grin. "Now, sweet . . . why do you assume I was rescuing *you*?"

32

Instead of returning to the Green Maiden, they drove to the cotton mill to interview Biddle. Maybe not telling her that he'd been a player in the card game where Turner had accused Stone of cheating had been entirely innocent. Or maybe not. Either way, Kendra needed to talk to him again.

She wouldn't be talking to him at the mill, however. Though the mangled frames had been cleared away, and the factory had resumed its operation, they learned that Biddle had left for home twenty minutes earlier.

Kendra shook her head as they returned to the cart. "I'm surprised Biddle would leave in the middle of the day. I'd think he'd want to prove what a hard worker he is, to prove that he's ready for the manager position."

"*Dum felis dormit, mus gaudet et exsi litantro.*"

Kendra shot Alec a look. "You know Latin?"

He grinned. "Six years at Eton."

"When the cat sleeps, the mouse rejoices and leaps from the hole," Kendra translated, and smiled when she met his eyes. "Fourteen years of indoctrination by two hard-assed parents who thought there were still a use for a dead language."

He arched a brow, amused. "And did you find a use for it?"

"Oh, yeah, I was a big hit when my parents trotted me out at fundraisers. For some reason, my parents' associates were charmed by a ten-year-old spouting off Latin."

Alec looked at her as he reached over and grasped her hand. Her heart fluttered when he brushed a kiss over her knuckles. She'd never get used to Alec's romantic gestures.

"You are a marvel," he murmured.

She cleared her throat. "Not really."

Alec released her hand as he picked up the reins. "Let's pay a call on Mr. Biddle to find out just how much rejoicing he may be doing."

Biddle lived in a charming two-story cottage on a sloping hill, not far from the mill. When they used the brightly polished knocker on the black painted door, a round, middle-aged woman wearing a homespun cotton dress beneath an apron opened the door. She peered at them from beneath the shadow of her mop cap, a smile creasing her pleasant face.

"Good afternoon ter you," she greeted. "Can I help you with anythin'?"

"We've come to see Mr. Biddle," said Alec, withdrawing a small gold case from his inside coat pocket. He flipped open the lid and slid out a thick card, which he presented to the housekeeper. "I am Lord Morgan, the Marquis of Sutcliffe. This is Miss Donovan."

She scanned the calling card, impressed. "Oh, my. I heard that there was a duke and marquis visitin' our village." She bobbed a curtsy. "Please, come in. I'm Mrs. Ferguson. The master is in his study."

They followed her through the small foyer, with its dark-paneled wainscoting and white walls decorated with tasteful paintings, into the drawing room on the left. In contrast to Stone's ostentatious drawing room, Biddle's taste was elegant. The dark wood floor was covered by a Persian area rug woven in blue, brown, and gold, and the Chippendale furniture gleamed. A brown tufted sofa was positioned near a sash window. Two wing-backed leather chairs were angled in front of an unlit limestone marble fireplace. The walls were covered in ivory-embossed Chinese wallpaper, and decorated with several paintings. Most were landscapes in the style of John Constable.

Kendra took a couple of steps in order to peer closer. If she wasn't mistaken, the artist *was* John Constable.

"Please take a seat, sir, ma'am. I'll just go and knock on the master's door. It would do Mr. Biddle a world of good ter set aside his work." She made a clucking sound with her tongue. "Poor lad is always working. Came home earlier, and what did he do? Went right into his study ter toil away again." She planted her fists on her wide hips, obviously warming to the subject. "I say ter him, I say, 'Mr. Biddle, sir, yer still a young man. You need ter go out and find yerself a wife, not work yer poor fingers ter the bone.'"

Kendra eyed the housekeeper. "Did he say anything back?"

"Nay." She released a heavy sigh. "He sometimes goes ter the local assemblies, but with Mr. Stone cocking up his toes like he did, poor Mr. Biddle is working harder than ever. Doin' everythin' he can do ter keep the mill going, I reckon."

Kendra asked, "How long have you been employed by Mr. Biddle?"

"Nigh on ten years now."

"Do you live here?"

"Nay, I'm not a live-in housekeeper. My husband works at the haberdashery shop near High Street. I'll go and fetch—"

"Were you here last Friday when Mr. Biddle came home?" Kendra asked.

She paused. "Aye, I was. I'd just put the master's supper in the oven. I usually have it waitin' for him at the table. That and the glass of red wine that he fancies. But he was home earlier than the usual. Thank heavens, too! If he'd stayed at the mill, he'd have run into those ruffians, the Luddites." She gave a shudder. "Who knows what would have happened then, eh?"

"What time did Mr. Biddle get home that evening?"

Mrs. Ferguson frowned. "Must've been five. Half past five? I put the stew in the oven. It wasn't done, but Mr.

Biddle sent me on my way. Said the fog was something fierce, and he wanted me ter get home. He's a good man, the master."

"What about Sunday? Where was he on Sunday?"

The housekeeper looked puzzled. "I reckon he was here, working as he's doin' now. Why?"

Kendra eyed her. "You don't know?"

"The Sabbath is my day of rest. I prepare a dinner on Saturday for the master to eat on Sunday. Nothing elaborate, just salt fish or salted beef. But I think Mr. Biddle goes to the coffee shops and taverns. Mrs. Pratt and Mrs. Bolton are both fine cooks at the Green Maiden. I expect you know that, seeing how you're staying there.

"I'll go and tell Mr. Biddle that he has visitors. Will you sit, Miss Donovan, milord?"

They both remained standing as the housekeeper shuffled down the hall. Kendra wandered to the window. For the first time, she noticed that the light was fading, afternoon sliding into evening. Another day in East Dingleford—Halloween, she remembered. In America, kids would be dressing up to beg for treats. In England, Guy Fawkes was the holiday celebrated. East Dingleford would be celebrating it on Sunday.

Time is slipping away, she thought. And she was no closer to figuring out who murdered Stone, or his wife and housekeeper.

"Mr. Biddle has an excellent eye."

"What?" Kendra glanced over to see Alec examine an exquisitely carved marble figurine of Zeus preparing to throw his thunderbolt.

"This workmanship is amazing," said Alec, inspecting it.

Kendra came closer. "Much better than the cats that Stone collected."

"You are speaking of the carnage in Stone's drawing room?"

"Yes. He had more in his office." Kendra looked at the figurine in Alec's hand. "It's lovely. I wonder how an assistant manager of a cotton mill can afford something like that?"

"'Tis because I am thrifty with my monies, and invest on the Exchange wisely."

Kendra swung around, her gaze going to Biddle standing in the doorway. He seemed paler than the last time she saw him, shadows darkening his eyes. "Then you are a lot smarter than most people, Mr. Biddle," she said, summoning a smile. "May I introduce Lord Sutcliffe?"

Biddle's light blue eyes slid to regard Alec. He came forward, and executed a polite bow. "Good afternoon, my lord. Please be seated. Mrs. Ferguson will bring tea."

"I'm surprised you're not at the mill today, Mr. Biddle," Kendra said as she and Alec sat down on the sofa. "Does Lord Bancroft know that you're playing hooky?"

"Playing what?" He frowned, puzzled, as he sat in one of the wingbacks.

"You've decided to spend the day at home rather than working."

He lifted his hand to smooth down his hair. Kendra remembered the nervous gesture from the last time she'd interviewed him. "You misunderstand, Miss Donovan. I was at the mill earlier, but with Mr. Stone's death, there is a tremendous amount of correspondence that must be done. In that endeavor, I thought it best to devote a few hours to it every day in my study. 'Tis much easier to concentrate without the relentless noise of the mill."

For the first time, Kendra noticed the dark smudges on Biddle's fingers. Ink stains. She'd seen the same smudges on the Duke's fingers after he'd spent long hours writing notes for his scientific studies, or the endless stream of letters he wrote to family, friends, fellow philosophers, and his business concerns. An entire forest had probably been felled by the Duke's correspondence alone. Texting and typing were making the pen and pencil obsolete for most things in her era, except, she supposed, greeting cards. She remembered that her colleagues at the Bureau had scribbled their names on the get-well card they'd sent her after she'd been shot.

Biddle said, "The mill is not unsupervised. Mr. Marston is the foreman. And, of course, I shall return after I've finished with the correspondence."

Kendra looked around. "I can see that it would be easier to concentrate here."

"Shall I pour tea, then?" Mrs. Ferguson said cheerfully, coming through the door and setting the tray down on a nearby table.

"Yes, thank you, Mrs. Ferguson." Biddle settled back in his chair while the housekeeper inquired how Kendra and Alec took their tea. China and teaspoons clinked sharply as she prepared the tea, then passed around the cups and saucers.

"Here now, Mr. Biddle, a refreshing cuppa will revive you," Mrs. Ferguson said, handing him the last teacup. "He works entirely too much," she told Kendra and Alec again, shaking her head. "Always scribbling away—"

"That will be all, Mrs. Ferguson. Thank you," Biddle interrupted. He picked up his teacup, and took a sip while his housekeeper bustled out of the room. When she closed the door, he set his cup back on the saucer resting it on his knee. "What may I do for you, sir, ma'am? I'm certain this is not a social call."

Kendra gave him a long, measuring look. "You can tell us why you lied to us."

Shock rippled across his face. The teacup rattled on his knee. He put a hand on it. "I beg your pardon?"

"When I asked you about the altercation between Mr. Stone and Mr. Turner, you failed to tell me that you were present during the card game. You participated in the card game. Why didn't you say anything?"

Biddle reddened. "I . . . I apologize, Miss Donovan. It was so long ago."

"Last spring. May." Kendra nodded, keeping her gaze fixed on his. "A few months ago. You could hardly have forgotten the incident where someone accused your boss of cheating."

Despite the hand keeping it in place, the teacup jiggled again, a clear indication of nerves. Biddle appeared to realize it, as he stood up abruptly, depositing the teacup and saucer on a nearby table. He clasped his hands together. Kendra wasn't a body language expert, but she knew the gesture indicated anxiety.

"I do remember the incident," he said slowly. "I should have been honest with you when you first inquired about it, Miss Donovan. However . . ." Now he unclasped his hands, bringing them forward, palms up in a gesture of appeal, trying to convince her of his innocence. "I cannot explain exactly why I didn't say anything. I suppose I was still in a state of shock."

"Did you lose as well to Mr. Stone?" asked Alec.

Biddle nodded. "I did. However, unlike Mr. Turner, I removed myself from the game when the play became too deep. The game was at the assembly. Normally it's not quite so . . . intense. I can only attribute it to Mr. Turner."

"Oh?" Kendra shot him an inquiring look as she sipped her tea. "What do you mean?"

"If you've made the acquaintance of Mr. Turner, you will understand that he is an unpleasant character."

"I have made his acquaintance, and I agree with you, Mr. Biddle. Tell me what happened at the card game."

"There is little to tell, really. Mr. Turner kept losing. The more he lost, the more aggressive he became. We advised him to cut his losses, and be done with the game, but Mr. Turner was not open to counsel."

"No, I don't think he would be," Kendra murmured. "Did he really believe Mr. Stone was cheating?"

"He appeared to. He was quite enraged." Biddle lifted the teapot off the tray and topped off his tea. "But the constable and Squire Matthews could find no proof."

"Which might just mean Mr. Stone was clever at hiding his deceit," she pointed out. "Do you think Mr. Turner could have killed Mr. Stone?"

Biddle returned to his seat again. "I think Mr. Turner was angry enough that evening to do such a horrendous thing."

Kendra leaned forward, studying him. "And do you think he could have murdered Mrs. Stone and her house-keeper, Mrs. Trout?"

Several emotions chased across Biddle's face. Shock, first, followed by confusion, and then what looked like genuine sorrow.

"I cannot conceive anyone doing such a vile thing," he said finally. "Mrs. Stone was . . . was such a lovely lady. Why would anyone wish to harm her?"

Kendra asked, "How well did you know her?"

"Not well. She attended the local assemblies, and I had the pleasure of dancing with her on many occa-sions. Mr. Stone preferred the game room. Mrs. Stone's dance card was always full."

"Where were you on Sunday, Mr. Biddle?"

"I was . . ." He suddenly seemed to realize what the question implied, and gaped at her. "You can't possibly think I—that I would have anything to do with what happened to Mrs. Stone!"

"Everyone's whereabouts need to be verified."

He ran a hand over his hair, and shook his head. "I was here the entire day, and evening. You may ask Mrs. Ferguson."

Kendra said, "We did. That's her day off."

Biddle stared at her blankly. "Oh. Of course. I wasn't thinking. I have no proof, but I spent the day working here. There is much to do at the mill."

Kendra regarded him closely. "We've heard that the mill has been on a decline with shoddy equipment, infe-rior cotton, questionable safety standards."

Biddle flushed. "Ah . . . we've had a few difficulties. I am determined to reverse those."

"You expect Lord Bancroft to promote you?"

"I would not presume such a thing," he said, flustered.

"I'd think it's a natural presumption," Kendra said. "Did you go into Mr. Stone's office at all on the day he was killed?"

Biddle frowned, leaning forward to retrieve his teacup from the table. "I don't think so. Why?"

Kendra watched him closely. "Is there any reason why someone told us you did?" she lied, wondering if she could trip him up. But he only continued to frown.

"I can't imagine."

"Do you know what Mr. Stone might have been working on in his office?"

"I don't understand."

"Mr. Stone had something on his desk. Do you know what it was?"

Biddle shook his head. "No."

"Why don't you take a guess?"

"I couldn't do that."

She drank some of her tea, letting the silence pool. When Biddle didn't break it, she said, "We heard that Mr. Stone was upset on the day he came into the mill. You didn't mention that either."

"I said he was preoccupied. I don't remember him being upset."

Kendra set down her half-empty teacup, and stood up. "We should let you get back to your work, Mr. Biddle."

He looked surprised, pushing himself to his feet as well. "We're done?"

She smiled. "For now."

"I only wish I could be more helpful," he said, opening the drawing room door for her and Alec, and following them into the hall. "I pray that the fiend who murdered Mrs. Stone will be punished."

"And Mrs. Trout. She was murdered as well."

"Of course. 'Tis terrible."

He walked with them to the front door, and watched them as they climbed back on the cart. Alec flicked the reins and sent the horse moving down the lane. Kendra glanced behind her, but Biddle had disappeared back inside, closing the door.

Alec said, "Mr. Biddle's distress over Mrs. Stone's murder seemed sincere."

"Yes, it did."

"You don't believe it is?"

"I don't know," she said slowly. Something was off. But did it have any connection to the murders, or was it something else? "He was the last to see Stone alive. He has no alibi for Sunday. I think Mr. Biddle is keeping secrets. But . . ."

"But?"

She shook her head and sighed. "But that doesn't make him a murderer."

33

Lord Bancroft lied," said Sam, pausing to enjoy the sip of whisky.

Twenty minutes ago, he'd returned from Manchester. He'd gone straight to his bedchamber to strip out of his clothes, making use of the washbowl to rid himself of the scent of horse and sweat, and several layers of dust from his journey. He'd tossed the dirty laundry on the chair, hoping a shilling would be enough to ensure a thorough cleaning, and dressed in the spare set of clothes he'd brought with him. He did his best to wipe the grit from his boots. He only owned one pair; they'd have to do.

By the time he entered the private parlor where Kendra, the Duke, and Alec had gathered around the slate board, darkness had fallen outside. Someone had lit the wall sconces and candelabras around the room. A cheery fire crackled in the grate. Sam appreciated the warmth, even though the day hadn't been particularly cold. He appreciated even more the whisky Alec had handed him.

"Mr. Murray did not recommend Mr. Stone for his position as manager," he continued. "Nor did Mr. Murray hand in his notice voluntarily."

Kendra nodded, as though she'd expected the information. "Bancroft fired Mr. Murray and replaced him with Stone."

There was a knock at the door. Kendra and Alec threw a blanket over the slate board, a precaution that Sam understood. He'd been impressed at how the American had incorporated the slate board into their investigations, and had considered suggesting Bow Street begin using a similar system. But he also recognized that the notes on the slate board were sensitive in nature, and should be kept away from prying eyes.

After it was covered, the Duke opened the door to Mrs. Bolton and her granddaughters. As they marched in with the evening meal, Sam's mouth began watering, and his stomach rumbled. The tantalizing aromas of roasted lamb, buttered beans, and broiled turnips filled the air, reminding him that he hadn't eaten since breakfast.

"Ah, Mrs. Bolton, I'd end my bachelor days and marry you this instant if you'd have me," he said, his gaze on the innkeeper's wife as she carved meat off the bone. His comment caused Tessa and Lizzie to giggle as they moved around the table, uncovering side dishes and setting out bowls filled with mint sauce, jellies, and butter.

"You'd be marrying the wrong woman, Mr. Kelly," Mrs. Bolton informed him with a smile. "Mrs. Pratt is the one who cooked this meal."

"You'll need ter look for a new cook, then, 'cause I'll be persuading Mrs. Pratt ter run away with me."

"Give Mrs. Pratt our compliments," said the Duke, pulling out a chair for Kendra. "The meal smells delicious."

"Aye, your Grace." Mrs. Bolton curtsied. "Mrs. Pratt will be most pleased. I bid you good evening." She shooed her giggling granddaughters out the door.

Alec brought one of the candelabras to the table as they sat down. The amber glow played over the faces and food. Sam appreciated this too. Being in the company of a duke meant no one dared serve inferior food or whisky. What was it like to have your every whim catered to, your every wish granted? Sam would never know. As the son of a London baker, and now a Bow Street man, his own station was far below Polite Society. This was a nice side benefit to working for the Duke, he decided, picking up his knife and fork and cutting into the lamb with gusto.

"What else did Mr. Murray say?" Kendra asked, as she impaled a turnip with her fork.

Sam looked across the table at the American. The candlelight warmed her pale skin, and made her raven locks shimmer with golden highlights. She'd begun styling her hair differently from the peculiar way she'd worn it when he first met her. Her maid had twisted it into something elaborate, and the fringe above her dark eyes was swept back by a simple green bandeau that matched her silk dress. Sam wasn't a man to pay attention to the latest lady's customs, but he knew this was more fashionable, allowing Kendra Donovan to blend in with the other ladies of the Beau Monde.

Still, he knew she'd never really blend in. She was too . . . *odd*. And not only because of her strange desire to become involved in murder investigations. She didn't seem to give a wit over her spinsterhood. He'd never met a lass who didn't want to become leg-shackled, whether she was Quality or common folk. All three of his sisters had begun plotting to find husbands when they'd turned fourteen, and were now scattered around the kingdom, happily tending their husbands and increasing broods of children.

"Mr. Kelly?" Kendra raised an eyebrow.

"Pardon me. I'm woolgathering." He pulled his thoughts back to the conversation at hand. "Mr. Murray said he was surprised when Lord Bancroft let him go." He stabbed a piece of meat, swirled it in the mint sauce, and popped it in his mouth. He chewed and swallowed before he continued. "He said the mill's operation was going well. The earl had been heavily involved in it, which was a bit unusual. The gentry aren't known to get their hands dirty."

"I rather doubt the earl was on the floor carding the cotton, or whatever is done in a mill," Alec said drily, lifting his wine glass.

"Nay. But Mr. Murray said his lordship came ter the mill almost every day when the mill was first built. Then he took himself off ter London ter hunt for a bride."

"Well, I can certainly understand why his attention was diverted. He didn't just look for a bride, he found one." The Duke shrugged as he focused on cutting the lamb on his plate. "A new wife can demand your attention more than a mill. Besides, it sounds as though the mill was fully operational by then."

"I think the point here is Bancroft lied twice," said Kendra. "Mr. Murray didn't quit his job, and he didn't recommend Stone as his replacement. Did Mr. Murray know anything about Stone, like where he was originally from? The man was in his thirties when he first became manager at Bancroft Mills. He has a past."

Sam shook his head. "Nay, miss. And from what Mr. Murray said, the mill industry is small enough ter have done so. He also confirmed the rumors that Bancroft Mills was having difficulties."

"No one should be shocked about the mill's disrepair given Mr. Stone's incompetence," said Alec.

Sam nodded. "Mr. Stone was not well regarded by his fellow tradesmen. Or the workers at the mill."

The Duke looked at Kendra. "This supports your contention that Lord Bancroft was acquainted with Mr. Stone before he hired him, my dear."

"And the theory that Mr. Stone acquired his position through some type of blackmail," Alec added. "You don't give a lucrative venture like Bancroft Mills to someone who does not have the fortitude to continue its success."

Sam frowned. "If it was blackmail, why didn't his lordship just buy off Stone? Why have him at the mill, always underfoot, so ter speak?"

"I'd say the manager position was Stone's idea," Kendra said. "It's actually brilliant. He gets a wage—probably a nice wage, too—on a regular basis. Better, it's legal. And it put Stone in a position of power. People relied on him for their livelihood. He got a kick out of that."

"Bancroft hired Mr. Stone twenty years ago." The Duke picked up his wineglass. "Even if he did use blackmail to get in his position, how does that relate to his murder? Or those of his wife and housekeeper?"

Kendra shrugged. "Blackmail is one of those crimes that never ends. Maybe Stone was becoming more aggressive. He was going to Manchester . . . maybe he crossed a line with his demands. It's connected to whatever he had on his desk. It's also connected to their past." She looked at Sam. "Is there any way to track down where Stone was from?"

"Without the name of a village or his family name?" Sam shook his head. "Nay."

Alec said, "We can't even be certain Harry Stone is the man's real name."

Kendra stared at him. "My God. You're right." She put down her fork. "So that's a dead end."

"In my opinion, I think the key to this is figuring out what was on Mr. Stone's desk," the Duke said. "What is it most likely to be? A map? Or some type of document? A bill of sale?"

"A book or painting," added Alec. "Or a box."

Kendra shook her head. "I think it's too low to be a box."

"Not a box, but a case," the Duke pointed out. "Like the cases that dueling pistols are stored in. That could fit the dimensions, if the case was open."

Kendra appeared intrigued by that. "And dueling pistols are usually a matched set. Is there any way to identify ballistics—connect a bullet to a specific gun?"

Sam nodded, wondering where the American was going with this. "Of course. But what gun? What bullet?"

"Hypothetically, what if someone kept the two pistols that might have been used in, say, a murder that happened decades ago? Could the weapons be used as blackmail?"

Alec raised his eyebrows. "Are you suggesting that Mr. Stone witnessed Lord Bancroft murdering someone during his travels, and kept the weapons to blackmail him years later?"

She let out a heavy sigh. "Put like that, it seems a bit farfetched." *For 1815.*

"You'd need the bullet to match ter the weapon," Sam added. "Something that long ago . . . the evidence is most likely at the bottom of the Thames, or wherever the sawbones would put the ball he dug out of the poor sod."

Kendra pushed aside her plate and rose from the table, looking frustrated. "This is impossible," she said, moving to the slate board.

"Just ter add ter the hypothetical, gold coins or jewels can fill a dueling case just as much as pistols," Sam pointed out. "Greed is always a prime reason for murder. And it would connect the two crime scenes if Stone had more hidden away. Could account for Mrs. Stone being tortured."

Kendra pulled the sheet off the slate board. "We can come up with a hundred guesses as to what's on the desk. We need to focus on our suspects and their motivations. In that, Mrs. Stone is the key."

"How so?" The Duke stood as well, and wandered over to the desk. He picked up his pipe, but more to hold in his hand—a habit Sam had observed a couple of months ago when he'd first been employed by the nobleman—as he regarded his ward.

"Anyone can snap and bludgeon someone, as gruesome as that sounds. But not everyone can torture another human being," she said grimly.

"Thank God," murmured the Duke.

Alec said, "I can't see Mr. Biddle doing what was done to Mrs. Stone. Or the housekeeper, for that matter."

"He does seem like an unlikely torturer," she agreed. "But you never know. The mild-mannered man living down the street could be exhuming corpses from their graves and making lampshades out of their skins and bowls from their skulls."

Sam choked on the whisky he'd just sipped. "Good God." He stared at her. "Have you encountered such a fiend?"

"I never encountered that particular fiend, but his name was Ed Gein, and he was quite real."

Sam had to control himself from making the sign of the cross. What kind of monsters did they have in America? Then he thought of Mr. Murray's teeth, which had either come out of the mouths of dead criminals or dead soldiers. Having lampshades made out of a corpse's skin suddenly didn't seem so peculiar.

"I've encountered resurrectionists, some mild-mannered," he admitted finally. "But their main purpose was ter dump the bodies off at the sawbones ter get the blunt, not ter skin the corpse."

"What about the sheep farmer?" asked the Duke suddenly. "Do you think he could have been cold-blooded enough to torture Mrs. Stone?"

Kendra's face hardened. "Yes. The man's a sociopath."

Sam had never heard the term before, but by the glint of temper he saw in Kendra's dark eyes, he knew it wasn't good.

Alec cleared his throat. "Yes, as to Mr. Turner, we've discovered something distressing."

Kendra gave a surprisingly bitter laugh. "Distressing is getting a stain on your favorite sweater. The bastard was using his wife to pay off his debt to Stone."

Sam frowned, but it was the Duke who asked, "How?"

"Turner allowed his wife to become Mr. Stone's mistress until the debt was paid," Alec said without any inflection.

Aldridge gaped at his nephew, his eyes widening with shock. "You are saying that the arrangement between Mr. Stone and Mr. Turner was . . . his own *wife*? My God, the man is a monster."

"Yes," Kendra said, and Sam saw the look in her eyes, and knew what she was thinking. A man capable of such evil against his own wife was certainly capable of the evil that had been done to Mrs. Stone.

34

Kendra propped herself up on one elbow, watching Alec as he slipped out of bed. The fire had died and the bedchamber was still thick with shadows. She thought it was probably near five A.M. She couldn't see the clock, but heard the steady tick of its minute hands. Funny how it was becoming a familiar sound. She'd only had digital clocks in her Virginia apartment. If there was any noise, it was the nearly imperceptible buzz of electricity. Now she regretted the lack of light emitted by all digital gadgets, only because it deprived her of watching Alec walk naked across the room.

"Is there anything we can do to help her?" she asked. She heard the rustle of material, and caught his shadowy movement as he pulled on his breeches, sensed him twisting to peer at her.

"Who?" he asked.

"Flora—Mrs. Turner."

Alec said nothing for a moment. "What do you propose?"

She sat up, pulling the blankets with her. "I don't know. Bring her with us when we leave? There's got to be a position for her at Aldridge Castle. Or at Monksgrey, or the Duke's townhouse in London. She's one woman. It can't be that hard to find her a position somewhere."

"She'd be a runaway wife."

Kendra could tell by his movements that Alec was buttoning up his shirt, tucking the tails into his breeches.

Anger flared inside her. "Christ, she's going to be a dead wife if we don't help her. He's not going to suddenly stop beating her. One day he'll go too far. Maybe he won't mean to kill her, but he will. Maybe he'll be remorseful, but it will be too late. She needs saving *now*."

Alec moved back to the bed, carrying his boots, cravat, and jacket. The feather mattress dipped as he sat down. "Why does this one woman mean so much to you? Not to make light of the matter, but there are many women in similar situations. What is it about Mrs. Turner that has you wishing to intervene?"

"I don't know those other women."

But I don't know Flora either. Not really. Why *was* this so important to her? She couldn't explain it to herself. "She doesn't have anyone, Alec," she finally said. "She's trapped in a miserable marriage with a piece of shit for a husband. She needs *someone* to help her."

Alec stared at her, not saying anything for a long moment. Then he lifted a hand, brushing her hair away from her face, his fingers drifting down to caress her neck. "Perhaps you see something of yourself in her," he said, his tone gentle. "You have told me that you often feel trapped by your circumstance, your inability to control the situation—"

"Oh, my God." Kendra jerked away from him, annoyed. "I don't need you to psychoanalyze me, Alec. I'm not transferring my situation to Flora. I'm *not* a victim. She is."

He said nothing.

Tension tightened Kendra's skin. She held her breath, then released it in a long sigh, loosening. "I'm sorry. I didn't mean to snap at you." She caught his hand, lacing her chilled fingers through his warm ones, and thought of what the Duke had said to Bancroft a few days earlier. "Maybe a part of me does identify with her, but there's more to it than that. The world needs justice, Alec. There need to be people who step forward to balance the scales."

He brought their laced fingers up to his mouth and pressed a kiss against her hand. "You do that. You step forward to protect the weak. And it terrifies me."

"I can take care of myself," she said, striving for a lighter note. "I'm a special agent for the FBI. I know how to kick ass."

He laughed. "The Federal Bureau of Investigation."

"Bringing justice to the world."

He was silent for a long moment. Then he asked quietly, "Is that why you chose such a dangerous profession for a woman? Because you wanted to bring justice to the world?"

She drew back a little. "Let's get one thing straight: the danger is equally divided between men and women." But she considered his question. They'd never talked about this before. "My decision to join the FBI is complicated."

"Tell me."

She said nothing for a long moment. "I suppose I've always been interested in solving puzzles," she said slowly. "Maybe that's genetics. Both of my parents are scientists. My father is focused on cognitive behavior—what makes people tick. My mother is involved in studying the mysteries of the universe. They're both solving puzzles." She shivered a little, thinking about her unhappy childhood. Alec's hand tightened on hers.

"It's also circumstance," she continued. "When I was at the university, two girls in my dorm went missing. The FBI was called in. I followed their investigation, watched the agents work. I found what they did interesting."

"Did they find the girls?"

"Yes. And the unsub who had taken them. Both girls were alive. Traumatized. But the outcome was good. Not all of them are, you know. But the fact that it was a success certainly made the FBI appealing. I was fifteen at the time."

"Justice."

"Or maybe a happy ending. But there were other factors. When I began to research the Bureau, I discovered they had a lot of rules. A lot of structure." Her lips twisted into an ironic smile. "Most of the agents hate that, but I loved it. I'd spent my entire life following my parents' rules."

"You needed some structure."

She nodded. "When my parents cut ties with me, I was so young. It was strange not to have someone pushing me to behave a certain way, to accomplish certain goals. I . . . freaked." She drew in a shaky breath. Why did this still knot her stomach? "Most kids would've rebelled, reveled in the lack of routine. I did the opposite. It felt comfortable to me to *have* rules. Do you understand?"

He let go of her hand, and drew her into his arms. His chin rested on the top of her head. "Yes."

"Maybe if I'd been older, I would have started drinking, or doing drugs," she murmured. "That's what happens to a lot of kids who suddenly find themselves independent of parental authority. But I was only fourteen, and no one wanted to bring a fourteen-year-old to a frat party."

"Hmm. What's a frat party?"

"Oh. A fraternal organization—like clubs at universities."

"Like the Freemasons and Stonemasons."

"Yes."

"You were fortunate, then. So many young gentleman of the Ton resort to decadence when they leave home after years of being under the thumb of a governess or tutor . . . or a controlling parent."

She shifted back and lifted a hand to touch his face, seeing the shadows in his eyes. "You're thinking of Gabriel."

"I shall always regret not recognizing the demons driving my brother." His voice was low and harsh. "You were wise to create the structure you needed."

Her heart ached at Alec's misery. "I don't know if I was wise, so much as I was conditioned to want that routine. Luckily, there's both routine and structure within the university system. Classes, tests, research, things familiar to me. If I wasn't given a schedule, I made one myself. Color coded with graphs and pie charts." Now she smiled. "I was a complete nerd. It took me a couple of years to rebel."

"How did you rebel?"

She laughed. "Mostly by watching a shitload of TV. My parents had banned TV when I was a child. So once I was on my own, I made sure I watched a lot, especially the shows that I knew they wouldn't approve of. I could almost feel my brain rot inside my skull—not literally," she added when she saw him frown.

His mouth twitched. "I'm relieved. TV—television. You've spoken of this. A play inside a box."

"Pretty much. Anyway, the FBI ticked all my boxes. I liked the structure and rules. I was attracted to the end goal—justice. I liked being part of investigations, which are basically puzzles. And, as I said, it's probably in my DNA with my parents . . ." She tensed.

"What are you thinking?"

"Maybe I could try to send my mother a message. She's in Switzerland, studying the universe. If anyone could help me, it would be my mother."

Alec released her, and stood up abruptly. "How would you send her a message?"

"I don't know. Maybe bury some sort of time capsule in a place that would be excavated. God knows, England always has some kind of archeological dig going on, usually looking for Roman ruins."

"How could your mother help you?"

She heard the anger in his voice, and reached out to grasp his hand. "Alec . . ."

His fingers tightened almost painfully around hers. Then he sat down on the bed again. "Don't ask me to be happy for you, Kendra, for any possibility that you could leave. I love you." He twisted to look at her, his hand reaching up to cup her face. "I can't bear to think of life without you."

Her heart squeezed at the thought of losing him too. She threaded her fingers through his silky hair. Could anybody be in a more impossible situation?

She was silent for a long moment. "I don't think you have anything to worry about," she said slowly, her voice unsteady. "If I was going to write to anybody, I should write to myself in the future—a warning to stay away from England."

He drew back, frowning. "You are not setting my mind at rest."

"It should. Because I can tell you if I got that letter, I'd never believe it. I'd assume it was a joke or a scam. No matter what."

This was the craziest conversation she'd ever had. But she continued. "The paper would be old. I would recognize my handwriting. I could even put in facts that only I knew. But . . . I know myself, Alec. There are ways to get paper from this era, and forgery only requires expertise. The hardest thing would be for me to figure out how someone knew intimate details." She shrugged. "Systems can be hacked. I might've been under surveillance. I *know* myself. I would think it was a clever hoax, and I wouldn't listen." She caught his gaze. "Would you believe it if you got a letter from yourself from two hundred years ago?"

Alec looked startled, then thoughtful. "I know myself too," he admitted after a moment. "I don't know how to test for paper, but . . . I would not believe it."

"I don't even believe it *now*. It's too . . . insane." And that's how her mother would view it as well. Who wouldn't?

He gazed at her in such a way as to make a lump rise in her throat. "I'm selfish, I know," he said softly, wrapping his arms around her again and pulling her against him. "I know you want to go back to your world, Kendra, but I can't wish for it. Don't ask me to."

Kendra's head was tucked against his chest. She heard the strong, steady beat of his heart. If the positions were reversed, she would be just as selfish, she realized. Oddly, she felt like crying.

"I have a question," he murmured.

"Hmm?"

"What's a nerd?"

Kendra laughed, and allowed herself to snuggle closer. "*I'm* a nerd. And you'd be the hot quarterback. If we were in the twenty-first century, there wouldn't be a chance in hell that I'd be able to get near you." Because she was near him now, she lifted herself, and devoured his mouth with a kiss that sent a shaft of heat straight through her.

When they drew apart, slightly breathless, Alec asked, "What's a quarterback, and why are they hot? Do they have some sort of fever?" His clever fingers were beginning to roam in a way that made it hard for her to concentrate. "Why wouldn't you be able to come near me?"

She laughed again. Kissed him again. "Hot means handsome, in my era's lingo, which you are. Quarterback. . . we'll save that for another time. And I wouldn't get near you because you'd be with the bouncy, beautiful cheer-leader, or a homecoming queen."

His green eyes gleamed at her. "You are either over-estimating me, or underestimating yourself. Unless I was a complete nodcock in your timeline, I'd be pursuing you. And . . ." His breath feathered her lips as he leaned closer. ". . . if you don't want to be forced into marrying me, I must go."

He smothered Kendra's groan with a kiss. The bed rose as he drew away. Snatching up his boots, cravat, and jacket, he crept to the door.

"Wait," she said. "What about Flora?"

"Keep your voice down, woman. I shall find a position for your Flora at one of my estates if the Duke does not."

"You'll help her?"

"Shh. Yes. Now go to sleep, darling." He opened the door a crack and peered out.

Kendra released a sigh. "You know, this is ridiculous. We're adults."

He glanced over his shoulder at her. "You are the one who wanted rules and structure, sweet."

"Not *these* rules," she muttered, but he was already gone.

Without Alec's warmth to share, the bed was too cold, even with the blankets. Kendra shifted, trying to get comfortable, as her mind replayed their conversation, racing forward and circling around like a cat chasing its own tail.

The idea of sending a letter to the future was certainly intriguing. But she'd been honest with Alec. She couldn't imagine herself believing such a letter. What if she sent it to her fourteen-year-old self? Would she have been more open-minded then? Probably not. She'd been dealing with the shock of figuring out how to navigate her life without parental authority. It had been like she was in a freefall. If she'd received a letter from 1815—*Help, I accidentally traveled through time, and now I'm stuck in Regency England*—she'd have tossed it in the trash, thinking it was some sort of weird hazing.

The fact that she was here at all must mean that she had never—*would* never send her future self a letter. She'd remember getting such a letter. Even if she was in some sort of time loop, that would be part of her memories *now*, wouldn't it? So that could only mean she never sent the letter . . . *or* something had prevented her future self from receiving it. Fate? The universe? A higher power conspiring to keep her in the nineteenth century? She didn't know, couldn't even begin to imagine.

Her head was beginning to hurt, and yet now that she'd begun to consider the matter, she couldn't turn it off. Her mind spun with the scenario that she could get a letter to her mother. But, what then? It wasn't like her mother could whip up a time-travel machine and rescue her. And she suspected that her coldly rational parent would also dismiss such a missive. But maybe she'd try to call Kendra. When she couldn't locate her, she'd contact the FBI to trace her whereabouts. Or had the FBI already contacted her mother? Her father?

Kendra's stomach clenched. She hadn't told Alec or the Duke how she'd spent her final moments in the twenty-first century—plotting the death of a valuable asset of the United States government, laying false trails, creating new identities, and opening overseas bank accounts. The Bureau wouldn't have wanted to spread that information, but she was certain that they would have contacted her parents as part of their investigation. Or maybe they had invented a story to explain a manhunt for one of their own. If she ever made it back to her own timeline, would she see her own face staring back at her from an FBI's Most Wanted poster?

She let out a heavy sigh, and rolled out of bed. It would be time to get up soon, anyway . . . well, in another two or three hours, maybe. She would do some yoga stretches, and then go to the private parlor. Review her notes. Maybe beg a cup of coffee out of Mrs. Bolton or Mrs. Pratt. Screw the cup; she'd ask them for a full pot.

Because it was freezing, she grabbed the cotton robe from the chair and hastily pulled it on. Tying the sash, she stumbled across the dark room to the window, shoving the curtains open.

It was still dark, but not the inky darkness of night. In an hour, the sun would begin its daily climb toward the heavens. Whether East Dingleford would actually see the sun was another matter though. She could see the shape of low-hanging clouds, and fog, silvery-gray, shifting like the souls of the damned across the ground, winding around the barn and outbuildings and through the trees.

She gazed into the backyard of the inn, remembering how Mrs. Bolton had drifted across the frost-covered ground a few days ago in her nocturnal journey. Kendra had pushed the incident to the back of her mind, distracted by other events. Like a double homicide.

She tapped her fingers along the windowsill as she recalled the first evening at the inn, when Freddie had accused Mrs. Bolton of sympathizing with the Luddites. And she remembered the old woman's panic. Like a mosaic, bits of stone were falling into place to create a pattern, a picture.

Would Mrs. Bolton have ventured out to meet a brother who had radical sentiments?

There was only one way to find out if her suspicions were right. Kendra turned away from the window, and moved to the wardrobe. Twenty minutes later, she opened her door and slipped quietly into the hallway.

35

The inn was silent and dark. There was a small window at the end of the corridor near the stairs; otherwise the hallway was so dark that she couldn't see more than a few inches in front of her. She moved slowly, cautiously, her hands outstretched so as to not bump into any furniture or the wall, using the light of the window to guide her. She almost regretted not lighting a candle, but she'd been afraid someone might see the flame. Besides, it always took her too damned long to strike the flint to light the wick anyway.

Deprived of sight, her hearing became more acute. She heard the soft swish of her morning dress and cloak as she crept forward. A floorboard creaked underfoot as she reached the stairs. She winced, held her breath, and waited.

Silence.

She exhaled slowly. The shadowy light from the window gave her a measure of comfort that she would be able to descend the stairs without breaking her neck. The fan window above the door helped direct her down the hall, but halfway down, the meager light disappeared, and she once again had to proceed more cautiously. She summoned the layout of the downstairs from her memory and followed the mental map. Past the private parlor. The kitchen on the left. Another room with the door closed on the right. A short stretch to the back door.

Her hand encountered the smooth wood of the back door. She allowed her fingers to drift over it, to feel the cold outline of the iron lock. She threw open the bolt and eased it open, relieved when there was no noisy squeak. She stepped out into the cold and the damp, closing the door behind her.

Somewhere nearby, an owl hooted. Kendra clutched the velvet cloak closer to her throat and struck out across the uneven ground, the grass crisp with early morning frost. The mist was slightly disorienting, obscuring the stone buildings she knew were ahead. As she drew near, they took shape behind the curtain of fog, and solidified when she was within a few feet of them. Kendra recognized the low stone structure on her right—an ice house. The small building to the left was a chicken coop. She wasn't sure what the next building was, but it didn't matter. Her attention was already shifting back to the stone barn looming ahead of her.

She hurried over to the barn door. The strong scent of hay, manure, and animal assailed her nostrils as soon as she opened the door. Three small square windows were cut into the stone, offering some relief against the dark interior, but not much. She hesitated in the doorway, allowing her eyes to adjust to the murkier light. She got the impression of a dirt floor, two stalls, and a high ceiling that soared to a hayloft. A large shadow moved in one of the stalls, lower and wider than a horse. A cow. She hadn't give much thought to what it took to run an inn of the Green Maiden's size. But as she moved farther into the barn, she realized how smart it was for the Boltons to have a cow for milk and chickens for eggs.

She approached the second stall and paused, then reached out, pushing the wood gate inward. It was darker in the stall, the meager light from windows unable to reach the area, but she could see something dark lying against the lighter hay.

"Mr. Thackeray . . ." she whispered, remembering Mrs. Bolton's maiden name. The dark shape didn't move. She bent down, her hand just brushing the blanket, when a noise behind her made her straighten and swing around.

A man emerged from another door, buttoning up his breeches. He stopped in surprise as he spotted her. Kendra recognized him as the large, burly Luddite from the road, the one who'd been carrying the pickax.

"Mr.—" she began, but her greeting was transformed into a cry as the man suddenly exploded in movement, racing forward and catching her square in the chest as he gave her a hard shove that caused her to fly backward. Her body slammed against the gate, which cracked loudly against the stall's wall. Disturbed, the cow in the next stall issued a plaintive moo. The straw and the blankets softened her fall, but she still gasped in agony as her tailbone hit the ground.

"*Fuck!*" She bit her tongue, tasted blood in her mouth. She heard the man's pounding feet as he ran toward the door. Despite the pain lancing up her spine, Kendra scrambled to her feet in time to see the man dive out the door. She yanked up her skirts and gave chase.

Mrs. Bolton's brother had to be in his fifties, Kendra calculated, which gave her the edge, because she was younger and faster.

Except she hadn't considered the fog. The sky was lighter, but the mist clung to the earth with tenacious fingers. She was forced to stop, her gaze scanning the area. She turned sharply at the sound of running feet, and she caught a glimpse of the Luddite racing toward the woods before his figure was swallowed by whorls of fog. She sprinted after him.

The mist was worse in the woods, reducing the visibility to a monochromatic gray. The chilly dampness snuck beneath her cloak and dress. She shivered, and stopped. Her gaze swept the area. She caught a quicksilver movement in the darkness, heard the snap of twigs. She ran in that direction, then went skidding on a batch of wet leaves. Arms flailing, she managed to keep her balance.

"Mr. Thackeray!" she called out. Her voice sounded loud and alien in the forest. She pivoted. Listened. A cacophony of noises seemed to drift out of the fog. Tree branches stirred above. She caught the occasional coo of a bird, the rustle of damp leaves on the ground.

"I know the Luddites didn't kill Stone!" she shouted.

She paused, waiting, and heard nothing but rustling and cooing.

"I just want to talk to you!"

There came a sound from behind her, and she spun again. Her heart thudded as she squinted, trying to see beyond the mist.

A wild boar burst through the vapor, and came to a stop about fifteen feet from her. The creature was the size of a large dog, with bristly fur and a long snout. Its small, beady eyes regarded her. Then it twisted its body, which seemed too bulky for its short, skinny legs, and bolted back into the fog again.

Kendra let out the breath she hadn't realized she'd been holding. She wasn't sure how dangerous wild boars could be to humans, but she wasn't about to find out if the creature had family nearby, or if there were bigger and more dangerous animals just waiting to pounce on her. She snatched up a thick branch from the ground, and held it like a baseball bat. *Just in case.* She may not have been a survivalist, but she knew how to survive.

It took her a while to make her way out of the woods. Some of her tension eased when she spotted the shadowy outline of the barn and outbuildings ahead. The mist was thinner here, she thought, away from the woods. She hurried past the barn and crossed the clearing to the inn. She let out a relieved sigh, tossing aside the branch, as she opened the back door and slipped inside. The glow of oil lamps and a soft murmur of conversation came from the kitchen. The inn was waking up.

Rubbing her arms beneath her cloak to drive the chill away, Kendra approached the doorway. Inside the kitchen, Lizzie and Tessa were beginning their domestic duties, with Lizzie black-leading the stove, while Tessa poured water into the teakettle. Kendra spotted the clock near the fireplace. Almost six o'clock.

Tessa let out a screech, which she quickly stifled. "Gor! Miss Donovan, ye startled me somethin' fierce!" She hastily set down the pitcher and reached for a rag to sponge up the water she'd spilled when she'd jerked the pitcher away from the teakettle.

"Sorry."

"Have ye been outside?" Lizzie asked incredulously, eyeing her cloak.

"Yes, and I'm frozen." Kendra removed the cloak, draping it over her arm. She was becoming aware that her half boots and the bottoms of her skirt and cloak were soaked. Her feet inside the boots were numb with cold. She gravitated toward the fire blazing in the hearth and held out her hands to the warmth.

"Whatever were you doin' outside at this time, Miss Donovan?" Tessa blurted out, earning a frown from her older sister. "Beggin' yer pardon, miss . . . Is yer chamber pot full, and ye needed ter go ter the privy?"

"*Tessa*!" Lizzie hissed, mortified. "Gentry have their own ways ter go about their business. I apologize, Miss Donovan. My sister is young, and still needs ter be schooled with the proper respect for her betters."

Kendra had to suppress a smile at Lizzie, only two years older than Tessa, taking such a grownup stance. "Where's your grandmother?" she asked.

"Oh, she'll be here shortly, as will Mrs. Pratt," Lizzie said. "Can we help ye with anything, Miss Donovan?"

"No." She stepped away from the fire, then paused. "Actually, I'd love a pot of coffee, if it's no trouble."

Tessa said, "Oh, it's no trouble at all, miss. I'll make ye up a tray"

"Thanks. I'm going to change my clothes and shoes . . . I'll meet you in the private parlor in twenty minutes." She started for the door, but paused, glancing back at the sisters. "If you see your grandmother, tell her I need to see her."

The inn was still quiet but not quite so dark when Kendra retraced her footsteps back to her room. It took her ten minutes to wiggle out of the loose-fitting blue muslin morning gown, take off the half-boots, and strip out of her white stockings; another seven minutes to wiggle into a lilac cotton muslin gown and pink stockings, and shove her feet into embroidered slippers. She ran a brush through her hair, but knew that she didn't have the skill to do anything more than that, and had no intention of waking up Molly just to style her hair.

She made it down to the private parlor with a minute to spare, and then realized that the door was locked. When Tessa came down the hallway carrying a tray, she asked, "Do you have a key?"

"Nay. His Grace has the key ter the parlor."

"Maybe your grandfather has a spare."

"Nay. Leastwise, I don't think so." Tessa frowned. "I can find him ter ask."

"Never mind." She eyed the young girl. "Do you happen to have a hairpin?"

"Aye. Why?"

"Do you mind if I borrow one?"

Tessa fixed her gaze on Kendra's loose hair. "Ye're gonna need more than one, if ye want ter do anything, miss."

"Actually, one will be sufficient, but if you could spare two, it would be easier."

The girl gave a shrug, and deposited her tray on a nearby side table. She dug around under her mop cap, then produced two long, lethal-looking hairpins. Kendra took them, and tried not to think about the time they'd saved her life. Under Tessa's wide-eyed supervision, she inserted the hairpins into the lock.

Tessa gasped when Kendra straightened and pushed open the door. "How did ye do such a thing, Miss Donovan?"

Kendra grinned as she handed the hairpins back to the girl. "It's a skill that comes in handy if you don't want to wake up anybody." *Or if you need to save yourself from a serial killer.* She looked around the gloomy room. "Unfortunately, I don't have the skills needed to get a fire going."

"Oh, I can do that!" Tessa hauled the tray in from the corridor and put it on the table. The maid snatched up a tinderbox from the nearby shelf and slid back the lid. "Ye just arrange the tinder inside. Ye must have tinder in America."

Kendra thought of the popular dating app, and had to smile. "We do, but it creates a different sort of fire."

Tessa shrugged, as if she couldn't bother to find out about the oddities of a country she'd most likely never set foot in. She concentrated on striking the flint against carbon steel. The shower of sparks fell on the tinder in the box. She blew on it. Smoke billowed, and within seconds, a blaze flared. She brought the box over to the hearth, and, kneeling down, transferred the fire to the logs and kindling.

Kendra shook her head, feeling amazed and incompetent. "You make it look so easy."

"It is." Tessa scrambled to her feet. "I can light the candles and lamps, if ye wish, Miss Donovan."

"That I can handle." She brought a candle over to the fireplace. "Fire begets fire," she murmured, and lit the brace of candles on the table. She was crossing the room to light the lamp when a knock came at the door, and Mrs. Bolton poked her head in.

"Miss Donovan," she greeted. "Lizzie told me that you wished to see me."

"Yes, thank you. Please come in." Kendra pushed the curtains back to let in the day's dreary light. The parlor's window didn't face the barn and outbuildings, but was angled more toward the forest. The fog was slowly evaporating. Silvery ribbons still wound their way around the trees and ground, but Kendra suspected that much of that would burn off by noon. She narrowed her eyes on the trees beyond, and wondered if it was her imagination or if she actually saw a shadow gliding between them.

"Tessa, your sister needs your help in the kitchen," Mrs. Bolton told her granddaughter.

"Aye, Gran!" The young girl hurried out of the room, but returned for a quick curtsy directed at Kendra. Then she sprinted off again.

"Ah, to be young again," sighed Mrs. Bolton, shaking her head. An affectionate smile played about her mouth, as she turned to look at Kendra. "You are awake early, Miss Donovan."

Even though it wasn't a question, Mrs. Bolton's tone turned it into one. Kendra crossed the room to the table. "I couldn't sleep," she admitted, pouring herself a cup of coffee. "I found myself looking out my window. I did the same thing a couple of nights ago."

The innkeeper's wife only smiled.

"My bedroom window faces the barn," Kendra said. She lifted her coffee cup and took a sip, wincing as the hot liquid hit her tongue where she'd bitten it. Iced water would have been better. "I know your brother has been staying in there."

Mrs. Bolton inhaled sharply. "My brother?"

"Your brother—who was fired from the mill. Who is part of the Luddite movement." Kendra set down her cup. "I went out to the barn to talk to him."

Mrs. Bolton couldn't stop her eyes from flicking to the window and back again, and her fingers twisted the material of her skirt. She pressed her lips together, and remained silent.

"I know your brother didn't kill Mr. Stone. I tried to tell him that, but he wasn't interested in discussing the matter. He knocked me down and fled." Kendra frowned. "I'm not sure why he's afraid—or why you are. Constable Jameson may be an idiot, but even he realizes that the Luddites weren't responsible for the murders."

Mrs. Bolton finally spoke. "Not the murders, no. Do you not see, Miss Donovan? Being part of the Luddite movement is enough to have a person arrested, and, if convicted, hanged. Or transported to Botany Bay.

Machine-breaking is a capital offense!" She was twisting her skirt in earnest now. "The Crown has sent spies everywhere to uncover evidence against men. Joseph—my brother—is a good man, Miss Donovan. He is a weaver, and yet he can no longer support his family because of these filthy machines!"

"Mrs. Bolton." Kendra crossed the room and grasped the old woman's agitated hands. "I'm not looking to hurt your brother. I only wish to speak with him."

"He didn't kill Mr. Stone. You said so yourself. He would never do such a thing. I know there are others in the movement who go too far, but most are like Joseph. They just want a fair wage for their service. Is that so very difficult?"

"I need to speak to Joseph."

Tears glinted in the old woman's eyes. "But why?"

"I know he didn't kill Mr. Stone," Kendra repeated firmly, "but he was at the mill around the time of Mr. Stone's murder. I need to interview him. Or one of the other Luddites—"

Mrs. Bolton was already shaking her head. "No one else. Joseph would never allow it. He would never risk betraying another."

"Do you think you could convince Joseph to talk to me?"

"Only you?"

"Yes."

Mrs. Bolton bit her lip, looking uncertain. "I think it's a fool's errand. Joseph would have told me if he'd seen something."

"Sometimes people don't even realize what they've seen or heard." Kendra held her breath, and waited. She sensed the old woman was wavering, but if she pushed too hard, she might retreat entirely to protect her brother. But when the silence lengthened, Kendra couldn't stop herself. "We're not just talking about Mr. Stone," she said. "Whoever killed him also killed his wife and their housekeeper. They deserve justice, don't they?"

"Yes." Mrs. Bolton whispered the word so quietly that Kendra had to lean forward to hear.

"Yes?"

"Yes." Mrs. Bolton said it louder this time, and her gaze lifted, locking on Kendra's. "I don't know where my brother goes in the morning, Miss Donovan. He has been sleeping in the barn, and I have brought him food when I'm able to slip out. But my husband knows naught of this. And he must not know. Do you understand?"

"I understand."

"Your guardian, the Duke, cannot know, nor his nephew, Lord Sutcliffe. Do you understand?"

"Yes."

"And the Bow Street Runner—"

Kendra heard the rising tension in the other woman's voice, and cut her off. "This will be our secret, Mrs. Bolton. You arrange a meeting, and I will be there. Only me. I promise."

The old woman stared at her with such intensity that she wondered if she'd be asking her next for a blood oath. *This is serious*, she thought, and was suddenly chilled. The Luddite movement had once been a distant rebellion in her history books. Now it was part of her life.

"I will do what I can," Mrs. Bolton nodded slowly, and her hand reached out to grasp Kendra's arm. Kendra was startled at the strength in the bony fingers. "Keep your word, Miss Donovan. You may be investigating the deaths of Mr. and Mrs. Stone and their housekeeper, but it will be my brother's *life* that you hold in your hands."

36

By the time the Duke and Alec walked into the parlor at
eight o'clock, a headache was thrumming behind Kendra's
eyes. On the plus side, it distracted her from the literal
pain in her ass, where her tailbone had smacked against
the barn floor.

Aldridge looked at her in surprise, then at the key in
his hand. "My dear . . . Does Mr. Bolton have a spare key
for this room?"

"I don't know, but his granddaughter had two hairpins
that she allowed me to use."

"Two hair—ah." He grinned, his grayish-blue eyes
twinkling. "I forget how resourceful you are, my dear."

Alec eyed her as he sauntered over to the coffeepot,
lifted it, and put it down with a frown when he realized
it was empty. "How long have you been here?"

"Long enough to drink that pot," she told him. She
couldn't tell him about her encounter with Mrs. Bolton's
brother. "I've gotta admit, I'm hungry."

Aldridge nodded. "We shall break the fast . . . Ah,
good morning, Mr. Kelly," he said when the Bow Street
Runner came into the room. He yanked the bell-pull. "I'm
about to order breakfast. Miss Donovan has already drunk
a pot of coffee, but I'll request another pot, and tea. Or
would you prefer ale?"

Sam's face lit up, but he managed a modest, "Ale,
would be lovely. Thank you, sir." Sam joined Kendra at

the slate board. "Have you come up with any new theories, Miss Donovan?"

"Only old theories." Kendra studied the board, jiggling the piece of slate in her hand. Her vision had blurred from staring at the board. Behind her, the door opened, and she heard the Duke's soft murmur as he gave Mrs. Bolton instructions for breakfast.

"Why did he smash all the cats?" she wondered out loud.

Sam looked at her. "Pardon?"

"In the second crime scene. All those porcelain cat figurines that Stone had collected were shattered."

"He was obviously looking for whatever he had tortured the poor woman for," the Duke said, coming to stand beside them. "If Mr. Stone had some sort of treasure, our fiend may have believed he'd hidden it within one of the figurines."

"The treasure would have to be limited to loose gems." Kendra tapped the piece of slate against her chin as she remembered the collection from their visit with Lavinia Stone. "Many of the figurines were too small to contain coins."

"What's troubling you, miss?"

Kendra glanced over and caught Sam's perceptive gaze. "I can't help but think that there was more to it," she said. "There was a lot of rage behind the destruction of Stone's collection."

Sam shrugged. "It's like we said before. If the killer didn't find what he was lookin' for, he'd have a lot of rage."

"You're right." Still, she felt that she was missing something. Her eyes shifted to the Victimology column. "Stone was the kind of man who liked to boast," she said slowly. "If he got his hands on something valuable, it would fit his profile to brag about it."

"Not if the treasure was obtained by illegal means," Alec said. He was sprawled in one of the chairs, his long legs stretched out and crossed at the ankles.

"*If* there was a treasure, I think we can make the next leap and conclude that Stone got it through illegal means,"

Kendra said. "If everything was on the up-and-up, Stone would not only have boasted about it, he would have been spending it."

The Duke nodded. "Excellent point."

Alec said, "Well, there are usually two people that men boast to—their wives and their mistresses."

Kendra shook her head. "We interviewed Mrs. Stone. She didn't know anything."

"If the treasure wasn't rightfully hers, she wouldn't have wanted it known," said Sam.

"I agree with Miss Donovan," the Duke put in. "I met Mrs. Stone. I didn't get the sense that she was being deceptive."

"She was an actress," Alec reminded them.

"Yes, but she would have told her torturer," Kendra argued. "The destruction that followed indicates she didn't. But it fits Stone's profile that he might have confided in Flora. He had power over her, could intimidate her into keeping silent. He would have felt comfortable boasting to her."

"You've already spoken to her," the Duke said. "Wouldn't she have told you?"

Kendra thought of the frightened woman, and shook her head. "She wouldn't have even told me about her relationship with Mr. Stone if I hadn't realized it myself and asked. I'll need to interview her again, and it has to be without her husband around. We can't wait until next Monday for him to go to market. He must leave the farm for other things." She had to stifle a frustrated sigh. How did you set up any type of surveillance in 1815?

"I'll make inquiries, miss," Sam spoke up. "People tend ter be a predictable lot with their routines."

Kendra nodded, her gaze drifting back to the slate board. The Bow Street Runner was right; people were predictable. Figuring out patterns was part of profiling.

"If Stone had gotten a hold of some sort of fortune, he wouldn't have hoarded it," she said. "Maybe he couldn't spend huge sums without raising suspicions . . . but he could spend a little here, a little there. There are all sorts of ways to boast, you know."

She thought of how Stone decorated his office, like a gentleman. It wasn't too different in the twenty-first century, the corporate raider wanting a fancy corner office or a flashy new car. *Hey, look at me! I can afford a Tesla!*

"If a man like Stone found himself sitting on a fortune, what would he spend it on?" she asked. "Something special for himself."

Alec said, "Buy new livestock."

Kendra found herself smiling. *The nineteenth-century version of a Tesla.*

But Sam shook his head. "I saw his stables. He wasn't spending any money on horseflesh."

"I've known plenty of gentlemen who will make an appointment with their tailor," said the Duke. "Mr. Stone didn't appear to be a dandy, but . . ."

"It's another avenue to pursue," Kendra finished. She frowned. "We're basing a lot on the assumption that whatever had been on Stone's desk had some sort of monetary value."

"It's a reasonable assumption, miss," Sam pointed out. "The killer took somethin' after Mr. Stone's death, then tortured his wife for somethin' more. What else would connect the two?"

Kendra didn't have an answer to that—or much of anything else. And that was the problem.

"Mr. Stone was an excellent customer," said Mr. Edward Shannon of Shannon & Son, the only tailor shop in East Dingleford, located on the north end of the high street.

Mr. Shannon was a small, wiry man who looked to be in his early sixties, blessed with a full head of gray curls that he brushed back from his forehead, and sporting a mustache he'd waxed into razor-sharp points. The coat he wore was a burnt orange, his waistcoat a beautifully

embroidered yellow silk, his shirt white, his cravat—
surprisingly, Kendra thought—black, which matched his
pantaloons. His black eyes, behind the silver spectacles
that he wore perched on the end of his narrow nose, had
eyed Kendra and Alec with a merchant's shrewdness
the moment he swept into the shop area from the open
doorway framed by dusky brown curtains that lead to the
back workshop.

Kendra had saved Alec from the sales pitch she saw
forming on the tailor's face by stating the purpose of
their visit. Mr. Shannon's smile had dimmed somewhat,
but Kendra gave him points for not losing it completely.
He invited them into the next room, where he could
continue to work while they asked their questions. Here,
mahogany drawers shared the walls with shelves con-
taining bolts of fabrics. There was a full-length mirror
tucked in the corner, and a table used to cut fabric.
Molly, who was once again in her role as chaperone,
remained in the retail portion of the shop, entertaining
herself by peering into the glass display cases and fin-
gering the fabric swatches strewn about the room.

"How long did you know Mr. Stone?" Kendra asked.

Mr. Shannon was busy pinning a canvas of horsehair
and wool to the shell of a coat on a headless dummy.
"Oh, years. Who can remember the exact number?" He
smoothed the stiff canvas. "Mr. Biddle was kind enough
to recommend my services to Mr. Stone."

Kendra lifted her eyebrows. "Mr. Biddle? I thought
that he came to East Dingleford a year after Mr. Stone."

"Hmm. Yes, I believe you are correct, Miss Donovan.
From what I recollect, Mr. Stone had previously been
traveling to a tailor in Manchester for his wardrobe. Perhaps he noticed the cut of Mr. Biddle's coat. Mr. Biddle
has always been a man of exemplary taste. He has an
exceptional eye for quality."

Kendra commented, "Which he found in your shop."

"Shannon & Son has always provided the best quality.
Mr. Biddle's only fault is that his taste, while refined,

tends to be bland." Mr. Shannon ran a hand down his own vibrantly hued lapel, unconsciously preening. "I've tried to coax Mr. Biddle to consider bolder choices, but . . ." He shot Kendra and Alec a look that seemed to say, *What can you do?*

"Some people lack vision," Alec murmured.

The tailor peered at him over the top of his glasses. "Exactly. Most of the gentlemen in East Dingleford tend to be a cautious sort. Except, perhaps, Mr. Matthews. Now that young man is a tulip!"

Kendra eyed the tailor. "If you say so."

Alec's lips twitched. "A tulip is a well-dressed gentleman, Miss Donovan."

"The squire also patronizes my shop, of course," Mr. Shannon went on, "but he does not have his son's sense of style."

"I can see why you have all the gentleman in East Dingleford as your customers, Mr. Shannon—your skill as a tailor is obvious," Alec complimented, allowing his gaze to wash over the embryonic jacket on the headless dummy. "It is comparable to London proprietors."

"Oh, thank you, sir! I do *try*." He beamed, but the smile faded quickly. "However, to be perfectly honest, I cannot claim that *every* gentleman in East Dingleford patronizes my shop. Since returning to the village, Lord Bancroft has chosen to travel to Manchester for his wardrobe." This last was said with pursed lips.

Alec raised an eyebrow. "That is odd. It seems an unnecessary journey."

Mr. Shannon frowned. "I agree. I cannot conceive what we did to offend him. Shannon & Son has been in my family for three generations. My father and my father's father served the late Earl of Langfrey and his father—well, before he chose to make his home in London Town. We served Nat before he had his dreadful falling out with his father, and left East Dingleford. All over a young girl who should have known better. So silly!"

"Love can make you do silly things," Alec drawled, and deliberately caught Kendra's eye.

Kendra focused on the tailor, ignoring the leap in her pulse. "You knew the earl as Nat?"

"We grew up together. Oh, we belong in different social spheres, but East Dingleford was much smaller back then, and . . . well, the earl was not the man that he is today. In fact, I shouldn't speak of him in such a slipshod manner. He has not been Nat for many years, not since he returned to Falcon Court as a viscount, when his father was dying."

"I heard Lord Bancroft's father died a week after he returned, falling down the stairs," Kendra said, her gaze on the tailor.

"Yes. Such a tragedy! My father and I attended the funeral, of course." He frowned. "Perhaps we were too free in our memories with Nat . . . Lord Bancroft. Too familiar. We may have overstepped our place, remembering Lord Bancroft as a boy, not seeing him as the man he'd become."

"Funerals often bring forth memories," Alec said. "It's odd that Lord Bancroft would be offended for you doing so."

"But that's just it. I remember him being perfectly pleasant." Mr. Shannon paused, then shook his head. "But we are talking many years ago. And my memory is not as good as it once was. I only know Lord Bancroft does not patronize my shop—although his son, Lord Drake, has come in for several fittings over the years. Still, he is rarely in East Dingleford, since the earl sent him away to school as a young boy."

Kendra asked, "Did Mr. Stone ever speak about Lord Bancroft?" She wasn't familiar with how long a gentleman's fittings might last. But maybe tailors were like bartenders; their customers might use them to vent or gossip.

Mr. Shannon returned to pinning the horsehair canvas to the lining of the jacket. "Mr. Stone was an excellent customer, but he was not a gentleman," he said, casting a sideways glance at Kendra. "I'm not referring to his status. I'm speaking of his manner. He could be coarse. I must admit that when Mr. Biddle first pointed him in my direction, I rather thought of him as—forgive the pun—an unpolished stone."

"I see." Kendra arched her brows. "And you managed to polish him?"

"I'm a tailor, Miss Donovan, not an alchemist."

Kendra had to smile. "But did Mr. Stone talk about the earl?"

"Not in a flattering light. He would talk about Lady Bancroft more often." A dull flush rose up on the tailor's face, and he glanced quickly at Kendra. "I cannot speak of what he said in your presence, Miss Donovan. Mr. Stone was a rake when it came to the ladies."

"That's all right. I have a pretty good idea what he was saying about the ladies. Did he ever mention meeting Lord Bancroft before he came to East Dingleford?"

He looked surprised. "No. Did they have a previous connection?"

Kendra ignored his question, asking instead, "Is there anything else you can tell us about Mr. Stone? Anything you noticed about him?"

"He lived life to excess. Throughout the years, he required more material."

"Did Mr. Stone ever tell you where he was from? Where he was born? His family?"

Mr. Shannon finished pinning the material, and looked at her. "He did not mention family, but I know he was from the London area. He spoke of the amusements he'd found there, and often lamented the lack of such frivolities to be found here."

"If he was so bored with village life, why do you think he stayed?"

Mr. Shannon lifted one shoulder, and let it drop. "I cannot say, but for all his complaints, Mr. Stone appeared content."

Kendra changed the subject. "Did he mention his altercation with Mr. Turner?"

Mr. Shannon frowned. "Turner . . . I do not recall the name."

Kendra waited—sometimes it took a second for people to remember—but when Shannon said nothing more, she asked, "When was the last time you saw Mr. Stone?"

"A fortnight ago."

"A week before he was murdered," Kendra specified.

Instead of answering immediately, the tailor crossed the room and opened a drawer. He removed a thick, leather-covered ledger, and brought it to the table. Kendra watched as he thumbed his way through the pages until he found the one he wanted.

"Mr. Stone had an appointment on Thursday, October 19, to pick up an order. Two white shirts, a vermillion waistcoat, and a new puce-colored greatcoat for the winter, with a lovely sable collar, and three caplets. It was really quite grand."

Kendra exchanged a look with Alec. "Would you say that it was more extravagant than usual for Mr. Stone?" she asked Mr. Shannon.

"What do you mean?"

"Was Mr. Stone spending more than usual?"

He rubbed his chin. "No," he said slowly. "I cannot say I observed any such a change. As I said, Mr. Stone was an excellent customer. He allowed me to . . . shall we say, guide him in selecting his wardrobe. He never balked at any of my recommendations, although I did not exploit the situation and persuade him into purchasing something he should not have. And his credit was always good. I never feared that he would not pay his account."

"When Mr. Stone came in for his last appointment," Kendra said, "can you describe his mood?"

"I remember him to be in high spirits. He had planned a journey to Manchester." Mr. Shannon hesitated, and blushed again. "I got the impression he would not be there alone."

Kendra said, "You mean, he wouldn't be there with his wife."

It wasn't a question, but Mr. Shannon nodded. "Yes. I made the error of mentioning Mrs. Stone and Mr. Stone laughed, and made the comment that there are certain matters best done without a wife in tow. I assumed he had other entertainment in mind, but I did not inquire." He closed the ledger, and returned it to the drawer. "In my profession, discretion is vital."

Kendra eyed the tailor closely. "When Mr. Stone was here, did he mention anything about money or jewels? Or finding something valuable?"

The black eyes behind the spectacles glinted. "No. But that would certainly be interesting."

"Do you think Mr. Stone was the kind of man to keep a secret like that?"

Mr. Shannon pressed his lips together. "I suppose it would depend on how Mr. Stone came into the fortune. However . . ." He shrugged. "I've always found that sooner or later, secrets tend to come out. If Mr. Stone had such a secret, I think he would have eventually told someone."

Maybe he did, Kendra thought. *Maybe he told his killer.*

37

Something was taken from Stone's desk. Lavinia Stone was tortured for a reason. Those two facts were irrefutable, Kendra reflected. She could also reasonably assume that the missing item had been valuable. People did not commit torture and murder over worthless items. But that didn't mean it had to be gems or coins or anything of monetary value. By pursuing that angle, were they going down a rabbit hole? In her own time, she'd chased down plenty of leads that had turned into dead ends. Of course, then she could take some comfort in being part of a task force, with multiple agencies involved, as someone else could've uncovered something important where she'd failed. Here, she could only continue her inquiries, and hope something would work its way to the surface, like a sliver under the skin.

At least that was what she thought later that evening, when she found herself again seated at Lord Bancroft's elegant table, spooning up her bouillabaisse. As rain tapped at the windowpanes, Kendra's gaze traveled the length of the table to where Bancroft sat as the host. The rest of the seating arrangements were typical of the era, assorted by rank. The Duke and Alec flanked Bancroft. Seated next to Alec was Lady Winifred, looking beautiful in a flimsy, low-cut gown of the palest lavender. A simple pearl necklace circled her throat. The firelight in the room teased out the gold in her tawny hair, which had been

swept up in an elaborate style of braids and curls and
sprinkled with seed pearls, and cast a golden haze over
Lady Winifred's alabaster skin.

Of which there is a considerable amount showing, Kendra
thought with some asperity. The woman's breasts seemed
to defy gravity, the way they swelled out of her bodice.
Her sleeves were long, but transparent, tied with ribbons
at her delicate wrists. Kendra caught the flash of Lady
Winifred's pale skin whenever she moved her arms,
which she did often, lifting her hand to lightly touch
Alec's sleeve as she spoke to him. The woman would
be out of her half-mourning period soon and destined
for London, to hunt for husband Number Two. If the
woman's flirtatious manner was anything to go by,
Kendra suspected she was getting a jump on her search
for a new spouse.

Kendra had never been one for jealousy—partially
because she'd never had cause to be jealous—but she realized that was what she was feeling now, a slow burn in her
stomach. Deliberately, she yanked her gaze away from the
pair. Mr. Matthews sat opposite Lady Winifred. His father
had been invited, Kendra knew, but the squire's gout kept
him housebound. Without the squire, the numbers were
uneven, with Dr. Poole and his wife facing each other.
Kendra was in the unfortunate position of sitting next to
the grumpy doctor, who was currently quizzing Matthews
on whether the squire was following the diet that he'd
prescribed.

Kendra furtively studied the doctor's wife, mainly
because she couldn't imagine living with Dr. Poole. Mrs.
Poole was a stout woman, who looked to be around her
husband's age. She wore a gauzy yellow gown that, even to
Kendra's less discerning eye, seemed to be at least a decade
out of date. She'd concealed her décolletage with a lace
fichu that matched the full lace cap that covered her gray
hair. Her face was plain, her expression pleasant. Kendra
wondered if the pleasantness was a façade, something
the woman had adopted as a form of defense over her

husband's more quarrelsome demeanor. Or maybe she'd taken to using a couple of drops of laudanum, which Kendra had discovered wasn't unheard of for women in this period of time.

The conversation at the table was light and gossipy throughout the first course, with Lady Winifred quizzing the Duke and Alec about the latest happenings in London. It didn't surprise Kendra that they knew some of the same people. While the Duke and Alec had never met Lady Winifred or Lord Bancroft, they belonged to the same social circles, and therefore had overlapping acquaintances. Lady Winifred appeared to have a better understanding of the London social scene than her father. Lord Bancroft remained silent, alternately sipping his soup and his wine, leaving his daughter to carry the conversation.

Every once in a while, though, Kendra caught the earl's dark eyes on her, his expression intense but impossible to read. During those times, Kendra strove to keep her own expression indecipherable. She refused to look away or be intimidated. Bancroft's gaze would eventually slide away, but not before she saw a thin smile curve his mouth. It both made her shiver and pissed her off. She was even more certain that he was playing some strange game with her.

Kendra remained quiet until the first course was cleared away, and the main course, which consisted of a variety of meats—roast beef and several platters of partridge and pheasant—and jellies was served.

"I'm curious, Lord Bancroft . . ." She picked up her wineglass and surveyed the nobleman over the rim. He wasn't the only one who could play a game. "Where did you travel after you left East Dingleford?"

He paused in cutting into his roast beef. "It was such a long time ago, Miss Donovan."

"Still, it must have been an exciting time. You couldn't have forgotten." She lifted her eyebrows to telegraph her skepticism.

"No, but I have more pressing concerns to occupy myself these days."

She smiled. "Well, we know that you were around London in those days."

He studied her from across the table. Kendra wondered if she imagined his sudden tension or not. "And how do you know such a thing?" he asked, his tone revealing nothing.

She took a sip of wine before she answered. "You said that you met the Duke's father at Aldridge Castle," she reminded him.

Something flickered in his eyes, then was gone. "Ah, yes. I think I told you that it was a brief encounter. I was passing through Aldridge Village at the time." He waved his hand, a gesture of dismissal. He turned to the Duke. "Your father invited me to share a glass of wine with him in his study. Unusual room, from what I remember. Octagonal in shape."

The Duke nodded. "It was part of the castle's original construction, when my ancestors fought for William the Conqueror."

"We discovered Mr. Stone was originally from outside London," Kendra lied, watching Bancroft closely. "You never had an encounter with him during your time there?"

Bancroft huffed out a dry laugh. "London has millions of people, Miss Donovan. If I had a chance encounter with Mr. Stone, I do not remember it."

Lady Winifred looked at Kendra. "Why do you persist in trying to see some sort of connection between my father and Mr. Stone, Miss Donovan? The very idea is absurd. I told you, Mr. Stone did not occupy our social sphere."

"Maybe I'm curious why a man like Mr. Stone, who enjoyed the pleasures of London, ended up in a village like East Dingleford." She kept her gaze on Bancroft. "Something must have lured him here."

Dr. Poole grunted. "I would imagine a lucrative position as manager of the mill."

"This is not appropriate dinner table talk," Lady Winifred cut in firmly. "I still shudder to think what happened to Mr. Stone and his wife."

"And Mrs. Trout," said Kendra.

Lady Winifred flicked her a look, then turned to the table at large. "I fear Mrs. Poole and I lack Miss Donovan's robust nerves. I must insist that we speak of less grisly topics while having our meal. Now, my lord . . ." She brushed her fingertips against Alec's arm, as she leaned in close, "Tell me, is there any truth to the rumor that Lady Byron fears her husband is quite mad . . . ?"

"Where do your people hail from, Miss Donovan?"

Surprised, Kendra looked at Mrs. Poole. The old woman hadn't said one word at dinner. Throughout the many courses and stilted conversation, she'd kept her pleasant expression focused on the courses laid out by the footmen.

Now the women were in the Chinese drawing room while the men lingered in the dining room with their port and pipes. A footman came around with a tray, serving cut crystal glasses about the size of a shot glass filled with Madeira to the women.

"America," she told the old woman. "Virginia."

"I have a cousin who immigrated to America after the war. The first one. Not this recent skirmish," she said placidly, and took a sip of her Madeira. "Donovan is an Irish name. Do you have family in Ireland?"

Kendra was lifting her glass to take a sip of the Madeira, as well, but her hand froze midway to her mouth. It had never occurred to her that she might actually have family in this world, that she might not actually be alone. Holy crap, her ancestors were *alive.* Her parents had always been interested in their genetic history, not their ancestry. But she could travel to Ireland and meet her great-great—hell, how many greats would that be?—grandmother or grandfather. The Donovan family wouldn't immigrate to the United States until around 1840, when the potato famine would force five million desperate souls to flee the island.

She could meet them, study their personalities . . . and completely screw up her own familial timeline. It was the Grandfather Paradox—taking an action in this era that could ultimately prevent her own birth.

"Are you all right, Miss Donovan?" Mrs. Poole was looking at her with concern.

"Yes." *No.* Hell, so much for her robust nerves. She tossed back the Madeira like she was at a bachelorette party in Vegas. A footman hurried forward and refilled her glass. A strange sensation stole over her as she met the servant's dark eyes. Then the footman retreated, and she had to stop herself from downing that drink too. She became aware of Lady Winifred regarding her with curious eyes.

Get a grip, Donovan. She drew in a deep breath, and let it out.

"I'm foolish," Mrs. Poole shook her head. "Of course, you don't have family in Ireland. If you did, your father would never have asked his Grace to be your guardian. You are fortunate. His Grace will undoubtedly provide a substantial dowry on you. That should help your circumstance."

Kendra took a sip of wine so she didn't have to answer. She'd never get used to being considered ancient at twenty-six. In her own era, she'd had to work hard to overcome the stigma of being too young to lead an investigation.

"It's not too late for you to marry and set up a nursery," Mrs. Poole continued cheerfully. "Do not be discouraged, my dear."

"Do you and Dr. Poole have children?" Kendra asked a bit desperately.

"Oh, children and grandchildren, and now a great-grandchild." Mrs. Poole's eyes misted with her happiness.

"Our granddaughter recently had a baby. A son, thank heavens! Unfortunately, Dr. Poole and I only had girls. Five of them, all a blessing, to be sure. But it was my greatest disappointment never to provide Dr. Poole with a son to carry on the family name and profession." The old woman glanced at Lady Winifred. "How is your daughter, my dear? Jane, is it not?"

"Doing quite well, thank you." Lady Winifred's smile was wintry. "I received a letter just the other day from Mrs. Tover, who said Jane has begun to crawl."

Kendra stared at the countess. "A letter? Your daughter isn't here with you?"

"Good heavens, no. Jane is with her wet-nurse. I understand that a few ladies in the Beau Monde have begun to bring the wet-nurse into their household or even nurse the babe themselves . . ." She gave a tiny shudder at the idea. "'Tis baffling to me as to why any lady would wish to change a practice that has worked quite well for centuries."

Now I know why I don't like you, Kendra thought. *You remind me of my mother.*

She was relieved when the door opened and the men filed into the drawing room. Lady Winifred rose from the sofa, and glided to the pianoforte, glancing at Alec with a smile. Kendra didn't think it was her imagination that the countess's smile was warmer. "Lord Sutcliffe, may I call upon you to turn the music pages for me?"

"I would be delighted, my lady."

Kendra caught the gleam of amusement in Alec's green eyes as he passed her. She wished that she could at least silently sneer at the woman's playing, but she had to concede that Lady Winifred was actually quite good. The pianoforte's delicate notes drifted across the room, blending with the soft tapping of rain against the windowpanes.

"My dear, Lord Bancroft was informing us how he had invested in the Middleton Railway, which has been using steam locomotives to haul coal," the Duke said to Kendra. "His lordship is an advocate of steam to power engines on land. Very progressive. Hardly surprising, though, from someone who has installed gas lighting in his home."

"Steam—bah!" Dr. Poole's fuzzy brows lowered, shadowing his eyes. "Mark my words, 'tis nothing but a passing fancy. And harmful to boot! Breathing in all that steam can't be good for the lungs."

"I think it's marvelous," Matthews supplied. "Steam is not as odorous as horses can be."

The doctor shot him a dark look. "A horse is one of God's creatures! Not some dreadful, clanking monstrosity that has no discretion, no wits, and will most likely roll right over everyone in its path!"

"Your uncle Ted was killed when his prized stallion threw him," Mrs. Poole said in her calm, pleasant manner.

"What does that have to do with anything, Mrs. Poole?" demanded her husband.

"I was merely pointing out that horses have harmed their riders on occasion as well."

"That is an asinine comparison to make. A horse is neutral, and is responding to the commands of its rider. My uncle was a fool to attempt to jump his horse where he should not. The horse wisely balked. One cannot blame the horse for being more intelligent than the rider."

The Duke jumped into the fray. "The same thing could be said regarding the steam locomotive, sir. It shall be manned by someone. If the contraption rolls over anyone in its path, surely it's the driver's fault—not the conveyance. In that, it is no different than a carriage."

Kendra glanced at Bancroft and deliberately walked to the window. In the glass, she saw her wavering reflection. She didn't have to wait long before Bancroft's image rose up behind hers.

"You have no interest in the future, Miss Donovan?" he asked with faint mockery.

She turned to look into the dark eyes. "At the moment, my interest is on finding a killer. We located Mr. Murray."

His expression, as always, was inscrutable. "Did you?" He lifted his wineglass and took a sip.

322   JULIE McELWAIN

"He said you dismissed him."

Bancroft pursed his lips and shook his head. "He was an excellent manager. Why would I dismiss him?"

"Because you wanted to hire Mr. Stone. See, here's the thing: Mr. Murray denies recommending Mr. Stone, and he denies resigning from his position."

"That is not what happened."

"Why would Mr. Murray lie?"

"Perhaps he's misremembering. It was more than a quarter of a century ago, Miss Donovan. The mind plays tricks on a person."

"And maybe it's not the mind that plays tricks . . ." She lifted her eyebrows, openly challenging him.

Lord Bancroft fixed those dark, enigmatic eyes on her. Kendra could feel herself tensing as she stared back. For a strange moment, it was as though they were the only two people in the room. The sounds around them—the thrumming rain, the placid notes from the pianoforte, the murmur of conversation—seemed to recede into the distance.

Kendra drew in a sharp breath, breaking the spell. "Do you know what I think, my lord? I think you and Mr. Stone knew each other from before he came to East Dingleford." She kept her voice low, but there was no mistaking the steel in it. "I think something happened in that time. Something that Stone could use to hold over your head."

"You have a vivid imagination, Miss Donovan."

"It doesn't take much imagination to connect the dots, my lord."

He smiled. "I think you will need to do more than connect the dots, Miss Donovan. Even here you need proof."

"I'll get it."

The smile vanished, and for a moment he looked grim. "I did not kill Mr. Stone. I was here, in my study. And then I joined my daughter for dinner."

"My dear . . . my lord . . ." The Duke joined them, his gaze flicking between them. If he noticed the tension, he chose to ignore it. "I apologize for interrupting, but I fear the rain will make our journey back to East Dingleford hazardous if we do not leave now."

The smile returned as Bancroft turned toward the Duke, once again the affable host. "Of course, sir." The dark eyes slid to meet Kendra's. "I believe Miss Donovan and I are done here, aren't we?"

She met his gaze. "For now."

38

The rain eased up sometime in the night. By morning, the only things left of the storm were muddy puddles, dripping leaves, and glistening grass. Clouds still moved across the sky, slow as a sloth, nudged on by a faint, icy breeze coming down from Scotland. Still, if the tinge of blue in the northern horizon was anything to go by, Kendra suspected that East Dingleford would be seeing sunshine sometime in the late afternoon. That should put a bounce in the villagers' steps, Kendra thought.

Her own bounce came when Sam Kelly informed her at breakfast that East Dingleford held a market every Thursday, which Flora routinely shopped. "The information that I have is Mr. Turner drops his wife off at the market, and goes ter wait at a tavern."

Kendra nodded. "That fits. Turner would view shopping the market as women's work."

"I shall be accompanying you," Alec said, his tone steely.

Kendra shot Alec an exasperated look. "I don't need you as a chaperone. I've already got one. Besides, it's not like we'll be alone. It's a *market*."

"Miss Donovan is right," the Duke said, calmly buttering his bun. "There will be hawkers there, not to mention the other shoppers."

"Aye. Markets tend ter be crowded, milord," Sam added.

Alec's eyes narrowed. "Then one more person shan't be a problem."

"Two."

Kendra glared at the Bow Street Runner. "I can take care of myself!"

"Aye, that you can," Sam agreed hastily. "But if Mr. Turner brings his wife ter the market, I thought I'd follow him. We've never met. Maybe it's time ter get acquainted."

"That is an excellent notion, Mr. Kelly." The Duke nodded approvingly. "You can keep Mr. Turner occupied while Miss Donovan speaks with his wife."

Kendra leaned back. "It's not a bad plan," she conceded gruffly. She glanced at Alec. "And where will you be, my lord?"

The cool green eyes regarded her steadily. "Around."

She huffed out a faint laugh. "Fine. I just don't want you breathing down my neck while I'm talking to Flora. She's a fragile woman."

"I shall attempt to control my breathing, and certainly will not do it down your neck."

The dry tone made her smile. "It's an expression."

"I suspected as much."

Kendra shifted her gaze to the Duke. "I suppose you'll be coming too."

"Actually, no. I think the three of you have the matter well in hand. Mr. Harding forwarded me a packet of correspondence that I must attend to regarding estate business and a few investments that need my attention."

She felt a pinch of guilt. The Duke had an estate manager and a man of affairs, but nothing could be done without his knowledge and signature. "I'm sorry. You have more to do in your life than investigate murders."

Surprise flashed in his blue eyes. "My dear, I have no regrets. If you recall, I was the one who insisted on becoming involved." He picked up his teacup. "I shall expect to be kept informed of what transpired when you return."

Kendra smiled. "Of course." She tipped back her coffee cup, drained it, and then pushed herself to her feet. She looked at Alec. "How far is the market? Can we walk?"

"We could, but the carriage is more convenient," Alec said, and rose as well. "I'll have it brought around."

The East Dingleford market reminded Kendra of the farmer and flea markets in her own era—it had the same energized, chaotic vibe. Voices carried along the twisty street, some bickering, some haggling for better deals, some peddlers shouting their wares. Colorful knots of people swirled around, up and down the street, pausing at stalls, moving on. Tinkers sold everything from bolts of fabric and haberdasheries to medicine to produce, teas, and coffee beans. Even though she'd eaten breakfast, Kendra's nose quivered in appreciation as the scent of frying bacon and yeasty pies drifted over to her.

They'd positioned themselves near a coffeehouse that gave them the best view of the street. Kendra scanned the people. Most of the peddlers were men, but the shoppers were women and children. The women were young and old, carrying straw baskets, and wearing homemade coats and dresses and sturdy shoes.

"I don't see Flora," Kendra said.

After fifteen minutes of surveillance, Kendra began to have her first doubts. Molly was getting fidgety, so Kendra sent her to buy some chestnuts. It stung Kendra that she had to ask Alec to give the maid a few coins. The only thing Kendra had in her reticule was a silk handkerchief and her muff pistol.

Another ten minutes crept by. Molly returned with a hemp bag filled with roasted chestnuts, and then Kendra spied Flora and her husband coming down the cobblestone street on a cart pulled by a mangy-looking pony. Kendra touched Sam's arm and nodded in the direction of the Turners as the sheep farmer pulled up on the reins. She watched Flora climb off the cart, without any help from her husband, and Turner pulled away. Her eyes narrowed when she noticed the bandage wrapped around the other woman's right wrist.

Sam gave her a nod, touching the brim of his hat before melting into the crowd. Kendra looked at Alec and Molly. "I'm going to approach her. I need you both to keep your distance."

She waited a moment longer, watching the other woman as she adjusted the straw basket on her arm. Then Flora began walking, her target apparently a cart selling loose leaf tea. Kendra caught up with her as Flora peered into a jar of shriveled leaves.

The peddler, a rotund man, approached Flora with a big, toothy grin. "Ah, dear lady, ye have exquisite taste! Ye are lookin' at the Darjeeling tea, cultivated in the plantations of India and brought to our great country from the East India Company. 'Tis a tea sipped by the Nawabs of Bengal themselves to ward off illness. If ye brew yerself up a cup, ye'll never suffer from ague, consumption, dropsy, or typhus. Why, if ye have but a twinge, sip this tea, madam, afore ye go to sleep, and I promise ye, ye'll wake up the next morning fresh as a daisy!"

Kendra snorted. "Tea has a lot of health benefits. Its antioxidants have been known to fight free radicals. But half of what you said is bull—boloney," she told the peddler. "Tea is more a preventative than a cure."

Flora gave a start, swinging around with wide eyes. The peddler peered at Kendra suspiciously, apparently not certain whether she was agreeing with him or not.

"And who might ye be, madam?"

"Kendra Donovan."

"An American, by the sound of ye. What's this about a . . . anti—what?"

"Antioxidants. Tea is filled with them."

He shot a look at the withered leaves. "Are ye certain? They wash the leaves, ye know."

Kendra decided she didn't have the time to explain. She turned to Flora. "I need to speak with you."

The woman licked her lips. "Oh, I . . . I don't think—"

"Let's walk."

"Here now, ye can't jest take away me customers!" the peddler protested.

Kendra glanced around. Alec was standing about ten feet away, giving her the space that she'd asked for. He lifted a sardonic brow as he met her gaze, and moved toward her.

"Do you need me, sweet?"

Kendra made a wry face. "Yeah. Could you buy tea for Flora while she and I talk?"

Flora blinked. "Oh, I couldn't . . ."

"Yes, you can."

"'Tis an excellent tea, sir," the peddler jumped in, his gaze assessing the cut of Alec's coat. "But if ye follow me, we've got another blend that's even better. Fights those radical buggers, ye know. A fine gentleman such as yerself should have the best."

Kendra drew Flora away from the kiosk, linking her hand firmly through the other woman's elbow to keep her from bolting. "Did he do that to you?" she asked softly, her gaze skimming Flora's bandaged wrist. "Sprain or break?"

"It just got twisted, is all," Flora mumbled, keeping her face averted. "'Tis fine."

"Did Dr. Poole look at it?"

"Nay. I said it's fine . . ."

Ignoring the other peddlers' cries to stop and test their wares, Kendra guided them toward a shadowy pocket between a tinker's stall and a small stone church. Coming to a halt, Kendra searched the other woman's delicate features, noting the pronounced pallor. Her bruises had faded to a sickly, but less obvious, green and yellow. The bandaged wrist was the only visible damage. Christ only knew what Flora concealed beneath her drab wool coat and dress.

"Flora, if you want to leave him, we can help you. Lord Sutcliffe has agreed to see about finding you a position in one of his households. I'm sure the Duke would as well. You can come with us—"

"I can't leave!" Flora shook her head, looking panicked. "'Tis wrong! I'm his wife."

"What's wrong is how he treats you." Kendra pulled back, frustrated. "You don't deserve to be beaten, Flora. Just think about it, okay?" She waited until the other woman nodded, then said, "But that's not all I wanted to speak to you about."

"What else?" Flora's aquamarine eyes darkened with fear.

"Mr. Stone."

It didn't seem possible, but Flora paled even more. "I—I cannot speak of . . . of him," she whispered, and cast a hurried glance around. "Please, I must finish me shopping. Me husband'll be seeking me out soon."

"Did Stone ever mention where he originally came from? About his time in London?"

Flora hesitated. She licked her lips, shot another frantic glance around. "He spoke of bein' born in a small village outside London," she finally said. "He didn't say the name. He said he left almost as soon as he was in breeches."

"What did he do? Before he came to East Dingleford?"

"I—I think he was a K-knight of the Road," she whispered fearfully.

Kendra frowned. "Knight of the Road?"

"Sh-sh! 'Tis a highwayman, miss," Flora whispered.

Kendra said nothing for a moment. "Why do you think this, Flora?"

"He told me, but he wasn't specific-like. He just said things. But it was in the past. What's it matter now, miss?"

"Flora, did Stone talk about knowing Bancroft from before he came to East Dingleford? Maybe when he was a Knight of the Road?"

A frown dug between the other woman's brows. "He spoke of the earl, of course. But . . . I don't know. I don't think so."

"Are you sure? Think about it. This is important."

But she was already shaking her head, agitated. "I can't remember. Truly, I can't."

"Okay. Did he talk about finding something recently? Something valuable?"

Flora frowned, puzzled. "What do ye mean?"

It sounded odd to her modern ear, but she said, "A treasure of some kind?"

Flora was quiet for a long moment, like she was thinking hard. Then she shook her head. "Nay. Why do ye think he had a treasure?"

Kendra wasn't about to explain blood spatter to Flora. "We believe that Mr. Stone had something on his desk that was valuable enough for his killer to steal. We think it's the reason he was killed, and why Mrs. Stone was killed too."

"Because there's more treasure?"

"Possibly."

"Do you think he could've had a map . . . ?"

Kendra stifled a sigh. Did everyone believe the myth of treasure maps? She ignored the inquiry to ask instead, "Did Stone ever mention anything to you?"

"Nay . . ." But her gaze was sliding away. "I—I can't help ye, Miss Donovan. Please, I must go."

Kendra put a detaining hand on her arm. "If you know anything, Flora, you need to tell us. We're dealing with someone who has killed three people to get what he wanted. I don't think he'd have qualms about murdering a fourth."

"I don't know anything," Flora whispered.

Kendra dropped her hand. "The offer still stands. If you want to leave East Dingleford, we can find a position for you. You won't be left to fend for yourself."

Flora hesitated, the expression in her aquamarine eyes almost painful. "Why would ye do such a thing for me? Ye don't know me."

"I know what it's like to be trapped somewhere you have no control. But I was lucky enough to get help."

Her lips twisted into a smile. "Even be given a position, of sorts."

Mrs. Turner just stared at her with those tragic eyes.

Kendra stepped away. Alec appeared at her side, and gave Flora a brown package.

"How much do I owe ye, sir?" she asked nervously.

"'Tis a gift. I was informed it will cure every ill."

"Thank ye kindly, milord." She bobbed a curtsy. She tucked the package into her straw basket. "Miss Donovan."

"He'll do it again, you know," Kendra said, when the other woman began to move away.

Flora hesitated, her hand automatically touching her wrist. Sadness dimmed her pretty eyes more than fear. "Me husband's a good man. He didn't mean ter hurt me, Miss Donovan."

"I'm not talking about the physical abuse." Kendra waited a beat, fixing her gaze on the other woman. "I'm talking about the arrangement. He'll do that again."

Flora turned so pale that Kendra thought she might pass out. "Nay," she said in a hoarse whisper. "Nay, it was the debt. It was too much ter pay without losing the farm. William didn't want ter do it. What choice did we have?"

"Your husband may gamble too much again. Or maybe he'll start to think about bringing in some extra money." Kendra felt a twinge of guilt at the stricken look on the other woman's face, but reminded herself that Flora needed a bit of tough love.

The other woman whispered, "Nay, he wouldn't do that."

"He's already done it. Maybe you need to remember that."

Kendra didn't wait. She swept past the woman and continued down the lane. There was nothing else she could do. She'd planted the seed. The rest was up to Flora.

39

After the crisp fall temperatures outside, the foyer of the Green Maiden felt overheated. In her bedchamber, Kendra stripped off her coat, bonnet, and gloves, and was in the process of handing them over to Molly when someone knocked lightly on the door. She crossed the room, opening it to find Mrs. Bolton standing on the other side. The expression in the old woman's eyes made her catch her breath; anticipation zipped along her nerves. Glancing over her shoulder to make sure Molly was occupied putting her coat and bonnet away, she stepped into the hallway and inched the door closed behind her.

Mrs. Bolton's eyes darted nervously down the length of the corridor. "My brother will meet with you in the barn," she said softly. "Forty minutes. You must come alone."

"I'll be there."

Mrs. Bolton hesitated. "I'm trusting you, Miss Donovan."

Kendra nodded. "I understand. Thank you, Mrs. Bolton."

When Kendra returned to the parlor, she found Sam had returned, as well, and was speaking to Alec and the Duke. He looked at her when she entered.

"I was just telling his Grace and his lordship here that I followed Mr. Turner ter a tavern," Sam said. "He joined a few other men and spoke about a card game that's happenin' on Guy Fawkes Night."

"Apparently losing to Stone didn't sour Mr. Turner on the game," Alec remarked drily, lifting the silver coffee pot. He poured two cups.

Sam looked at Kendra. "Did you learn anything from Mrs. Turner, miss?"

She accepted the cup Alec handed to her with thanks, then replied, "Flora could only tell us that she thought Stone came from a village outside London, and that he left when he was young." She took a sip of coffee. "She also thought he might have been a highwayman."

Alec's expression remained neutral, but only because she'd already relayed the information to him on the carriage ride back to the Green Maiden. Sam's eyes narrowed, and Kendra caught the hard gleam of suspicion.

"Why would he tell a thing like that ter Mrs. Turner?"

"Well, he only hinted at it, according to her. I can only speculate, of course, but Stone was about seventy. Flora is in her mid- to late-twenties, I'd say. He might have felt the need to impress her with his youthful exploits."

"Being a highwayman is not admirable, and it is more than a youthful exploit." The Duke leaned back in his chair, rolling the quill pen between his fingers. Kendra noticed the smudges on his fingertips, and was reminded of Biddle. "'Tis a hanging offense."

"We knew that Stone wasn't a saint," she said with a shrug, and moved to study the slate board. "What we need to know is if there is a connection between Stone's alleged highwayman activities from thirty-odd years ago and Bancroft."

Alec said, "Bancroft wouldn't be the first gentleman who took to the road to make a living through nefarious means."

"We cannot accuse the earl of such a serious charge without proof, Alec." The Duke shot his nephew a warning look.

Sam frowned. "Didn't Lord Bancroft leave England after East Dingleford?"

"He was gone for sixteen years," Kendra pointed out. "He could've become involved in anything during that time. And he was a kid. If he needed money, who knows? And we could be talking about more than robbery. In my—" she nearly said *era*, and cleared her throat—"America, armed robberies can turn deadly. What if Bancroft killed someone in the course of a robbery?"

"That would certainly account for Lord Bancroft paying a blackmailer for twenty years to keep quiet," Alec murmured. "But what proof could Stone have possibly had?"

They fell silent as they considered the problem.

Kendra finally sighed and shook her head. "Whatever it was had two pieces. The first was on the desk." She sipped her coffee as her gaze drifted over to the desk that the Duke was sitting behind, littered with his correspondence, an open leather-bound ledger, and the writing tray. Kendra's neck prickled with sudden comprehension. It couldn't be so simple.

She forced herself to move, to set down the cup and walk over to the desk. "What are you working on, your Grace?"

The Duke didn't seem to find her question odd. He sighed. "Balancing the household ledgers, my dear. I have been inspired by Lord Bancroft to install gas lighting in Aldridge Castle. But it's no small expense. I may be forced to trim some of the estate's more frivolous expenses so as not to become overextended."

Kendra's lips parted as she stared at the tidy columns of numbers. The air around her seemed to buzz, as though charged with electricity.

"It will be a sizeable undertaking," continued Aldridge, unaware of Kendra's distraction. "Undoubtedly, it will cause an upheaval with the staff."

"Because you operate Aldridge Castle like a business," she murmured.

"Well, yes, that is true." He leaned forward to replace the quill pen in its holder. "Thankfully, my estates are all profitable, and I cannot complain about the plumpness of my pockets. Still, I don't have the liquid assets to simply write a check to cover an endeavor this large."

She said, "Your funds are tied up in other investments."

Awareness flickered behind the Duke's blue gaze, as though he were suddenly realizing that something might be off. "Yes, much of my money is in the Exchange, as well as personal investments or group investments. What's this about, my dear?"

Kendra became aware of Sam and Alec's curious regard as well. She glanced at the clock. "I have an idea, but I need a moment." Her heart began thumping as she crossed the room, pulling open the door.

The Duke's eyebrows shot up. "Good heavens. Where are you going, Miss Donovan?"

But she only shook her head and closed the door to the private parlor, hurrying down the hall.

Adrenaline made Kendra's pulse jump. She had a momentary worry that Alec might follow her, but she made it to the back door without interference. She shivered as she stepped outside, the thin muslin walking dress no barrier against the cool breeze. The grass was still wet from the previous evening's rain, and the moisture soaked into the hem of her skirt as she crossed the yard to the barn. Pushing open the door, she paused to let her eyes adjust to the gloomy interior. Once again, she was assailed by the strong stench of the barn.

Mrs. Bolton emerged from the shadows, her gaze anxious. "You came alone?"

"Yes," Kendra said, though she was stating the obvious. She looked at the figure looming behind the old woman. The man was a dozen years younger than his sister, she estimated, but stress had aged him. His face was heavily lined. His hair was more silver than blond. The first time she'd seen him on the road, he'd smeared soot across his face, which had made his eyes blaze like a blue flame. Without that contrast, his eyes were an almost colorless blue. He wore a dirty work smock beneath an even dirtier tweed coat, with brown wool trousers and muddied boots so worn that Kendra could see the sole peeling away from the toe.

"Joseph, this is Miss Donovan," Mrs. Bolton introduced them.

"We weren't involved in Mr. Stone's killing," he said immediately, his eyes narrowed warily. "And I didn't see the fiend that killed Mr. Stone either. Laura says that's what you want ter know, but I don't know how I can help you."

The man looked ready to bolt. Kendra stepped forward carefully. "I know you had nothing to do with Stone's murder," she said. "But you were there at the mill. I need you to tell me what happened when you went there. You might have seen more than you realize."

"It's all right, Joseph." Mrs. Bolton put a hand on her brother's arm. "Please, tell Miss Donovan what you remember."

He gave Kendra a hard look. "I won't peach on my men."

"I'm not asking you to. Why did you choose that day to attack the mill?"

"They'd just ordered new frames, and fired seven good men. They have families. They'll be starving soon, and tossed into the poorhouse." Joseph scowled. "It's not right how his lordship let Mr. Stone cut back on safety measures. Ned Mann lost his right hand last month. How's he supposed to feed his family?"

"You used to work there, right? When did you start noticing the declining working conditions?"

"Stone fired me three years ago, when I started complaining about the poor wages. I don't remember when I first noticed things weren't right."

"But there was a time when things were good at the mill?"

"Aye, when Mr. Murray was runnin' it. He was a good man. Then he was gone and his lordship hired Mr. Stone." He turned his head, and spat into a clump of hay. "He couldn't run it proper, and Lord Bancroft brought in Mr. Biddle."

"It got better then?"

"For a time. Mr. Biddle was at least at the mill, tryin' to keep it runnin'. Mr. Stone wasn't around. Too busy pretending he was gentry. A mushroom, that's what he was."

Kendra had learned that a mushroom was someone who found his or her position suddenly elevated in society. By definition, *she* was a mushroom.

"I heard that you confronted Stone recently about the problems at the mill," she said.

"Aye, after Ned had his accident. Somebody had to do it!"

"How did Mr. Stone react?"

Thackeray snorted. "Like I was telling him a Banbury Tale! Why would I lie about that, eh? He dismissed my words like he was still my master."

"So you . . . the Luddites wanted to send a message to Stone by smashing the frames."

It wasn't a question, but Joseph nodded. "Aye. Stone and Lord Bancroft. Maybe they'd notice the worker's plight after losing all that fine equipment." His mouth twisted. "That's what they care about—money, not men."

"You had spies inside to let you know that the mill was closing early," Kendra guessed.

"Aye. They sent word that Mr. Biddle was closing the mill on account of the fog. We waited until everyone was gone. Then we went inside to smash the looms."

"But you didn't wait for Mr. Stone to leave."

Joseph frowned. "We thought he did. But the fog can confuse a person. We didn't know that he was . . . that he was still upstairs. Dead." He wiped a sleeve against the sweat that had suddenly sprung up on his brow. "Christ, I'd never seen so much blood."

Kendra regarded him with surprise. "You went upstairs?"

"Aye, me and a couple of me men. We had the thought of smashing up Mr. Stone's fancy office, all those cats he collected . . ." He scrubbed his face with hands that shook.

"We saw Mr. Stone. He was already dead. I swear on my mother's grave that he was dead!"

"I believe you. And there was no one else in the mill?"

"Nay."

"Did you go into Biddle's office?"

"Only for a moment." He hesitated. "We have no quarrel with Mr. Biddle, but if we destroyed their bill of sales and such, that could hurt the operation more than smashing the frames. But one man had gone into Stone's office and was yelling something fierce . . ." His face twisted in remembered horror. "I went to him. And . . . and there was Mr. Stone."

"I need you to think back very carefully, Mr. Thackeray. I want you to think about when you were in Mr. Biddle's office. Did you have a lantern?"

"Aye. We used the mill's lanterns and torches. We had to be careful. We didn't want to draw attention."

Kendra thought of that night, how she'd hurried past the open doorway to Biddle's office, intent on getting to the crime scene. Nausea curdled her stomach. That had been a mistake, she realized. If she'd treated the entire factory as a proper crime scene—not just Stone's office—would Mrs. Stone and Mrs. Trout still be alive?

She drew in an unsteady breath. "Okay, imagine you're in Biddle's office like you were that night. What do you see?"

Joseph stared at her like she was crazy.

"Please, Mr. Thackeray. This is very important."

He was silent for a moment, then shrugged. "I see his desk. Papers and books on it. His writing tray."

"Chairs," Kendra prompted when he fell silent. "The coatrack."

"His greatcoat, of course. And hat—"

"His coat was there. Are you sure?"

Joseph frowned at her. "What does it—" Comprehension lit his pale eyes. "Aye. His greatcoat was hanging on the rack. Who leaves their greatcoat behind when it's so cold outside?"

Kendra didn't say anything, but she knew the answer. *A murderer who was already wearing the coat of his victim to cover up his own bloody clothes.*

"*Mr. Biddle*? You think Mr. Biddle is the fiend?" Oliver Matthews stared at her in disbelief. "Pray tell, Miss Donovan, why do you think such a thing?"

Constable Jameson's lip curled. "W'ot's this about? Ye can't be flingin' accusations around without proof, Miss Donovan. A man's good name is at stake."

Kendra pressed her lips together to prevent herself from saying something she might regret. She took a moment, allowed her gaze to travel the room. The Duke, Alec, and Sam waited. She'd already laid out her suspicions to them. It was mostly conjecture, she knew, except for the greatcoat. If Joseph hadn't been mistaken, the greatcoat was a damning piece of evidence.

Now she looked at Matthews and Jameson, ready to lay out her theories again. "Biddle has always been the most obvious suspect," she said. "He was the last person to see Stone alive, and the last person to be seen with Stone. We have witnesses that saw Biddle with Stone."

"That's not strange, given Mr. Biddle worked for Mr. Stone," Matthews pointed out.

She nodded. "I know. That's why it never seemed like a big deal. It would have stood out if Biddle had denied meeting with Stone, but he never did. However, he told us that Stone came into his office to speak to him. I should have realized that was odd."

Matthews regarded her quizzically. "Why would that be odd?"

"Stone enjoyed being in control. He had an almost pathological need to make others feel small, and himself big by comparison. A guy like that would have demanded to meet in his office, not Biddle's. In the mill, his office was his kingdom."

She waited, but when no one challenged her, she went on, "Biddle was also the one who shut down the factory early."

"Under orders from Mr. Stone," the constable argued.

"Biddle *said* that he was acting on Stone's orders," Kendra corrected. "When we interviewed the workers, we never asked what Biddle was wearing when he gave the order. Who would have asked that?" She gave a shrug. Hindsight was a bitch. "Even if we had thought to ask the question, they would have told us that he was wearing a greatcoat. No reason for us to assume it wasn't *his* greatcoat.

"There's no way the murderer could have avoided getting blood on himself. He could clean up his hands and face, but not his clothes. Biddle's instinct—anyone's instinct—would have been to put on Stone's greatcoat to conceal his clothes before he left the office."

"Dear God," Matthews muttered. He appeared already convinced. He retrieved his hankie, and pressed it to his lips. "But why? *Why* would Mr. Biddle kill Mr. Stone?"

Kendra walked over to the desk and picked up the Duke's ledger. "For something like this—the mill's accounting books. Stone was the manager at the mill, but it's an open secret that he never really did any work. Biddle was responsible for running the mill, for ordering supplies and paying vendors, and keeping the accounting books and bank accounts."

"W'ot are you saying?" the constable demanded.

"I'm saying that Biddle has excellent taste. In clothes. In artwork. Furnishings. I noticed it when we called upon him. I had wondered how an assistant manager could afford his lifestyle. Biddle told us that he invested wisely and was frugal." She tossed the ledger back on the desk, where it landed with a soft thud. "But I think it was more than that."

Matthews said slowly, "You think he was stealing from the mill."

"We heard how the quality of the mill had suddenly declined—inferior products, cutting corners. Of course, everyone blamed Stone. Or Lord Bancroft. We forgot who was really running the mill."

"Mr. Biddle," Matthews breathed.

Kendra nodded. "I'm not sure how long he's been doing it. Based on his artwork alone, I'd say a couple of years. But it wasn't until recently that Stone figured it out, when someone confronted him about the shoddy products and safety conditions." She didn't need to identify Joseph. "I think it made Stone suspicious. He probably decided he should take a look at the mill's ledgers. I think that's when he realized that Biddle had been embezzling from the mill."

Matthews stared at her. "And Biddle killed him?"

"It wasn't planned. I think Stone called Biddle into his office and had the ledger open on his desk. We've heard the stories about how Stone enjoyed threatening his workers. I can't imagine him sparing Biddle."

"No, I can't either," Matthews agreed softly.

"Biddle must have panicked when he realized his embezzlement had been uncovered. He grabbed the bronze . . ." She lifted her shoulders. "Maybe he didn't even realize what he'd done until it was all over."

The Duke spoke up. "Mr. Biddle may not have meant to kill Mr. Stone, but afterward he did everything he could to cover it up."

Kendra nodded. "He put on Stone's greatcoat and closed down the mill. He left with the workers, taking the ledger with him. The inside pages also had Stone's blood on them. He knew he needed to get rid of the pages, and redo the figures. That's why he was spending more time at his house. It was too risky keeping the bloodstained ledger in his office. He could never be sure when Bancroft might come by, or one of the workers might come into his office."

Jameson remained silent, but Matthews looked shocked. "Good heavens. It all makes sense."

"We'll need a search warrant for his house," Kendra said. "That's where the ledger with Stone's blood will be."

"I'll send word to my father to issue one." Matthews hesitated. "And an arrest warrant."

"Wait." Jameson held up a hand, and scowled at Kendra. "Why'd Biddle torture and kill Mrs. Stone?"

Kendra frowned as she met the constable's brown eyes. "I don't know," she finally admitted. "But I promise you, that's going to be the first question I ask Biddle."

40

An hour later, armed with the search and arrest warrants, they went to Biddle's cottage. Mrs. Ferguson answered the door, her cheerful disposition sliding into concern when Matthews presented her with the search warrant. She allowed them to enter, but unfortunately, Biddle kept his study locked, and the housekeeper insisted she'd never been given a spare key. She also mentioned that until recently, her employer hadn't locked the door at all.

Jameson suggested breaking down the door. Though she knew it would only add to the constable's suspicions of her, Kendra took out two pins from the chignon that Molly had painstakingly twisted her hair into, and for the second time in two days, she bent down and picked a lock.

"'Tis a talent ter be found among those sent ter Botany Bay," the constable muttered darkly.

Kendra grinned. Straightening, she pushed open the door to a room done in tasteful maroons and charcoal grays. Hanging on the wall behind the desk was a Gainsborough. How much did a painting like that cost in this era? Thomas Gainsborough had been dead for about thirty years now. In her time, it would cost a small fortune.

They didn't have to search too hard to find the ledger, a large embossed leather-bound book sitting on Biddle's desk. Biddle had cleaned up the leather jacket, so the shadowy stains were barely noticeable on the cover. Kendra imagined it would light up like a Christmas tree if she had luminol and a black light on hand. But

she didn't need it. All they had to do was open the book
to see Stone's blood. Some pages were pristine, filled
only with columns—dates, accounts, debits, credits,
balances—written in a spidery hand. Others had tiny
black specks near the page's outer edges.

Matthews inhaled sharply. The book fell open easily to
the pages that had been exposed during Stone's murder.
They'd soaked up Stone's blood, stiffening the foolscap
and staining it so dark that the writing could barely be
seen beneath.

"Lookee here," Sam said, and they glanced over to
where the Bow Street Runner was dragging a puce-colored greatcoat with three caplets out of a black lacquered
chest. The light streaming in from the window caught the
sable collar, making it gleam.

"Mr. Shannon is right—it's a grand coat," she said.

"Why'd the fool keep it?" Jameson wondered. "He
should've burned it."

"Maybe he planned to, or maybe he thought he could
get rid of it at a second-hand clothing store in Manchester," said the Duke. "The workmanship is superb. I
think he would have received a nice price for it."

Kendra shoved away from the desk, and the book that
held Stone's blood on its pages. "I think you have enough
evidence. It's time to talk to Biddle."

The bits of cotton floating down from the gray sky
reminded Kendra of the first time she'd come to the
mill. It had been night then, and eerily quiet. It was day
now, and the noise coming from inside the factory was so
thunderous that Kendra could feel the vibrations through
the soles of her feet as they approached the doors. Kendra
covered her ears against the clattering of the machines
inside. The smell of linseed oil, dust, and sweat struck
her forcefully as soon as they were through the door.
The factory floor was a whirling dervish of activity: men

working the looms, racing around with bags of freshly carded cotton slung over their shoulders, leaping forward to pluck white fluff from the teeth of the machines, and jumping back before their fingers could be chopped off.

Kendra scanned the workers. Biddle wasn't among them. She moved forward, walking rapidly toward the stairs. Alec, Sam, and the constable were beside her, while the Duke and Matthews followed. Kendra picked up her pace when she saw Biddle coming down the stairs with another man. They were talking, but Kendra saw the exact moment when Biddle spotted them. His face froze as his eyes locked on the constable.

Shit. Kendra knew what was going to happen from the panicked expression that crossed Biddle's face, his eyes all but falling out of his head. Snatching up her skirts, Kendra dashed toward the stairs, the reticule, heavy with the muff pistol, banging against her thigh.

She made it to the bottom of the stairs when Biddle grabbed his companion's arm and shoved him hard. Caught off balance, the man flapped his arms urgently, almost like he was hoping to take flight. Then he came crashing down the stairs. Kendra leaped to the side to avoid him, and continued racing up the stairs. Behind her, she thought she heard Jameson cry out as the man bowled him over.

Biddle reached the top of the stairs and kept running. Kendra chased after him, knowing that Alec was probably not far behind her, unless he'd been knocked over as well.

"Stop! You can't escape!" she yelled. The walls acted as a barrier to the thundering noise of the factory, so she could actually hear her voice. *"Give it up, Biddle!"*

He didn't stop. He didn't look back. He plowed ahead, his footfalls loud as shotgun blasts as he ran past the offices and down the hallway, skidding around a corner.

Gritting her teeth—and silently cursing her shoes and skirt—Kendra followed. She yanked her skirts up even higher as she skittered around the corner. Ahead, Biddle jumped on the iron ladder bolted to the wall, scrambling upward. Her gaze traveled up the ladder, which soared into the shadowy catwalks. At the top, she noticed the door cut into the wall.

"*Stop*!" she shouted, her gaze fixed on the man climbing the ladder. "It's over, Biddle!"

"Kendra!" Alec yelled from behind her.

She ignored him, launching herself at the first rung, and began to scale the ladder after Biddle. He was about eight feet above her. Kendra's calves burned as she thrust herself upward. Halfway up, her foot caught in her skirt, nearly unbalancing her. She gripped the railing hard and kicked viciously, hearing the material rip. Freed, she kept climbing.

Biddle tossed a quick glance down at her as he reached the door. Panting heavily, he worked the bolts. Then he flung the door open, its hinges giving a rusty shriek. Light poured through the aperture. Kendra leaped to clasp the rung above her, pulling herself up two rungs at a time. Her breathing was ragged by the time she made it to the door. Then she was plunging through it to the roof.

Icy wind slapped her face, and whipped her torn skirt around her legs. She drew in great gulps of air as she scanned the roof. The top portion was a long, flat strip, five feet in width that ran for about fifty yards. The slates plunged at a steep angle on either side. Ahead, the mill's massive smokestacks rose up to bisect the roof. Kendra caught the dizzying sweep of countryside and East Dingleford—vivid autumn trees, a flash of the glimmering green-blue of the river, white and gray stone houses and cottages.

Biddle was sprinting down the flat strip of roof toward the chimneys.

"There's nowhere to run, Biddle!" she shouted over the screaming wind. Where the hell was he going? She grabbed fistfuls of material, yanking her tattered skirt high above her knees as she again dashed after him.

Biddle had reached the end of the strip. Stumbling to a stop, he whipped around to face her. "Let me go!" he yelled. His eyes were bright with panic and fear. "It was an accident! I didn't mean to kill him, I swear!"

Kendra skittered to a stop about seven feet from the man. Behind her she heard rapid footfalls, but she kept her focus on Biddle. "I believe you. Let's talk about it, okay? Come with me, Mr. Biddle. Let's go inside to discuss it."

She inched forward. Five feet between them.

"Stay back!" he shrieked.

Kendra dropped her skirt, lifted her hands, and stopped. "Okay, Mr. Biddle. Stay calm!"

"Calm?!" He gave a bark of wild laughter that was instantly carried away by the wind. "This was never supposed to happen! He never gave a damn about the mill! *I* cared! It was *my* sweat, *my* blood that went into this place! Not Stone's! Not the earl's!"

"You deserved something for your efforts." One step forward.

His eyes blazed. "You're goddamn right I did! I was giving my life for this place, and barely got a pittance! No one cares about us workers! Do you know what happened when I asked for an increase in wage? The bastard *laughed* at me! Said he could snap his fingers and the earl would find another man more appreciative!"

"I understand." Another step. "They failed to see you for who you were. An intelligent, resourceful man." Four feet.

"I deserved to be compensated!"

"So you increased your own wages. Took a little here, a little there."

"God helps those who help themselves. That's what the Bible says."

"Actually, no. That phrase isn't in the Bible."

Biddle glared at her. "I told you to stay where you are!" Suddenly he whirled around, his hands reaching out to steady himself against the smokestack. His fingers tried to dig into the brick as he slid, crablike, onto the section of the slate-shingled roof that sloped sharply downward.

Kendra's heart leaped into her throat. "What the fuck are you doing? You're going to get yourself killed!"

He ignored her, his attention focused on his feet.

"Kendra," Alec said from behind her, a low warning. "Let him go."

She didn't turn around, didn't acknowledge Alec. Instead, she kept her gaze fixed on Biddle. He didn't seem to notice that the wind was picking up strength, tearing at his jacket, fluttering his hair. Kendra could feel it buffet her, strong enough to rock her back and forth. Carefully, she moved forward. Less than two feet now.

"There's no escape, Biddle!"

He glanced at her, his expression fierce. "Are you certain?"

Another slide. Another scrape. Kendra was stunned when he started to grin. She didn't actually see him lose his footing, but she knew the moment it happened. She saw his body jerk, and his eyes go wide in a terrible comprehension. His fingers tightened on the bricks, his feet shuffling, desperate to gain traction, but the weight of his body tore his hands away. He screamed, and threw his hands out, clutching at air.

Instinctively, Kendra lunged forward, her hands outstretched to catch hold of his. He clawed at her arm, yanking her forward. His fingers locked around her wrist in a death grip that crushed her bones. A cry tore out of Kendra's throat and she tried to throw herself backward to break the momentum, to offer a counterbalance against his weight and the inexorable pull of gravity. For a shocking second, they teetered together, their eyes locked on each other's. The wind pummeled them. Then Biddle's feet went out from under him, and he plunged backward, his hands still wrapped around Kendra's wrists.

"*Kendra!*" someone—the Duke or Alec—yelled from behind her.

She cried out in pain as she fell forward, her body slamming against the roof's slate tiles. The impact knocked the breath from her lungs. Then she found herself being dragged forward as Biddle's weight pulled her headfirst toward the edge of the roof.

Her gaze was locked on Biddle's terrified face, and, beyond him, the ground that swam dizzyingly below. Desperately, she kicked her feet, trying to slam her toes into the slick slate tiles to stop their downward momentum. Her hands were useless. Biddle's fingers were shackled around her wrists, binding them together as they hurtled toward the edge of the roof.

Then suddenly her whole body wrenched, her ankles caught in a viselike grip. She screamed, her arms nearly ripped out of her sockets by Biddle's dead weight. Her breath hitched in her chest as her gaze shifted beyond Biddle's face, down the length of his body to where his boots were dangling off the roof.

"I've got her! Someone bloody well take hold of my coat, and *pull*!" Alec ordered. "Goddamn it, *pull!*"

Kendra gasped as her body was tugged back up the pitch of the roof, the tiles scraping painfully against her flesh. She tilted her head back to prevent her face from being scratched off completely. Biddle's weight brutally stretched her arms. She kept her jaw locked to prevent herself from screaming in agony.

The hands on her ankles shifted to her calves, then to her waist. Sam and the constable reached past her to pry Biddle's hands from her wrist.

"Let go!" Sam shouted. "Damn you! Let go, you bloody bastard!"

The next moment, Kendra was free, Alec's arms locked around her as they rolled onto the flat portion of the roof. Breathing heavily, Alec straightened, dragging her across his lap as he leaned against the brick smoke-stack. She could feel his body trembling. Or maybe it was hers. Kendra caught the intense flash of green in his eyes before he swept her into a hard, wild kiss.

"My God . . . Kendra!" The Duke said behind her.

"I swear it was an accident!" Biddle's voice rose up. "I didn't mean to kill him!"

"Shut it, ye son of a whore!" Jameson yelled.

Kendra saw the constable shove Biddle toward the door.

"Are you all right, miss?" Sam asked, his golden eyes bright as they roved over her.

"I might need longer sleeves, otherwise I'm fine." Still, she had to catch her breath. "I want to talk to him."

"Aye. I'll just assist the constable in taking the basta—the prisoner ter jail." The Bow Street Runner grinned and gave her a jaunty salute before spinning around, hurrying to catch up with the constable and Biddle.

The Duke stared down at her and Alec. "How are you really, Miss Donovan?"

"Now I know how people felt when they were put on a torture rack." She regarded him. "You know, I heard you call me Kendra. Do we really need to be formal again?"

A smile split his face, and his blue eyes were bright as they drifted over her and Alec. "No, I don't believe we do. I think I shall go and explain what has happened to Mr. Matthews. He wisely stayed inside the mill."

They watched as he jogged the distance to the door. He turned to smile at them again before disappearing inside.

"Alone, at last," she huffed out with a laugh.

"Hell and damnation, Kendra." Alec's arms tightened around her. "I nearly died when you tried to grab the bastard. You are a courageous, foolish woman."

"Why, thank you." She stroked her fingers through his thick, dark hair, even though the movement caused her shoulders to ache. "I'm glad you were here." She leaned in and kissed him, then sighed. "I need to interview Biddle. There are still unanswered questions."

"Later. First, I'm sending for Dr. Poole to examine you."

"Hell, no."

"Kendra."

"No. He'll probably try bleeding me, or he'll tell me to snip a lock of hair and burn it under a full moon"

"He's not a witch."

"You could've fooled me," she muttered. "I'm fine. Just a little sore, okay?" She shifted, and winced. "Maybe a lot sore. But it's nothing that a hot bath won't cure."

Alec helped her to her feet. As they stepped away from the protection of the smokestack, the wind pummeled them. Alec kept his arm around her. "I'm bringing you back to the Green Maiden. You'll have to change your clothes anyway."

Kendra glanced down at her ragged skirt. He was right, she realized. It was ripped so badly in places that she could see her legs. She'd shocked East Dingleford enough.

"And mayhap Mrs. Bolton has some liniment for your shoulder."

"I wouldn't object to that," Kendra said, and smiled.

"You're limping," Alec observed as they reached the door.

"I banged up my knees when I fell. The bath and liniment should take care of it."

Alec went down the iron ladder first. Kendra bit her lip to keep from gasping as she clutched the ladder's railing firmly, each downward step jerking her bruised shoulders. A hot bath and liniment didn't sound so bad, she decided. Then she'd interview Biddle.

The hot bath and liniment oil helped ease some of Kendra's soreness. Mrs. Bolton's apricot brandy did the rest. She didn't want to overindulge. She had every intention of interviewing Biddle in the jail, but one small glass wouldn't hurt, she decided, as she, the Duke, Alec, and Sam sat in front of a crackling fire in the private parlor.

"I thought he was mad, when he went up ter the roof," said Sam. He shook his head as he stared into the glass of whisky he cupped in his hands. "I thought he was gonna jump, the bloody fool." He glanced at her. "Pardon me, miss."

Kendra smiled wryly, looking at the Bow Street Runner. "I think we can let go of the formalities. I'm hardly going to swoon when you say the word 'bloody.'"

Sam grinned. "Nay, you're made of sterner stuff than that, Miss Donovan. But you are also a lady, so I must apologize."

"Oh, don't go all missish on me now, Mr. Kelly."

Sam laughed. "Forgive me, but I think I *am* missish. God's teeth, my heart nearly stopped beatin' when you jumped forward ter save Mr. Biddle. My nerves haven't recovered."

"Neither have mine," drawled Alec, giving Kendra a hooded look. "I can only hope that Miss Donovan will temper such heroic impulses in the future, or someone ought to carry smelling salts, because I shall be the one swooning."

Kendra eyed the marquis. He'd bathed and changed his clothes as well, and was looking outrageously handsome in a bottle-green superfine jacket that fit his broad shoulders perfectly. He wasn't sitting so much as he was sprawled in his chair in his preferred pose, his long legs stretched out in front of him, his boots crossed at the ankles.

"Somehow I think you're made of sterner stuff, as well, my lord," she murmured.

"Well, apparently Mr. Biddle wasn't quite as mad as we thought," said the Duke, circling back to the earlier discussion. "There is another set of stairs that can be accessed on the other side of the roof. I imagine he thought if he could get around the chimneys to the other side, he could escape."

Alec shook his head in disbelief. "He was still mad if he thought he could flee East Dingleford without us giving chase."

"He panicked—classic fight-or-flight response," Kendra said, and began to lift her shoulders in a shrug. Because they were still sore, she settled for a half shrug. "When he saw us coming, his instincts kicked in and he ran. He knew he couldn't get by us, so he ran for the roof." She thought of the twisted grin and glint in his eyes as he stepped out onto the peaked portion of the roof. "I blame myself for bringing Constable Jameson. I don't think Biddle would have reacted in the way he did if Jameson hadn't been along."

"There is little point in second-guessing our decisions." The Duke took a sip of his brandy. "We have the fiend, that's all that matters. To think he was embezzling from Lord Bancroft and the mill for all those years, and no one noticed."

"Actually, the workers noticed," Kendra corrected. "Not that Biddle was stealing, but that corners were being cut. They simply attributed it to Stone."

"I'm surprised Lord Bancroft didn't review the books at least once a year," said the Duke. "He is actively involved in his business and investments."

"Mr. Murray said his lordship was involved when he was runnin' the mill," Sam put in.

"But then he fired Mr. Murray, and hired Stone." Kendra frowned. "I think there's still a connection between Stone and Bancroft."

The Duke shrugged. "Even if there is—or was—it had nothing to do with the murder."

Kendra said nothing, but a whisper of unease teased the back of her neck.

"Once the earl hired Mr. Biddle, he began ter stay away from the mill," Sam said.

"I wonder if the earl was responsible for the new machines or if Biddle suggested them," Alec murmured. "It would be an easy way to skim money and make a substantial profit. I don't know how much one of the frames cost, but if Biddle put it in the books that he had bought five looms, when in fact he'd only purchased four—"

"He would pocket the rest of the blunt," Sam finished, his golden eyes glinting. "Ah, clever scheme."

"It was—until Stone figured it out," agreed Kendra.

"Given Mr. Stone's personality, I'm rather surprised he didn't suggest some sort of partnership with Mr. Biddle when he discovered his manager's larceny," the Duke remarked. "They could have stolen from the mill—and Lord Bancroft—together."

Kendra shook her head. "Stone would have felt like Biddle played him for a fool. The mill was *his* territory."

Alec twirled his empty glass in his hands. "So it was all for greed? Stone, and his wife and the housekeeper? Biddle had already stolen the ledger that was on Stone's desk. Why torture Mrs. Stone? What was he looking for?"

"Maybe there are more ledgers?" Sam suggested. "Biddle had been stealing for years."

"There's only one way to find out." Kendra pushed herself to her feet. "Ask him."

41

East Dingleford didn't have a jail. Instead, the village had what was called a lockup. It was exactly what its name implied: Villagers who broke the law were locked up until they could be hauled before the magistrate. The East Dingleford lockup had probably housed plenty of disorderly drunks, maybe a thief or two. But Kendra suspected that it rarely held a murderer within its walls.

The building itself was strange: a single-story, round structure, only eight feet in diameter, with a spire-shaped roof that looked like the top of a witch's hat. A thick, nail-studded plank door was cut into the stone wall, about a foot deep. Three narrow slits served as windows.

The lockup was located next to the Norman church. Kendra couldn't decide if that was odd or diabolically clever. Was it meant serve as a warning to churchgoers? Or an extra humiliation to the prisoner confined within the lockup, forced to gaze upon the church and think on his sins while awaiting his sentence?

"W'ot do ye need ter talk ter him about, anyhow?" asked Constable Jameson as he pulled out the key for the heavy padlock on the door. Kendra tried not to let it bother her how the man's gaze slipped over her head to look at the Duke, Sam, or Alec for an answer.

She snapped, "Mr. Biddle murdered three people. I think questions need to be asked."

Jameson's jaw tightened. "Don't know why; w'ots done is done."

Metal scraped against metal, and Jameson shoved the door inward and stepped back, allowing Kendra to brush past him. She paused just inside, squinting into the squalid, gloomy room. The waning afternoon light beamed across the dirt floor from the open doorway and window slits. Her eyes bounced from the built-in privy, which reminded her of a seat in a porta-potty, to the narrow cot shoved against the left wall. Biddle was lying on the thin straw mattress, his body twisted away from the door. She could hear the rattle of his breathing, but he was still.

"Mr. Biddle?" Kendra came forward and gripped Biddle's shoulder, easing him onto his back. He gave a muffled groan. She let out a gasp as her gaze slid over the man's face. In the murky light, she could see that his left eye was swollen shut, and the lower half of his face was caked in dried blood. His nose had an odd, smashed appearance, tilted to the side. Broken, she was sure, which accounted for his labored breathing. He probably had a few broken teeth as well. She slipped her fingers beneath his bloody cravat to search for his carotid artery. His pulse was weak.

Fury made her tremble. She snatched her fingers away, and before she knew it she was out the door, slamming her palms against Jameson's chest, hard enough for him to stumble, lose his balance, and fall on his ass.

"Oy!" He stared up at her with wide eyes. "W'ot's that for?"

"What the fuck did you do to him?" she demanded.

"Kendra!" the Duke exclaimed.

The constable shoved himself to his feet, glaring at her. "You're mad!"

"You fucking bastard!" She took another step forward, but Alec caught her arm. She yanked it free and whirled to face the Duke. "Someone needs to get Dr. Poole," she said through clenched teeth. "Biddle has been severely beaten." Her mouth tightened as she lowered her gaze to Jameson's hands. His knuckles were swollen, the skin broken, with specks of blood congealed across the stretched flesh. She had a feeling most of the blood wasn't his. "He's unconscious."

"He slipped and fell," Jameson said, rolling his shoulders in a shrug.

"You're an ass."

The constable's eyes nearly bugged out of his head. "'Ere now! You mind yer tongue, miss!"

The Duke held up a hand. "I think we need to calm down."

Jameson reddened, matching Kendra's glare. "He's a sodding murderer. Don't know w'ot you're getting so het up about. His neck'll be stretched soon enough anyhow."

"I'll go and get the doctor," Sam volunteered.

The Duke pointed at Jameson, "Constable, it will be a speedier endeavor if you show Mr. Kelly the way to Mr. Poole's address. Take the carriage."

Jameson looked like he wanted to protest, still glaring at Kendra. "Aye, yer Grace," he finally huffed, and fell into step beside the Bow Street Runner.

Kendra spun around, pinching the bridge of her nose in frustration. *"God."*

Alec disappeared into the lockup, emerging a couple of minutes later. He shook his head when he met the Duke's eyes. "Mr. Biddle does not look good."

Kendra stared up at the darkening sky. Down the street, she saw two men begin the nightly ritual of lighting the lampposts. "Why did he do it?" she finally asked. She turned to look at Alec and the Duke. "Why?"

Alec regarded her. "Biddle, or Jameson?"

Kendra opened her mouth, hesitated. She thought of Mrs. Stone and Mrs. Trout. She shrugged. "Both. Damn it."

42

I don't know what you think I can do," Dr. Poole said, his fuzzy eyebrows meeting as he came out of the bedchamber, wiping his hands with a towel. The doctor had reluctantly allowed Biddle to be transferred to a spare bedroom in his cottage, although even at the lockup, he'd taken one look at the unconscious man and given a shrug, pronouncing Biddle all but in the grave. He hadn't seemed too eager to stop that from happening, and was bewildered over Kendra's desire to save him.

"Most of the injuries are to his face, but he's got several nasty gashes on the back of his skull. His color ain't good. He's not responding to stimuli." He paused, as though to weigh his words. "Doubt if he'll wake up again. He probably won't last the night."

Kendra lifted her hand to rake her fingers through her hair, but remembered the hairstyle Molly had pinned. She let her hands fall, her gaze moving over Alec, the Duke, Sam, and finally Dr. Poole.

"If Biddle dies, Jameson should be brought up on charges," she said.

Dr. Poole stared at her. "Do you have feathers for brains, madam? From what I heard, Biddle is the fiend that we've been seeking."

"He deserved a fair trial," she snapped.

"The constable said that the prisoner slipped and fell."

"Yeah—at least twenty times."

Dr. Poole's eyes narrowed at her. "Maybe Mr. Biddle attempted to escape, and Mr. Jameson was forced to subdue him."

Kendra looked at Sam. "You accompanied the constable when he brought the prisoner to lockup, Mr. Kelly. Did Mr. Biddle attempt an escape?"

"Nay, but . . ." The Bow Street Runner glanced away. "I didn't tarry. I don't know what happened after I left."

She sighed, rubbing the ache that had begun pounding between her brows. "Did Mr. Biddle have bruises on his face when you left him and the constable?"

This time he looked straight at her, no obfuscation. "Nay."

Her lips tightened. She recognized the look on Sam's face. *The thin blue line.* Bow Street Runners preceded any official police force in London, but that didn't mean they weren't cops. And cops—whether you were a Runner in London or a part-time constable—stuck together. Sam hadn't participated in the beatdown, but he wasn't going to point fingers at Jameson either.

"What's all this nonsense? If Mr. Biddle cocks up his toes, it'll save East Dingleford the cost of the hemp and building a scaffolding," groused Dr. Poole.

"You have such a warm and gentle bedside manner, doctor," Kendra said drily.

"Forgive me, young lady, for not shedding tears over a murderer."

He had her there. She held up a hand, a gesture of concession, and looked beyond the doctor into the bedchamber. She couldn't see anything, really, except the soft glow of firelight. "I'd like to stay with Mr. Biddle. He might wake up."

Dr. Poole frowned. "You are an unmarried lady, Miss Donovan. I hardly think it proper for you to spend the night in a bedchamber with a man."

Kendra stared at him. "The man is at death's door," she finally said. "What the hell do you think he's going to do to me?"

Dr. Poole's mouth knotted in disapproval. "Nevertheless, proprieties must be observed. East Dingleford may be a country village, but we are respectable people. You may come back tomorrow."

"That's ridiculous."

The fuzzy brows lifted. "What, pray tell, would you be able to do if Mr. Biddle woke and needed assistance? You are not a doctor, Miss Donovan. I doubt you have had much practice as a nursemaid either. Still, I can set your mind at rest on one score: Mr. Biddle shall not be alone. Either myself or Mrs. Poole will keep an eye on him throughout the night. He is not the first patient we've had in our home, you know. Although, I reckon if he survives, he'll be the only patient we've nursed through the night whose hanging we'll be attending."

Kendra glanced across the room and caught the glint of amusement in Alec's eyes. *He sees how absurd some of these rules are too.*

"I can spend the night with Mr. Biddle," Sam offered. "If anything changes, I shall send word ter you immediately, miss."

"Mr. Kelly has hit upon an excellent solution," said the Duke, laying a hand on Kendra's arm. "I suggest we return to the Green Maiden and seek a good night's rest."

Kendra supposed that was the only thing she could do. Still, she hesitated, her gaze locking on Sam's. "If he wakes—"

"I'll send word ter you."

"No." She shook her head. "Get him to talk about the murders. You need to ask him why he tortured Mrs. Stone." She wanted to ask Biddle these questions herself, but she had to be prepared for the just-in-case. Just as she had to be prepared that Biddle might never wake up.

Biddle didn't wake up during the night, but at least he was still alive the next morning when she arrived to relieve

Sam. The Bow Street Runner looked tired, the shadows beneath his eyes giving him a bruised appearance. After he reported that Biddle was still unconscious, Sam left. Molly had insisted on accompanying Kendra to the Poole residence, and her eyes were round as they entered the sick room.

It was a decent size room, with pale yellow painted walls, low ceiling beams, and sturdy pine furniture dusted to an inch of its life by either Mrs. Poole or an efficient housemaid. The fireplace was plain but functional, though the coal had apparently died out hours ago. Two chairs were in front of it, facing each other. Kendra noticed the blanket and pillow crumpled on one, and assumed that's where Sam had spent the night. Someone—Sam, most likely again—had opened the damask curtains on the two windows, allowing sunlight to slant into the room and across the bed. One sunbeam fell across Biddle's bruised and swollen face.

"'E looks just awful, don't 'e?" Molly whispered, peering down at the patient.

"He'll need to stay away from mirrors for the foreseeable future," Kendra admitted.

If he has a future, she amended silently. She gazed at Biddle. As far as she could tell, the only thing Dr. Poole had done was clean the blood off him and bandage his broken nose, which eased his breathing somewhat. It still sounded like he had a blockage.

If Biddle didn't wake up, he would die. It was as simple as that. In the twenty-first century, coma patients were given fluids, nutrients, and medicine intravenously or through a feeding tube. If they stopped breathing, they could be attached to a ventilator to keep their lungs pumping. But here? Dr. Poole was right; what could he do? It was simply a waiting game. Biddle could die of the head injury, or starvation and dehydration.

A wave of helplessness washed over her. For the first time, Kendra regretted her decision to pursue a career in criminology. Her parents would have approved if she'd chosen to become a doctor. And twenty-first-century medical skills would have been invaluable right now.

On the flip side, if she had become a physician, she wouldn't be there; presumably, she wouldn't have flown halfway across the world to take down Sir Jeremy Greene.

Were all her life choices just links on a chain that inevitably led her into the Duke's study in the twenty-first century? Was it her destiny to flee into the stairwell, and into the wormhole or vortex? Or was it a random event? The thoughts crowded her brain, frustrating, tantalizing—and ultimately unanswerable. *So let it go*.

She released a long sigh, and turned away from the bed. "You don't have to stay, Molly. I don't need a chaperone here."

Molly hesitated. "Well, Oi saw a sweet shop around the corner . . . Maybe Oi can nip out and get us somethin'?"

"Sure—oh. I don't have any money to give you."

"Oi 'ave money, miss."

Kendra frowned. "You have money? How do *you* have money?"

"'Tis me wages, miss."

"Oh. Of course." Kendra was careful to keep her expression neutral. She didn't begrudge the maid her wages, but that was another thing that was becoming intolerable. A fifteen-year-old had more money in her pocket than she did. "Okay," she finally said. "You can go to the sweet shop while I stay here."

"W'ot do ye want me ter bring ye?"

"I'm fine. You go, and don't feel like you have to come back anytime soon." She glanced at the still figure in the bed. "I have a feeling this is going to be a long day."

Unfortunately, her prediction turned out to be true. After Molly left, Mrs. Poole arrived, and plopped herself in a chair with an embroidery hoop. Kendra wondered if the doctor's wife was acting as her new chaperone.

"Did you bring any of your needlework with you, Miss Donovan?" the old woman asked in her placid manner.

"No." She wished that she'd brought her murder book. Even though Biddle had essentially confessed on the rooftop, something was troubling her. She wanted to review her notes, the timeline.

"I have another hoop, if you wish to embroider."

Kendra glanced at the rather intricate flowers, leaves, and stems that the other woman was creating, and shook her head. "I'm afraid that I don't have that kind of talent."

Mrs. Poole eyed her with surprise. "You do not do needlework?"

"Not so far."

The day dragged on. Dr. Poole came in to examine Biddle, which meant taking his pulse and pronouncing that nothing had changed. He shot Kendra an irritable look, but didn't say anything. Molly returned with a brown paper package, which she opened to reveal marzipan shaped into tiny animals. Mrs. Poole left, then returned an hour later with a tea tray.

The Duke and Alec arrived. They tried to convince her to abandon her vigil, certain that Mrs. Poole or her husband would send word to her if Biddle's conditioned changed. Kendra was tempted, but decided to stick it out a little longer.

Boredom finally made her accept Mrs. Poole's offer of another hoop, cloth drawn tight across it, and needle and embroidery threads. *How hard can this be?*

Once again, the skills of the nineteenth century foiled her, and she discovered that a task that looked simple was deceptive. She was staring at the tangled threads and lopsided flower when Biddle suddenly moved, his legs churning under the bedclothes, his arms flailing.

"*No!*" he cried. "*No . . .*"

Kendra dropped the embroidery hoop. Racing over to the bed, she grasped his shoulders to stop his thrashing. "Get your husband!" she ordered Mrs. Poole, her gaze on Biddle. She saw that his swollen eyes had opened, mere slits. The whites of his eyes were demon-red.

"Mr. Biddle, you're going to be fine." *Biggest lie I've told*. "Calm down, please."

His eyes slid back and forth.

"Dr. Poole is coming . . ." But even as she said that, Biddle's eyes rolled backward, then closed. The terror twisting his features began to fade.

"Mr. Biddle?" she said, resisting the urge to shake him. "Mr. Biddle? *Wake up*!"

Dr. Poole hurried into the room. "Move aside, move aside!"

Kendra stepped back and watched as the doctor did a cursory examination, checking Biddle's pulse, pulling his eyelids up. After a moment, he shook his head, and moved away from the bed.

"He's unconscious now. He woke up?"

"Yes. He cried out, and opened his eyes briefly before lapsing back into unconsciousness," Kendra said. "Do you think he's coming out of the coma?"

"How would I know? Head injuries are the most mysterious kind. Personally, I didn't think that he would wake up at all." He shrugged. "But if he woke up once, he could wake up again."

He wandered away, and Mrs. Poole, Molly, and Kendra resumed their vigil in a room silent but for Biddle's rattled breathing. Kendra didn't pick up her embroidery though. Instead, she went to the window. The sun was beginning to sink behind the moors, the shadows lengthening.

No . . . no, what? She prayed that Dr. Poole was right and Biddle would wake again.

But those prayers went unanswered. She wasn't sure exactly when it had happened, but eventually the sensation creeped over her that something had changed. She became aware of the silence in the room. Kendra flew over to the bed again, her fingers going to Biddle's neck. But she already knew.

Biddle was dead.

43

There would be an inquest, of course. The news caused a bit of a flurry around the Green Maiden. Apparently inquests were rare in East Dingleford. Even the old earl's death hadn't required one.

It was decided that the Green Maiden's tavern would be used for the inquest. Kendra wasn't sure she'd heard that right. But she was quickly informed by Sam that holding inquests in taverns wasn't quite as strange as Kendra thought, especially in the countryside. A village like East Dingleford was sizeable, but, like a jail, it wasn't big enough to have a courthouse.

"We shall have to stay for the inquest tomorrow, as we are witnesses," the Duke told her while they were both having tea in the private parlor. "Although ladies are not required to attend such proceedings, given their delicate sensibilities." He hid a smile when her dark eyes fired up.

"I'd really love to know which man started the myth about women having such delicate sensibilities," she muttered. "And then kick his ass."

Now he did laugh. "I cannot help you, my dear." He lifted his teacup and added, "You may instruct your maid to begin packing. I do not think it would be wise to leave immediately after the inquest, so we shall spend the night. And since the next day is Sunday—"

"There's no travel on the Sabbath."

Aldridge smiled. "Precisely. Besides, we ought to stay for Guy Fawkes Night, which I hear promises to be quite a celebration. We shall travel to Monksgrey on Monday morning, weather permitting." He took a sip of tea and waited. When Kendra said nothing, he set his cup back on the saucer with a clink. "Are you quite all right, my dear? You appear to be in rather a brown study."

Kendra glanced over at the slate board, which had been wetted and wiped clean. The investigation was finished.

So what was bothering her?

"I'm fine, just—I don't know . . ." She sighed, unable to put the sensation she was feeling into words. She was silent for a long moment, then picked up her teacup, and drank. Lowering the cup, she admitted, "I hate that I didn't have a chance to interview Biddle."

"You wanted him to confess about Mrs. Trout and Mrs. Stone."

"Yeah." She scowled into her tea. "It bothers me that the first crime scene was so different from the second one. Stone's murder was disorganized, sloppy. But Mrs. Stone and Mrs. Trout? That one was organized and calculated."

"Mr. Biddle clearly panicked when he realized Mr. Stone had discovered his theft, and he killed him. Afterward he had time to calm down, to think rationally."

Kendra nodded. "But what's the other piece of the puzzle? Biddle tortured Mrs. Stone for a reason."

"Obviously, Mr. Stone had more proof that Mr. Biddle had embezzled," said the Duke. "Maybe he taunted him with that. It could have contributed to the man snapping."

"I suppose. It's the only thing that makes sense."

He regarded her quizzically. "And yet you are still troubled."

She shifted impatiently in her seat. "It's unfinished business, a thread dangling."

"And you want to snip it off."

Kendra smiled slightly. "Yeah, I'm anal that way."

The Duke choked, having just taken another swallow of tea. *"Anal?"*

Kendra laughed. "Sorry. I don't mean . . . it's just an expression."

"It's a very *graphic* expression."

She'd never really thought about it before. There was so much she'd taken for granted, things that were just part of her world.

"I suppose it is," she said. She finished off her tea and set the cup aside. "It also bothers me that I never thought Biddle the type to do what was done to Mrs. Stone. I can see him snapping and killing Stone, and maybe he could've been cold-blooded enough to slit a woman's throat. But torture?" She shook her head. "I didn't see that. And if I didn't see that . . . what else am I missing?"

"I would agree with you on that score, my dear. However, you tell me often enough that people hide parts of themselves. And everyone can be fooled."

She nodded. "Maybe that's the thing that's bugging me. No one wants to be a fool." She moved toward the door. "I just feel . . ." She searched for the word, but nothing came to her. She shrugged. *Let it go.* "I'll tell Molly that we'll be leaving on Monday morning."

Unsettled. That was the word that she'd been searching for.

She needed to walk. She needed to brood. And because she wanted to do it alone, she snuck her spencer out of her bedchamber while Molly was occupied in the dressing room.

Outside, she struck out across the open field. In her haste to leave the bedchamber, she'd forgotten her bonnet and gloves, but it was warm enough not to need them. The fact that she even considered wearing a bonnet worried her a little. *Wearing bonnets is becoming part of my life.* She fought back a shiver, and once again her stomach tightened in the fear that she was losing herself, becoming unrecognizable.

She didn't pay any particular attention to where she was going until she crested a hill that sloped down toward the river. Her gaze traveled to the paddock near the edge of the forest. About a dozen people—kids mostly, she realized—were stacking wood into a pyre. Fixed to a stake at the center of a pyre was a straw-filled dummy, presumably, Guy Fawkes—the Catholic conspirator who had tried to blow up Parliament.

The forest behind them was brilliant with reds, oranges, yellows, and greens. The mill towered above the trees in the distance. The sight of the peaked roofs and enormous chimneystacks had greasy knots tightening in her belly. She'd never been afraid of heights, but she wondered if she might start suffering from the phobia now.

The pounding of hooves drew her attention away from the building. She turned, and felt a quick stab of disappointment that the man on horseback wasn't Alec.

"Miss Donovan," said Lord Bancroft, sweeping off his beaver hat as he reined in the large black stallion beside her. "Good afternoon. You are out alone."

"So are you."

He smiled. "I shall walk with you," he said, swinging off his horse.

Kendra didn't particularly want the earl's company, but since she didn't know how to avoid it without being rude, she waited. He kept hold of the reins, and the horse docilely trailed behind him as they walked.

Bancroft spoke. "I heard about Mr. Biddle." His expression was grave. "I cannot believe that he's a murderer. And I am shocked to learn that he was embezzling from the mill."

"Are you?" Kendra shot him a curious glance. Bancroft's dark eyes gave nothing away. "Rumor has it that the mill had become more rundown, and wasn't producing the quality product that it once did. I'm surprised you didn't notice or question it."

He was silent for a long moment. "I am guilty of negligence, I'm afraid," he admitted finally, expelling a sigh of regret. "My interest in the mill waned as other interests took precedence. The gas lighting craze. Steam engines.

I put the mill in Mr. Stone and Mr. Biddle's hands, and . . ." He shrugged. "I received a consistent dividend from the project, so I didn't inquire too closely."

"It seems a little odd that you didn't check in occasionally, since you practically live next door," she commented, studying him carefully.

"Ah, but I did occasionally put in an appearance, and speak to Mr. Stone about the mill's operation," he corrected her smoothly. "I relied on him to give me a fair report. I would say that he failed in his duty. However, it would seem that Mr. Stone only became aware of the embezzlement last week."

Kendra said nothing. Bancroft was right.

The earl asked, "Will you be attending the inquest tomorrow, or will you and your party be leaving East Dingleford?"

"I'll be at the inquest. We're leaving on Monday."

"Will you be coming to our Guy Fawkes celebration on Sunday evening, then?" He gestured to the activities in the paddock below. "Everyone attends, villagers and farm folk. I give my servants leave to go to the festivities. Even my daughter, Winifred, shall be there."

"Everyone?"

She wondered if Mr. Turner and his wife would be there, if she would have another opportunity to speak to Flora, at least to get word to her that they'd be leaving on Monday. Would Flora take her up on her offer to leave her husband? She doubted it, and that left a weight on her. *Is that why I feel so unsettled? The certainty that Turner will eventually kill his wife?*

But what can I do?

"Everyone," Bancroft confirmed. "There will be food and drink, and I shall supply a wild boar for the feast."

An image of the ugly beast she'd encountered in the forest a couple of days earlier came to mind, and she wondered if the animal's existence had ended on a roasting spit. For some reason, that depressed her.

"We plan to attend," she said.

"Very good. I'm certain you will enjoy it." He came to a stop, and regarded her with his intense gaze. "I must return home. I am reviewing the mill's operation. I also must advertise for another mill manager, and begin the interview process."

"Sounds like you're busy," she said, watching him swing himself onto his horse.

"I am." He sat, looking down at her; his expression was unreadable. Some emotion flitted behind his eyes. Then he inclined his head. "Good day, Miss Donovan."

Kendra stared at him as he wheeled his horse around. The stallion's hooves kicked up clumps of damp earth as Bancroft sent the animal into a gallop. She shivered a little, thinking of the expression she'd seen in his eyes. It didn't make any sense, but she thought it might have been regret.

44

Kendra had never attended an inquest quite like the one held at the Green Maiden the next day at noon. For one, she'd never been at in inquest where alcohol was served. And the proceedings seemed almost . . . *festive*. The tavern was crowded with villagers, men and women alike. Tessa and Lizzie and the dark-haired barmaid were kept busy, hopping between the tables, serving drinks.

Kendra sat down at one of the scarred tables, flanked by the Duke and Alec. They were lucky to find seats. A lot of people weren't so fortunate, standing with their backs pressed against the wall. She spotted Sam standing across the room. Even though he was drinking ale, his expression remained flat and hard. *Cop-like.*

Kendra tensed when her gaze moved beyond the Bow Street Runner to another familiar face. William Turner.

Maybe he felt her gaze on him. Whatever the reason, his eyes swung in her direction, his expression darkening with malevolence. After a long moment, he jerked his gaze away, looking toward the area of the bar that had been cleared except for fifteen empty chairs for the jurors.

"It's a circus," she said with a frown. "A man's dead."

Alec's mouth twisted. "We're a ghoulish lot, aren't we? It wasn't long ago that the French delighted in watching their aristocrats' heads roll."

"We English are hardly pure, Alec." The Duke looked at his nephew. "How many tavern owners and peddlers have increased profits every time there's a hanging at

Newgate?" He glanced at Kendra. "I pray that mankind has advanced beyond this form of amusement in your America."

"We don't have public executions," she murmured. *At least not government-sanctioned ones*, she thought. There had been murderers who'd live-streamed killing their victims, and a media frenzy always surrounded famous trials. "I don't think anybody can claim to be pure."

Dr. Poole came into the room, jostling his way over to the bar, where the dark-haired barmaid poured him a pint. The crowd hushed when Squire Matthews was carried in by two burly men.

"Clear the way! Clear the way!" one of the men shouted, making a path through the throng of people.

"Get away from my toe, you fool!" the squire yelled, and used the cane he was holding to jab at bodies that were too close. "Stand back! Stand back, I say!"

His son followed with a pillow, and there was more jostling as another chair was acquired, displacing its current occupant, so the squire could have a footstool. Matthews placed the pillow on the seat, and helped his father prop up his bandaged foot.

Kendra's attention was caught by fourteen men filing into the tavern. By their dress, she guessed them to be from all walks of life: merchants, field hands, farmers, a couple of mill workers. The last person to arrive was Constable Jameson. He swaggered in, earning cheers and back slaps. Another chair was hurriedly acquired and Jameson sat down, feet spread, arms crossed.

"Oy! Quiet now!" the squire shouted at the room. "We're here about the untimely death of Mr. Biddle."

"*The murderer!*" Someone shrieked from the back of the room. "Fiend! *Demon!*"

The squire addressed the heckler. "Yes, he was that, but we're here because the Crown says we have to have an inquest for any prisoner who cocks up his toes in custody, so an inquest we shall have!"

A slender man hurried over and handed the squire several sheets of foolscap. The squire lifted his hand and snapped his fingers impatiently. Matthews broke from the crowd, and handed his father a pair of spectacles. The squire took a moment to put his glasses on, then scanned the papers. He cleared his throat and shifted his gaze to Jameson.

"Now, Constable, what say you? Were you alone when you brought Mr. Biddle to lockup?"

"Nay, Mr. Kelly came with me. He's a Bow Street Runner from London Town."

"I see. And Mr. Kelly . . . where are you?" The squire scanned the crowd.

"Here, sir!"

"Come closer, sir. Please tell this inquest what state Mr. Biddle was in when you accompanied the constable to the lockup."

Sam set down his tankard of ale, and strode forward until he faced the seated men. "He was fine, sir. Not a mark on him."

"I see. And did you leave Constable Jameson with the prisoner?"

"Aye, that I did."

"Thank you, sir. That will be all." He shifted his attention back to the constable. "Now, sir, tell us in your own words what happened."

"Well, sir, I was ready ter lock the bastard up, I was, but then he went mad. Attacked me, he did."

"Oh, this is bullshit," Kendra muttered beneath her breath.

"I was afeared for my life," the constable said, "and had ter subdue the murderin' bastard."

"You struck him?"

"Aye. Defendin' meself." He lifted his beefy shoulders and let them drop. "Then Mr. Biddle slipped and fell. Must've hit his head."

"You did not maliciously attack the prisoner?"

"Nay! As I said, I was defendin' meself against Mr. Biddle. Didn't wanna end up like Mr. Stone, did I?"

"Understandable," said the squire.

Kendra leaned toward the Duke and whispered, "If Mr. Biddle attacked him, I'd like to see his defensive wounds."

"Oy! Quiet!" The squire shot her a look before turning his attention back to Jameson. "Is it your contention, sir, that Mr. Biddle died from his head injury, which was caused by him slipping and falling? And not any blows you may have done in the course of defending yourself from the fiend's attack?"

"Aye. That is me contention, sir."

"Dr. Poole, please step forward." The squire waited until the doctor drained his glass, slammed it on the bar, and stepped forward. "Can you tell us how the prisoner died?"

"Mr. Biddle died of his head injury," Poole said, his fuzzy brows lowering. "Most likely by slipping and falling."

"Thank you, doctor. Now we shall take a recess in order for us to go to Dr. Poole's house to view Mr. Biddle. We shall resume again in one hour."

"You've *got* to be kidding me," Kendra snapped as the room exploded around her with noise. Chairs scraped back and everyone began to talk. She looked at Alec and the Duke. "This is a farce."

"Would you like to leave, Miss Donovan?" Alec asked.

"No." *Damn it.* "I'm staying until the end."

It took another three hours for the end to come. The Duke was called upon to describe how Biddle had tried to flee up to the roof, and had nearly killed his ward in the process.

"Why aren't they asking *me* these questions?" Kendra muttered to Alec. But she knew, and it pissed her off. Alec wisely kept his mouth shut.

Kendra sat fuming while the squire questioned the Duke about how Biddle had nearly dragged her off the roof. The Duke answered the questions posed to him with painstaking honesty. In the end, the squire credited Biddle's actions as an attempt to escape, and decided it was an extension of his lunacy. A man who was so crazed that he'd drag a maiden to her death, he reasoned, could attack a constable in the same fit of madness.

"A constable," he added, "who was working hard to ensure the safety of East Dingleford's citizens."

The squire was forceful and convincing. Hell, Kendra would've believed him if she hadn't been there.

They broke up for a late nuncheon. Kendra was too annoyed to eat. She went up to her bedchamber, and shocked Molly when she stripped down to her chemise and stays, and forced herself to do several yoga stretches. It helped. By the time she was in corpse pose (the irony was not lost on her) she was feeling both limber and relaxed. After Molly buttoned her up again, she returned to the tavern.

Alec was standing in the doorway. He caught her hand, his thumb stroking the inside of her wrist. "Are you all right?"

She nodded. "Yeah. I just needed to release tension."

They returned to their seats, and waited until the inquest reconvened. The squire banged his cane against the floor to draw everybody's attention. Kendra held her breath as Squire Matthews pronounced Biddle's death to be the result of a fall, which had come about because of his own folly.

The room burst into applause. Men launched themselves at Constable Jameson, laughing and thumping him on the back. Kendra caught the exchange of money between several groups. More backslapping. More laughter.

"I think I need a drink," Kendra said.

The Duke gave her a look. "You didn't think the jurors would have punished one of their own for the likes of Mr. Biddle—a murderer—did you?"

"I suppose it was too much to ask for some semblance of justice."

"Justice does not always have a clear line, my dear."

Kendra stared at the people celebrating, and nearly shook her head in disgust. Then she remembered her own line in the sand. She'd gone after Sir Jeremy Green because of her own idea of justice. Who was she to judge?

She met the Duke's eyes. "No, it doesn't."

45

Flora Turner was scared.

She concealed her fear, though, as she put on her Sunday best, and coat and bonnet. The one pair of gloves she usually wore had to be abandoned; she couldn't fit the knit wool over the bandage on her wrist. She concealed her fear during church service.

She was good at concealing her fear. She'd been doing it all of her life.

Lowering her head, she prayed over her tightly clasped hands. Praying was another thing she'd been doing as long as she could remember, the same thing over and over. *Save me.*

Though she kept her eyes downcast, she could feel her husband's big body beside her. She listened to him as he joined the congregation, repeating the verses of the Bible. His voice was a low rumble for the words, then lifted for song.

She wasn't the only one hiding things. Her husband had demons inside him that no one knew about. Standing here, in the church, before God, he looked like a paragon. Handsome in his newly laundered Sunday best, his face clean-shaven and his hair combed back. It was easy to overlook the puffy redness around his eyes.

He'd been gone most of yesterday, into the village for the inquest and then—then, she didn't know. He'd left her to milk the cow, a chore she often did, but it was more awkward with her wrist hurting the way it was.

Still, she'd managed. Just as she'd managed to scrub the
kitchen floor and wash both of their Sunday best. She'd
cooked their supper, even though she'd had a feeling
deep inside that he wouldn't be home for his. If he *had*
come home and she hadn't had his supper cooked and
waiting . . . well, that just didn't bear thinking about.

She'd been in bed when he'd finally come home.
Asleep, but she rarely slept deeply. She'd woken the
moment he'd stumbled into their bedchamber, reeking of
whisky. The odor was enough to send a dart of paralyzing
fear through her. Long before William, she'd learned to
become afraid of that smell. It had clung to her father
every time he'd become enraged at his wife and children.

She'd pretended to sleep. When William had discarded his clothes and crawled under the covers, she'd
feared his carnal appetites would emerge, as they sometimes did. But God had been looking after her, and William had fallen asleep.

Save me.

Sometimes prayers were answered.

But that was temporary, she knew. Today, standing
before God with Bible in hand, Flora sensed the demons
roiling within her husband, and began to tremble. She
hoped that he was only suffering from a headache. She'd
made a physic out of basil and honey that usually eased
his suffering, but sometimes her husband's mood went
beyond his discomfort.

Save me.

The church service ended. The vicar began his walk
down the aisle, but stopped next to the pew where the
Duke of Aldridge sat. To have someone as exalted as the
Duke in their country church was a great honor, and the
vicar's face glowed as he escorted the nobleman down
the aisle. As they passed, Flora caught the tightening of
William's lips, and dread rolled through her stomach.

Head bowed, she followed William and the flow of the
congregation toward the exit. Around her, people spoke
of the Guy Fawkes bonfires later that night. That meant

another night of drinking for William, and cards or games of chance, another night to wonder if the demons would rise up in her husband and turn against her.

The vicar was standing next to the Duke of Aldridge near the door. She sensed William's impatience as the crowd jammed up, everyone trying to leave at once. Flora overheard the Duke tell the vicar that he and his ward and nephew would be attending Guy Fawkes Night, and leaving for his estate the following morning.

Flora's mouth dried up, and she stumbled. She quickly straightened, but she saw the narrow-eyed look that William shot her. She was relieved when they were out of the church, walking to the cart and pony.

Save me.

Miss Donovan had offered to save her, to take her away from East Dingleford and find a position for her at one of the Duke's estates. But Flora was married, bound by God to William. It was wrong of her to think about running away.

Still, Miss Donovan's warnings swam through her head as she climbed into the cart and sat down. Flora wasn't as worried about the beatings. She'd spent her life having a man lift his hand to her, first her father and then her husband. But William's demons seemed to be getting worse. Maybe Miss Donovan had the right of it. Maybe someday William *would* kill her.

Yet that worried her less than the other thing. A beating could only hurt her body. But her soul . . . William had forced her to lay with another man. He didn't want to do it, she knew, but they'd needed to pay off the debt, or else be sent to the poorhouse. They'd had no choice, but it was still a sin.

Her body burned with shame whenever she thought of Harry. She'd heard about his reputation at the cotton mill and with women. He'd married an *actress*, virtually a strumpet. And he was old, older than her father. She'd felt sick when the arrangement began, but Harry had been surprisingly gentle. He may have ignored the bruises on

her body, but he'd never added to them. That said something, didn't it?

Flora gave a small start when she realized they were
already back at the farm. William jumped off the cart,
and shot her another dark look as he began unharnessing
the pony.

"W'ot are ye doin' jest sittin' there?" His eyes narrowed
suspiciously. "W'ot are ye thinkin', wife?"

For a second, Flora froze in terror, wondering if William could see inside her head. She forced herself to
scramble off the cart. "Just thinkin' about tonight." The
lie felt ungainly on her tongue. "Will we be goin' ter the
Guy Fawkes fire later?"

"*I* may be goin'," he said, tossing the harness over his
shoulder as he regarded her. "Some of the fellas will be
gettin' together for a game. Can't very well go ter that and
watch over ye at the bonfire, can I?"

"Nay," she whispered, lowering her eyes so that her
husband wouldn't see the horror turning her bones to ice.

She hurried into the house, her movements automatic as she slipped out of her coat and took off her
bonnet. She went upstairs to carefully put them away.
She started to shake as soon as she closed the wardrobe.
With a sob, she sank onto the bed.

What if William used her to pay off more debt? Her
soul would burn in hell.

Flora pressed a hand to her mouth, and rocked back
and forth. She was already a whore in William's eyes,
she knew. He'd made the arrangement, had given her
to Harry, but ever since the first time she'd lain with the
other man, she'd seen the hatred in her husband's eyes.

Shuddering, Flora rose from the bed, and wiped the
tears from her face. She needed to cut meat and bread, and
pour ale for William's nuncheon. Yet when she returned to
the kitchen, she didn't go to the cupboards where the knife
and bread were kept. Instead, she went to the cupboard
that held the tin flour bin. Her heart stuttered painfully
in her chest as she lifted the container down, setting it

on the counter. Before she lifted the lid, she darted over to the window. William had brought the pony into the stables and was now walking toward the barn.

Drawing in a nervous breath, she hurried back to the flour bin. She removed the lid, pushing her hand through the silky mixture until her fingers closed over the soft oilskin roll that Harry had given her a month after they'd begun the arrangement. He'd told her that his wife had come across it once. He'd hidden it, but that hadn't stopped his wife's snooping. Flora hadn't asked what it was. *She* knew better than to pry into a man's business. Harry seemed to know that about her, to know he could rely on her to do what he asked without pestering him.

She'd hidden it, just as Harry had asked. She'd actually forgotten about it until the other day, when Miss Donovan had mentioned that Harry might have something valuable. A treasure. She'd brought it out after Miss Donovan had gone, her fingers trembling as she untied the ribbon and unrolled the oilskin. Inside the material was a letter, folded and sealed. Guilt had squeezed her stomach, but she'd broken the seal and smoothed out the single piece of foolscap. The paper was large, with wiggly lines all around the page. Words, she supposed. She'd never been taught to read, so the flowing ink baffled her.

Continued to baffle her, as she wiped the flour from the oilskin, once again unfolding the paper. She bit her lip, squinting at the odd squiggles. It wasn't a map, she knew. She'd seen maps before. But maybe it was directions to a treasure? She shot a nervous look at the window. If she brought this to Miss Donovan, would the other woman tell her? She'd said she'd wanted to help.

Carefully, Flora folded the paper again and slipped it into her pocket. She needed a plan. Miss Donovan would be leaving on the morrow. That left Flora only tonight.

Save me.

Prayers were sometimes answered.

46

Kendra was not really in the mood for the Guy Fawkes's celebration, but she dutifully accepted the spencer jacket, bonnet, kid gloves, and reticule that Molly handed her. Outside, the Duke, Alec, and Sam mingled with the rest of the staff: the Duke's valet, Wilson; the coachman, Benjamin; the groom Stanley; and the stable boy Dylan. Molly eagerly joined them, and began to bounce on her toes. Whether it was because she was excited or wanted to keep warm, Kendra couldn't be sure. The evening sky was clear and the moon brilliant, still in its waning phase, casting a silvery light over the landscape, but it was cold enough to turn their breath into puffs of vapor.

"'Tis a glorious evening." The Duke smiled at her. "I thought we could walk to the celebration."

She summoned an answering smile. "An excellent idea, your Grace."

Alec proffered Kendra his elbow, his gaze on her face. "What's the matter?" he asked in a low voice, as they began walking.

She shook her head. "Nothing." *Everything.* Something had been bothering her all day, but she couldn't pin it down.

"Oh, this is ever so excitin'," Molly exclaimed, grinning. "Tessa says there'll be musicians. I wonder if they'll 'ave fireworks like we 'ave back in Aldridge Village."

The Duke said, "Have no fear, young Molly. Mrs. Bolton told me that there will be fireworks. It won't be Vauxhall, but I'm certain it will be entertaining."

"Will there be sermons, sir?" wondered the maid.

"Possibly." The Duke looked at Kendra, and explained, "The local vicars often use it as an opportunity to preach against the evils of popery."

"Hopefully, the parson'll be quick about it," Sam muttered. "But I've learned ter have a pint of spiced rum in me hands *before* he begins his prattle."

Aldridge laughed. "Clever notion, Mr. Kelly. I shall have to borrow that from you."

"And do ye think they'll 'ave bonfire toffee, yer Grace?" Molly asked, her eyes shining in the moonlight.

"What's Guy Fawkes Night without bonfire toffee?" He smiled, and the maid giggled.

It occurred to Kendra that before their stay in East Dingleford, Molly would never have felt so free to speak directly to the Duke like this. Aldridge Castle's housekeeper, Mrs. Danbury, was a great believer in keeping the rigid rules of the Beau Monde, and enforced the policy that servants were supposed to be invisible to their betters. If the housekeeper could see the Duke and Molly converse like they were now, she'd probably accuse the maid of being too familiar. That had been Mrs. Danbury's reaction when Kendra had unwittingly called the Duke, *Duke*, when she'd first stumbled out of the vortex, she remembered. How was she supposed to have known that *Duke* was a title for family or close acquaintances? The housekeeper's head had practically exploded.

But the teasing sensation was back, that something . . . something . . . *What am I missing?*

They had reached the crest of the hill. Kendra stared down at the paddock in amazement. It appeared as though Lord Bancroft had been right. The entire village of East Dingleford really did turn out to celebrate Guy Fawkes Night.

The field had been transformed into something that reminded Kendra of a country fair or carnival. Torches and lanterns bore bright flames, flickering in the darkness. About two dozen tinkers had set up their carts to sell food, beverages, and an assortment of merchandise. The unlit pyre was a dark mountain, a staggering ten feet high near the bank of the river. People—probably two hundred men, women, and children—milled about the area. Conversation, laughter, the delighted shrieks of children, and music—violins and flutes—swirled around them, and there was a cacophony of smells in the air. Roasting meats and chestnuts. Baking pies. Smoke from the torches. The brackish odor from the river. The strong scent of pine and foliage from the forest.

"Wow," was all she said.

"I think the good folks of East Dingleford need this more than ever, given the recent tragedies," said Alec. He captured her hand, and brought it to his lips in a display of affection that sent heat shooting straight to her toes. Or maybe it was the glitter in his green eyes.

Beside her, Sam snorted, but didn't say anything. She caught his eye, and knew what he was thinking. The good folks of East Dingleford weren't mourning Mr. Stone. And while his wife was probably better liked, especially by the village's men, no one was crying over her demise either. If there was anything that East Dingleford was feeling, it was relief that the murderer had been caught so they could get on with their lives.

Except . . . Damn it, what *was* it?

The Duke said, "The villagers are fortunate to have such an excellent evening. Look at that sky!" He pointed. "Look, there's Alpha Draconis—Thuban. Are you aware that thousands of years ago, Alpha Draconis was the star that held up the heavens? The true north star. Ancient man may have stood where we are standing now gazing at these very stars."

"It's beautiful," Kendra breathed, and was struck by how she'd never taken the time for this simple pleasure.

She'd been too busy with her career, too busy trying to prove herself. Plus, she'd lived in urban areas where light pollution washed out about seventy percent of the universe.

"I think young Molly is more interested in earthly delights," Aldridge said, giving the maid a smile.

Molly blushed. "Ooh, yer Grace, pay me no mind. Oi like doing nothin' better than stare at the moon and such."

The Duke laughed and started forward. They followed him down the sloping hill, joining the throngs of people.

"There's Tessa and Lizzie," Molly said, spotting Mrs. Bolton's granddaughters with a group of other young people.

"Go on, Molly," Kendra encouraged. "Go and have fun!"

"Oh, but me duties—"

"Nonsense," she cut her off, and gave the maid a gentle push. "Everybody deserves a night off."

It still bothered Kendra that she had no money to pay for any of the goodies in the tinkers' carts. She had to rely on the Duke to purchase her the dense, dark brown bread topped with seasoned pork that they ate while walking. The servants wandered away, and Sam joined a cluster of men Kendra recognized from the Green Maiden stables. She caught the whirl of familiar faces. Mr. and Mrs. Bolton were standing in the same group as Mr. Matthews and Mrs. Hearnshaw. Dr. Poole and his wife were standing in line for pasties.

Lady Winifred materialized in front of them, looking beautiful in a dark purple velvet hooded cloak, held together at the throat with silver frog enclosures. Her face was a pale cameo, shadowed by the sable-trimmed hood. Her hands were tucked inside a sable muff.

"Good evening, your Grace, my lord," she said, and smiled in that small, practiced way of hers, as though she feared the lines that could develop if she smiled too much. Her gaze slid over Kendra. "Miss Donovan." Once the chilly acknowledgement was made, Lady Winifred dismissed her, turning to Alec. "How delightful that you could come out to East Dingleford's celebration."

"Are you here alone?" Kendra asked, surprised. But she knew that there were more lax rules for widows.

"My maid is with me." She glanced briefly over her shoulder to where a small, lonely figure stood hunched against the cold several feet away. "My father ought to be here shortly. He went to the mill today, and has yet to return."

"There is much work to be done, I'm certain," murmured the Duke. "Please, won't you and your maid join us? It appears that they are about ready to light the pyre. Mayhap we can find ourselves a better position."

"Thank you." This time Lady Winifred didn't bother to smile at Kendra. She withdrew a gloved hand from the sable muff to hold out for Alec. "Mayhap over in that area? Hopefully the direction of the wind won't shift, and we can avoid the smoke."

"Sound reasoning, my lady," the Duke agreed, and gave Kendra a wink when he offered his elbow to her.

"My father tells me that you shall be leaving East Dingleford tomorrow?" Winifred tilted her head to look at Alec, letting her hand linger on Alec's arm as they arrived at the viewing spot. There was nothing Alec could do but stand and accept the countess's attention, Kendra knew, but it irritated her nevertheless. The woman looked like a Madonna, but she was brazen.

"Yes," the Duke answered. "We shall continue on to Monksgrey as we had originally planned, before the fog and other matters waylaid us."

"And you, my lord?" asked Lady Winifred. "Will you be accompanying your uncle, or will you be venturing back to London?"

"With Duke's permission, I think I shall accompany him and Miss Donovan to Monksgrey for a spell," Alec told her. "Ah, they have begun to light the fire. And there goes Guy Fawkes."

Kendra turned to watch two men throw the Guy Fawkes dummy on top of the pyre, and two others light the kindling below. They must have used some sort of accelerant, because the flames soared and the fire spread rapidly. The crowd broke out into cheers.

"Would you ladies like a glass of spiced rum?" Alec asked with a crooked smile. "I have it on good authority that it's best to have in your hand before the sermons begin."

"That would be lovely," Lady Winifred said, and finally released his arm.

"I shall assist you, Alec," the Duke said. "If you will pardon us, ladies, we shall return shortly."

As soon as they left, an awkward silence fell between Kendra and Lady Winifred. Kendra racked her brain for something to say to the other woman, then wondered why she should bother. Lady Winifred didn't seem inclined to converse, her attention fixed on the fire, now soaring a good fifteen feet high. Besides, it was far from quiet, the high spirits of the crowd a steady noise that rose and fell around them.

The vicar approached the platform next to the roaring fire—or tried to. He kept pausing here and there to exchange words with the villagers. At the rate he was going, Kendra calculated it would take him an hour before he would be able to give his sermon. At least she should have her spiced rum by then.

The light from the roaring bonfire spilled across the paddock, gilding everything with an orange glow. Her gaze drifted over a group of teenage boys huddled near the riverbank. She wasn't surprised when she caught the metallic glint of the flask being passed back and forth between them. Her eyes shifted to where a handful of smaller children chased each other in circles at the edge of the forest. Kendra smiled slightly, observing two kids off to the side. They were simply spinning around like a pair of figure skaters. When they stopped, they stumbled across the grass like drunken sailors before toppling to the ground. She was too far away, but she imagined their giggles.

She started to look away, but stiffened suddenly, her gaze swinging back to the trees. She caught a pale flash in the darkness. Frowning, she took three steps forward, scanning the trees.

"Where are you going, Miss Donovan?" Lady Winifred asked from behind her.

Kendra ignored the woman. She searched the trees. Maybe it was her imagination . . . no. Something moved in the shadows. She saw a face.

Flora Turner.

47

Flora was going to have a seizure, she just knew she was. She'd seen it happen once when she was a child. A tinker who'd come to her hamlet had gotten into an argument with a local merchant. They'd shouted at each other, their faces turning purple in rage, when the tinker's eyes had suddenly bulged and his face twisted in a spasm of pain. Flora had watched as he clutched his chest before collapsing on the ground. It had been a terrible thing to witness, and later her mother had told her that high emotions sometimes caused seizures.

Flora's emotions had been high all day. Not from anger like the tinker's, but from a terrible fear that kept her stomach churning. Guilt and worry over her decision to leave William made her heart beat so fiercely that she worried it would pound right out of her chest. The paper that Harry had given her for safekeeping, in her pocket, seemed to burn her thigh.

In her head, she'd begun counting down the minutes. She'd packed a small satchel, storing it deep inside the wardrobe. There wasn't much in it: her Sabbath dress and her nightdress, her hairbrush. She'd have to wear a maid's uniform, she supposed, if she worked in the Duke's household. And she'd be getting a wage. Her heart leaped at the notion. She'd never had money before. Her father had certainly never believed in sharing his hard-earned coins with his wife and children. William was much like her father. The only time he gave her money was on market day. He would count the coins as he laid them on her palm. And he always made her show him the insides of her pockets and reticule to make sure she wasn't hoarding any coins after market.

It was one of the reasons she'd never thought about running away. That, and because it was a sin for a wife to leave her husband. But if William forced her to lay with other men, that was a sin too. She couldn't stay. And for the first time, she had someone who offered to help without requiring money in return. As soon as she started working, she'd be able to earn her own keep.

Yet her thoughts flitted time and again to the paper in her pocket. What if it really was instructions to a treasure? She didn't know how such things worked, but surely she'd be entitled to a small portion? Was she being too fanciful?

William had noticed her distraction, of course, which only added to her skittishness. He seemed to linger longer at the table, even after he'd eaten his nuncheon, his gaze tracking her as she cleaned up the kitchen. She'd dropped a plate, and thanked the Lord when it didn't break. But she'd seen William's eyes narrow. She'd held her breath for so long, awaiting his reaction, that she'd felt dizzy. When he didn't punish her, she'd carefully exhaled, and, though her bandaged wrist throbbed, began vigorously scrubbing the counters. William had finally hefted himself up, and stomped out of the house without a word.

The rest of the day, she'd occupied herself by scrubbing the floor and then the laundry. William had come in several times during the day to stare at her. The attention had nearly shattered her nerves. As the sun sank down, she began to worry that he'd changed his mind about going out, that all of her planning had been for naught. But then he'd come into the house, demanding she fix him a bath. After washing, he'd changed into a shirt and cravat, and shrugged back into his coat. His gaze was on her as he picked up his purse and stuffed it into his pocket. Then he slammed out the door.

Flora sat down then, just for a short spell, to steady her heart and trembling hands. She prayed for courage. After a long moment, she stood and went upstairs to grab the satchel with her dress, nightgown, and one hairbrush. She put on her coat and bonnet, feeling a little like one of those windup toys she'd seen peddlers bring to the market, her movements stiff and automatic. Her gaze swept the kitchen one last time, and she hoped to never see it again.

Still, Flora's chest felt tight when she left the house. The farm was quiet, the chickens in the coop for the night and the animals stirring quietly in the barn as she set off down the road. She wished that she could carry a lantern, but didn't dare call attention to herself. Luckily, the moon and stars were bright enough to guide her. She didn't stay on the country lane long, as she had no wish to encounter anyone. And there was always a chance that William might return.

Shuddering at that thought, Flora leaped off the road, toward the woods. It was a little less than two miles to the squire's paddock on the edge of East Dingleford. She often walked that route to the village on market day when William was too busy to bring her. Unless the weather was bad, she always enjoyed those long walks through the woods.

But she'd never before walked the woods at night. The moon and the stars didn't penetrate the canopy of leaves, so it was much darker, and the forest was filled with noises that made her heart gallop in her chest. Just the breeze rattling the leaves? Or some beast stalking her?

She swallowed hard and increased her pace. She prayed she wouldn't trip on roots and stones. Dear heaven, William was right. She was stupid. Stupid and fearful . . .

She nearly went back. But she thought of Kendra Donovan. The American was so fierce, and fearless. She'd stood up to William. Of course, she was Quality. The gentry knew that William was beneath them. It was easier for them to stand up to him, even a woman.

In the darkness, the journey seemed endless. She didn't like being in the woods at night, but she liked it even less when she reached clearings or had to cross roads, feeling too exposed. At least she was hidden in the shadows. She picked up her skirts and ran through such clearings until she reached the next stretch of woods. She was beginning to lose her breath, the satchel with its meager contents feeling like it was filled with stones, when she finally saw the orange light flickering through the trees.

In a final burst of energy, Flora ran, the satchel bouncing awkwardly against her leg. Caution—and lack of breath—halted her at the edge of the forest. She sucked in cold air and peered out from behind the trees. Children were playing only a few yards from where she lingered. Beyond them was the bonfire, enormous in size, a circle of tinkers' stalls, and crowds of people—so many people! Flora's stomach twisted. She hadn't thought of that. How would she ever find Miss Donovan? Even worse, what if William was in that crowd? If she encountered her husband in her search for Miss Donovan, he would kill her.

Tears sprang to her eyes. She dashed them away, but more came. She'd come so far. How could she go back? But how could she go forward and risk meeting William?

With a sob, Flora sat down on a fallen log. She covered her face with her hands and rocked back and forth. It was too much. William was right. She was weak and stupid. If she returned home now, William would be none the wiser—

"Flora?"

Flora stilled. Her hands fell away and she turned toward the voice. She let out a ragged gasp as her eyes focused on the figure entering the woods. *Miss Donovan.*

Save me.

48

Kendra had never been a big fan of the woods in the dark, probably because she'd watched too many horror movies in her rebellious stage, and they always seemed to take place at an isolated cabin in the woods, where a bunch of teens and twentysomethings did the most idiotic things. By the end of the movie, she'd usually wanted to shoot them all herself. But at least in the twenty-first century, she could enter the dark woods with a good flashlight and her trusty Glock.

As she pushed aside the prickly branch of a pine tree, she wondered if she should retrieve the pistol from her reticule. Her gaze scanned the woods. Her ears strained to identify noises. A shuffling movement over there. A snap of a twig to the right. A soft sob to the left.

She moved to the left. Her gaze locked on the forlorn figure sitting on the log. "Flora?"

Flora stared at her, her face wet with tears. Then she leaped off the log and ran toward Kendra.

"Thank heaven," she cried. "I—I didn't know w'ot ter do!"

Kendra grasped the other woman's slight shoulders, searching her face. "Are you all right? Your husband didn't—"

"Nay." She gulped. "I want ter go with ye. I can work hard, I—I can."

Kendra ordered, "Take a breath."

Flora regarded her anxiously. "Ye haven't changed yer mind, have you? Maybe I can pay . . . pay me way . . ." She unbuttoned her wool coat and thrust her hand through the opening in her skirt to the pocket.

"Flora—"

"Harry gave me somethin'."

Kendra raised her eyebrows. "Stone gave you something?"

"Aye. For safekeeping. He said it was important." She fished out the folded foolscap, and held it out to Kendra. "It's not a treasure map. I know that. But maybe it's a letter that leads ter a treasure?"

"I doubt it." Frowning, Kendra took the paper, turning it over to peer at the address. It was so dark that it took her a moment to read. *Mrs. Farnsworth, Toad & Scythe, Hammersmith.* Kendra noticed the seal had been broken. "Did you read it? What does it say?"

Flora shook her head. "Nay, I . . . I don't know how ter read. But I know it ain't a map. Maybe it's ter something important, something I can use ter pay ye ter take me with you."

"I already promised to take you with us. You don't need to pay me. Don't worry, Flora, I'm not going to break that pro—" She broke off when Flora's eyes widened in terror. Flora screamed, stumbling back.

Kendra started to spin around, but was sent flying when something hard slammed into her back. She landed in the dirt, gasping in pain.

"Bitch!"

Heart thudding, Kendra rolled over to meet William Turner's glittering eyes. He towered over her, his mouth knotted into an ugly snarl, his gaze moving from Kendra to his wife.

"Ye think ye can leave *me*?" he demanded. "After all I've done for ye, ye ungrateful trollop!"

Kendra scrambled to her feet. Out of the corner of her eye, she saw the reticule and Stone's letter on the ground, where they'd fallen. Too far away to retrieve the muff pistol. "Step back, Mr. Turner."

He glared at her. "I'm gonna teach *ye* ter mind yer own bloody business. I don't care whether yer the ward of some fancy Duke. No one but God can come between a man and his wife!"

Kendra kept her eyes trained on the sheep farmer. "See, here's my problem with that. You call yourself a man. But real men don't hit defenseless women." She moved closer, circling, drawing his attention away from Flora.

He shifted around to keep his eyes on her. "Ye're not gonna look so pretty after I'm done with ye, bitch," he snarled.

"You think I'm pretty?" She showed her teeth in a tight smile, her eyes fixed on his face. Then, she struck, rushing forward and putting her entire body behind the punch. Turner's nose cracked, and blood spewed forth as his head snapped back.

She danced backward, out of his reach, while Turner grabbed his nose and howled. Behind her, Flora screamed.

"Go, Flora! Find Alec or the Duke!" Kendra ordered. She kept her gaze locked on her opponent. Now that she'd lost the element of surprise, she needed all her attention on the sheep farmer.

He came at her with a roar, swing his arms in a poorly constructed move that she easily blocked with her left arm, allowing her to bring up her right fist for another punch. If his nose wasn't broken before, it was now, she thought, hearing the satisfying crunch. She jumped back again, ignoring the sting in her knuckles.

"Fucking Satan's whore!" he yelled. He stumbled, and shook his head like a wet dog. Then he rushed at her to knock her down, like he had earlier. Kendra leaped to the side, grabbing his arm and twisting it viciously behind his back. Turner screamed. She yanked his arm higher, and used the leverage to drive him to his knees.

"*Miss Donovan!*"

Kendra jerked her head up, her eyes finding Lord Bancroft. The darkness of the forest and the shadow cast by his tricorn hat made it impossible to see his expression. But she had no trouble seeing the gun in his hand.

"The woman is bloody mad!" Turner shouted. His damaged nose made his voice sound nasally. "She's runnin' away with me wife!"

"Indeed? I heard your threats against Miss Donovan . . . You can release him, Miss Donovan." The earl's eyes flicked to her. "I don't think he'll try anything. Will you, Mr. Turner?"

Adrenaline was still making Kendra's blood hum. It took her a moment to let Turner go. She sprang back to avoid a renewed attack from the sheep farmer. But his gaze was on Bancroft and the gun, which was pointed at his heart.

Turner shoved himself to his feet, licking his lips nervously, swiping at the blood on his face. "Here now, sir. It ain't w'ot ye heard, I swear. She's the one that needs ter be locked up. Stealin' me wife! She's mad, she is." He swung his damaged face around to glare at Kendra. "I've gotta right ter protect me property!"

"Shut up," the earl snapped. He glanced at Kendra. "Are you all right, Miss Donovan?"

"I'm fine. Where did you come from?"

Bancroft gave a thin smile. "Your Duke believes in fate. He talked about it the afternoon he came to Falcon Court. I've always been a man who believes in making my own destiny—regardless of life's misfortunes." He laughed when she frowned. "I've changed my mind. Don't move, Mr. Turner. That's right—stay very still." He kept his eyes on Turner, but said to Kendra, "I have this gun in my hand because I was working at the mill today. The troubles with the Luddites have made me more cautious. Yet it's come in handy, don't you think, with Mr. Turner?"

"I guess so," she said, flicking a look at Turner's bloody face. "But I was handling it."

"Perhaps," he shrugged. "But think of this. I left the mill later than I intended. If I had left five minutes earlier or later, I would have missed seeing you go into the woods, Miss Donovan. That's fate."

"W'ot the bleeding hell does fate have ter do with me and me wife?" Turner interrupted with a growl. He was getting his swagger back, thrusting out his jaw belligerently.

"Probably nothing," admitted Bancroft.

Kendra jolted when the night sky was filled with a series of explosive pops, washing the woods in greens, blues, and reds, the promised fireworks of Guy Fawkes Night.

Bancroft smiled slowly. "Actually, you might be tied to fate after all, Mr. Turner."

He pulled the trigger.

49

The line for spiced rum had been longer than Alec or the Duke had anticipated. By the time they made their purchases, Alec had to tamp down his impatience. Both men carried a glass in each hand, careful not to spill any as they threaded their way through the jostling throngs of people.

"I believe the vicar has begun his sermon," the Duke said.

The vicar was shouting above the cacophony of the crowd. As they neared the bonfire, Alec caught the words *Guy Fawkes* and *the evils of revolution*. He smiled at his uncle. "Let us hope that one glass will be sufficient."

Pushing their way through a group of people, Alec saw Lady Winifred, the flames from the pyre bathing her beautiful face in gold. Her maid stood a couple of feet behind her mistress. When Lady Winifred noticed their approach, she smiled and fluttered her lashes, experienced in the coquetry of the Ton. He'd been aware of her attempts to engage in a flirtation since they'd first been introduced. She was a beautiful woman, but she left him cold. The countess was like all the other women of the Beau Monde who'd eyed him as a potential husband. Before Kendra, he might not have regarded her so dispassionately. He might have been amused, and not entirely averse to a light flirtation.

"Thank you, Lord Sutcliffe," Lady Winifred said. "I have discovered I am quite thirsty."

He glanced around. "Where is Miss Donovan?"

She gave a tight smile, looking at the Duke. "I do not mean to offend, your Grace, because I know Miss Donovan is your ward. But I found her behavior quite peculiar. No doubt it's because she is an American."

"Where is she?" Alec repeated impatiently.

"I don't know," Lady Winifred lifted her shoulder in a dainty shrug. "One moment she was standing here, and the next she simply walked away. It was ill-mannered."

The Duke frowned. "Miss Donovan didn't say anything to indicate what had caught her attention?" he asked the countess.

"No. I told you, she simply walked away."

Ice formed in Alec's stomach. Kendra wouldn't think twice about dismissing proprieties that she considered ridiculous and wandering around without a chaperone. But she'd known they'd be returning with the spiced rum. She wouldn't walk away without a good reason.

"Which way did she go?" he demanded.

Lady Winifred hesitated. "I don't know."

"How can you not know? You must have seen which direction she walked!"

She stiffened at his tone. "I was not paying any attention to Miss Donovan, my lord."

Alec bit back a curse.

"Alec—" the Duke began, but whatever he had been about to say was drowned out by loud booms and crackles as the Guy Fawkes's fireworks lit up the night sky.

Alec shoved the glasses of spiced rum into the hands of the surprised man standing next to him watching the fireworks display.

"Oy!"

"Alec!"

"Something's wrong."

He didn't know if his uncle heard him. He was already plunging into the crowd.

❧

Kendra stared, shocked, as Turner clasped his chest, a look of surprise on his face. Blood seeped through his fingers. He staggered back and fell over the log that Flora had been sitting on moments before.

"What the hell?" She spun around to face Bancroft. Further words dried up in her throat as her gaze lowered to the gun the earl was holding. It was now pointed at her.

The night had taken on a surreal quality. She could smell the gunpowder, sulfur, and nitrate in the air, both from Bancroft's gun and from the cloud drifting over them from the fireworks. The sky lit in red, green, gold, and blue with each bang and crackle. The varied hues created a strobe effect, flashing over Bancroft's face.

"This is unfortunate," Bancroft said with eerie calm. "I would have spared you this, Miss Donovan, but you have something that is mine."

"What are you talking about?"

"Fate, Miss Donovan. Give me the letter." He paused, lifting the flintlock pistol slightly. His hand was steady. "Now."

Kendra glanced at the reticule and Stone's letter on the ground.

"Yes," he said in answer to her unspoken question. "If you please . . ."

Slowly, Kendra walked over and snatched them up. "What's this about?"

"All in good time, Miss Donovan. Kendra. You don't mind if I call you, Kendra, do you?" He approached her. He was old, but there was nothing frail about the man, she thought. His tread was firm as he approached her, his gaze dark and dangerous. "Formalities can be so tedious here. Turn around. Slowly, please. And walk."

She swallowed. "I thought you wanted the letter."

"Don't be clever, Kendra. My gun may be old, but I can assure that it will put a sizeable hole in your head. And I really do not want to do that. At least not until we have a conversation. Now, turn around. *Walk*."

Kendra forced herself to pivot and move forward. Adrenaline was replacing the shock. Her heart was pumping loudly in her chest. Her skin felt clammy in the night air. She needed to keep calm. *Breathe in; breathe out.*

The weight of the muff pistol inside her reticule was comforting. If she could slip her hand into the pouch and get hold of the weapon—

She stumbled to a stop when she saw what was ahead of her.

The muzzle of the gun poked her spine. "Keep going."

Slowly, she forced herself to move forward, her eyes locked on the black stallion that stood next to a tree, its reins tied to a branch. As they approached, the beast snorted, ears twitching. The eyes rolled toward them. Dread squeezed Kendra's stomach.

"Get up," Bancroft said, and untied the reins. He huffed out a dry laugh when she hesitated. "You're not afraid of my horse, are you, Kendra?"

She looked at him, her mind racing with possible defensive maneuvers. Yet whether it was coincidence, luck, or smart strategy, the earl had positioned himself far enough away from her that there was no way she could close the gap before he pulled the trigger.

"Get on Alba, Kendra. Please, don't make me tell you again."

"Well, since you said *please* . . ." she muttered.

She slid the strings of her reticule over her wrist and clutched the letter with one hand. With her other hand, she took hold of the pommel. Her heart hitched when the beast shifted impatiently. Still, she managed to slip her foot into the stirrup, and haul herself up, swinging her leg over. Her skirt hiked up past her knees as she sat astride the horse, but modesty wasn't her concern at the moment. Briefly, she considered using the horse to escape, but every scenario involving that idea that flitted through her mind didn't end well for her. Either she'd be trampled to death under the beast's hooves, or Bancroft would shoot her in the back.

The earl laughed as he swung up behind her. His body pressed against hers. "You really should learn how to ride, Kendra."

She held onto the pommel for dear life as he clicked his heels to the stallion's flank, and the horse shot forward into a hard gallop. Only last month, she'd been in a similar position, holding onto Alec and hurtling across the countryside. She'd been terrified then, too, but she'd been preoccupied with saving her friend, Lady Rebecca. Now she forced her mind to think of something other than the ground below, which was a blur.

Suddenly, Falcon Court was before them, and the earl yanked on the reins, hard enough to cause the stallion to rear back. Kendra's fingers tightened on the pommel, and she couldn't stifle a gasp. Bancroft laughed as he swung down. He already had the gun out and aimed at her before she could recover.

Kendra glanced around the courtyard and at the mansion as she slipped off the horse, but Falcon Court was eerily quiet. The gas lighting hissed around them. The gargoyles above the door seemed to mock her in the mottled light.

"Everyone is at the Guy Fawkes celebration," he said, correctly interpreting her look. "We shall have complete privacy, Kendra. I have a secret to share with you."

Kendra turned slowly to meet his dark eyes. "I know your secret. I know you're not Lord Bancroft."

50

Flora stumbled out of the woods. Her legs were shaking so badly that it took all her effort not to collapse on the ground. She pushed herself forward, running past the children. Fear clutched her heart at the size of the crowd ahead. She sucked in a deep breath and dashed over to the first person she saw, a man standing with two companions on the outskirts of the milling horde.

"*Please*! Oh, please! I need yer help, sir!"

He gaped at her, but recovered quickly. "Oi can help ye, lass. But w'otcha gonna do fer me, eh?" The wink he sent the other two men made them burst out laughing. "Oi need some sort of boon ter make it worth me while. But don't ye worry. Old Matthias'll make it worth yer while too."

Flora flinched as the foul odor of whisky hit her. "Nay! Ye don't understand. Miss Donovan . . . Ye have ter help Miss Donovan—" She yelped when the man lurched forward and grabbed her arm, yanking her against him.

"We'll take care of yer Miss Donovan, too, doncha worry, lass. But first a kiss."

Terror clutched Flora's heart. She struggled against the man's embrace, but her efforts only caused the drunken men to laugh louder. The world swam around her. She tried to twist away, and then gasped when she was suddenly free. She stumbled back, her eyes widening as a stranger yanked her attacker away and plowed his fist into the other man's paunch, causing him to double over. Her savior then brought up his fists in a pugilist pose, squaring off against her attacker's two companions.

"'Oo the 'ell are ye?" one of the men growled, his eyes narrowed.

"Sam Kelly—Bow Street. And you're interfering with Crown business. Unless you want ter speak ter the magistrate and spend the night in lockup, you'd best be on your way!"

The man hesitated, glaring at Sam. Sam stared back, his gaze hard, his muscles tense.

"It ain't worth it," the other man finally said, and grabbed the arm of the man that Sam had punched. That man lifted his head to stare at Sam, initially resisting his friends' efforts to drag him away. But whatever he saw on the Bow Street Runner's face had him spitting on the ground, before turning and walking away with his friends.

Sam tracked their retreat for about half a minute. When they kept walking, he spun around to look at the woman he'd just rescued. "I heard you speak of Miss Donovan."

"Aye! She—" Flora's eyes went wide as the sky flashed with vibrant colors. The ground seemed to vibrate beneath her feet.

"Miss?" Sam snapped impatiently. "What's this about Miss Donovan?"

Flora jerked her gaze back to the Bow Street Runner. "Please, ye have ter help her! He's goin' ter kill her!"

Bancroft's dark eyes flickered, but the gun didn't waver. He cocked his head to regard Kendra. "Well, well, well. This is very interesting. I didn't expect this."

Kendra said nothing.

"I always knew you were a clever girl. You had to be, didn't you?" His mouth curved into a thin smile. "Let's talk in my study. We might as well be comfortable." He gestured with the pistol. "You first. And please don't make any attempt to escape. I saw what you did to Mr. Turner—and you saw what I did. I think a gun has an unparalleled advantage in our situation, don't you agree?"

Kendra pressed her lips together, and swung around. Inside, a few of the gaslights had been left on, bathing the entrance hall in soft amber light. She walked to the earl's study, all the time intensely aware of the gun pointed at her back. The only light in the study was from the moon and stars, streaming through the French doors and windows.

"There's a tinder box on the desk. If you would light a fire, Kendra."

Bancroft went around the room turning on the gas lamps. Kendra slid her reticule off her wrist, and briefly considered retrieving the pistol in its depths. But Bancroft was watching her, and she didn't want to risk him taking the purse away from her before she could get her hand on the weapon. She carefully set the reticule down on a chair, and placed the letter on top of it. Then she went to work, striking the flint and lighting the tinder. Someone, a footman probably, had already put kindling and logs in the hearth.

Kendra glanced at Bancroft, leaning his hip against his desk, studying her. The gun was still in his hand, still aimed at her.

"You really are a novice at these things, aren't you?" he said, and she caught the gleam of amusement in his dark eyes.

Kendra gritted her teeth, and after a few more strikes, managed to actually create a spark that lit the tinder. She knelt down and coaxed the kindling in the grate to catch fire. Out of the corner of her eye, she saw the fire poker.

"Very good. I would applaud, but . . . well, you understand my hand is occupied," he mocked. He straightened, and without taking his eyes off of her, walked over to the reticule.

Kendra held her breath as his hand brushed over the purse. If he should nudge it, he'd become aware of the weight. But he was only interested in the folded foolscap on top of the purse. Kendra watched him closely as he scanned the address. He smiled.

"Ah, Millie. I had wondered where she'd disappeared to."

Kendra lifted a brow, striving for nonchalance. "A friend of yours?"

"You could say that." His gaze returned to Kendra. "She was someone I knew a long time ago, in another life."

"What's in the letter?" asked Kendra.

"It doesn't matter. You still haven't told me when you realized my secret."

The letter had mattered enough for Bancroft to kill two women and torture one, Kendra thought. But she let the line of inquiry go for now. "A couple of things have been bothering me for a while now," she finally answered him.

"Oh? Please, tell me."

"I kept hearing stories about Nat. He was charming, warm, basically a nice young man. It was difficult to reconcile that description with . . . you."

"You wound me, Kendra."

"I doubt it." She went on, "Of course, people change. Nat left East Dingleford when he was seventeen years old and he was gone for sixteen years. There would be physical changes from boy to man; it was even plausible that there could be personality changes. It was assumed Nat had a difficult time while he was away. Life is hard. He found that out and grew up, became harder, colder. It happens."

"Fascinating. Go on. You haven't yet told me what gave me away."

"I began to realize that you kept a lot of people from the past at a distance. Why wouldn't you go to the tailor here in East Dingleford? He's skilled. But Mr. Shannon grew up with Nat. He said that he and his father spoke to you at the earl's funeral, sharing memories. Except they weren't *shared* memories, were they?" She forced a smile at him. "You were afraid that there might be more stories swapped during fittings. If you failed to recall a significant event, he might become suspicious."

She paused. He said nothing, so she continued, "Same with your housekeeper and butler. You pensioned them off as fast as you could. And then there was Mrs. Bolton. You really had to keep her at a distance, given her romantic involvement with Nat. The possibility that there were memories that only she and Nat would know was too great."

He snorted. "I didn't think any of these people would figure out my charade. But why tempt fate?" He smiled slowly, his eyes gleaming. "There's that word again, Kendra—fate. You still haven't told me how you figured out my secret."

"I told you it was a lot of little things. The earl—the real Nat's father—figured out the truth, didn't he?"

He stared at her, saying nothing.

"Names are funny things, aren't they?" she said after a moment. "What people are known by, formal names, nicknames." She thought of tonight, when she'd observed Molly's familiarity with the Duke, knowing that the maid would never be relaxed enough to call him *Duke*. She said, "The Honorable Nathan Bancroft—that was Nat's formal address before he became a viscount and then an earl. But the people of East Dingleford called him Nat. I was told that his father even called him Nat."

"Is this story going somewhere?" Bancroft drawled.

"*Nat-son*," she said, locking her gaze on his. "Mrs. Hearnshaw told me how the earl had a stroke. He slurred his words, could barely talk. She thought he was saying Nathan. But he wasn't, was he? He recognized that you were an imposter. He wasn't saying Nathan or Nat-son—he was saying, *not son*. He was trying to warn everyone that you weren't his son."

Bancroft's black eyes reflected the fire from the gas lamps and fireplace. She could see her own face wavering in the dilated pupils.

"You *are* a clever girl," he murmured. "I don't know how the old man knew. He could barely move, barely function. Half the time he was drooling and the other half of the time he was pissing in the bed. I did him a favor by breaking his neck."

"What did you do to the real Nat?"

"I killed him, of course."

"Was Stone with you when you killed him? Is that what he was blackmailing you with?"

Surprise flickered across Bancroft's face. "No, Harry never met my predecessor. Our association predated my chance encounter with Nat. But I saw an opportunity and took it. I left Harry and Millie and the rest of my associates behind. Or so I thought." His mouth twisted, though with either irony or bitterness, Kendra couldn't be certain. "I suppose that was fate as well. Harry chanced to see me while I was once in London, and approached me. For a loan, he said, given my new status in life."

"How did he know that you weren't the real Nat? For you to have pulled off your charade, the resemblance between you and Nat must have been astonishing."

His dark eyes flashed with temper. "It was like the old man. Unfortunately, Harry, for all his faults, was not a fool. He knew certain things about my person and threatened to bring me to the authorities. I couldn't take the chance of closer scrutiny."

"Then I'm surprised you didn't kill him too. Eliminate the threat."

"You think I didn't consider that? I told you, the bastard wasn't stupid. He wrote our past association down. Times, dates . . ."

"Misdeeds," Kendra finished for him when he trailed off with a shrug. "Stone boasted to Flora that he'd been a highwayman. I assume that's your past association."

"Among other things."

Kendra glanced at the letter. "And if anything happened to Stone, the letter would be sent to your old friend, Millie," she guessed.

It was the nineteenth century version of the fail-deadly concept, a strategy created as a deterrent between nuclear powers. If an aggressor launched a first strike, it would trigger a second-strike response, overwhelming and devastating. Or, perhaps more accurately, it was the digital dead man's switch, which kept an aggressor in check by threatening to expose their secrets on the Internet if anything happened to the blackmailer. Either way, Stone's tactic had forced Bancroft into an uneasy détente—though neither man had counted on Biddle's attack.

Bancroft seemed to read her thoughts. He lifted his shoulder, let it drop. "I couldn't take the chance of that letter surfacing."

"So you tortured Mrs. Stone." Kendra's face tightened as she thought of what the woman had endured.

"It made sense that Lavinia had the letter. She knew of it—but not its contents. She told me where she thought Harry might have hidden it—after I applied the right motivation." He smiled coldly. Then the smile vanished, and his face hardened. "Except the letter wasn't there. Harry had obviously already given it to Mrs. Turner."

And Bancroft smashed the porcelain cats in his temper, Kendra thought.

"Was it your idea to fire Mr. Murray and hire Stone?"

He grunted. "Hardly. Do you think that I wanted the son of a bitch on my doorstep, taunting me? The position appealed to Harry."

"You mean the power appealed to him."

Bancroft conceded with a small nod "You are clever, Kendra, figuring out that I had assumed Nat's identity. But you don't know my real secret, after all."

"What are you talking about?"

His gaze was locked on hers, so intense that it sent a chill down her spine.

"Fate, Kendra. I will tell you my story. You and I are connected. I want you to understand and live. But I will kill you if I must—though with great regret."

"Well, as long as you have regret," she replied
sarcastically.

He continued to look at her with his penetrating gaze.
"It will be fate if my bullet ends your life," he said quietly.
"My bullet should have ended your life thirty-eight years
ago."

Kendra stared at him.

Bancroft said, "The night I killed Sir Jeremy Greene."

51

Sam's heart thumped with terrible fear. He grabbed the woman, his fingers digging into her arms so hard that she cried out in pain, and he released her abruptly, but kept her pinned with his gaze. "Who's gonna kill her? Where is Miss Donovan? *Who are you?*"

The woman licked her lips. "I'm F-Flora . . . Flora Turner. Me husband, William—he found me. M-Miss Donovan stopped him. But now he has her!"

"Mr. Kelly!"

Sam pivoted and saw the Duke, Alec, and Coachman Benjamin approaching. Their expressions were grim.

"Mr. Kelly," the Duke said again, his eyes moving briefly to the agitated woman. "Miss Donovan appears to be missing. It might not be of any concern, but—"

"It *is*!" Flora cried. Her eyes were wide and glassy with shock. "Me husband William's got her and he's gonna kill her. We must save her like she was saving me!"

"Mrs. Turner." Alec recognized the woman, even though terror contorted her pretty face into something dreadful. "Where are they?"

"In the forest, near where the children are playing."

Alec didn't wait. He spun away, and heedless of the stares, began running across the field to the forest. Sam raced after him. They sprinted past the children and plunged into the woods. The darkness made Sam curse, wishing he'd brought a torch.

The marquis came to a stop ahead, panic tightening his features as he spun in circles. "Kendra!" he yelled. *"Kendra!"*

Sam wasn't sure if it was smart to alert the man who held Kendra hostage that they had arrived. He glanced over as the Duke and Benjamin came crashing through the trees.

Alec called the American's name as he walked forward.

"Wait!" The Duke held up his hand for silence. "I think I heard something."

Sam listened intently, but heard nothing.

Alec said, "Where would he—" He stopped suddenly, and Sam heard it as well. A groan.

"Over there!" the Duke pointed to the left, and moved forward, pushing through prickly tree branches.

Sam followed, his gaze traveling over overgrown bushes, trees, and a fallen log. It didn't register initially, but then his eyes swung back and he saw a boot extending beyond the log. He jogged over to stare at the man on the ground, his shirt stained dark with blood.

The Duke joined him, followed by Alec and Benjamin. "My God!"

"It's Turner." Alec reached across the bloody chest to search for a pulse.

"Bastard," the man whispered, his voice faint, but filled with hate.

Sam squatted down next to the man. Turner's eyes fluttered open, and he groaned again.

"Where's Miss Donovan?" Sam demanded, capturing Turner's pain-filled gaze.

Turner didn't seem to hear the question. Or he didn't care. He muttered, "He shot me, the bastard."

Sam asked, "Who? Who shot you?"

"His lordship." Turner's chest heaved, and he turned his head and spat out blood. "The earl."

❖

It was as if all her facial muscles and bones had melted, completely slack with shock. There was a strange buzzing in her ears. She didn't know how she made it to the chair, but suddenly she was sitting, the reticule on her lap. She bent over and drew in deep breaths. *Inhale . . . exhale.*

Bancroft laughed. "Oh, my God, I know *exactly* how you feel, Kendra. It's the same way I felt when I first saw *you*."

Kendra thought of how Bancroft had frozen, his eyes locked on her, his face seemingly carved from stone. She'd picked up the strange vibe in the air then, and the countless other times she'd been in his presence. *He gave me the heebie-jeebies.*

"It's been thirty-eight years since I last saw you, Kendra. You haven't changed at all."

She sucked in a breath, straightening. Her throat was so dry she barely got the words out. "You have."

He ignored that. "Look at you, the Duke's ward. How did you accomplish such a feat?"

Her gaze roved over the old man's features, the sparse, white hair, the sagging, speckled flesh, trying to see any resemblance between this old man and his younger self—the assassin dressed as a footman who'd shot Sir Jeremy Greene three months ago. Three months ago—two hundred years into the future. Was the bladelike nose the same? The heavy-lidded eyes? *Yes, the eyes . . .*

"I've thought of you often, Kendra."

She realized that he was inspecting her as closely as she was inspecting him. It made her shiver.

"The woman I followed into the stairwell . . . " He shook his head. "Who are you? Obviously law enforcement. CIA? DEA? FBI?"

"FBI," she mumbled.

He laughed softly. "I had always thought you were one of Greene's paramours, waiting for him in the study. I thought you were there for *amor*."

The Spanish word rolled perfectly off Bancroft's tongue. She remembered the accented voice murmuring in the hallway before a mortally wounded Sir Jeremy had fallen into the room.

"I realized my mistake when you began investigating Harry's murder," he said, eyes fixed on her. "I thought maybe you were a homicide detective in our world. But a homicide detective would have no authority to go after Greene."

Kendra sucked in another deep breath, felt her lungs expand. The buzzing in her ears was slowly receding. "Who the hell are you?"

He smiled. "Mateo Hernández."

Kendra leaned back in the chair, carefully putting her hands on top of the reticule. "I think it's time you told me your story."

He nodded. "I *want* to tell you my story, Kendra. I never thought I'd be able to tell it to anyone. Do you know what it's like to keep a secret like this for thirty-eight years?" He walked behind his desk, sinking into the chair without ever taking his eyes off her or dropping his gun. The long barrel of his flintlock remained steady.

Kendra found herself staring at the pistol he held, noting the polished walnut with inlaid silver. "My gun may be old . . ." she murmured now, lifting her gaze to see his wicked grin.

"My little joke, Kendra. I purchased this flintlock only last year. As far as technology goes, it's quite modern. Personally, I miss my SIG Sauer. What about you?"

"Tell me your story," she said instead.

"It's a long story. Why don't you pour us both a drink? And please, do not attempt any heroics. I miss my SIG Sauer, but I'm quite good with this pistol."

"And yet you used a knife on Mrs. Trout and Mrs. Stone," she said as she stood. She set the reticule back on the chair and walked over to the sideboard. "Whisky?"

"Brandy. A knife was quieter. In my day, I was quite good at wet work."

"Wet work." She poured two glasses of brandy. "A term used by assassins. And the KGB."

"Set my glass down on my desk. Slowly," he cautioned when she returned. "I would dislike shooting you before I've told my story. I have no one else to tell."

Kendra did as he asked, then returned to her seat, glass in hand and reticule back on her lap. She lifted her glass in a mocking salute. "I'm all ears."

He picked up his glass, returned her salute, two comrades sharing war stories.

"As you are aware, I was hired to eliminate Sir Jeremy. We figured out he was the one leaking our intel regarding our shipping routes." He tilted his head curiously. "What were you doing there? You never said."

"You could have saved yourself ammunition, and we'd both be back in the twenty-first century. I went there to kill him."

Bancroft—she couldn't think of him as Hernández—raised his eyebrows. "Why?"

"He pissed me off." She took a sip of her own brandy, just enough to wet her mouth. "Continue with your story."

There was a flare of surprise and appreciation in his eyes. "I told you we have much in common, Kendra. Anyhow, I am not one to leave witnesses, so when you ran into the stairwell, I followed." Just for a moment, his hand trembled. "Christ, what an experience. I thought I was being flayed alive."

Kendra had to suppress an empathetic shudder. It had been more than three decades since Bancroft had experienced the vortex, and it looked like it still gave him nightmares.

"When it finally ended, I got the hell out of there. It took me a few minutes to understand that everything had changed. Sir Jeremy's body was gone. Things were . . ."

"Different," Kendra breathed, remembering how she thought she'd gone crazy.

He nodded. "I was dressed as a footman, and when I left the study that night, I was treated as such." He took a gulp of the brandy, his eyes darkening with memories.

"I met the Duke—your Duke's father. I did not lie about that."

"Another joke?"

"A small one, perhaps." Bancroft's lips twisted. "Of course, he barely saw me. I was a servant. But I knew that I wouldn't be able to fool the other servants for long. My accent . . . it brought scrutiny." Another sip. "I spent two days dodging most of the staff. Then I stole several fine pieces of jewelry and silver candlesticks, and left." He looked at Kendra. "Money is always important, isn't it?"

"Tell me about it," she muttered beneath her breath. "I don't like not being able to earn my own money."

"Ah, yes. You're an independent modern woman, aren't you? And yet you fell on your feet quite nicely. How did you become the Duke's ward?"

"I got lucky." *Very lucky.*

"And his nephew, the marquis. Are you his mistress?" She stiffened. "No."

"The way he looks at you . . . well, no matter." He waved the hand holding the glass, causing the brandy to swirl dangerously. "My story. I stole the jewelry and silver, and left Aldridge Castle. I walked; it seemed like forever. I finally stole a horse. Unlike you, I knew how to ride horses in the twenty-first century." He gave her a smug look. "I made it to London and pawned enough of the jewelry to stay in a flash house. That's where I met Harry. He was nothing more than a sewer rat. But he helped me pawn the rest of what I'd stolen and introduced me to his contacts."

"All upstanding members of society, I'm sure."

"We formed our own association, you could say. They were pickpockets, carried out petty crimes. No vision."

"You changed that."

"I did. It was a tidy operation. Then one night I stopped in a tavern and met Nat Bancroft. The other patrons mistook us for twins. Believe it or not, I never thought to kill the fool that night. He told me how he and his father had argued over a girl, and he'd left home to seek his fortune. He traveled the world and lost the girl. God, how the simpleton whined about his beloved Laura. But he was returning home. His father was sick. He wanted to mend the rift in their relationship before it was too late."

Kendra tried to discern if the gun barrel had shifted slightly downward as he told his story.

"Do you know when I decided to kill the bastard?" Bancroft asked suddenly.

"When?"

"I brought him back to the hostelry he was staying at late that night, and put him to bed. No one was around. When I came back the next morning, the stable hands and the innkeeper thought I was Nat. You should have seen how they scraped and bowed. They knew he was a viscount, in line for an earldom. Treated me like Christ Almighty descending from the cross." He paused, the smile that curled his mouth ice-cold. "That's when I decided to kill him.

"It was like a lamb to the slaughter. I brought him into the woods, promised to show him something—I don't even remember what. And I slit his throat and buried him in a shallow grave. Then I went back to the hostelry and gathered Nat's—*my* things."

"And you became Viscount Nathan Bancroft of Langfrey."

His smile was as sharp as a scalpel. "I've been a better earl than that idiot Nat would ever have been if he had inherited the title. The old earl lost land, and his bank account was pitiful. Do you think his weak son could ever have done what I have? *I* knew where to invest. Gas. Coal. Steam engines. Mill manufacturing. *We* know the future, don't we, Kendra?"

"Didn't you ever try to figure out some way to return to our world?" Her lips felt numb as she asked the question. "Christ, you've spent almost forty years here!"

"Why would I ever have wanted to go back? I was born in Cuba. I grew up in a two-room shack. I rode a fucking donkey! I joined the army when I was fifteen and the Mexican cartels when I was twenty-one. I became one of Luis

Gomez's top lieutenants." He looked at her, his eyes seemed to burn. "Here, *I* am the top lieutenant. I control an earldom. My daughters have married into the aristocracy. My son will take over Falcon Court and the estate. He is my legacy."

"Did your wife know your secret?"

"Don't be a damn fool," he snapped. "Her father was an earl, and she married into an earldom. If I had told Victoria that I was Mateo Hernández from a shack in Cuba, that I was from the future, what do you suppose she'd have done? If I told her after I married her, she would have had me committed to a madhouse."

"And life was good until Harry Stone."

"I should have killed the son of a bitch when he first approached me. But I couldn't take that chance."

"I still don't understand what Stone could have done. He was a . . . 'sewer rat.' You had assumed the identity of an earl. Aristocracy wins the battle against a commoner in this era."

"You haven't been here long, Kendra, but surely you know how this world operates?" He gave her a contemptuous look, then took a swallow of brandy before continuing. "Rumor and innuendo can destroy reputations. Many of my fellow investors are sanctimonious little pricks. If there was even a hint of scandal, even a thought that I was an imposter, doors would close, and my line of credit would dry up. The scandal would destroy my son. Everything I worked for would be lost."

Kendra wasn't buying it. "Harry must have had more than your word against his."

He said nothing for a moment. "I have a tattoo on my chest that could be incriminating," he finally admitted. "If Millie had testified in court that her former lover, Mateo Hernández, had such a tattoo, it might have been difficult to explain away."

Kendra thought about that. Not just one voice, but many voices whispering that Bancroft was an imposter. "I can see where that could ignite rumors. Just curious, what's the tattoo?"

"A panther."

She nodded, then said, "I wondered what motivated Stone's strange collection. He did it to taunt you."

A muscle bunched in Bancroft's jaw. "Yes."

They fell silent for a long moment, their eyes fixed on each other. "So, you've told me your story," she said finally. "What now? Are you going to shoot me here in your study? Think of the blood. The servants will talk."

His mouth curved. "I don't want to shoot you at all, Kendra. Fate brought you to me. Think about it. If Biddle hadn't murdered Harry, you would have left the next morning, after the fog lifted. Our paths would never have crossed."

"Yeah, things have worked out so well for me," she said acidly.

"You and I are connected. We share something unique, a bond that cannot be denied. Think about that, Kendra!"

Kendra said nothing. He was right. They had a history—or, rather, a future.

"I have been alone here for thirty-eight years." His eyes took on a feverish glow. "I have never been able to speak the way I am now with anyone. We could marry." His lips twisted when he saw her jolt. "I know I'm old to you, Kendra, but I am the only man on this earth—*in this time*—that truly understands you. That is powerful."

She was surprised to feel sadness well up inside her. She'd shared her secret with the Duke and Alec, yes, but they could never truly understand her like the man sitting across the desk from her. She and Bancroft—Hernández—shared a common existence.

"Consider what I am saying very carefully, Kendra."

She had to clear her throat. "Or else?"

He was eyeing her closely. "Or else we shall take a walk out those French door to a secluded spot in the woods. There's a small lake, and a gazebo that my wife Victoria had built."

"I see. Would I be buried or thrown in the lake?"

"The gardeners would notice freshly turned earth, I'm afraid."

"Ah, the lake, then," she murmured. Her heart beat heavily, painfully. She wanted to cry. She forced herself to shake off the malaise. "You're quite the planner, aren't you, Mateo?"

Humor gleamed in the dark eyes, and he smiled. "I always plan—"

The bullet ripped apart the fabric of the reticule when she squeezed the trigger. She'd managed to work her hand into the purse during their conversation, but she wasn't able to aim. She'd tilted the gun into a position that she calculated would send the ball's trajectory into his chest. *Center mass.* If she was wrong . . . well, the servants would have some cleaning up to do. Bancroft wouldn't be bringing her to the lake. At least not alive.

Her calculations were wrong; the trajectory was higher. The ball hit Bancroft in the middle of his forehead. The scent of sulfur hung like a rotting blanket in the air. Her stomach clenched as she stared into Bancroft's wide eyes. She remembered when their eyes had met across Sir Jeremy's body.

Bancroft fell forward, crashing onto his desk. The brandy glass shattered. The gun, still clenched in his hand, clattered against the surface of the desk. Kendra sprang to her feet and dove out of the way, just in case the pistol went off accidentally. Being shot by a dead man would be such a waste.

Slowly, she straightened. Her ears were ringing. She stared at Nathan Bancroft—Mateo Hernández. *Whatever.*

"I guess you didn't plan for everything, did you?"

52

Alec was opening the door to Lord Bancroft's mansion when he heard the gunshot. Ice-cold fear lanced through him. He sent one panic-stricken glance behind him. The Duke and Sam were only now galloping into the courtyard, yanking hard on their reins, causing their horses to snort and buck. Alec tore down the hall. He saw the light wavering from a half-open door, and aimed his body toward it. His shoulder connected with the sturdy panel, the door slamming loudly against the wall as he burst into the room.

"Kendra!"

Relief flooded through him as his gaze focused on her. She was standing—God, that was all that mattered—while Bancroft lay slumped across his desk. Bancroft was unnaturally still, but Alec's fingers tightened around the blunderbuss he'd borrowed from Benjamin, just in case.

"He's dead," Kendra said with eerie calmness. "I'm going to need a new purse."

"My God." Alec set the blunderbuss down on a chair. He turned and gathered her into his arms when the Duke and Sam came running into the room. Despite Kendra's composure, Alec could feel the tremors racing through her body. "Are you all right? You're not injured?"

"No . . . no, I'm fine." Her arms went around him. "God . . ."

Sam walked over to the body, shifting Bancroft so that his head flopped back. He whistled low, staring at the bullet hole in the earl's head. His golden eyes narrowed as he scanned the room, his gaze landing on the reticule with the blackened hole punched through the bottom. "Clearly self-defense. I reckon the constable and the magistrate need ter be sent for, although Jameson is busy at the moment with Mr. Turner."

"Bancroft shot Turner." Kendra looked at them. "Flora found you."

It wasn't a question, but Sam nodded. "Seemed ter think you were in danger from her husband. Mr. Turner told us that the earl shot him."

"He's alive, then?"

"Aye. Don't know for how much longer though."

The Duke added, "Dr. Poole was summoned, but we didn't stay to find out. You were our first priority, my dear. We feared we'd already lost too much time getting here."

Alec tightened his arms around Kendra. They'd been forced to run back to the Green Maiden to saddle their horses to travel to Falcon Court. They'd left Benjamin to round up the constable and Dr. Poole for Turner. "It was a hell of a ride," he murmured. With a sigh of regret, he loosened his arms from around Kendra, but didn't let go altogether, proprieties be damned.

The Duke asked, "Can you tell us what happened, my dear?"

Alec could feel Kendra's chest rise and fall. She was quiet for a long moment, her gaze drifting to Bancroft's body. "It's a hell of a story."

There were two stories, of course.

The first began thirty-two years ago, when Nat Bancroft lost his life at the hands of a ruthless man. Stone's letter detailed how the man he'd known as Mateo

Hernández had taken over Nat's identity. He'd included the times, dates, and crimes.

In the guise of Lord Bancroft, Mateo had built a mill that the town of East Dingleford had come to rely on. He'd created an empire with tentacles in investment firms and conglomerates across England. The ownership of the mill and stock in his many business interests would most likely go to his son, Phillip. The kid wouldn't be destitute, Kendra knew, but he would be devastated. How could he not be? He'd lose Falcon Court and the earldom. He'd also lose the memory of the man he'd always thought of as his father.

When the scandal broke, it would break over the entire family. Kendra might not like Lady Winifred, but her father's perfidy would affect her and her daughter, and her sisters and their children. How many lives would be destroyed if the truth came out?

Kendra didn't want to think about it. She was almost glad when Dr. Poole and Constable Jameson arrived fifteen minutes later, forcing her to focus on them—especially since Jameson wanted to arrest her for murder. He spotted her blackened and shredded reticule, which he declared damning evidence against her, conveniently overlooking the gun still in the dead man's hand until the Duke, Sam, and Alec all pointed it out. Surprisingly, Dr. Poole spoke up in her defense, of a sort, reminding Jameson that the earl had gone mad earlier and shot Mr. Turner. The sheep farmer had died no less than twenty minutes earlier.

That announcement left Kendra feeling a little queasy, mostly because she was empty of any sort of sympathy over the man's death. At least she wasn't rejoicing at the news. Maybe she hadn't gone over to the dark side—yet.

Dr. Poole examined Bancroft's body briefly. He examined the letter, which the Duke handed over to him, for much longer. Kendra watched the doctor's fuzzy brows dip lower and lower as he scanned the contents, but his expression remained as grumpy as ever. When he finally finished, he declared the matter urgent enough to wake the magistrate.

"W'ot does it say?" demanded Constable Jameson, eyeing the letter suspiciously.

Dr. Poole ignored him, his gaze passing over the others as he pocketed the letter. Then he turned and looked at Bancroft. Kendra suspected he wasn't seeing the slain man, but the friend he'd known. Maybe he was also thinking about the real Nat, dead in a shallow grave somewhere. After a moment, he sighed.

"Nothing else to do here. We must wake the squire, and tomorrow summon an inquest. Again." He spoke to the constable. "The jurors can come here to look at the body, see the crime scene. Let's turn off the gas lamps and close up the room."

It felt strange to close the door to the study and walk down the hall to the foyer knowing that Bancroft would remain where he was, slowly stiffening with rigor mortis, until the jurors came tomorrow to examine him. But Kendra was too tired to argue.

Three men from East Dingleford had come with the constable, and were standing on the step outside. Kendra recognized one of the men from their first evening in the village—Freddie, who had been so eager to bring the Luddites to justice. The servants had begun to trickle back to Falcon Court from the Guy Fawkes celebrations, as well, shaken to be greeted with the news of their master's death.

Lady Winifred followed five minutes later. Her beautiful face went white with shock when Constable Jameson informed her of her father's death. Dr. Poole and Lady Winifred's maid hustled her off to her bedchamber, and no doubt into the mindless slumber of laudanum.

Kendra noticed that Dr. Poole didn't show Lady Winifred the letter. Maybe he would tomorrow, after she'd had a chance to absorb the shock of her father's death. Maybe he never would. Kendra supposed it depended on what Squire Matthews decided.

It was nearly one o'clock in the morning by the time they made their way to Acker Manor. The butler was surprised, but didn't question Dr. Poole, who demanded that the butler rouse his master while they waited in the drawing room.

Ten minutes later, the magistrate was carried in by two footmen. He was wearing a ruby dressing gown over his nightshirt and a nightcap. One foot was clad in a slipper. The other was propped up, swollen big toe thrust into the air. Oliver Matthews joined them, wearing a rather flamboyant turquoise and green floral silk dressing gown. Mr. Shannon was right, Kendra decided. The younger Matthews was definitely a tulip.

Dr. Poole made *tsk*ing noises as he inspected the squire's big toe. "Have you refrained from drinking alcohol and eating red meat as I instructed you over two weeks ago?"

The son said, "Father had tripe for dinner and a bottle of red wine."

"Poppycock! Half a bottle."

"A bottle."

"Bah! Unless Dr. Poole is suddenly making house calls in the middle of the bloody night—with an entourage—I suspect he's not here to lecture me about my menu," the squire snapped at his son. He frowned at his unwelcome guests. "What is this about, and why couldn't it wait until morning?"

Jameson said, "Lord Bancroft is dead."

"Good God!" Squire Matthews's eyes widened. "What? *How?*"

"I shot him," Kendra replied, earning a frown from the doctor.

The squire stared at her. "Why would you go and do that?"

"Lord Bancroft murdered Mrs. Stone and her house-keeper," the Duke spoke up. "He was searching for evidence that would incriminate him. Miss Donovan had recently come into possession of that evidence."

"What evidence?"

Dr. Poole handed him the letter. "This is the evidence his Grace is referring to. If you read it, I think you shall see what motivated Lord Bancroft . . ." He hesitated, lips twisting as he realized the title was misplaced. "What motivated the man to kill."

While his father read the letter, Matthews poured drinks and encouraged everyone to take a seat. Kendra took him up on the suggestion, feeling suddenly exhausted. The night's events were beginning to weigh her down. Bancroft—Hernández—had been a psychopath. But they'd shared a link that went beyond time and space. Hernández had recognized that. It was why he'd offered her a choice. Of course, if she'd told him no, she'd be the one with a bullet in her head. Was that really a choice?

"Hell and damnation," the squire finally uttered, his gaze lifting to view his audience. "This is . . . this is . . . quite incredible."

"What are we going to do?" asked Dr. Poole.

Matthews looked at his father. "What is it?"

The squire pursed his lips. He ignored his son, looking at everyone. "Who has read this letter?"

"Miss Donovan, my nephew, Mr. Kelly, and myself," said the Duke.

"And I," Dr. Poole added.

"W'ot's in the bloody thing?" Jameson demanded, irritated at being kept out of the loop.

"Something I must consider carefully," the squire said. "I shall tell you what I decide tomorrow. For now, I suggest we go to bed. Miss Donovan, you will most likely need to give a statement tomorrow on Lord . . . ah, Bancroft's death, since he died by your hand."

Kendra was surprised when Dr. Poole said, "I shall be announcing my verdict tomorrow at the inquest. A clear case of self-defense."

"It *was* self-defense," she said.

Dr. Poole stood, and he looked over at Kendra with narrowed eyes. "Perhaps you ought to take up more ladylike pursuits in the future, Miss Donovan," he said nastily. "Then you wouldn't be embroiled in an inquest, needing to claim self-defense at all, would you?"

There was, of course, the second story.

Kendra was forced to wait until Sam finally bid them goodnight before she was able to tell the Duke and Alec. It was near three o'clock in the morning by then. They'd rehashed Bancroft's deception, and his part in the murders, until nothing more could be said. The way Sam fixed her with his cop-like stare before he finally departed made her think that he knew she was holding something back.

She felt a pang of guilt over that. She knew what it was like to be an outsider. But how could she tell him that Hernández had been a time traveler? How could she tell him that *she* was?

"All right, my dear," the Duke said, and settled his intelligent blue eyes on her after the door closed. "I sense you have something else to discuss privately."

"Yes." Her gaze fell on the glass she held in her hand, which still held a splash of Mrs. Bolton's homemade apricot brandy. She had also been half drunk with brandy when she'd first told Alec about being a time traveler.

She lifted her eyes, drew in a deep breath, and told them Mateo Hernández's story.

"This is . . . extraordinary," the Duke marveled fifteen minutes later. "*Two* of you? And he *followed* you into the stairwell? Why didn't he come out when you did? Why did his journey through your wormhole take him further into the past?"

Kendra gave a weak laugh. "Christ, I wish I knew. But I'm as much in the dark about this as you are. I think it's safe to say that traveling through time is precarious."

And if I ever went into another vortex, there's no guarantee where I'd end up.

Her eyes met Alec's gaze across the room. He'd taken up his habitual position against the fireplace mantel. *And if Alec joined me, there would be no guarantee that we'd end up together.*

The thought made her shudder.

She said softly, "He didn't want to kill me. He didn't want to lose the connection to our world. It's hard to know that I am the one who cut the link in that chain."

"You had no choice," Alec said, his voice harsh. "He would have killed you."

"I know that, but . . ." She lifted her shoulders in a weary shrug. She couldn't explain the sadness she was feeling, even to herself. "I didn't know that he existed until a couple of hours ago, but I feel like I lost something. He and I were the same."

"No." The Duke shook his head. "You may come from the same period of time, but you are nothing alike. Since you came through the wormhole, your instinct has always been to save lives. To stop evil. When Lord—when Hernández came through, he stole and killed, exactly as he had done when he had lived in the future as an assassin.

"He stole a young man's life," he added quietly, his blue eyes filled with sorrow. "Everything he built as Lord Bancroft was built upon a horrible lie."

Kendra's lips twisted as she looked at the Duke. "I'm building my life here on a lie. You took in the daughter of your good friend, remember?"

"We didn't murder anyone to create our fabrication."

She drank the rest of the brandy, and set it aside with a sigh. The Duke was right, of course. There were fine lines between lies. It occurred to her that if she hadn't been caught in this bizarre adventure, she'd be building her life on lies back in the twenty-first century, with multiple identities after killing Sir Jeremy.

But she hadn't killed Sir Jeremy, she realized. Would she have been able to return to the FBI? Or, if the vortex hadn't opened when it did, would Mateo's bullet have found her, leaving her body to be discovered in the stairwell?

She looked up at the Duke and Alec. "I was lucky to have ended up with you, to be able to share my secret with you and have you accept me."

Love me.

It was a gift. Unexpected tears pricked her eyes. "I don't know what I would have done otherwise."

"You would have survived," the Duke said gruffly, and his eyes were brighter than normal when he looked at her. "You are a remarkable young woman, Miss Donovan . . . Kendra." He gave her a slow smile. "I think it's time I call my ward by her Christian name, don't you think?"

"I think it is exactly the time."

It was past four when Kendra finally tumbled into bed. She didn't think Alec would come to her. In another hour and a half, the servants would begin to stir, and he wouldn't want to compromise her reputation. But she was wrong. The door opened quietly, and he slipped across the room and into bed, his arms going around her.

"I won't stay long," he whispered. "I needed to hold you."

"I love you."

She didn't know that she was going to say the words until she said them. And when she did, they sounded right.

His arms tightened. "I love you too. Now go to sleep. We'll need our wits about us tomorrow." He paused. "Kendra?"

"What?" The word sounded mushy. She was already drifting into sleep.

"It was a hell of a story."

53

Late Monday afternoon, Kendra stood alone on top of the same slope that she'd stood upon with Lord Bancroft—Hernández—only two days before. The wind, which hinted at the cold months that lay ahead, whipped her skirts against her legs, and sent the big, fluffy clouds scuttling across the blue sky. Her gaze drifted to the squire's paddock below, where the only evidence of the Guy Fawkes celebration was the remaining burnt logs and ashes from the pyre.

Early that morning, Squire Matthews and Dr. Poole had met with them in the Green Maiden's private drawing room. The squire had come to a decision. As much as he disliked an upstart like Mateo Hernández taking over the life of one of his betters, he saw no reason to create an upheaval in the lives of his children and his children's children. The squire had also once met the earl's cousin, who would be the rightful heir to the estate if scandal broke. The cousin was a wastrel and a debaucher.

"Of course, our meeting took place nearly forty years ago," the squire acknowledged. "The man may have changed. But why take the chance?"

Apparently, Phillip Bancroft, the young viscount, was well-liked by everyone in East Dingleford, despite the fact that he'd spent most of his time away at school. Maybe that was the reason he was a nice guy, Kendra thought. As she listened to the squire speak of the young man, she realized that he sounded a lot like the real Nat.

The squire and Dr. Poole spoke of not wanting to disrupt the lives of Phillip and his sisters, but Kendra wondered if they worried more that the wastrel cousin could leave Falcon Court in shambles and fight for control of the mill. A lot of villagers were employed at both places. Kendra had always found self-interest to be a powerful motivator in decision-making.

The inquest had been held earlier in the afternoon in the Green Maiden's tavern, and she'd given her statement to Squire Matthews. Only twelve jurors were called to the tavern this time, and they trudged out to Falcon Court to view Bancroft's body before the dead man was hauled away. Dr. Poole gave his evidence. Lord Bancroft had suffered from lunacy, he said, causing the man to murder Mrs. Stone and Mrs. Trout. He had been struck with the same madness when he'd killed Mr. Turner, and nearly killed Kendra, he insisted. For the second time in less than a week, the jurors handed down a decision of self-defense. The jurors disbanded immediately thereafter, except for those who stuck around to drink.

Flora Turner visited Kendra. Besides Dr. Poole and Squire Matthews, she was the only other person in East Dingleford who'd seen the contents of the letter. Of course, since she couldn't read, the point was moot.

With her husband dead, Flora had decided to sell the sheep farm. But the task was beyond her, so Kendra enlisted the Duke's help, who offered the services of his land steward, Mr. Kimble, to guide the sale. Unfortunately, Turner had been heavily in debt, and it was questionable whether the widow would end up with any money at all. She might even end up owing. But the Duke reminded Flora that he'd promised to find her a position at Monksgrey or Aldridge Castle. Either way, she wouldn't end up in the poorhouse. Life for Flora was looking up.

The same couldn't be said about Lady Winifred. She was just coming out of mourning; now she'd have to return. Her search for another husband would have to be put on hold, maybe indefinitely, if rumors about Lord

Bancroft's sudden lunacy reached the ballrooms. No one wanted to marry into a family tainted by madness.

Kendra turned around on the hill, and her heart flipped over when she saw Alec walking toward her. The capes on his greatcoat flapped in the breeze. He hadn't put on a hat, so the wind teased his silken hair, making her fingers itch to do the same.

"Molly is looking for you," he said, his mouth curving into a smile as he reached her.

She'd deliberately ditched her lady's maid. "I needed to be alone to think."

His gaze searched hers. "Do you want to talk?"

She shrugged. "My head is still spinning. Bancroft spent half his life here. I guess it's starting to sink in that this—*here*—will be my life."

Alec brought his hands up, palms gently framing her face. He stared into her eyes. "Is that such a terrible thing?"

She reached up to clasp his wrists. She hadn't bothered with gloves, so she could feel the strong pulse of his heart. "Some things here aren't so bad," she admitted, looking at him through veiled lashes. She gave a slow smile. "In fact, I'd say some things are pretty wonderful." She raised herself on tiptoes and kissed him.

"Hmm."

"But . . ." She broke off, gazing at him. "I hate not having any money. Money"—she cut him off when she saw his expression—"that I earn. I was thinking I could get a loan from either you or the Duke and invest in the Exchange. If Hernández could use his knowledge of the future to become financially independent, I don't know why I can't."

Alec lifted one eyebrow. "What about all your talk about changing the future?"

"I won't be changing the future. I'll be profiting from my knowledge *of* the future." It occurred to her that this plan might also change the future. "Or maybe I can use my other skills."

"What other skills?"

She poked him. "Please. I'm a special agent for the FBI. Maybe I can open a detective agency. I can't call it that—that word won't be part of anyone's vocabulary for several years. But maybe Mr. Kelly and I can become partners."

Alec paled. "What are you talking about?"

She kissed him again, because he looked like he needed comforting. "I'm talking about offering my services to people to investigate crimes."

"Go into trade? As a Bow Street Runner? Do you have any smelling salts on hand, Miss Donovan? I think I may swoon."

Kendra laughed, and realized her spirits felt lighter.

He regarded her closely. "You're not serious. Are you?"

"Maybe." She smiled, and laced her fingers through his. "I think I have time to figure it out."

ACKNOWLEDGMENTS

As I finished the third installment of Kendra Donovan's adventures in Regency England, I was reminded once again that I am not alone in this journey. In fact, I have a whole team of amazing professionals who have invested their time and energy to make this endeavor happen. I am so thankful to my agent, Jill Grosjean, who has been a graceful and tireless champion of Kendra since the beginning. And I can't even begin to express the comfort that I've felt sending *Caught in Time* into the world, knowing that it would land first in the extremely talented hands of my editor, Katie McGuire. I am also eternally grateful for the tremendous support that I have received from my publisher, Claiborne Hancock, and the entire team at Pegasus. Once again, I am blown away by the talent of Derek Thornton of Faceout Studio, who is responsible for designing all of the *In Time* book covers.

Researching this particular time period often means paging through countless books and scrolling through countless blogs. Louise Allen's *Regency Slang Revealed* was particularly helpful, as was Joanne Major's and Sarah Murden's blog, *All Things Georgian*. And I was again grateful to be able to turn to Regency researcher Nancy Mayer for the odd inquiry whose answer I simply could not find elsewhere. For the modern-day research, I was thrilled to come across Geoff Symon's forensic book, *Blood Spatter*. As always, any errors are mine, and mine alone.

While I strive to make the books as historically accurate as possible, there are a few areas in which I take creative license. Thanks to *All Things Georgian*, I learned that Guy Fawkes Night was actually known as Guy *Faux* Night during 1815. After much contemplation, I decided to use the modern spelling that is more familiar to readers to avoid confusion—and possibly messages telling me that I had misspelled the celebration held in the Catholic radical's name.

One of the best things that has happened to me in writing these books is my increasing circle of friends and supporters. From my original circle, Bonnie McCarthy, Karre Jacobs, and Lori McAllister—you continue to inspire me with your courage and talent. Ethan McCarthy—your wisdom belies your age, and I appreciate your help in clarifying my sometimes tangled thoughts on blood spatter and the like. A special thank you to Lesley Heizman for taking me in hand, and helping me with social media, which is still a bit of a mystery to me. A big and sincere thank you to everyone who has reached out to me via Facebook. Your kind words and encouragement have meant more to me than you will ever know. I also want to thank the people in my hometown of Max, North Dakota. Your continued unconditional support takes my breath away.

Finally, I want to give a giant thank you to librarians and LibraryReads, who again put *A Twist in Time* on their Must-Read list. You are the giver of dreams to so many children, who pick up a book for the first time. I cannot—do *not* want to—imagine this world without you.

ABOUT THE AUTHOR

Julie McElwain has freelanced for numerous publications from professional photography magazines to those following the fashion industry. Currently, Julie is West Coast Editor for *Soaps In Depth*, a national soap opera magazine covering the No. 1 daytime drama, *The Young and the Restless*. Julie lives in Long Beach, CA.